Fair I.

NORWAY

Samfiere
Bergen

Stotmen
Syek
Carmen
Buckenford

DES I.

Notten
Ec. de Soult

head

Kynards Head
Buchan Nesse

Aberdeen

The Nese of Norway

Jutland

TH of FORTH

bar
bbes Head
oly I.

newcastle

A CHART
shewing the several
Places of Action between the
ENGLISH and SPANISH Fleets,
with the Places where several of
the SPANISH Ships were destroyed in their return to SPAIN,
North about the
BRITISH ISLANDS.

ch. I.

full

otton I.

Vlieland

Texell

Frisland

H O L

Yarmoth
Lyn Regis
Norwich
Aldborough
Harwich

Malden

Amsterdam
Gravesande

L A N D

LONDON

D

Gravesend
Rochester
Sandwich
Deal
Dover

Thames R.

Flushing

Z E Island D
Bergen

I Wight

Antwerp

Lewis

Rye

Flushing
Ostend
Newport
Dunkirk
Graveline
Calais
Boulogne

nd

F L A N D E R S

Estaples

NNEL

Somener

uvre de Grace
Seine R.

Diepe

Rouan
St Sauveur

Quilbeuf

Abbeville

F R A N C E

CALCITRARE DV
COECAS HOMINVM
O PECTORA COECA
CONTRA STIMVLOS

ARMADA

Armada

DUFF HART-DAVIS

BANTAM PRESS

LONDON · NEW YORK · TORONTO · SYDNEY · AUCKLAND

TRANSWORLD PUBLISHERS LTD
61–63 Uxbridge Road, London W5 5SA

TRANSWORLD PUBLISHERS (AUSTRALIA) PTY LTD
15–23 Helles Avenue, Moorebank NSW 2170

TRANSWORLD PUBLISHERS (NZ) LTD
Cnr Moselle and Waipareira Aves,
Henderson, Auckland

Published 1988 by Bantam Press,
a division of Transworld Publishers Ltd
Copyright © Duff Hart-Davis 1988

British Library Cataloguing in Publication Data

Hart-Davis, Duff
Armada.
1. Armada, 1588
I. Title
942.05′5   DA360

ISBN 0–593–01231–3

Phototypeset by Wyvern Typesetting Ltd, Bristol
Printed in Great Britain by
Butler & Tanner Ltd, Frome

Contents

Acknowledgements

I should like to thank Victor Oristano, Chairman of Alda Communications Corp., Palm Beach, Florida, USA, and a director of Croydon Cable Television PLC, Croydon, England, for suggesting the idea of this book, and for supporting its publication so enthusiastically.

A grant from Alda enabled the National Maritime Museum at Greenwich to commission special research into the design and construction of the ships that fought on both sides in the Armada campaign, and funded the drawing of scale plans by David White, a naval architect on the staff of the Museum. These represent the best possible reconstruction of how the ships of 1588 were built, and give the book – I believe – unique authenticity. These reconstructions are superbly brought to life in Jonathan Potter's full-colour illustrations, also specially commissioned for the book.

I am most grateful to Dr Alan McGowan, Chief Curator at the Museum, for directing this work, for his guidance throughout the project, and for eliminating errors from the text.

I am also grateful to Tom Graves, an expert picture researcher, for seeking out suitable illustrations so diligently.

Duff Hart-Davis
August 1987

Foreword

The 400th anniversary of a famous battle is not the moment for chauvinistic breast-beating or self-congratulation. Rather, it is the occasion for fresh evaluation of an event that profoundly affected the course of history in Europe, and for an attempt to imagine what it was like to fight in the Spanish and English fleets of 1588. In this account I have tried to bring that distant age to life by quoting as much as possible from the reports of men who took part in the campaign.

For more than three centuries it was fashionable in England to present the conflict as a clash between David and Goliath, and to portray the gallant little English ships as overcoming fearful handicaps of size and weight when they defeated the far-larger Spanish galleons. Modern scholarship has now proved this picture to be fantasy, and shown that, in size at least, the ships of both sides were evenly matched. Yet in the past twenty years the discovery and excavation of wrecks off the Irish coast have revealed that the Armada was undermined by deficiencies never suspected by earlier historians. It was their equipment, rather than any lack of courage, which let the Spaniards down.

A word must be said about language. English documents are quoted in their original form, except that I have modernized spelling and punctuation, both of which were so erratic as to obstruct a modern reader's comprehension. The Elizabethans' modes of expression and thought were subtly but markedly different from those of their descendants four centuries later, and I believe that extensive quotation of their language alone gives some idea of what sort of people they were.

The translations from the Spanish, on the other hand, were almost all made late in the nineteenth century, so that they are couched in solid Victorian prose. To have restored archaic touches, or invented new ones, would obviously not have been satisfactory – so that a slight loss of authenticity has to be accepted.

A note about the calendar is also necessary. By 1588 most of Europe had gone over to the new calendar, which had been proclaimed by Pope Gregory XIII six years earlier, and is still in use today. England, however, was still using the old Julian calendar, and was ten days behind her continental neighbours. Thus in Spanish reckoning the first of the Armada battles took place on 31 July, but in English reckoning on 21 July, although the days of the week were the same to both sides. To avoid confusion, I have used new-style, Gregorian dates throughout the narrative.

Chapter One

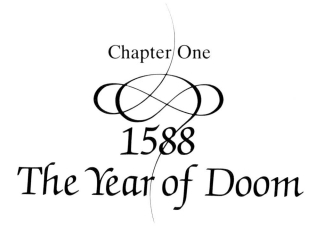

1588
The Year of Doom

For more than a hundred years astrologers, seers and divines had given warning that the year would be one of disaster. The first to do so was Johann Müller, the German mathematician and astronomer born in Königsberg, who styled himself Regiomontanus (King's Mountain, a Latin version of the name of his birthplace), and who in a famous prophecy of 1475 singled out 1588 as a year of ruin and catastrophe. It was Müller who, in January 1472, observed a moving, fiery star and recorded its track precisely enough for later astronomers to identify the body as Halley's Comet; and it was he who worked out the astronomical tables on which Christopher Columbus relied when he sailed to discover America in 1492. Thus Müller was a man whose word commanded respect, and his predictions were taken up by many who came after.

One such was Philip Melancthon, the German theologian, scholar and reformer, whose scriptural researches led him to the conclusion that although the world would not end in '88, it would be severely shaken:

> *Tausend fünfhundert achtzig acht,*
> *Das is das Jahr das ich betracht:*
> *Geht in dem die Welt nicht unter;*
> *So geschiet doch sonst gross merktlich Wunder.*

English versifiers soon produced their own translation:

> *If not in this year all the wicked world*
> *Do fall, and land with sea to nothing come,*
> *Yet Empires must be topsy-turvy hurled,*
> *And extreme grief shall be the common sum.*

The same sentiment was expressed in Latin verses, frequently quoted in spite of the execrable scansion of the hexameter line:

Octogesimus octavus mirabilis annus
Ingruet, is secum tristia fata feret.

(The miraculous year of '88 rushes on, bringing dire events with it.)

Another common prophecy forecast that the 'black fleet of Norway' would appear in English seas – but even that great sage Francis Bacon, who was 26 in the year of the Armada and a student of such arcane utterances, confessed himself baffled by it, unless 'Norway' could be interpreted as one of the King of Spain's surnames. Another forecast again was that England would fall to soldiers 'with snow on their helmets' – a prediction taken to warn of invasion in winter or early spring.

As the dreaded year drew nearer, alarm was fuelled by both religious and astronomical speculation. Protestants calculated that 'a grand climacterial' was approaching. In his *Hours of Recreation* published in 1576, James Sandford concluded that because the captivity of Babylon had lasted for seventy years, the 'same time may be thought to prefigure the captivity of the Gospel in these later days'. Since it was in 1518 that Martin Luther had begun to preach God's word (which 'forthwith became captive with fire, sword and all cruelty'), the crucial period of seventy years would end in '88.

On the astronomical front, it was immensely sinister that 1588 would bring a conjunction of the planets Saturn, Jupiter and Mars. Still worse, an eclipse of the sun on 16 February would be followed, in only two weeks, by a 'universal' eclipse of the moon on 2 March, and then by a second total eclipse of the moon on 26 August. Three eclipses in a single year were themselves a recipe for disaster; and had not the Hermetic Books of the fourth century AD laid down that whenever sun and moon were eclipsed in one month 'there ensue manifold mischiefs in the world'? As if to confirm the worst expectations, an unparalleled sign appeared in the sky during March 1587. According to the historian William Harrison, who by then had become Dean of Windsor, 'a star was seen in the body of the moon . . . whereat many men marvelled, and not without cause, for it stood directly between the points of her horns, the moon being changed not passing five or six days before'.

Such was the general anxiety that in London the Privy Council – the main executive organ of government – tried to suppress all reference to the prophecies, and forbade the compilers of popular almanacs to mention them. Nevertheless, ministers of the Church urged people to repent before judgement, as a means of preparing themselves against the 'prognosticated dangers' of the year, and books were published instructing their readers on how to face up to the end of the world. John Harvey, for instance, produced a discourse 'especially in abatement of the terrible threatenings and menaces, peremptorily denounced against the kingdoms

12

John Dee, the astrologer, mathematician, mystic and magician of Mortlake, to whom Elizabeth would resort for advice in times of crisis. In 1588 he was on an extended trip to Bohemia, but in November he sent the Queen an effusive letter congratulating her on the 'triumphant victory against your mortal enemy', and expressing the hope that he would soon be home in her 'British earthly paradise and monarchy incomparable'.

and states of the world'.

For Queen Elizabeth and her people the prophecies had a specific meaning, for there was not the slightest doubt as to the source from which doom – if it came – would emanate. For years relations with Spain had been deteriorating, and it was well known in England that for much of 1587 King Philip II had been preparing a mighty Armada whose purpose was to invade the country and finally crush the Reformation there. No doubt the Queen sought guidance from the celebrated mathematician, astrologer and charlatan Dr John Dee, whom she was wont to consult in times of crisis, both about her own health and about general matters.

Looking back from the vantage point of 1624, George Carleton, Bishop of Chichester, recalled how 1588 had seemed at the time:

> Some said it was the climacterial year of the world. And they that trust not in the *Living God* took the opportunity of this *fatal year*, as they supposed, now utterly to overthrow the *Church of England* and *State*. Which before they could not do. The *Pope* and *Spaniard* laid up all their hopes upon this year's destiny.

The accuracy of this recollection was borne out by Thomas Taylor, whose sermon 'Eighty-eight' was written in 1631:

> It was a year of strange expectation before it came . . . Some
> designed it to be the end of the world . . . Others designed it
> to be the doomsday of England, the ruin of our Church and
> religion, and the funerals of the Prince, people and Kingdom,
> all on one day.

For churchmen of all persuasions the year was one in which religious
beliefs were on trial as never before. Just as King Philip had no doubt that
in setting out to crush the arch-heretic Elizabeth, whom he disparagingly
described as 'the English woman', he was acting as an agent of the
Almighty, so too the English were perfectly certain that God was on their
side and would smash His enemies, who happened also to be theirs. Logic
must have suggested to some detached observers that both sides could not
be wholly correct in their expectation of divine support, but this did not
deter them. Both countries went into the encounter with absolute confidence that God would see them through.

Chapter Two

I, The King

Philip as a young man: portrait by Titian.

To understand why King Philip II of Spain committed the most disastrous mistake of his reign, one must briefly trace the events and policies that led him to attack England; for by the time he despatched the Armada he had already reigned for thirty-two years and had made numerous attempts to resolve by stealth or diplomacy the problem which he ultimately sought to settle by force. At the beginning of 1588 he was almost 60 years old – a man of middle height, still slim and upright, with a high, strong forehead, heavy-lidded eyes, and the full lips of his Hapsburg ancestors. His hair and beard, once a striking light brown, had turned grey-white, a colour which accurately suggested the pallor and coldness of his temperament. Never exuberant or vivacious even in youth, he had now become a melancholy recluse, immensely conscientious and industrious, but utterly lacking in humour or imagination. Only once in living memory had his courtiers seen him laugh, and that had been sixteen years before, when he learnt of the St Bartholomew's Day massacres in the autumn of 1572. It took the news that 30,000 Protestants had been slaughtered in Paris to jolt him out of his habitual heavy gloom, and he laughed so immoderately that those around him were amazed.

His kingdom was the most powerful in Europe, his empire the greatest in the world. Thanks to the brilliant flair of his subjects for exploration and conquest, which had flowered as never before during the previous two generations, he was master not only of Spain, the Netherlands and much of Italy, but also of the whole of South America, parts of North America, and outposts in Africa and the Caribbean. His countrymen had pushed back the frontiers of the known world by margins hitherto inconceivable. From South America, via the Spanish Main – the contemporary and entirely appropriate name for the West Indies – such a stream of silver, gold and jewels came pouring back to Europe on board the treasure fleets that Philip was able to equip and maintain the most powerful army and navy in existence.

Yet from this great wealth and power he derived little joy, for his twin missions in life, as he saw them, were to impose Spanish domination on the whole of Europe and to make the Catholic faith supreme; and in neither aim – by 1588 – had he enjoyed the least success, even though he had devoted himself selflessly to the cause. Above all he was a practical politician, endlessly manipulating and scheming for territorial advantage; yet he was also a religious zealot who came to see himself more and more as the instrument of the Almighty, chosen to further His designs on earth. In Philip political instinct and religious faith were inseparably fused together: he was thus perfectly prepared to sanction murder and inflict untold cruelties on fellow humans – as he did through the Inquisition – provided such crimes were committed for the greater glory of God.

The path of his private life had been scarcely less rough. Four marriages had brought him no serviceable heir to the throne. His first three wives had all died, and the brief life of his only son Carlos had been wretched from start to finish. Born epileptic and mentally defective, the boy had become increasingly violent, his behaviour ever more grotesque, until his father had found it necessary to have him locked away in a tower of the palace in Madrid, where he died at the age of 23. The King was suspected by some of having had him murdered, but it seems more likely that he expired from his own physical excesses, alternately swallowing jewellery, starving himself, and then gorging on partridges and iced water.

The Escorial, the huge palace-monastery built by Philip II on the lower slopes of the Guadarrama mountains, north of Madrid. The four corner towers represented the legs of the upturned grid-iron on which the early Christian martyr St Lawrence was put to death.

Letter from Philip II to the Duke of Medina Sidonia, February 1588. The letter was written by a secretary, but at the end the King added a few lines in his own bold hand – as he often did – and signed himself 'Yo, El Rey' – 'I, the King.'

It would not have been surprising if this tragedy, piling on top of political setbacks, had left the King embittered; but all the reverses he suffered seemed only to drive him down into a lower gear of dogged determination. If sheer industry and perseverance had been all that were needed, he must have been triumphantly successful, for no one worked harder than he. Night after night, until the early hours, he sat up in his bare office in San Lorenzo del Escorial, the immense palace-monastery in the mountains north of Madrid whose construction he had supervised over a period of twenty years. Often he dictated to his secretary Juan de Idiaquez, but for much of the time he was reading and making notes himself, endlessly poring over despatches and reports, scribbling remarks in the margins, adding extra instructions, writing and writing and writing in his large, strong hand, signing himself at the end of every document,

YO
EL REY

Any of his subjects who received an order signed 'I, the King' would certainly be galvanized into action; but what most of them could not know was that their master had one drastic failing – his inability to delegate. Like a spider at the centre of a gigantic web, he sought to maintain control of every scheme that he launched, every order that he sent out, busying himself with a thousand small matters which would have been better left to subordinates. No detail was too small to escape his attention. He sought to shape every facet of his people's lives, laying down what they might or might not wear, how many servants and horses they might own, how they should address each other. His obsession with minutiae not only robbed his executives of initiative: often it positively crippled operations that might otherwise have succeeded – and none more fatally than the Armada.

As years went by his tendency towards centralization grew: dispensing first with the parliaments of Spain's member-states, he progressively ignored the Cortes (or Parliament) in Madrid itself, and reigned more and more as an autocrat. Formally, the government was made up of eleven departments, presided over by four secretaries of state; but in practice every important decision was taken by the King, advised only by his closest confidant and friend, Ruy Gomez, Duke of Pastrana and Prince of Eboli, and by his harsh but widely-experienced commander-in-chief of the armed forces, the Duke of Alva.

In the thirty-two years since his father Charles V had handed over the throne to him, Philip could count only three major military or political successes: the Spanish victories at Lepanto and Terceira, and the annexation of Portugal. At Lepanto – or Navpaktos, on the Gulf of Corinth – on 7 October 1571 the allied forces of Spain, Venice, Genoa and the Pope, commanded by Philip's illegitimate half-brother Don John of Austria, had finally smashed the sea-power of the Turks, against whom, until then, it had been necessary to maintain constant eastward vigilance. The battle was on a colossal scale, the allies sailing to the attack with more than 200 galleys, 29,000 soldiers and 50,000 mariners and oarsmen. Don John, aged only 24 and wonderfully handsome, led the forces of Christendom clad in white velvet and gold, with a crimson scarf across his chest. In a grand charge, made in line-abreast formation, the forward-firing galleys of the allies rammed the Turkish centre, broke through, came to close quarters, grappled with the enemy, and in hand-to-hand fighting annihilated their right wing, with the result that the Muslim navy was routed, and some 20,000 of its men were killed. (In the course of the battle the young Miguel Cervantes, then a regular soldier of 24, was wounded in the left hand.) The form of the victory, and the tactics that succeeded, were of the utmost importance, for they dominated Spanish ideas on naval warfare for the next twenty years.

The annexation of Portugal was accomplished in 1580, with little bloodshed, but not without a great deal of ill-will on the part of the Portuguese. The sudden death of the young King Sebastian in 1578 on an expedition against the Moors left no firm succession to the throne. The official claimant was his uncle, the aged Cardinal Henry, last of the Aviz dynasty; but although he succeeded briefly, the strain overcame him and he soon expired. Next in line was Don Antonio, a grandson (though illegitimate) of the former King Emanuel, and a man of great popularity among ordinary Portuguese. For a few months he reigned as king; but Philip was also a grandson of Emanuel, and, with at least as good a claim to the throne, he sent down the ruthless Duke of Alva to sweep aside opposition. Antonio fled into the mountains, and Philip, having marched across the border, was proclaimed king at Tomar, near Santerem, on 3 April 1581. Thus at one stroke he added to his own empire both Portugal itself, with its invaluable Atlantic port of Lisbon, and the huge overseas territory which Portuguese sea-captains had been winning ever since Prince Henry the Navigator had begun to colonize the coast of Africa in 1415.

The third great Spanish triumph – at Terceira, in the Azores – came about as an indirect consequence of the annexation. Don Antonio, having escaped first to France and then to England, returned to France in 1583 and solicited the support of Catherine de Medici, the Queen Mother, who helped him fit out a fleet. With this he planned to recover the Azores, and then, using the islands as a base, to make an attempt on the mainland; but in August that year his hopes were wrecked by the Spanish fleet under the command of the formidable Don Alvaro de Bazan, Marquis of Santa Cruz, who scattered the French ships after a fierce battle. Once again, grappling and hand-to-hand fighting were what won the day, and in a never-to-be-forgotten exploit the dashing young Don Miguel de Oquendo saved the life of his commander-in-chief by personally boarding the French flagship.

Apart from these successes, Philip's reign had been a dour struggle; and in the three countries that concerned him most – the Netherlands, France and England – he had failed almost entirely to make progress, either political or religious.

No country had been more dear to Charles V than the Netherlands, which Spain had taken over from the Dukes of Burgundy at the end of the fifteenth century. The Spanish possession comprised parts of the countries that are today Holland, Belgium and France; and ever since Philip made his own state entry into Brussels in 1549, to spend two years there, he himself had retained a strong sentimental attachment to the low, flat territory along the southern shore of the English Channel. It is hard to see why. In economic and political terms the Netherlands were vital to Spain: the taxes from their rich trading cities were indispensable to the Exchequer, and their physical presence acted as a barrier cutting off the French both from access to the Channel and from contact with the English, with whom – given a more direct approach – they might have formed an alliance threatening to Spain. These advantages were undeniable; yet they were not easily held, for the Netherlands gave Philip endless trouble, and were in almost every way alien to him. Their flat, wet, cloudy landscape was infinitely less stimulating than the high, dry mountains of Spain; their people ate and drank and swore with a coarse relish that did not commend them to him, abstemious and reticent as he was. Worst of all, in spite of every effort that he made to convert them – no matter how cruelly his agents might slaughter and torture them in attempts to extirpate heresy – they remained unshakeably Protestant.

The ruthless Don Fernando Alvarez de Toledo, Duke of Alva, sent by Philip to subdue the Netherlands in 1567: a portrait by Titian.

'You know how the Spanish Inquisition is hated here', wrote his sister Margaret, Duchess of Parma, Governor of the Netherlands, when he insisted on sterner enforcement of the Catholic religion in 1566; and in 1567, when he sent the Duke of Alva to help her crush the rebellion led by William the Silent, Prince of Orange, she had no hesitation in telling the King: 'As he [Alva] is so detested in this country, his coming itself will be enough to make all the Spanish nation hated.'

Margaret's prediction proved an understatement. Although Alva ruled the Netherlands in splendour from a gold-covered throne in Antwerp, his brutal method of trying to silence all opposition by armed force succeeded only in stepping up the general loathing for Spain, and in 1572, at his own request, he was recalled, his policy of blood and iron a failure. Under the milder Luis Requesens, who replaced him, things were less stormy; but William proved a resilient and resourceful opponent, and the permanent deployment of a large army – which was needed to keep the country under control – put such a severe strain on Philip's finances that when Requesens died in March 1576, the Spanish troops mutinied for lack of pay.

Don John, victor of Lepanto, was sent as governor, but in November the mutineers ran amok in Antwerp, sacking the city and putting 6,000 people to death. To reinforce the command, Philip next despatched his nephew Alexander Farnese, son of Margaret, with a force of veteran Spanish and Italian infantry; and he, together with Don John, won a great victory over the Protestant forces on the Plain of Gemblours. When Don John died of fever on 1 October 1578, Farnese took over his command.

Thus there assumed control in the Netherlands Spain's ablest, most dedicated and imaginative soldier, who over the next decade brought to the task of re-conquering the lost provinces not only personal courage and physical endurance of a very high order, but also an intellectual curiosity and analytical approach exceptional among military commanders. Besides fighting and organizing for the present, he was constantly thinking and planning for the future, reading the minds of his colleagues and opponents with rare perspicacity, and recording his own observations. It is a thousand pities that the one mind which he did not analyse on paper was his own; for he became a crucial figure in the Armada campaign, and it was his failure to carry out the role assigned him that, more than any other single factor, sent Philip's mighty enterprise to its destruction.

While Philip kept control of the Netherlands by force, he sought to influence affairs in France more by dynastic marriage, by diplomacy and by intrigue. His aim – largely destructive – was to keep the country as weak as possible, and to prevent it forming alliances with other nations, principally England and Scotland, that might constitute threats to Spain.

CLAVDE DE
LORRAINE DVC
DE CVYSE

Claude de Lorraine, Duke of Guise: a portrait by Jean Clouet. Leader of the Catholic faction in France, Guise was sustained by Spanish gold, and won such widespread support that the effete King Henry III was forced to flee from Paris. For years the English were afraid that, if the Spanish tried to invade, Guise would cross the Channel in support; but when the Armada came, he made no move.

In this he was greatly helped by the fact that France herself was riven by debilitating internal dissensions, both political and religious.

The cardinal weakness lay in the Valois monarchy, which was never in control of the whole country, still less of the powerful, extreme Catholic faction led by the Dukes of Guise. Philip's first major attempt to control French affairs came with his marriage to Elizabeth of Valois, eldest daughter of King Henry II, in 1560. The betrothal had been made in Paris the year before by Alva, acting as Philip's proxy, when the princess was still only 16, and before she could be brought to Spain the whole future of France was clouded by the sudden death of King Henry, killed by an arrow in the eye at a tournament. In spite of this disaster, the wedding went ahead; and in the eight further years for which she lived, Elizabeth played no small part in preserving the precarious balance of relations between France and Spain. Although she never produced a son and heir, she did bear Philip two daughters, and by her very presence on Spanish soil limited Philip's designs against her country.

During that time, however, allegiances shifted with bewildering rapidity. In 1558 the Dauphin of France had been married, at the age of 14, to Mary, Queen of Scots, who was herself only 16. On the death of his father a year later, he succeeded as King Francis II, but during his brief reign the country was in effect ruled by Mary's uncles, the Duke of Guise and the Cardinal of Lorraine. When Francis died in 1560, and Mary returned to Scotland, the throne passed to his younger brother, who became Charles IX; but since the new king was only 10 years old, effective government fell into the hands of his mother, Catherine de Medici, who became regent.

The French Queen Mother was an intelligent and able politician, not blinkered by religious bigotry, but ready to play any faction off against another to the advantage of her own family. Hating the extreme Catholic Guises, she tried to balance the opposing forces by leaning towards the Protestant Huguenots – and for the next thirty years France was torn apart by religious strife, first under her own domination, then under Charles IX, and finally under her third son Henry III. In the early 1570s there emerged as leader of the Huguenots the dissolute but able and popular Henry of Navarre, who remained the main obstacle to Philip's designs for more than twenty years. The three terrible weeks of the St Bartholomew's Day massacre in August and September 1572 – touched off by the attempt to murder Gaspard de Coligny, Admiral of France, which Catherine had instigated – were merely the most savage manifestation of the almost ceaseless civil war between Catholics and Protestants that racked the country.

Seeing that he could not control Catherine, Philip concentrated his attention on the Duke of Guise, whom he bribed, threatened and cajoled to carry on the internal struggle against the Protestants. Bolstered by Spanish gold, Guise won such strong support – first from the mob in Paris, then all over France – that the effete Henry III was forced to flee from his own capital. As a front for his own political ambitions, Philip encouraged the formation of an ostensibly religious body, the Catholic Holy League; and when Henry of Navarre refused to join it, he got Pope Sixtus V to excommunicate him. For a time it seemed that his dream of turning all France forcibly Catholic might become reality, only for it to be shattered when Henry III managed to have Guise murdered.

For Philip, the effects of this bitter struggle were mixed. Although his efforts to impose Catholicism on France were frustrated for many years, the internecine warfare which he financed so crippled the country that it was no threat to him or anyone else; and when at last his plans to invade England matured, France was *hors de combat*, unable to give him, or his principal enemy, any help.

With his plans to win over – or subvert – England, Philip had even less success. After a promising start, his relationship with England fluctuated sharply before it degenerated into ever-increasing hostility and ended in open war.

At least he began in style. In 1553, at the instigation of his father, who

still ruled Spain and the Netherlands, he formally asked for the hand of Mary, Queen of England, in marriage; she accepted his offer next January, and on 20 July 1554 he landed with great ceremony at Southampton, clad in white velvet, bringing extravagant wedding gifts, and accompanied by a large contingent of retainers. His bride was no beauty – even well-wishers described her as a faded little woman with thin red hair and no eyebrows – but she seems to have responded to her southern prince with enthusiasm, even with love. Philip himself behaved impeccably, taking care to maintain an open and polite demeanour with all he met. Yet no one could disguise the hostility which the English felt towards him and his companions. The 8,000 soldiers who had come with him were not even allowed to disembark, and by the time he and the Queen made their State entry into London on 27 August, it was clear to his courtiers that the English had no intention of ever letting him govern their country.

Cynics remarked that all he wanted was to sire a son and heir, and that once he had done so, he would depart. They were not far wrong – for Charles V's grand dynastic design was that a strong Anglo-Spanish dynasty, ruling in England and Flanders, should control the Channel and all the wealth of its trade. Yet the old king's dream was never realized, for, after several times believing she was pregnant, Mary failed to produce a

The St Bartholomew's Day massacre, which began in Paris on 24 August 1572. During the next three weeks some 30,000 Protestants were massacred – the only event known to have made Philip laugh out loud.

Philip II of Spain and Mary Tudor were married at Winchester in 1554; but the presence of the Spanish prince and his followers excited great hostility in England, and the attempt at a dynastic alliance failed when it became clear that Mary could not produce a son and heir.

child, and when she died in 1558 her successor, Elizabeth, at once took steps to distance herself from Spain and Spanish support, rejecting the overtures of Philip's special envoy, and – a gross insult to the proselitizing Spanish king – re-establishing the Protestant religion.

Philip never came to England again; but at first he made it a central part of his foreign policy to maintain good relations with Elizabeth, and he did so for as long as his other commitments allowed. Heretic though she was, he would rather have her kingdom independent than joined together with France. Thus in 1560, when Elizabeth sent a strong amphibious force to attack the combined armies of Scotland and France at Leith, on the Firth of Forth, he ignored strident calls for help from the Duke of Guise, for at that stage the last thing he wanted was that Elizabeth should be deposed and the way opened for a potentially-threatening Anglo-Scottish-French alliance.

For ten years relations between England and Spain remained reasonably cordial; but then in 1568 Philip provoked Elizabeth's furious resentment by dismissing the English ambassador to Madrid on religious grounds. By then she was openly supporting the Protestant resistance in the Netherlands, and when Spanish ships carrying money to pay the Duke of Alva's troops were scattered by pirates and ran into Plymouth, Falmouth and Southampton, she condoned the seizure of the gold – pretending that it had been taken ashore purely to protect it – and in spite of repeated demands from Spain, she never returned it. In retaliation Philip ordered the seizure of English ships in Spanish ports.

Still he did all he could to avoid open hostility; but from now on he began to condone and even promote plots to free Mary, Queen of Scots (who was by then under arrest in England) and have Elizabeth murdered. Such clandestine intrigues did not trouble his conscience, for he persuaded himself that an assassination, if it were carried out, would promote the service of God; yet equally they availed him nothing, for in whatever way he sought to harass England – whether he was banning her traders from Spanish ports, having her seamen tortured by the Inquisition, or encouraging plans for the capture of Ireland – his schemes remained ineffective.

Yet inevitably, as the monarchs manoeuvred for advantage, relations between their subjects deteriorated. The English, having once looked on the Spaniards as friends, began to hate them, and vice-versa. No doubt every story that came back to Plymouth or Portsmouth, of how an innocent sailor had been flung into gaol or put upon the rack, was suitably embellished and exaggerated; but it is certain that no small number of English subjects were burnt at the stake (twenty-six in 1562 alone), and that the mutual loathing between the two sides provoked appalling atrocities. Thus when Thomas Cobham – a member of the well-known Protestant family of Cowling Castle – captured a Spanish ship in the Bay of Biscay, he had the captain and crew sewed into their own mainsail and cast overboard. Days later they were washed ashore dead, still trapped in their outsize winding-sheet. Even the Elizabethans found this outrage a little disturbing, and Cobham was ordered to explain himself; but there is no record of him ever being punished.

For this progression of hostility the Queen herself was in no small measure to blame, since she secretly encouraged privateers to prey upon Spanish shipping to such a degree that among the English piracy became a national sport, both in the Channel and further afield, and adventurous young bloods conceived the idea that in attacking Catholic vessels they were working not only to their own advantage, but to that of God and the country as well. Many of them, from Sir Francis Drake downwards, made vast profits, but in doing so they were unwittingly contributing to the long-term danger which threatened their country; for their activities, compounding all Philip's other irritations, gradually increased his resentment to the point at which he felt compelled to launch a full-scale attack on England.

Chapter Three

The
Virgin Queen

Elizabeth: a portrait from the collection of Her Majesty the Queen. As a young woman Elizabeth was strikingly attractive. Numerous attempts were made to marry her off to members of the European royal families, but, although a perennial flirt, she resisted every suitor.

At the beginning of 1588 Queen Elizabeth was 54, and in the twenty-ninth year of her reign. Having succeeded to the throne at the age of 25, she had managed, by means of her courage, her shrewdness, her intelligence and the loyal support of her people, to rule alone for almost as long as Philip, surviving no small number of attempts on her kingdom and her person. In youth she had been strikingly attractive, and for years she had been seen as the most splendid match in Christendom. Everyone, both in England and abroad, had expected her to marry, and pressure to do so had been put on her from every side; just as many a potentate in Europe had sought to arrange a dynastic alliance with England, so her own counsellors had ceaselessly urged her to take a husband and secure her succession with a son and heir. Suitor after suitor had appeared on the horizon – none more imposing than King Philip – but she had sent every one of them away, and gradually consolidated her status as the legendary Virgin Queen.

By 1588 her appearance was startling, for although her looks had faded and her few remaining teeth were yellow or black, she got herself up in deliberately fantastical fashion, wearing a large auburn wig, brilliantly coloured clothes, and a riot of jewels about her person. No one left a more vivid glimpse of her than André Hurault, Sieur de Maisse, who came to London in 1597 as ambassador extraordinary from Henry IV of France. Although he saw her nine years after the Armada, it is likely that this is very much how the Queen would have appeared to a distinguished visitor in 1588. At the first of Maisse's several audiences:

This allegorical portrait of the House of Tudor and the Protestant succession in England, painted during the reign of Elizabeth I, shows Henry VIII on the throne, flanked on his right by Mary and Philip, behind whom is Mars, the God of War. On the King's left is Prince Edward (later Edward VI), kneeling, and next to him Elizabeth, backed up by Flora and the fruits of prosperity.

She was strangely attired in a dress of silver cloth, white and crimson, or silver 'gauze', as they call it. This dress had slashed sleeves lined with red taffeta, and was girt about with other little sleeves that hung down to the ground, which she was for ever twisting and untwisting. She kept the front of her dress open, and one could see the whole of her bosom, and passing low, and often she would open the front of this robe, as if she was too hot. The collar of the robe was very high, and the lining of the inner part all adorned with little pendants of rubies and pearls, very many, but quite small. She also had a chain of rubies and pearls about her neck.

On her head she wore a garland of the same material, and beneath it a great, reddish-coloured wig, with a great number of spangles of gold and silver, and hanging down over her forehead, some pearls, but of no great worth. On either side of her ears hung two great curls of hair, almost down to her shoulders, and within the collar of the robe, spangled as the top of her head. Her bosom is somewhat wrinkled . . . but lower down her flesh is exceedingly white and delicate, as far as one could see.

After the shock of the pearly Queen's appearance, the most memorable impression Maisse got was of her restlessness. She was for ever opening her robe, twisting her sleeves, getting up, sitting down, complaining of the heat or lack of air; and perhaps this jumpiness reflects the trait which, above all others, had enabled her to rule with such success: her endless capacity for prevarication, improvisation and changing her mind. Maddening to those who worked for her, but immensely effective at defusing dangerous situations, the habit (or device) of playing every situation by ear had brought her through crises innumerable.

Although herself highly gifted – able to read and write in Greek and Latin, and to converse fluently with the ambassadors of France and Italy in their own languages – she depended heavily on a small circle of advisers, and in these she was extraordinarily fortunate.

The closest to her was Robert Dudley, Earl of Leicester, whom she had first met when they were both in the Tower. He became established as a favourite at Court in 1559, the year after her accession, and remained her greatest moral support for the rest of his life. When first he took her eye he was only 26, and had already been married for nine years: a splendidly handsome man, of bounding ambition, but a *nouveau riche* of moderate intellectual endowments, a selfish and unscrupulous courtier whose abrupt elevation gave rise to spiteful stories. These by no

AN · DNI
1562

ÆTATI
SVÆ 30

RESPICE

FINEM

Closest to the Queen of all her courtiers was Robert Dudley, Earl of Leicester. As the threat of invasion grew, she placed him in supreme command of the land forces, but he died in September 1588, just after the crisis had passed, to her inconsolable grief,

The Queen's faithful servants. William Cecil, first Baron Burghley (left), the Lord High Treasurer, who devoted his life to the service of monarch and nation, and his son Robert.

means decreased when his wife Amy Robsart was found dead, with her neck broken, at the bottom of the stairs, in November 1560; gossip held that Leicester was a man of unbridled lechery, and that when the Queen left London on her summer Progresses through the kingdom she went to bear his children in secret. Such rumours, however, failed to unsettle his relationship with Elizabeth; even though baffled contemporaries could not imagine what she saw in him, it is clear that his friendship – even love – brought her untold comfort over the years.

A still longer-serving retainer was William Cecil, first Baron Burghley, who had formed a secret understanding with Elizabeth and helped protect her when she fell under suspicion of plotting to murder her half-sister Queen Mary. Immediately after her own accession, Elizabeth made him Secretary of State, and then, in 1572, Lord High Treasurer: for almost the whole of her reign he devoted himself with the utmost loyalty to the twin tasks of maintaining financial stability at home and strengthening England's position abroad by the discreet support of Protestant movements in Scotland, France and the Netherlands.

By the year of the Armada Burghley was 68, a spare, sombre, white-bearded figure, usually dressed in grey or black, whose sheer sobriety made him stand out among the peacock figures of the Court. Secretive and self-possessed, he preferred to live in his own house, rather than occupy official lodgings and be swept up in the brilliant, superficial glitter that surrounded the Queen. Yet in private he was an attractive character, faithful to friends and family, an immensely generous entertainer, and an inveterate gardener who imported foreign trees regardless of expense.

The earliest of risers, he had a phenomenal capacity for work; and this, with his lifetime's experience of high office, made him indispensable to the Queen. His selfless patriotism gave him an unique hold over her mind, for she saw that his ambition was entirely on behalf of his country, rather than of himself, and she trusted him absolutely. Even if he was known to others as the Old Fox, the Queen called him her Spirit, or Sir Spirit; and in many ways he was the spirit of the country, for he was *the* administrator of Elizabethan England.

In his days as Secretary he had built up an efficient information system which bribed secret agents all over Europe to send information to London; and to help run this combination of espionage service and news network he had taken on as a protégé Francis Walsingham, a young man whose burning Protestant faith had driven him into exile during Mary's reign. Soon, however, Burghley found he was creating a rival to himself – and in due course, after a spell in Paris as ambassador to France, Walsingham himself became Secretary of State in 1573, holding the post until his death.

He, the third member of Queen Elizabeth's inner circle, held a key position in government, for the Secretary was the intermediary between the Crown and the Privy Council – the permanent executive body (fore-runner of the modern Cabinet) which dealt with affairs of State. Not only did he run the diplomatic service and administer foreign policy: he also controlled the espionage system both at home and abroad, watching the post and the ports with equal assiduity. Thus, quite apart from his value

1. The Escorial: the Hall of Battles, decorated for Philip II with scenes of Spanish victories, including the triumph at Lepanto.

2. Philip's study-bedroom in the Escorial, where he worked far into the night, reading, dictating and writing.

3. The Battle of Lepanto, 7 October 1571. The Turkish galleys, meeting those of the Catholic allies at close quarters, were utterly defeated. In the generation that followed, the Spanish never broke away from this concept of using ships as battering-rams and of fighting hand-to-hand battles at sea; and their failure to develop new tactics played a large part in the defeat of the Armada.

4. Don John of Austria. illegitimate half-brother of Philip II, and commander-in-chief of the victorious Catholic forces at Lepanto. Philip later sent him to suppress the revolt in the Netherlands, but he died of fever there in 1578.

FRANCISCUS WALSINGHAM Reg: Elis: a Secretis
A.D. 1573. Obiit A.D. 1590.

'None alive did better ken the secretary craft, to get counsels out of others and keep them in himself . . . Quick his ears, who could hear at London what was whispered at Rome': Sir Francis Walsingham, the Queen's Secretary, adviser on foreign affairs, and head of an efficient intelligence-gathering organization.

as an administrator and shaper of policy, Walsingham was a vital factor in preserving the Queen's own person, since it was he who, through his spies, uncovered the main plots to assassinate her. Not for nothing did she call him her Moon, for his calm gaze seemed to miss nothing.

If Walsingham yielded nothing to Burghley in terms of patriotism, his religious convictions made him a much sharper character. Although of complete personal integrity, he did not hesitate to use the most treacherous and brutal means, including torture, to obtain the exposure and confession of supposed enemies. The seventeenth-century historian William Camden gave a good idea of his penetrating nature:

A man exceeding wise and industrious . . . a most sharp

maintainer of the purer religion, a most diligent searcher of hidden secrets, who knew excellent well how to win men's minds unto him and to apply them to his own uses, insomuch as in subtlety and officious service he surpassed the Queen's expectation.

'None alive did better ken the secretary craft, to get counsels out of others and keep them in himself,' wrote Thomas Fuller.

Marvellous his sagacity in examining suspected persons, either to make them confess the truth, or confound themselves by denying it, to their detection. Cunning his hands, who could unpick the cabinets in the Pope's conclave; quick his ears, who could hear at London what was whispered at Rome; and numerous the spies and eyes of this Argus dispersed in all places.

As the threat from Spain increased, Walsingham and Leicester formed a war party within the Council, opposing more cautious spirits such as Burghley, who, like the Queen, sought to avoid direct confrontation. Behind Walsingham was the ever-growing force of the militant Protestants known as Puritans, whose leading spirit the Secretary became.

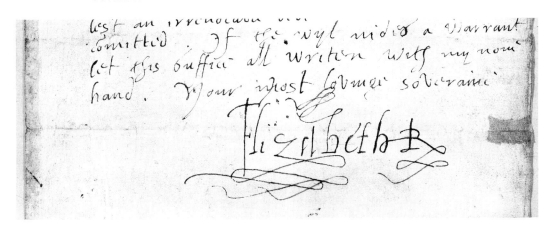

Letter from Elizabeth I to Burghley, her Lord High Treasurer, agreeing to defer the execution of the Duke of Norfolk (who finally went to the gallows, for treason, on 2 June 1572). It is said that the extravagant flourishes under the Queen's signature were designed to prevent forgeries being added to the document.

By the 1580s the Council was meeting almost every day, including Sundays; yet although it played an essential role in threshing out policy and putting decisions into effect, it was in the end the Queen who ruled. Like all the Tudors, her ambition was to centralize power into her own hands; she could always, if she wished, impose her will, and her ministers were responsible to her rather than to Parliament, which held only occasional sessions.

The Queen herself never wanted war. Indeed, at the start of her reign the idea of an all-out war against Spain would have been unimaginable. She had neither the territorial ambition nor the passion for forcing religious ideas on other nations that drove Philip relentlessly on; the sole aim of her foreign policy – if indeed she can be said to have had one – was no more ambitious than to undermine threats to her own kingdom by judicious subsidy of Protestant movements in other countries. She had problems enough on her own northern border, for although in 1568 she placed her cousin Mary, Queen of Scots under arrest, and never again released her, the mere fact that the deposed monarch was still alive incited Catholic conspirators everywhere to brew plots for her release and to stir up revolution in Scotland. Another continuous worry to Elizabeth was Ireland, which was strongly Catholic, thinly garrisoned by English troops, and under imperfect control – potentially an ideal base for Spanish mischief-making.

And yet, no matter how keen Elizabeth might be to keep clear of Philip's religious wars, the side-effects of his dogged manoeuvring in Europe gradually drove her into a more and more extreme position. One critical event came in 1570 with the issue by Pope Pius V of the Bull *Regnans in Excelsis*, a copy of which was nailed to the door of the Bishop of London, denouncing the Queen as a heretic and a bastard, depriving her of her 'pretended right' to reign, and absolving her subjects from the need to show allegiance.

Until then her reign had been distinguished by its religious tolerance. Although Mary had left the Catholic religion established in England, Elizabeth had taken the momentous decision to break from Rome, as her father Henry VIII and her brother Edward VI had done; and yet the early years of her reign had been remarkable for their freedom from religious persecution. Her aim was to foster a national Church, Protestant yet tolerant, under the control of the crown. But now came this grossly offensive attack from Rome, and instruction that it was a mortal sin to attend Protestant services. This put English Catholics in an impossible position: from now on they either had to defy their Church or become traitors to their country.

The Bull was utterly inept – a political disaster, and entirely counterproductive, for it not only made war between England and Rome inevit-

The Popes bull against the Queene.

An engraving to commemorate Pope Pius V's Bull of 1570, which excommunicated Elizabeth, denounced her as a heretic and a bastard, deprived her of her 'pretended right to reign', and absolved her subjects from the need to show her allegiance. This clumsy proclamation had an effect exactly opposite to the one intended, and greatly strengthened the Protestant cause in England.

able, but also set off a train of legislation against Catholics in England which culminated in the vicious measures of the 1580s. The Act of 1581 made it high treason to withdraw from the Church of England to Rome, and anyone convicted of hearing or saying Mass became liable to a heavy fine and a year in gaol. Serious fines -- of £20 a month -- for absence from church forced most Catholics into line; but the number of executions for religious crimes went steadily up, from 2 in 1583 to 15 in 1584 and 34 in 1588.

Puritans such as Walsingham urged the Queen to take a more aggressive religious stance by giving overt assistance to the French Huguenots and Philip's Protestant enemies in the Low Countries; she, however, was too cautious to risk an all-out war. She might seize Spanish treasure ships in the Channel to gain immediate financial advantage, as she did in 1568; but only four years later she suddenly expelled Count la Marck's Sea Beggars, the Dutch privateers who had been launching attacks on Spanish ships from English ports. This magnanimous gesture led, in 1573, to the restoration of trade with Spain, and in 1577 to the re-establishment of diplomatic contact for the first time in six years. Officially, at least, Anglo-Spanish relations were more cordial than for some time; yet still the Queen privily encouraged her ocean-going sea-captains to prey upon King Philip's ships, and when one came home with a tremendous haul of Spanish gold and silver – as Francis Drake did after his circumnavigation of the world made between 1577 and 1580 – she pocketed part of the proceeds and rode out the diplomatic storms that inevitably followed.

It needs a strong effort of imagination to see the land over which

Elizabeth ruled. 'The most famous island, without comparison, of the whole world', wrote Camden modestly in his survey *Britannia*, first published in 1586. Even though the population had recovered strongly since the ravages of the Black Death two centuries earlier, in England, Scotland and Wales combined there were scarcely five million people, and of these 300,000 were concentrated in London. The second city in the kingdom, Norwich, had fewer than 20,000 inhabitants, and the land as a whole was sparsely populated. Birmingham was nothing but a village, and Southampton, which had been a flourishing little town of 300 houses when Philip came to marry Mary in 1554, had since fallen on hard times and was much decayed.

The countryside itself must have seemed almost empty of people. In general it was much wilder than today: there were still huge tracts of natural woodland and miles of moor, bog and down, rough and uncultivated. Around the villages crops were grown by local people, but settlements were cut off from each other by the forests. To the eyes of visitors from the south of Europe, used to greater heat, the land looked incredibly green. Greenness was perhaps its most pronounced physical feature, no matter the season of the year. Even at the height of summer, although the patches of wheat, oats and barley turned yellow, there were still bosky woods and verdant pastures as far as the eye could see. Kent, already the garden of England, was dappled with orchards of apples and cherries, and in the fields, everywhere, grazed the great big, fleecy white sheep whose wool had been the mainspring of England's prosperity for the past hundred years. The absence of wolves, which still flourished in Wales and Scotland, made husbandry simple, and English wool was of such high quality that it was in demand as far afield as Turkey. 'In these wolds' wrote Camden of the Cotswold hills,

> there feed great numbers of sheep, long-necked and square of bulk and bone, by reason (as it is commonly thought) of the weally and hilly situation of their pasturage; whose wool being most fine and soft is had in passing great account among all nations.

There were also huge numbers of rabbits, many wild, but some kept in special warrens for their meat and fur.

Roads were few, and those that existed were so dreadfully rutted, waterlogged and deep in mud that travellers on foot or horseback usually took the straightest possible route across the fields. In winter people did not travel at all unless they were forced to, so that news often did not reach country communities for weeks on end.

Communications, in any case, were very poor. There was no postal service, except for the Royal Mail, which conveyed government corre-

English costumes of about 1580. From left, well-to-do merchant of London, noble young lady of London, woman of the people, young man.

Court dress in the reign of Elizabeth I.

Adrianus Matham sculpsit 1620.

spondence only, and no public transport of any kind – except that well-to-do individuals in a hurry could ride one of the post horses, and by this means travel relatively fast – for instance, from Plymouth to London in thirty-six hours. Newspapers did not exist, and the only written intelligence normally available came in the form of the pamphlets and broadsheets which were sold by itinerant pedlars in towns and at country fairs; but as these were bawdy and fanciful, mixing the wildest rumours with facts, it was impossible for most people to get any accurate idea of what was going on outside their own area. Even educated people spoke in what would now sound like fruity rustic accents – 'o's sounded as in 'raw' rather than 'road', so that Plymouth Hoe was known as Plymouth Haw – and Sir Walter Raleigh, for one, retained his broad Devonshire drawl throughout his life.

Country people, who made up the bulk of the population, lived in extreme simplicity. Although they cultivated crops in open fields, they depended heavily on the many thousands of acres of common land which were still unfenced, not only for grazing, but also for firewood and building-timber. The best-off ate bread made of wheat, but the poorest had to survive on bread made from barley, rye or even peas and acorns. Most houses were made of wood, and almost all household artefacts were home-made – plates, bowls, spoons and mugs carved from wood, clothes woven from wool, hemp and flax, furniture rough and ready, built by their own hand.

The balance of agriculture fluctuated a good deal during Elizabeth's reign. By the middle of the century the great prosperity of the cloth industry, and the ever-increasing demand for wool, had taken thousands of acres out of cultivation and put them down to pasture; but then, to increase the supply of grain, the Government brought in a series of Tillage Acts, and so pushed the arable acreage up again. In good seasons there was not too much hardship, but the failure of one harvest set hundreds of new vagabonds wandering the country – and poverty, in the form of vagabondage, was the greatest social problem of the age. Attempts to deal with it by savage legislation were ineffective: persistent vagabonds could be branded through the ear, whipped till their backs were bloody, and sent back to where they had come from – but still their numbers increased, and the first system of poor relief gradually evolved.

The poor formed the lowest level of society. Next up were labourers, and next again the freeholders. Then came the yeomen, or well-to-do farmers, with 100 or more acres of land to their name. Above them were the gentry, and at the top of the pyramid the nobles, who built themselves palatial country houses like Burghley or Hatfield. The classes were sharply differentiated, but it was perfectly possible for go-ahead individuals to move up from one to another – and indeed many yeomen, buying

The Booke of Faulconrie or Hau-
KING, FOR THE ONELY DE-
light and pleasure of all Noblemen and Gentlemen:
Collected out of the best aucthors, asvvell Italians as Frenchmen,
and some English practises withall concernyng Faulconrie, the contentes
whereof are to be seene in the next page folowyng.
By *George Turberuile* Gentleman.
NOCET EMPTA DOLORE VOLVPTAS.

Imprinted at Londen for Christopher Barker, at the signe of
the Grashopper in Paules Churchyarde.   *Anno.* 1575

Falconry was a favourite pastime among Elizabethan nobles and gentry.

up more land whenever they could, rose to become gentry through the sheer volume of their possessions.

Even though most of the population was engaged in agriculture, the first industrial revolution was starting to bring in momentous changes. The forests of Kent, Sussex and Surrey became the centre of a flourishing iron industry, and the discovery of good calamine near Bristol in 1560 led to the large-scale manufacture of brass. These two developments had a direct and important bearing on the Spanish Armada, for they helped make English gun-founders pre-eminent at their craft. Although nobody realized it at the time, the excellent quality of Sussex iron derived partly from the fact that the ore contained a high proportion of fossilized grey shells, with the result that it yielded an iron free from slag and gave the finished product its characteristic light colour. Gunpowder was manufactured in Surrey from about the same date.

Coal-mining, particularly in the Newcastle field, developed at a fast pace, many thousand tons being shipped out of the Tyne to London and ports abroad. (The Queen herself would not have coal burnt in her palaces, preferring wood, but already a pall of coal-smoke was liable to hang over the capital.) Engines driven by horses or by water were developed for draining the mines. The cloth industry branched out into fresh fields, producing many new materials, especially from its strongholds in East Anglia, where large numbers of immigrant weavers had settled after being driven out of the Netherlands by religious persecution (in 1572 there were 4,000 aliens in Norwich alone). Altogether, the two decades from 1570 to 1590 were most prosperous for budding industrialists.

In social terms, no industry was more important than the fishery; for not only did fishermen provide much of the nation's food but they also, by making frequent deep-sea voyages to Icelandic waters, maintained a sizeable fleet and trained themselves in maritime skills, thus furnishing the nucleus of the nation's sea-power. An Act of 1548 had designated Friday and Saturday compulsory fish days, on which no meat might be

The Queen being carried in a litter during one of her royal progresses. In the early years of her reign she made extensive journeys through the kingdom, accompanied by a huge retinue and taking her own bed; but as the threat from Spain increased, she curtailed her travels and stayed in or close to London.

View of Elizabethan London, including the Tower, from an engraving by Cornelius Visscher. Almost all the city was strung out along the north bank of the Thames.

London Bridge, covered with shops and houses, was the only connection between north and south banks of the river. On pikes that sprouted from the gateway at the southern approach the heads of recently-executed criminals and traitors were exhibited.

eaten; but Burghley got Parliament to increase the number to three, for purely secular reasons – 'so that the sea-coasts should be strong with men and habitations, and the fleet flourish more than ever'.

Just as most country people never in their lives set eyes on their Queen – unless she happened to come by on one of her Progresses – so very few of them ever visited the capital. London was another world, the greatest city not only in England but on earth.

Almost all its buildings stood on the north bank of the Thames, their western extremity at Westminster, the eastern at the Tower, and the whole dominated by the hugely-long outline of St Paul's Church (predecessor of Wren's cathedral) on Ludgate Hill, whose steeple had never been repaired since being struck by lightning a generation earlier. Places such as Paddington and Islington were still hamlets out in the country. The capital's main thoroughfare was the river, in which salmon and sturgeon abounded, and on its banks were built not only the Queen's palace of Whitehall, flanked by a park containing white fallow deer, but also the great houses of the nobility and the merchants who had grown fat from trade. The Queen's favourite palace was eight miles down-river from London at Greenwich, where her living apartments were on the first floor, for fear of floods, and her windows looked down on the ships passing up and down the great waterway that led to her capital.

In London itself the streets that ran down the river were narrow and stinking. The whole place bustled with life and vigour, seething with hawkers, pickpockets and prostitutes. In the taverns people drank good English beer or Spanish wine, and smoked leaves of the weed first brought by the sea-captains from America little more than ten years earlier, tobacco. Yet the feature that most struck newcomers was London Bridge, whose twenty arches carried a complete row of houses and shops, and a gate-house tower sprouting long poles on which were exhibited the heads of recently-executed traitors.

The city had grown huge on commerce, but it had also become a flourishing centre for the arts, and chief among its glories were its two theatres. Foreigners were amazed to find that on any afternoon two or even three different plays might be performed simultaneously, *in competition with one another*; and posterity will for ever be indebted to the Queen for the way in which she defied Puritan critics, who damned 'the play' as pagan idolatry, and fostered the emergent theatre.

In 1583 she gave a lead by bringing together twelve of the best actors to form her own company, Queen Elizabeth's Men, and others soon followed, among them the Lord Admiral's Company, set up by Lord Howard of Effingham a couple of years later. It was this team, led by Edward Alleyn, that gave the moody young playwright and poet Christopher Marlowe his chance – and by the time the Armada came, an astonishing array of dramatic and literary talent had begun to manifest itself in London. Marlowe completed *Tamburlane the Great* in 1587, and in 1588 was working on *Dr Faustus*. Also in London was the 24-year old son of a butcher from Stratford-upon-Avon, William Shakespeare, who had deserted his wife and twin children to join one of the new theatre companies. The cheerful Thomas Dekker, who later wrote dozens of plays, was then about 18, and John Webster, who sometimes collaborated with him, only 10. Another budding dramatist, Ben Jonson, was 16, and that astonishing polymath Francis Bacon was already a Member of Parliament at the age of 24. Of course the Queen did not directly encourage all these bright talents, but she did by her own example create the atmosphere in which they could flourish, and so made possible the inexhaustible glories of Elizabethan literature.

But the age was one of violent contrasts. As that outstanding Shakespearean scholar Leslie Hotson pointed out, besides being articulate and creative, the Elizabethans were exceedingly tough people:

Unable to reduce or control physical suffering, they had to

William Shakespeare was about 24 in the year of the Armada. By then he had left his wife and twin children in Stratford-upon-Avon to join one of the theatre companies which flourished in London under the enlightened patronage of the Queen and members of the Court.

face the worst. Consequently education of children was severe, and they were taught not to fear the hardships of life, and to tackle them young. Their way of life sharpened their senses, quickened their wits, and gave them a grasp of human experience that we can only envy.

It also made them – by the standards that prevail four centuries later – fiendishly cruel. The Spanish Inquisition has always been a byword for barbarity, yet there is no doubt that the English of the day, from their Queen down, were not far behind when it came to inflicting pain on fellow-humans. After Elizabeth's troops had put down the northern rising of 1569 she celebrated the occasion by writing a poem, allowing the richest of the mutineers to buy themselves off, and ordering the execution of 800 'of the poorer sort' as a reprisal and a warning. When in 1578, after her flirtation with the Duke of Alençon (who at 23 was half her age) the Puritan John Stubbs wrote a tract which said that she was too old to be contemplating marriage, he and his publisher William Page had their right hands severed by mallet and cleaver in front of a crowd at Westminster. In 1587, after the exposure of the Babington conspiracy – which aimed to free Mary, Queen of Scots and murder Elizabeth – she ordained, even before the conspirators were tried, that their deaths should be the most ghastly that the law permitted. The first seven, after hanging for a short time, were cut down, disembowelled and mutilated while still alive; and the rest, by a special royal reprieve, were not mutilated until they were dead.

In and around London, public executions were commonplace popular entertainments: there were gallows on Tower Hill, at both ends of Fetter Lane, and at Tyburn. Particular crimes attracted a variety of special penalties: poisoners were boiled to death in water or molten lead, and felons who refused to speak at their arraignments were (according to Harrison) 'pressed to death with huge weights laid upon a board, that lieth over their breast, and a sharp stone under their backs'. Bear- and bull-baiting regularly drew full houses (of women as well as men) to a circular arena, open to the sky, with boxes for spectators round the perimeter. The bear, with his teeth broken off short so that he could not bite lethally, was tethered to a pole in the centre, and baited by specially-trained mastiffs, six or seven at a time. Bulls were similarly tormented, and the Queen herself was no rare spectator.

The miracle was that in her own being she somehow combined almost all the elements that gave the Elizabethan age its tremendous head of steam. She was subtle, intelligent, a scholar with a relish for words, an accomplished musician, an exhibitionist, an actress, a lover of masque and spectacle (especially the tilt), a perennial flirt, a good rider and competent shot with the crossbow; above all, she was a ruler who elicited the most astonishing devotion from her subjects. And yet her slender frame, feminine and graceful as it was, harboured also the masculine traits of cruelty, coarseness and physical courage. She would swear atrociously when crossed, and engage her courtiers in bawdy repartee – as in the exchange with Edward de Vere, Earl of Oxford, inimitably chronicled by John Aubrey in *Brief Lives*:

> The Earle of Oxford, making of his low obeisance to Queen Elizabeth, happened to let a Fart, at which he was so abashed and ashamed that he went to Travell, 7 yeares. On his returne the Queen welcomed him home, and sayd, My Lord, I had forgott the Fart.

She herself recognized the duality in her nature, and never expressed it more memorably than in her speech to the troops at Tilbury during the Armada campaign, when she proclaimed that although hers was 'the body of a weak and feeble woman', she had 'the heart and stomach of a king'. It is not surprising that to Philip and the militant forces of Catholicism 'the English woman' became the personification of her people, the arch-enemy, the being whose free existence they could no longer tolerate.

The Queen in Parliament. Although the importance of Parliament increased during Elizabeth's reign, it met irregularly, and the main instrument of government was the Privy Council.

46

Chapter Four

Countdown
to War

The idea of a full-scale attack on England was by no means new. The plot
to assassinate Elizabeth in 1570, led by the Florentine financier Roberto
Ridolfi, had the backing of both Philip and the Pope, and an integral part
of it was that the Duke of Alva should cross from the Netherlands to
reinforce the insurgents with a force of 30,000 men. The blundering
intrigue was easily unmasked, but the concept of a mass invasion lived
on: the presence of powerful Spanish forces just across the Channel was a
constant temptation to Philip's commanders there, and Don John of
Austria, for one, was obsessed by the idea of a strike against England
during the late 1570s. Gradually the plan for an invasion became known
as 'the Enterprise of England', or merely as 'the Enterprise'.

Catholics everywhere busied themselves in stirring up anti-English
agitation, not least Vargas, the Spanish ambassador in Paris, who in 1580
told Philip:

> Such is the present condition of England, with signs of revolt
> everywhere, the Queen in alarm, the Catholic party
> numerous, Ireland disturbed, and distrust aroused by Your
> Majesty's fleet . . . that if so much as a cat moved, the whole
> fabric would tumble down in three days.

No doubt the King perceived this for the exaggeration it was; yet
tension between the two sides steadily built up as each traded insults and
provocations. After Philip had annexed Portugal in 1580, Elizabeth gave
asylum to Don Antonio, the exiled monarch, housing him in state in
London and Eton, paying him a pension and encouraging him in
attempts to recover his lost kingdom. From the Continent, Catholic
penetration of England increased with the despatch in June 1580 of the
Jesuit missionaries Edmund Campion and Robert Parsons, both former
Oxford men. Their arrival was seen as a serious threat to the stability of
the country, and Campion's attack on Protestantism, *Decem Rationes*,

The Jesuit martyr Edmund Campion, executed on the Queen's orders at Tyburn in 1581 'for conspiring the death of the Queen and to raise sedition'.

Don Alvaro de Bazan, Marquis of Santa Cruz, Spain's most celebrated military commander, was appointed to lead the Armada against England. He demanded a truly colossal force – twice the size of the one that eventually sailed – but died during the final preparations in February 1588.

published in 1581, led swiftly to his arrest, torture in the Tower and execution at Tyburn – the Enterprise's first martyr. Parsons escaped, to join forces with the other mainspring of the English Catholic movement abroad, William Allen.

In spite of the violent hatred which his name provoked in England, Allen seems to have been a scholarly man, drawn into political warfare against his better inclinations. A former principal of St Mary Hall in Oxford, he had fled the country soon after Elizabeth's accession, and had established a college for the training of Catholic refugees as seminary priests. His institution – first at Louvain, then at Douai – enjoyed enormous success, attracting many exiled students who, after indoctrination, filtered back into England on missions of subversion. When war became inevitable, Allen was summoned to Rome to help with preparations for the attack; in 1587 he was created a cardinal, and then nominated by the Pope to become the Catholic Archbishop of Canterbury, once England had been conquered.

Among the Spanish military commanders invasion fever rose to a peak after their great defeat of the French in the Azores in August 1583. If the victorious commander-in-chief, the Marquis of Santa Cruz, had had his way, the Enterprise might have gone ahead there and then, for, with a triumph behind him, and confidence alight in his forces, he wrote to the King begging for permission to conquer England in the 'name of God and Spain'. His proposal was that he and the Spanish navy should hold the English Channel while the Duke of Guise, under their protection, crossed with an army to land in Sussex – whereupon (he hoped) the English Catholics would rise in arms, set Mary free, and make her queen.

For the moment Philip shelved the idea; but soon events put new pressure on him. In July 1584, after surviving three earlier attempts, William of Orange was assassinated by a Spanish agent, and this disaster to the Protestant cause precipitated England's direct involvement in the Netherlands. Parma began to gain ground rapidly, and the fall of Antwerp – captured by his forces on 7 September 1585 – so alarmed Elizabeth and the Privy Council that they at last abandoned their neutral stance and concluded the Treaty of Nonsuch, whereby they agreed to send an army under the command of Leicester to stiffen Protestant resistance, and to garrison the ports of Flushing and Brill. The decision can be interpreted either as a courageous initiative and a calculated challenge to Spain, or as a desperate measure taken as a last resort to prevent resistance in the Netherlands crumbling altogether and leaving Spain free to turn against England. Either way, the intervention was not a success, for Leicester could not work with the Dutch, and fell out with William's son, Prince Maurice of Nassau; moreover, his poorly-trained troops were no match for Parma's battle-hardened professionals, many

Alexander Farnese, Duke of Parma, Philip's nephew and supreme commander in the Netherlands. He was to command the military attack on England, and assembled a huge invasion force in the Low Countries; but although a military genius, he undermined the Armada campaign by unaccountably failing to provide support at the critical moment.

of whom had been fighting on and off for thirty years.

Leicester was recalled in 1587; but the presence of an English army in the Netherlands had finally goaded Philip into accepting that the Enterprise must go ahead, and early in the spring of that year Santa Cruz sent him an estimate of the forces which he thought would be required. The veteran commander, who had been in service for fifty years, had no illusions about the magnitude of the task, and outlined a truly colossal force, consisting of more than 550 large ships, 240 small craft, 30,000 seamen, 64,000 soldiers and 1,600 horses. Seeing at once that he would never be able to mobilize so vast a force in Spain alone, Philip took the decision – which ultimately proved fatal – that half should be raised at home, where Santa Cruz would collect the large ships and the men to sail them, and the other half in the Netherlands, where Parma would assemble the invasion army and a fleet of flat-bottomed boats to transfer them across the Channel.

As preparations were put in hand at both ends, a memorandum was drafted for the King setting out various possibilities for the Enterprise.

Many people had advised His Majesty to make such an expedition (said the anonymous writer), as it seemed essential for completing the pacification of Flanders and safeguarding the Indies and their trade, 'apart from the service which would be rendered to Our Lord in extirpating the heresies of that kingdom'. Thus the invasion was seen as a means of furthering both political and religious ends simultaneously – a political and territorial campaign made respectable by its guise as a crusade.

The writer went on to outline possible courses of action. The first was to form an alliance with France and raise a joint expedition; the next, to make a league with the Pope, who would help by furnishing men and money, and 'would proclaim a crusade as being a war against heretics, and attempt to come to an understanding with the English Catholics so that they would rebel against the Queen'. Another suggestion was that His Majesty should 'make an agreement with the King of Scotland [Mary's son, James VI], offering to place him in possession of England and to marry him to a member of the House of Austria. The extirpation of the heresies of England should be adopted as a war-cry.'

Others again thought that the King should make the expedition alone, and that 'the whole of the equipment for the attack should be got ready in Spain with great secrecy, giving out that the preparations were being made for other reasons'. The army should consist of 50,000 men, of whom 15,000 would remain at sea to guard the Channel while the rest disembarked at Dover (which 'being weak, could be taken in two days') and advanced on London. Yet another faction favoured an attack on Ireland first, on the grounds that 'the Irish would rebel against the Queen on the slightest pretext'.

In such terms did the Spanish leaders discuss the future of England, as though the rulers of northern Europe and their nations were mere pieces on a chessboard. Yet it seems that by the time this memorandum was written, the King had already decided on his plan of a two-pronged attack. The author of the document warned, with no small prescience, that great dangers would attend the undertaking: England would without difficulty be able to arm fifty or sixty large ships, and the Armada would have no refuge in a storm: 'It would go in evident and grave danger of being lost.' On land the English would be able to keep up guerrilla warfare for a long time, during which 'there will be a thousand inconveniences and embarrassments'. If the Turks saw Philip occupied with 'the English affair', they might well take the opportunity of attacking him in the back.

None of these considerations stopped Philip, however much they might worry him; and there was one point on which the anonymous writer was definitely wrong. 'The Pope would not dare to proclaim a crusade against the English,' he wrote; but Sixtus V, who had succeeded

Guile and malice ooze from this bronze bust of Pope Sixtus V. He promised to pay King Philip a million gold ducats when the Armada landed in England, but whenever anyone tried to exact the money from him he threw childish tantrums – and the crockery.

Secret correspondence: a typical cypher letter from '30' to '10' – Sir Robert Cecil. By such cryptic means did Walsingham's agents send him news from abroad.

to the Papacy in 1585, did just that, promising Philip a million ducats the moment the first Spanish soldier set foot on English soil.

A man of immense energy and grandiose ideas, the former Felice Peretti had been an outstanding student, and a preacher celebrated for his eloquence in the pulpit; he was also a harsh disciplinarian, and when he became Pope launched a purge against bandits and other criminals, exhibiting their heads on the Sant' Angelo bridge in Rome. His main mission was to make the Catholic faith pre-eminent in Europe, and to tighten up clerical discipline; but he also inspired such an immense pro-

52

gramme of building and re-building in Rome that during his five-year tenure of office the grandeur of the city was reborn. Under his direction the dome of St Peter's was completed, and he marked each of the years 1586–89 by re-erecting one of the ancient Egyptian obelisks brought to Italy in the days of the Roman Empire. His fanatical meanness also helped to make him one of the richest rulers in Europe.

All this contributed to give Sixtus a formidable public persona. In private, however, his behaviour was often puerile and ridiculous, especially when he was threatened with having to part with money. Traces of this weakness are visible in his portrait: the eyes are sly, avaricious and shifty. The Spanish ambassador at Rome, Count de Olivares, did eventually wring out of him a warrant promising that he would pay the promised million as soon as the Enterprise succeeded, but every time the matter was brought up he made a scene. 'His Holiness was in a great rage at table,' Olivares reported to the King on 30 June 1587, 'railing at those who served him and throwing the crockery about furiously, which he is rather in the habit of doing.' Later the ambassador wrote that the Pope's 'extreme and extraordinary perturbation' at the idea of having to disburse the money was evident to everybody, and later still, when the expedition had already sailed, he reported that mere mention of the Armada made the Pope 'babble the most ridiculous nonsense at table, and to everyone that comes near him, such as would not be said by a baby of two years old':

> He possesses no sort of charity, kindliness or consideration, and his behaviour is attributed by everyone to the repulsion and chagrin that he feels as the hour approaches for him to drag this money from his heart.

Needless to say, Philip's explosive partner in the Enterprise never paid up; yet his backing was invaluable, for it invested the expedition, if not with funds, at least with the credibility of a religious undertaking.

In England the sense of impending danger was sharply increased by discovery of the Babington conspiracy, with its plan to murder the Queen, in 1586. The exposure led directly to the ignominious expulsion of the Spanish ambassador, Don Bernadino de Mendoza, who decamped to Paris deeply embittered. Thereafter his detailed knowledge of English affairs, sharpened by hatred, made him a dangerous enemy: through him passed all the reports from and to Catholic spies in England, and he forwarded a ceaseless stream of information to the King. No one was more eager than Mendoza that the Enterprise should succeed, for the defeat of Elizabeth and her ministers would constitute personal revenge for the humiliations he had suffered, and a chance to return to his former haunts in triumph.

The collapse of the Babington plot led almost as directly to the death of Mary, Queen of Scots. For months Walsingham and others had been trying to convince Elizabeth that Mary's continued existence was a menace to the kingdom. The scale of the conspiracy uncovered leant fresh weight to their arguments, and in February 1587 they at last persuaded her to sign an execution warrant. On the morning of 18 February Mary Stuart was beheaded in the great hall of Fotheringhay Castle, in Northamptonshire, to Elizabeth's great distress and confusion, but also – after the shock had worn off – to her profound relief.

The murder of so prominent a Catholic was a severe affront to Philip, and he felt it also as a personal blow. 'I have been deeply hurt by the death of the Queen of Scotland,' he wrote to Mendoza in March. Yet it also cleared the way for him to proceed with the Enterprise. Now, if he managed to dislodge Elizabeth, there would be no chance of England, under a half-French monarch, joining forces across the Channel with France. Instead, Philip would be able to exercise his own claim to the English throne, based on his descent from John of Gaunt, and he planned to install his daughter, the Infanta, as queen.

As Santa Cruz and Parma pressed ahead with their respective preparations, Catholic spies in England and Scotland were working overtime. One valuable source was Antonio de Vega, a Portuguese traitor attached to Don Antonio, the exiled king, who, though arrogant and boastful, nevertheless gleaned much interesting information. Other anonymous 'Advices from London' were of variable reliability. In spite of the vigilance of Walsingham's own agents, and the fact that in times of crisis the ports were closed to all shipping, their reports kept filtering out across the Channel in fishing boats and smacks and on to Paris, whence Mendoza forwarded them with his comments to the King. Some time in 1587 a Scot signing himself 'Jacobus Stuart' furnished a list of 'Heretics, Schismatics and Neutrals in the Realm of England', including under the heading 'The Principal Heretics' Leicester, Burghley and Walsingham, among others, and adding: 'These are the principal devils that rule the Court, and are the leaders of the Council.' Some of the messages went in code, some in clear, and most of the principal agents had cover-names.

For all their efforts, however, the agents failed to pick up the intelligence that most vitally concerned the Enterprise in the spring of 1587. Before the end of February they reported that 'a great fleet' was being fitted out 'by the Lord Admiral', but they did not know its destination. On 28 March Mendoza wrote:

An Italian merchant, well known to me as a trustworthy

Sir Christopher Hatton, Elizabeth's Lord Chancellor, one of the English aristocracy named as 'principal heretics and devils' by the Spaniards.

man, who left London on the 11th, tells me that the merchant ships they are equipping reach the number of fifteen . . . [they are] being got ready with furious haste . . . said to be bound for the coast of Brazil.

On 5 April Mendoza wrote that the fleet was 'ready to sail', and advices from London on the 9th, 11th and 12th confirmed that Sir Francis Drake had gone on board near Dover and sailed with the fleet to Plymouth. Yet still the ships' destination remained a mystery. Some informants thought they were going 'to prevent the junction of His Majesty's fleet in Spain', but most concluded that they were planning to intercept the treasure fleet on its way home from the West Indies.

The true purpose of the expedition was skilfully kept secret until the last, and the Spanish fell victim to a carefully-prepared scheme of disinformation. The trap was laid in London by Burghley and in Paris by Sir Edward Stafford, the English ambassador to France, who was in the pay of the Spaniards, but not (as they thought) in their pocket, and who, creeping about the city at night in disguise, fed them carefully selected information, enough of which was genuine to keep their money flowing. On this occasion he first hinted to Mendoza that the purpose of the expedition was to help Don Antonio attack Portugal; but then, in an apparent act of treachery, he pretended to betray the fact that Don Antonio was merely a stalking-horse, and that the true object was a raid on the Indies.

Thus, when Drake suddenly sailed into the Spaniards' great southern harbour of Cadiz on 18 April, and carried out the brilliantly audacious raid that 'singed the beard of the King of Spain', the defenders were taken completely by surprise. The attack – a triumph of deception – is described in more detail in Chapter Seven; suffice it here to say that the damage Drake inflicted on ships and stores set back the whole programme for the Enterprise by several months. News of the raid caused incredulity in Paris, where Mendoza hastily sought to defend himself by writing: 'I can assure Your Majesty, and call God as my witness, that so far as lies in my power I do not lose an instant in reporting what I hear.'

In spite of this setback, Spanish preparations ground forward; but they were interrupted again early in July, when Santa Cruz sailed from Lisbon with some thirty-five ships to meet the incoming treasure fleet and protect it from pirates. 'If God should allow him to encounter Drake,' the King wrote grimly to Mendoza, 'I trust he will give him what he deserves.'

This hope was not fulfilled. But on 4 September the King told Parma that the Armada was almost ready, and that Santa Cruz would take charge of it and sail for England as soon as he returned, which should be any day. As the project so dear to him drew nearer, Philip again went over its main points with his commander in the Low Countries.

The aim, he said, was 'to cut the root of the evil', and his plan for doing so looked good enough on paper. It was simply that Santa Cruz would sail up the Channel and 'anchor off Margate Point', having first sent word of his approach. Parma, meanwhile, was to have his forces 'quite ready', and as soon as he saw his 'passage assured by the arrival of the fleet', he was to ship the army over immediately. Thus united, he on land and Santa Cruz afloat, they would together, 'with the help of God, carry through the main business successfully'.

Several times the King stressed the paramount need for Parma to be fully prepared:

The most important of all things is that you should be so completely ready that the moment the Marquis arrives at Margate, you may be able to do your share without delay . . . You must not forget that the forces collected, and the vast money responsibility incurred, make it extremely difficult for such an expedition to be got together again if they escape us this time.

In fact Parma's preparations were well advanced, and he had already collected a very large force on or just inland from the coast of Flanders. At its peak his army amounted to nearly 30,000 men, including 700 renegade Englishmen and 4,000 cavalry, with a large number of barges and flat-bottomed boats for transporting humans, horses and their equipment and ammunition. In a clumsy attempt at deception it was put about that the force was being assembled for an attack on Ostend, but this did not fool the English, who in September appointed a team of peace commissioners to go and treat with Parma under the leadership of Dr Valentine Dale.

The extent to which each side genuinely wanted peace has been endlessly debated. The most cynical view is that both opened negotiations and kept them going for as long as they could to give themselves a breathing-space in which to complete their preparations for war. Certainly Walsingham delayed the departure of the commissioners for more than four months, until February 1588, and during their deliberations Philip never faltered in his plans for launching the attack; towards the end, Parma kept Dale and his colleagues in play with patently mendacious evasions when the Armada was already on its way. Yet it is also clear that Elizabeth wanted to avoid war if she possibly could, and she hoped that the commissioners might be able to exploit the uncertainties which had been detected in the behaviour of Parma.

Of all the leading figures in the Armada campaign, Parma's motives were – and remain – the hardest to interpret. Although in 1587 he appeared to be doing all the King asked him, it is obvious from his later actions and letters that his heart was never really in the Enterprise, and the frame of mind in which he carried out royal orders was more dutiful than enthusiastic. Some of the reasons for his coolness were undoubtedly practical: he knew that an invasion of England would leave his rear dangerously exposed, and he did not want to commit a large force across the Channel until the pacification of the Netherlands was complete. He also realized that the King's plan – so simple on paper – had severe weaknesses, and foresaw that it might well fail. What would happen, for instance, if the Armada were caught by a storm as it was approaching, or lying off, Margate? Without a port that could accommodate its big ships, it would be in dire trouble.

Apart from these practical considerations, however, Parma seems to have been inhibited by personal grudges, which he could not articulate in his letters to the King, even though Philip was his uncle. For one thing, he was aggrieved that the rights of his own children to the throne of Portugal had been passed over. For another, he probably resented the fact that command of the Armada had been split between two officers, rather than being invested in him alone. The result was that although he went through the motions of making his invasion troops ready, as the King demanded, he did so more to cover himself against possible charges of negligence than out of any real hope that England could be conquered – with results that ultimately proved the Armada's undoing.

The English had an inkling of his disaffection, and tried to exploit it by suggesting that he should make peace with them in return for their recognition of him as independent sovereign of the Netherlands. The chances of thus prizing him away from Spain must have seemed very slim; but the exceptionally emotional nature of Philip's letters to Parma suggests that the King was aware of the possibility, and trying to scotch it before birth.

Anxiety on this score may also explain the abrupt desire for haste which overtook the King at the end of 1587. Normally the slowest and most ponderous of movers, he suddenly became frantic for the expedition to sail; and it was said to be his uncharacteristic chivvying which contributed to the illness and death of the veteran Santa Cruz. Some Spanish historians put the blame on the forceful and dashing young Don Alonzo Martinez de Leyva, who, it is said, wrote to the King and his ministers complaining that the build-up of the Armada was too slow, and asking that someone should 'put the spurs into the Marquis'. Other sources say that the King sent the Condé de Fuentes to Lisbon with orders to speed up departure. Whatever the truth, Santa Cruz fell ill, apparently from exhaustion and over-work, and died on 9 February 1588 at the age of 73. His death sent a shock-wave of dismay through the fleet, for besides his proven courage and ability, he was popularly supposed to command that elusive but essential commodity, good fortune.

His demise, however, caused only the merest hiccup in Philip's preparations, and in England it did nothing to diminish the general alarm. Even though the peace commissioners had crossed to Flanders at the end of February, the Queen and her Council were belatedly bracing themselves for war.

Chapter Five

The Enterprise Assembles

It is hard to know how the announcement of Philip's new commander-in-chief struck his professional sea-captains; but they can scarcely have expected the choice to fall on Don Alonso Perez de Guzman el Bueno, the Duke of Medina Sidonia, whose two main claims to fame were that he was exceedingly rich and of the most illustrious ancestry.

The sole surviving portrait shows a man with a weak and unimpressive face – not unintelligent, but gentle, melancholy and lacking in authority. This likeness was made long after the catastrophe, which aged him greatly, and it is safe to assume that in 1588, when he was only 38, he must still have had a more vigorous and youthful air. A good rider and a keen huntsman, he was personally brave and said to be graceful in his movements, with a 'pretty, tanned face', though short in the body and thickset, with feet that turned outwards. But perhaps he already bore that essentially passive appearance which seems the key to his character. When threatened with a task which he did not want to take on, he would first try to avoid it; but then, if overruled, he would meekly give in and do his best.

In Andalusia, the southern province from which he came, he was well liked for his fairness and efficiency. Yet it is no clearer now than it was then why the King chose him. Certainly it was not for his military or naval achievements, of which there were none. If anything, it was *in spite* of his military record, for he had already failed, for no good reason, to take up one earlier commission – as Governor and Deputy of the State of Milan, to which he had been assigned in 1581; and at Cadiz in 1587, although in charge of the local militia, he had arrived on the scene too late to stop Drake's work of destruction in the harbour, thereby becoming the butt of much mocking criticism.

At the time the main reason for his appointment as Captain General of the Ocean Sea was said to be the sheer excellence of his pedigree. The Armada included so many military and naval officers of noble birth that only a man with the highest social qualifications – it was explained – would be able to command their respect and obedience. If this was true, the Spaniards paid dearly for their snobbishness; but certainly the new commander-in-chief could hardly have been more highly bred or better connected.

He came from San Lucar, just north of Cadiz, where for generations his family had derived a substantial income from their rents, their orange groves and their monopoly of the tunny-fishing (the word for tunny – *atún* – gave unfortunate openings for satirists, since it also means 'idiot'). He was the twelfth Señor and fifth Marques de San Lucar de Barrameda, the ninth Condé de Niebla, the seventh Duke of Medina Sidonia, Marquis of Casaza in Africa, Knight of the Noble Order of the Fleece. At the age of 8 he inherited one of the largest estates in Spain; at 18 he was betrothed, and at 21 married, to Doña Ana de Silva y Mendoza, who was $10\frac{1}{2}$ years old when the union was effected and consummated. (In the words of the family chronicler, she made up for her lack of years by 'good judgment and discretion'.) Doña Ana was the daughter of the King's favourite closest adviser and confidant, Ruy Gomez de Silva, Duke of Pastrana, and of the famous Princess of Eboli; through his wife's family Medina Sidonia was thus close to the throne, and malicious gossip ascribed his winning of the Armada command to the fact that the King had once been in love with his mother-in-law.

Even if he had – and there are many reasons to suppose that he had not – Philip would scarcely have made so vital an appointment on this account. Nor would he have created Medina Sidonia his Captain General merely to reward him for past generosity and patriotism in lending or giving bronze cannon to the royal fleet. It seems much more likely that he deliberately chose a commander who would not be too adventurous or aggressive, but would obey his own orders to the letter – for the truth was, whether he realized it or not, that the ageing recluse of the Escorial was determined to control the whole gigantic enterprise himself, from his stone eyrie on the side of the Guadarrama Mountains, no matter how impractical such an ambition might be.

It also seems likely that although the King was determined to bring Elizabeth to heel, he did not want the conquest of England to be a bloodbath, which it might have become under the tougher Santa Cruz; and it was perhaps this softness at the core that leant a fatal imprecision to his orders, immensely detailed though they were: for all the thousands of words of instruction with which he burdened his commanders, he never made it clear exactly what he expected them to do once they reached their goal.

When Medina Sidonia's mother heard about his appointment, she was horrified. A sensible woman with a sharp tongue, she knew his

The only known portrait of the Duke of Medina Sidonia, appointed to command the Armada on the death of the Marquis of Santa Cruz. Chosen because of his illustrious ancestry, rather than for any military achievement, he did not want the command, and told the King so plainly, but was over-ruled. Though often vilified by historians, and greatly hampered by the rigidity of Philip's orders, he did his limited best, showing no mean personal fortitude. In 1588 he was only 38, and must have aged greatly by the time this likeness was made.

limitations all too well, and was mortified by the certainty that his new role would expose them. He could manage his own household, she told her friends, but if he tried to command the Armada, such reputation as he had would be ruined.

In the Duke's defence, it must be made absolutely clear that he did not want the job, and tried in his half-hearted way to escape from it, both when he was first appointed, and then again after the Armada had put into Corunna on its way north. Whatever his faults, self-importance was not one of them: he knew he was not cut out for high military command, and told the King so.

Santa Cruz died on 9 February 1588; and when, on the 14th, the King wrote to Medina Sidonia confirming that he wanted him to succeed as commander-in-chief, the Duke immediately replied to the King's secretary, Don Juan de Idiaquez, begging to be excused:

> I wish I possessed the talents and strength necessary for it [the task]. But, Sir, I have not health for the sea, for I know by the small experience that I have afloat that I soon become sea-sick, and have many humours. Besides . . . I am in great need, so much so that when I have had to go to Madrid, I have been obliged to borrow money for the journey. My house owes 900,000 ducats, and I am therefore quite unable to accept the command. I have not a single real I can spend on the expedition.
>
> Apart from this, neither my conscience nor my duty will allow me to take this service upon me. The force is so great, and the undertaking so important, that it would not be right for a person like myself, possessing no experience of seafaring or of war, to take charge of it. . . . For me to take charge of the Armada afresh, without the slightest knowledge of it, of the persons who are taking part in it, of the objects in view, of the intelligence from England, without any acquaintance with the ports there, or of the arrangements which the Marquis has been making for years past, would be simply groping in the dark. . . . I should be travelling in the dark, and should have to be guided by the opinions of others, of whose good or bad qualities I know nothing, and which of them might seek to deceive and ruin me.

The pleading of poverty was nonsense, for the Duke was a millionaire, and in the end spent nearly eight million maravedis of his own on the expedition. But the rest came from the heart. With its painful, humiliating honesty, his response was utterly unlike the reply that might have been expected from a high-born Spaniard fired by arrogance or ambition. Yet the King simply brushed the objections aside.

'Duke and Cousin,' he wrote on 20 February,

> All of what you say I attribute to your excess of modesty. But it is I who must judge your capabilities and parts, and I am fully satisfied with these. . . . You yourself should proceed to Lisbon with the haste made necessary by the concentration there of a mighty Armada, uncaptained and awaiting your orders.

As speed was 'particularly important', the Duke was to sail 'within eight or ten days' if he found that everything was in order. So off he went, riding post-haste across country. In Lisbon, however, he found that the King's demand was absurdly optimistic. Far from being ready, the fleet was in a state of chaos. So great were its deficiencies, in fact, that more than three months passed before it could be made fit to sail, and another two went by on top of that before it cleared the Spanish coast. However distinguished a warrior Santa Cruz had been, he was no administrator. Yet such was the King's inflexibility that at no stage of the delay, as spring came and went, and summer merged into autumn, did he modify his orders to the Duke for the conduct of the campaign.

These opened with a sombre reminder that the whole Enterprise was a religious undertaking, and that it was 'the Service of our Lord' which had moved the King to collect his enormous fleet:

> As all victories are the gifts of God Almighty, and the cause we champion is so exclusively His, we may fairly look for His aid and favour, unless by our sins we render ourselves unworthy thereof. You will therefore have to exercise special care that such cause of offence shall be avoided on the Armada, and especially that there shall be no sort of blasphemy. . . . You are going to fight for the cause of our Lord, and for the glory of His name, and consequently He must be worshipped by all, so that His favour may be deserved.

Then came the most important paragraph, the crux of the entire matter:

> When you receive a separate order from me, you will sail with the whole Armada, and go straight to the English Channel, which you will ascend as far as Cape Margate, where you will join hands with the Duke of Parma, my nephew, and hold the passage for his crossing, in accordance with the plan which has already been communicated to both of you.

The task sounded simple enough. Yet the royal orders, though tremendously long, were dangerously flawed by Philip's failure to think them through. It was typical of the King that he went into minute detail about how Medina Sidonia was to communicate with Parma as the Armada approached the Channel – either by means of sea-borne letters couched in a special cypher, or through trusted messengers landed at night on the French coast. Philip had already bombarded Parma with equally long-winded instructions, and now, to his Captain General, he laboured through many incidental possibilities: that the Armada might be scattered by a storm on its way towards England; that Drake might sail to Spain in spite of it; that Medina Sidonia might be overtaken by a tempest in the Channel itself. For all these eventualities there were supplementary instructions. Yet never once did Philip explain clearly what he expected the invaders to *do* when they reached their destination.

The Armada was to cover Parma's passage across the Channel, if possible without engaging the English fleet; and if his invasion force did manage to establish itself on English soil, the Duke was to 'station a portion of the Armada at the mouth of the Thames and support him', some of his ships being deployed to hold off reinforcements. Provided Medina Sidonia's force had not been depleted in battle, he was to give Parma the 6,000 special troops he was carrying; but he was not to land unless the Duke agreed, his 'sole function . . . indeed the principal one' of the Armada being 'to fight at sea'.

Then what? How long was Parma supposed to remain on shore? What was he to do if he captured London? What if he took the Queen prisoner? What was to be done with all the other principal heretics – Burghley, Walsingham, Hatton – if they too were captured? How long was Medina Sidonia supposed to wait 'off the Cape of Margate' after Parma had disappeared up-river towards the capital? What happened if winter set in before the conquest were completed? How was the captured country to be garrisoned, or in what state was it to be left?

Parma himself may well have had specific orders on these points. In the documents that survive there are hints that he was already familiar with what the King called 'the undertaking' or 'the principal business'. But Medina Sidonia's orders contained no answers to the questions above. He had no opportunity of discussing them with the King. He had, as he himself protested, not 'the slightest knowledge . . . of the objects in view'. Nor did he have any chance of meeting his fellow commander to talk through the coming campaign: he sailed on the Enterprise without once seeing or speaking to his vital partner, and he never saw him again.

By 'the principal business', the King seems definitely to have meant that Parma should invade the country. Some historians have conjectured that he intended only that the Armada should parade up the Channel and terrify the English into submission by its mere appearance; but recent archaeological research has scotched this idea by showing that the fleet carried extensive siege equipment – 50-pounder guns (which were so big as to be almost useless at sea), scaling ladders made from pine-trunks with their branches sawn off short, and bundles of brushwood for filling in moats. Besides, the King certainly expected prisoners to be taken, for in a second set of supplementary instructions he told Medina Sidonia that if Parma managed to capture Don Antonio, they should be sure to place him 'in security, so that he shall not escape'. Yet he never said to the

5. Philip II, painted by Antonio Moro in 1554.

7. *Following page:* Elizabeth I in middle age: a portrait attributed to John Bettes the Younger. The fantastical elaboration of the Queen's clothes, jewellery and wig fits well with contemporary descriptions.

6. Plymouth in the sixteenth century. The town had been a centre of naval activity since the middle of the fifteenth century. During the civil disturbances of the 1540s Drake's family were said to have taken refuge on St Nicholas's Island (*left centre*) which was later renamed Drake's Island after them.

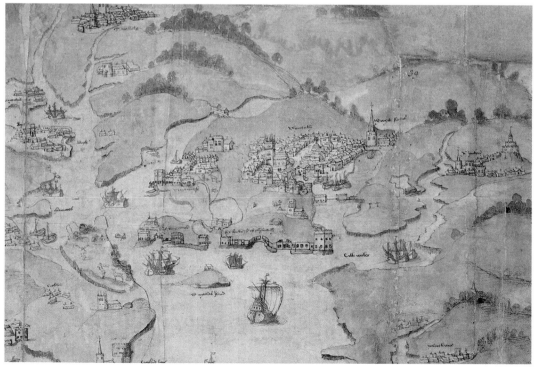

Captain General of the Ocean Sea, in so many words, that his aim was a physical take-over of England, and he gave only the vaguest recommendations as to what he should do after the conquest:

> You will have to stay there [in English waters] until the undertaking be successfully concluded, with God's help, and you may then return, calling in and settling affairs in Ireland on the way, if the Duke approve of your doing so, the matter being left to your joint discretion.

With Medina Sidonia's secret orders came a separate, sealed document, which he was to deliver to Parma only if he landed in England. In any other event the document was to be returned to the King. The packet contained yet more orders, designed mainly to cover the possibility of a stalemate. If (the King wrote) 'affairs be so counterbalanced that peace may not be altogether undesirable', Parma was to gain the best possible terms, bearing in mind 'three principal points'. The first was that in England 'the free use and exercise of our holy Catholic faith' should be permitted to everyone, and that all exiles should be allowed to return. The second was that all the places in the Netherlands held by the English should be restored to Spain; and the third that the English should recompense the King for injury done to him, his dominions and his subjects – 'which will amount to an exceedingly great sum'.

These sweeping conditions – which were to be exacted even if the English had not been defeated – perhaps represented the King's later thoughts, when he realized that an outright victory over the English fleet was most improbable. But Medina Sidonia did not know of them, any more than he knew what Parma's orders for the land-battle were; his sole task in commanding the Armada was to see Parma safely across the Channel.

To help him, green as he was, he did at least have the combined experience of seasoned sea-captains. One, Don Diego Flores de Valdes, was assigned by the King to be his special nautical adviser, and to sail with him in the flagship *San Martin*, where he acted as Captain of the Fleet, and in effect took control of the Armada's movements. It is hard not to feel that the King made a serious mistake in choosing Don Diego for the vital role of supporting a weak supreme commander; for although nobody denied his competence, either as seaman or as hydrographer and designer of ships, equally, nobody liked him, since he was a sour, unruly character whose worse nature often got the better of him. In 1581, for instance, he had led the fleet of twenty-three ships which went to fortify the Magellan Straits, but that expedition had broken up because of his jealous disagreements with his fellow-commander, the heroic Pedro

Lope de Vega, the Spanish poet and dramatist, who was on board the *San Juan* throughout the battle. Goaded (as usual) by the fires of love, he had joined the Armada to escape from a romantic entanglement, and spent his time aboard imperturbably composing verses.

Sarmiento de Gamboa, whom he abandoned, taking some of his men with him. The fact that he then fought a successful action against the French on the coast of Brazil to some extent redeemed him, but everyone (except, apparently, the King) knew that he was quarrelsome, jealous and difficult to work with.

A more extrovert stalwart was Admiral Don Juan Martinez de Recalde, a scarred old warrior of 62 from Bilbao, whose distinguished family claimed among its members Inigo Lopez de Recalde, otherwise Ignatius de Loyola, founder of the Jesuits. Recalde's experience was enormous: he had escorted the Indies treasure fleets, fought in almost every part of the known world, and served as Superintendent of the Royal Dockyards, and he had been generally reckoned as second only to the old Marquis of Santa Cruz in ability, being intelligent and personally fearless. Now that Santa Cruz was dead, he was without doubt the most formidable seaman in Spain. It is small wonder that he suggested himself as the new Captain General of the Ocean Sea – and one can only speculate on what the outcome would have been if the King had listened to him.

Another famous seaman from Bilbao was Martin de Bertendona, whose father (with the same name) had captained the ship which took Philip to England in 1554. For the past five years he had been in command of the guard on the coast of Portugal. Of equal renown was Don Pedro de Valdes – a cousin of Don Diego's, and in permanent feud with him – who had been admiral of the squadron sent to blockade Oporto during the conquest of Portugal, and had been wounded in a fight with two English privateers who had taken refuge in the Ferrol estuary. At Terceira he had landed himself in trouble by exceeding his orders: sent as admiral of the fleet to blockade the islands until reinforcements arrived, he grew bored with waiting and put ashore a party of men, who were defeated – a fiasco for which he was temporarily held prisoner in the castle at Lisbon before being restored to favour. Later he became general of the galleons of the Indian Guard.

Perhaps the most glamorous of the admirals was Don Miguel de Oquendo. An exceptional seaman, who was said to manage his ship as masterfully as if it were a horse, he had long been the terror of the Turks in the Mediterranean; in a dashing intervention at Terceira he had rescued his admiral, Santa Cruz, by charging the French flagship, grappling with it, capturing it, and hoisting his own flag on the poop. In 1588, the most eager of volunteers, he badgered the King for months with requests to be allowed to join the fleet, and in the end, a few weeks before it sailed, was granted his request. Contemporary accounts come alive with the magnetism of his character, comparing his valour with that of Hector of Troy.

An equally striking figure was that of Don Alonso Martinez de Leyva, commander-in-chief of the cavalry of Milan, and secretly designated Medina Sidonia's deputy, who would take over command of the Armada if the Captain General were killed or disabled. So famous was he as a soldier, so distinguished in birth and career (although still only 24), that when high-born young men volunteered to sail with the Armada their fathers wanted them all to serve under him. By the time the expedition sailed, no fewer than sixty *aventureros* had attached themselves to him on board his carrack *La Rata Encoronada*. A description of him given by an Irishman shows how sharply he stood out among his swarthy colleagues:

> Don Alonso for his stature was tall and slender, of a whitely complexion, of a flaxen and smooth hair, of behaviour mild

and temperate, of speech good and deliberate, greatly reverenced, not only by his men, but generally of all the whole company.

During their enforced wait in Lisbon, while the Armada got ready, he and his young men lived in some state. Don Alonso entertained in style, dining off gold and silver plate, and numbering Medina Sidonia among his distinguished guests on board. The fact that he brought thirty-six *criados*, or retainers, with him – and that several of his young hopefuls brought at least ten – shows that their expectations reached far beyond the voyage itself. They could not possibly need that many servants at sea; indeed, the flocks of staff were a menace, for they made the ship extremely crowded. No: Don Alonso and his acolytes were clearly expecting to settle down, at least for the time being, in the English mansions or palaces that would inevitably fall into their hands.

The admirals and other officers were splendidly dressed in silks, satins and fine linen, with much gold and silver embroidery; many also wore the blood-red diagonal cross which showed that they were going to a holy war. But they were not alone in their peacock colours, for even the lower ranks sported embroidered jackets and breeches. On Don Pedro de Valdes's *Nuestra Señora del Rosario* Sergeant Pelegrin had a pair of blue velvet hose with gold and silver lace, as well as 'a jerkin of wrought velvet lined with taffety'. Sergeant Marcos de Biber's breeches were of blue satin laid with gold lace, and even the 'ancient bearer' Cristobal de Leon had a leather jerkin perfumed with amber and laid over with gold and silver lace. Although most members of the crew probably made do with plain clothes and leather jerkins, others had breeches of black satin, yellow satin, black wrought velvet, cloth of gold; and another old servant, Bermudo, wore a 'blue stitched taffety hat', with a silver band and a plume of feathers.

Several of the ships carried very large amounts of money, part of it State funds, for paying the men, but much of it belonging to the officers. On the *Rosario* there were 52,000 ducats in a chest belonging to the King, of which Don Pedro had one key and the King's treasurer the other. Don Pedro took along 4,000 reals of his own, and 'many other gentlemen had good store of money aboard the ship. Also there was wrought plate of the Duke's and Don Pedro . . . and great store of precious jewels and rich apparel.' Most of the officers had gold coins sewn into their doublets, and several wore, slung round their necks, heavy gold chains which they could use as currency, cutting off a link or two when they needed to pay for something. One such chain recovered from the wreck of the galleass *Girona* was eight feet long and weighed over four pounds.

The *Rosario* was said to be one of the four richest ships in the

Armada, and was carrying much of the fleet's pay. But why did her officers take along such large amounts of their own? Again, the explanation seems to be that they felt confident that they would have opportunities of spending – and winning – money on shore. One man wrote to a friend in Andalusia asking him to 'pray to God that in England he doth give me the house of some very rich merchant, where I may place my ensign, which the owner thereof do ransom me in 30,000 ducats'.

Certainly expectations were high. According to Vicente Alvarez, captain of the *Rosario*, in Lisbon 'it was openly spoken' among the crews that 'the place of their landing should be within the river of London', and they had decided that 'in what place soever they should enter within the land, to sack the same, either city, town, village or whatever', putting to the sword anybody who resisted them. Like their monarch, they had fallen victim to the persuasions of their own propaganda: they had heard that the King would establish the Inquisition in England, and it was 'commonly bruited amongst them' that as soon as they landed 'a third part or one half of the realm of England' would rise to join them.

Among its 30,000 members the Armada included a bewildering variety of human beings. The Spanish empire itself was by no means homogeneous, and now Andalusians, Catalans, Castilians and Galicians were organized in separate squadrons, edgy with ancient feuds and not even able to understand each other perfectly. Besides the Spaniards there were several thousand Portuguese, who, not having been members of Philip's empire for long, would gladly have cut the throats of their masters had they thought they could get away with it.

As its name suggests, the vast force was predominantly an army: some two-thirds of its members were soldiers, only one third seamen. The regular troops were made up of five brigades of *tercios* or heavy infantry, of about 3,000 men each, and 5,000 light troops and pioneers (for construction work). Many of the light soldiers and seamen had been recruited forcibly – in effect, arrested. Sailors of the regular navy had seized the crews of many small merchantmen and fishing boats in the villages along the coast and pressed them into service. Soldiers who had deserted and been recaptured at places inland were marched on board and kept there by armed guards stationed on the quays. Long-range voyages, with their notoriously bad food and danger from the sea, enemy action and disease, were so unpopular that men constantly tried to outwit the guards, especially if they had been lucky enough to get some pay. So great was the wastage that during the two years in which the Armada was fitting out nearly 50,000 men were drafted in to yield the final complement of 30,000.

Now, more than ever, there was a dire shortage of soldiers, especially when illness began to thin the ranks; standards had to be lowered, and numbers made up with grooms, apprentices and pages. As time ran out, a frantic drive rounded up sundry stray Greeks, Portuguese, Venetians and other Italians, and at the last moment the crews of some captured Dutch hulks were brought straight from prison and put on board: enemies though they were, it was thought that, well split up, they would be more use than no one. Still some crews were below strength, and on the day before departure the Spaniards went to the desperate expedient of seizing by force sailors from French, German, Danish and other foreign merchant vessels which happened to be in Lisbon. Even then many of the ships, though carrying large complements of troops, were undermanned with hands capable of sailing them – a deficiency which told severely against them when they needed to manoeuvre for their lives in the Channel. To preserve the health of the multitude, both physical and spiritual, there was a hospital staff of 62, including five physicians and five surgeons, and 180 monks and friars.

All these men had joined the fleet either because they were professionals, or because they had fallen under duress. Besides them, however, a large number had volunteered, fired by religious fervour and the hope of gain to join the holy war. Altogether there were nearly 120 gentlemen adventurers, who brought with them 456 servants. From Spain itself came the young noblemen, camping with their retinues on the quayside, setting up cabins on board, generally getting in the way – a gay and glamorous crowd, bent on adventure. None among them excited greater interest than Antonio Luis de Leyva, Prince of Ascoli, believed by many to be a bastard son of the King, who brought 39 servants to sail with him in Medina Sidonia's flagship the *San Martin*. Another scion of a distinguished family was Martin Cortes, son of the conqueror of Mexico; but a more interesting figure, already well known in his own right, was the poet and playwright Lope de Vega.

This astonishingly prolific author, who wrote 1,500 plays (or about thirty a year during his working life), seems to have gone to sea partly to find intellectual stimulus, and partly to escape from the consequences of his own ceaseless love-affairs. In 1583, at the age of 20, he had seen service as a volunteer at Terceira, and now, at 25, he was on the run from a passionate involvement with Elena Osorio, daughter of a theatre producer in Madrid. When the five-year affair ended in bitterness and frustration, Lope had published a poem libelling Elena's father. For this he was banished from Madrid for eight years, but before he left the city fell in love with Isabel de Urbina, and she had scarcely become his wife in a marriage by proxy when he rushed off to join the Armada. Obsessed as he was by sex, immersed in his ideas for poems and plays, he can hardly have been any great help to the officers and crew of the *San Juan de Portugal*, on which he sailed.

From further afield came exiled English and Irish priests, traitorous nobles, the wild Caley O'Connor who spoke nothing but Gaelic, salaried officers such as Sir Maurice and Sir Thomas Geraldine, young Catholic gentlemen from England and Scotland, a German captain, Italian military officers, all gathering like vultures to feast off the carcase of the rich heretic in the north.

Just as the sheer numbers of men assembled in Lisbon were enough to strike terror into enemy hearts, so, on paper, the tally of ships seemed immensely impressive. When the fleet finally sailed, the number of vessels was 130 – a colossal force by the standards of those days. Closer examination, however, shows that only just over half these were fighting-ships. The rest were *urcas*, or load-carrying hulks, *pataches* (despatch boats, the equivalent of the English pinnaces), and *zabras*, or Biscay smacks, which were also used for running errands, transferring officers from one ship to another, putting messengers ashore, and so on.

Like the men, the ships had been collected from every quarter. The best of the fighting vessels were the nine galleons of Portugal – strongly-built, designed for the Atlantic, and used to any weather. Among them was the flagship *San Martin*, and they had been reinforced by the addition of the *San Francisco*, which had been appropriated, to his great dismay, from the Grand Duke of Tuscany. Next best were the ten galleons of the Indian Guard, from Castile, whose normal duty was to escort the treasure fleets.

The galleons were descended from the great ships, or carracks, which formed the other element of the front-line force. These were full-bellied and high-castled, with the forecastle built up like a two- or three-storey house over the bow, and the sterncastle towering still higher. Although they looked majestic and alarming, they were poor sailors (especially into the wind) and unmanoeuvrable. The galleons were narrower, lower, less cumbersome and more weatherly – but still no match (as will be seen) for the new galleons built by the English.

To bring the Armada up to strength, several merchantmen, known as *naos*, were converted at the last minute and built up into good imitations of great ships by the addition of extra decks fore and aft, and furnished with heavy armament. Four of them were attached to Diego Flores de Valdes, and the rest split into equal squadrons representing the maritime provinces of Andalusia, Biscay, Guipuzcoa and Levant. The extra weight, much of it high up, still further limited the sailing powers of the great ships; but even they were more manoeuvrable than the twenty-three hulks, or *urcas* – tubby cargo-carriers which had been chartered from Spain's Hanseatic allies in the Baltic.

The most powerfully armed ships were probably the four galleasses from Naples under the command of Don Hugo de Moncada. These were hybrid vessels – galleons with oars – created in an attempt to harness the mobility of a galley, which was not dependent on the wind, to the power and strength of a great ship. With their heavy complement of 50 guns, several of which fired forward, and 300 oarsmen to keep them moving in periods of calm, they were formidable weapons.

There were also four galleys, each powered by 222 oarsmen, but these carried only five guns each and were lighter vessels altogether. In his original proposal the Marquis of Santa Cruz had asked for forty galleys, and the fact that in the end only four sailed with the Armada seems to reflect a sharp change of policy induced by Drake's raid on Cadiz. On that occasion a few broadsides from Drake's *Elizabeth Bonaventure* had reduced the fleet of galleys in Cadiz Harbour to a shambles; and the demonstration of the fire-power of heavy ordnance apparently convinced the Spaniards that they must increase the weight of the armament on board the Armada. Not only did they decide to leave most of the galleys behind: they also re-equipped with heavier guns, and whenever possible substituted the big, load-carrying *naos* of the Mediterranean for the smaller and lighter ships built on the Atlantic coast in Guipuzcoa and Biscay.

All the big ships were ballasted with stones, the largest of them probably carrying 200 tons, the bulk of it concentrated forward, so as to trim the vessel and counterbalance the weight of the sterncastle. The stones, weighing up to 50 lbs each, were carefully laid, as in a dry-stone wall, so that they could not shift about with the movement of the ship. Some of the casks containing food and water were bedded in the ballast, and wedged tight (again to prevent movement) with bundles of brush-wood, which could be burnt to heat the cooking-pots as the stores were used up. The rest of the stores were loaded on the orlop deck above. Each ship also carried a substantial stock of lead in the form of boat-shaped ingots weighing 100 lbs each, from which the soldiers on board could cast fresh supplies of bullets, and larger ingots known as *planchas* of 300 lbs apiece, used to make plates for patching shot-holes in the hull.

From the King down the Spanish high command were aware that their country's ideas about naval warfare had scarcely developed since Lepanto. In 1588, as in 1571, their aim was to close with enemy ships, grapple them, board them and take them by storm – in other words, as nearly as possible to fight a land battle on the sea. Tradition claims that the Spaniards saw gunnery only as a means to this end – and none too respectable a one at that. Great ordnance could honourably be used to bring down masts and sever rigging, and thereby render a victim easy prey for the grappling hooks; but to aim at the hull was like hitting below the belt.*

Thus an Armada warship was essentially a floating fort, with a low waist and the decks fore and aft built up in tiers so that the defenders could pour small-arms fire into other vessels or down on to attackers who managed to clamber aboard amidships. The vessels' heavy ordnance was mounted on the gun-deck, which ran right through the ship, and the higher decks carried a variety of smaller, anti-personnel weapons. (A table of weapons is given on page 79.)

It is now generally accepted that there is no truth in the claim – which persisted for centuries – that the Spanish galleons were far larger than the English. They *looked* bigger, because they were so high out of the water; and the misconception was reinforced by records of their tonnages, the Spanish figures being consistently the larger. Now it is known that two different methods of rating were being used: reckoning was in any case very vague, but Spanish tons referred to displacement, and English ones to cubic capacity. Thus the converted *nao San Salvador*, which blew up and was captured in the Channel, was rated by the Spanish at 958 tons and by the English at 600.

With this misconception removed, it is clear that there was probably not much difference in basic dimensions between the ships of both rivals. The biggest Spanish vessel of all, the *Regazona* of the Levantine (or Italian) Squadron, rated at 1,249 tons, was probably no larger than the biggest English ship, the *Triumph*, of 1,100. It is likely that the flagship *San Martin* (1,100 tons) was of much the same dimensions as her English opposite number, the 800-ton *Ark Royal* – 100 feet long at the keel, and some 33 feet wide.

The chief disparity between them lay not in size but in shape, and in the way they were manned – for whereas the *San Martin* carried 177 seamen and 300 soldiers, the crew of the *Ark* was balanced the opposite way: 125 soldiers and 300 seamen. The difference in emphasis precisely reflected the role each side thought most important (the English ships are described in Chapter Seven).

The Spanish had no doubt as to how the English would try to fight, and in his orders the King warned Medina Sidonia explicitly what to expect:

> Above all it must be borne in mind that the enemy's object will be to fight at long distance, in consequence of his advantage in artillery . . . The aim of our men, on the contrary, must be to bring him to close quarters and grapple with him, and you will have to be very careful to have this carried out.

*Some authorities doubt the validity of this tradition, believing that the policy of aiming high was dictated not by sportsmanship but by the purely practical belief that it offered the best chance of disabling the enemy.

The Royal arms of Spain embossed on one of the 50-lb siege guns, cast by the master gun-founder Remigy de Halut in 1556. The weapon was recovered from the wreck of the *Trinidad Valencera*, which went down in Kinnegoe Bay, Co. Donegal, in 1588.

It was a measure of the Spaniards' conservatism that they could not do much to adapt their tactics or equipment to deal with the English threat, even though they perceived it so clearly. Yet in the last months of Santa Cruz's life, and now in the first weeks of Medina Sidonia's command, they made strenuous efforts to increase the weight of their armament, ordering thirty-six new big guns from the arsenal at Madrid and thirty from Lisbon. How many of these were completed in time is not certain; but deliveries fell behind schedule, and other guns were brought in from the Low Countries, Italy and Germany, often at grossly-inflated prices, as well as from foreign ships in Spanish ports.

In their last-minute scramble for heavier armament, the Spaniards seem to have sensed that the outcome of the combat might turn on gunnery, and in the end the Armada carried a grand total of 2,431 guns of all types, nearly 1,500 of them made of bronze. The exact composition of its armament will never be known, but there is no doubt that, since its principal aim was destructive battery, its officers favoured heavy-shotted, short-range cannon, demi-cannon and periers at the expense of long-range culverins and demi-culverins, especially in the final stages of preparation. On 14 March 1588 Philip ordered Medina Sidonia to strengthen the artillery of Oquendo's squadron; Pedro de Valdes asked permission to replace some lighter guns with ones of larger calibre. Partly on the orders of the King, and partly due to Medina Sidonia's own initiative, the supply of shot was increased from an average of thirty rounds per gun to fifty – a total of more than 123,000 rounds, the iron balls all smeared with animal fat to prevent them rusting. Stocks of powder were also stepped up, to more than 500,000 lbs. This was all fine-corned powder, suitable for use in small arms as well as great ordnance; and since it was more efficient than coarse powder, only two-thirds of the load would produce the same performance from a big gun as a full charge of the coarser cannon powder. Thus, on paper at least, the armament of the Armada was extremely powerful.

Yet archaeological research has now revealed that, just as the ships were less robust than they looked, so the sheer numbers of weapons concealed dangerous weaknesses. Some of the bronze pieces, such as those cast by the celebrated gun-founder Remigy de Halut at Malines, in Flanders, were beautifully made, even though more than 30 years old; escutcheons on top of the barrels bore the full arms of King Philip in the first year of his reign, and each weapon was a work of art. Other guns, however, were so poorly cast as to have been all-but useless, if not a positive danger to their users. Recoveries from the wrecks off Ireland have shown that the barrel of at least one culverin was by no means in the centre of the moulding, and it is impossible to say how many others may have been similarly flawed.

Another serious weakness, recently brought to light, lay hidden in the quality of the cast iron itself, which has been revealed as far inferior to the iron smelted in the Weald of Kent and Sussex. Nor was it only the guns themselves which were a potential liability: cannon-balls and anchors were similarly vitiated by poor manufacture.

Gun-casting was still a far-from-exact science; but in the generation preceding the Armada English craftsmen had outstripped their Continental rivals in skill and renown, so that their weapons were highly prized. The result was that, in spite of attempts by the Government to suppress it, a flourishing illicit export trade had grown up. From 1574 the six or seven English gun-makers were supposed not to cast guns without licence, not to sell to foreigners, and to send all finished weapons to Tower Wharf, the only official dealing-place for them. Such was the demand, however, that the rules were continuously broken – both by English merchant captains determined to arm their own ships adequately, and by unscrupulous dealers who sold to foreigners. Many big guns found their way abroad, and it was said that in 1587 alone

English merchants, many of them based in Bristol, supplied the Spanish with nine shiploads of goods, including big guns, muskets, powder and lead. Later Sir Walter Raleigh recorded that 'it was directly proved in the lower house of parliament . . . that there were landed in Naples above 140 culverins English . . . It is lamentable that so many have been transported into Spain.'

The task of preparing the immense and loose-knit force for sea, of making it fit to tackle a powerful enemy 900 miles to the north, had already defeated old Santa Cruz, and it would have taxed a more forceful commander than the Duke of Medina Sidonia. Even so, he soon impressed the admirals by his industry, and proved himself no mean administrator. Yet he was struggling against fearful handicaps, not least the elephantine central bureaucracy under which Spain was governed, and the stream of detailed instruction which flowed ceaselessly from the pen of his monarch in Madrid. A royal warning against allowing anyone to take women on board was relatively simple to deal with: 'As the presence of public or private harlots on board is a source of well-known scandals,' said the Duke's orders, 'we forbid them to embark.' The purge led to thirty females being evicted (although at least one must have escaped detection, for among the prisoners taken by the British on the *Rosario* there was listed 'one German woman'). Another source of worry to the King was the unofficial modification of the ships' living-space:

> Before the Marquis of Santa Cruz died [he wrote on 25 March], he told me that because gentlemen and private persons were enrolling for service in the Armada, each one desired to have constructed on the ships his private cabin; which was extremely inconvenient because space necessary for fighting and for the service of the ships was used.
>
> I ordered then that on no account were such cabins to be built. This tendency, however, seems to have increased because of the large numbers of the nobility who have come forward to serve me in the Armada. But it is not right that there should be such obstacles on those ships, which should carry men going with self-restraint, and with their arms in their hands to fight the enemy's fleet.

The cabins went overboard or were burnt, and men had to sleep on the open decks. This, however, was the smallest of Medina Sidonia's problems. By far the greatest was the general chaos and lack of organization which he found he had inherited. Many ships had fallen into disrepair; some had far too many guns for their size, some far too few. (The sheer physical difficulty of installing or removing cannon weighing 5,000 lbs or more, with primitive tackle, can easily be imagined.) Stores and men were equally ill-distributed. To sort out the mess the Duke formed an impromptu Council of War of Pedro de Valdes, Recalde and Oquendo, reinforced by an Italian gunnery expert and two further naval officers. Backed by this small staff, he set about strengthening the fleet by every means he could find. As he battled to apportion men, guns and stores in the most effective deployment, carpenters worked day and night to fit the merchantmen with extra fighting decks and to bring older ships up to scratch by the replacement of decayed timbers and planking.

The difficulties of provisioning so huge a force – in any case daunting – were increased to an almost unmanageable degree by the length of time that the ships had been lying, fully manned, in port. Already many of them had been in harbour at Lisbon or elsewhere since November; now the further delay meant that they had to remain in port right through the summer, and it was inevitable that food and water began to go bad. Only now did the full impact of Drake's raid on Cadiz begin to be felt. In the course of his depredations he had burnt an immense number of barrel-staves, so that the Spaniards had been forced to take into service many barrels of unseasoned oak, which was liable to shrink and let in the air, so ruining the contents.

The aim was that the Armada should sail with six months' food and water on board. Yet from an order to the fleet's shipmasters put out by Medina Sidonia on 21 April, it is clear that the fleet was in trouble many weeks before it left:

> You will carefully inspect the stores constantly, and anything that you see is becoming bad you will serve out at once, nothing else being distributed until that be finished; so that nothing shall be wasted. If any stores be wasted by your negligence, you shall pay for them. . . . You must not serve out more than the ordinary ration to any captain, ensign, sergeant, corporal or other official; nor to any drummer, fifer or other without my order. . . .
>
> If for any reason, of scarcity or other, rations are omit-ted or shortened on any day, the ration or quantity short is not to be made up by distribution of a large quantity on another day.

The 'ordinary ration' was minutely laid down. Each man received either 2 lbs of fresh bread or $1\frac{1}{2}$ lbs of biscuit every day. On Sundays and Thursdays he also got 6 oz. of bacon and 2 oz. of rice; on Mondays and Wednesdays, 6 oz. of cheese and 3 oz. of beans or chick peas; on

Tuesdays, Fridays and Saturdays, 6 oz. of fish (tunny or cod), or, in default of these, 6 oz. of squid or five sardines, with 3 oz. of beans or chick peas. On the fish days there was also an issue of 1½ oz. of oil per man, and quarter of a pint of vinegar. All this was washed down with watered wine, the daily ration being 'a third of an *azumbre*' (an *azumbre* being about half a gallon) of Sherry, Lamego, Monzon, Pajica or Condado, but only a pint if the wine was the stronger Candia. (These rations were markedly less substantial than those issued to the English fleet – see page 114.)

Medina Sidonia's regulations governing the issue of food give a vivid glimpse of the bureaucracy by which administration was gripped, and of the corruption which bedevilled attempts to get ready. All rations were to be served out not by eye, but strictly by the measures and weights supplied. Lists were to be made, and signed by the Inspector-General and pursers of the fleet, of the men in each ship, and all rations were to be issued according to these lists. Each ship's notary was to be present at the distribution of rations, 'his book to be signed every day by himself, and by the captain or ensign of infantry on board'. If any man died or was trans-shipped, his name was to be struck off the list, 'even though the captain or ensign may claim his ration'.

Later events make it clear that, in spite of all the regulations and checks, the inventories produced by the pursers for the benefit of inspecting officers were highly inaccurate, whether wilfully or as a result of incompetence. No matter how efficient he might try to be, the Captain General of the Ocean Sea could not possibly inspect every last cask himself, and there can be no doubt that in his efforts to establish how bad the position was he was often given deliberately misleading information. Thus the supplies of that most basic necessity, water – supposed to last for six months – began to run out before the fleet had been at sea for a fortnight.

With the making, signing and endless supervision of lists, with food going bad and having to be replaced, with men dying and deserting, it seems a miracle that the Armada ever made ready at all. But on 25 April – even though preparations were not yet complete – an elaborate ceremony was staged in Lisbon to launch the Enterprise on its way. Detachments of men were brought ashore from the ships to line the city's streets and squares. At six in the morning the Captain General of the Ocean went in solemn procession to the cathedral, the Iglesia Mayor, where, in the company of the King's representative, the Cardinal Archduke, Viceroy of Portugal, he formally took possession of the expedition's standard. On its snowy background, flanking the Spanish arms, this bore images of Christ Crucified and of His Holy Mother, and beneath them a scroll carrying words from the seventy-fourth psalm,

Exsurge, domine, et vindica causam tuam (Arise, O Lord, and champion Thy cause).

As the banner lay on the altar, the Archbishop of Lisbon said mass and blessed the whole Enterprise. Then Medina Sidonia held the sacred flag in his hands while the ships in the harbour thundered out a salvo. Next, the ritual was repeated at the Dominican convent across the square. Finally, as musket-volleys rattled off on land, and the great guns boomed again from the ships and harbour-forts, the banner was taken on board the *San Martin*, and the leading figures in the ceremony were free to go off to breakfast in the palace.

With brilliant colours everywhere catching the early sun, with the city decked out in festive array and the officers resplendent in their gaudy uniforms, with smoke from the salvoes rolling among the crowded masts on the river, the parade should have been deeply moving. But somehow it was not. Genuine emotion was inhibited by a sense of artificiality – a feeling that the ceremony was contrived, and lacked spontaneity. Certainly it was boycotted by the Portuguese aristocrats, and among the Spaniards perhaps too many people shared the secret fears of a senior officer who a few days earlier had confided to an emissary of the Pope that although he thought the Armada could beat the English, they would need a God-given miracle to do so.

PRINCIPAL WEAPONS

GUN	CALIBRE	WEIGHT OF SHOT	SHORT OR LONG RANGE
Cannon	$7\frac{1}{4}''$	50 lbs	S
Demi-cannon	$6\frac{1}{4}''$	30 lbs	S
Perier		c. 20 lbs (stone)	S
Culverin	$5\frac{1}{4}''$	17 lbs	L
Demi-culverin	$4\frac{1}{2}''$	9 lbs	L
Saker	$3\frac{1}{2}''$	5 lbs	L
Minion	$3\frac{1}{4}''$	4 lbs	L

The above were all muzzle-loaders. Smaller, breech-loaded weapons included the *falcon*, *falconet*, *esmeril*, *robinet*, *base* and *musket*. These were originally all swivel-mounted quick-firers for repelling boarders. But by the time of the Armada the musket had developed into the most powerful hand-gun on both sides.

The *harquebus* was the predecessor of the musket, originally fired from the breastbone, and then from the shoulder. The musket was more powerful and was reckoned able to kill a man in full armour at 100 yards, or 500 yards if he was unprotected. The *calliver* was a smaller form of musket.

The term 'harquebus shot', often used in descriptions of the naval battles, probably indicates a distance of about 100 yards.

The term *point-blank range* indicates the range at which a ball would hit its target if the barrel of the gun firing it were laid horizontal. The point-blank range of a cannon was about 250 yards, that of a culverin 300. At distances above these the power and accuracy of a shot rapidly declined.

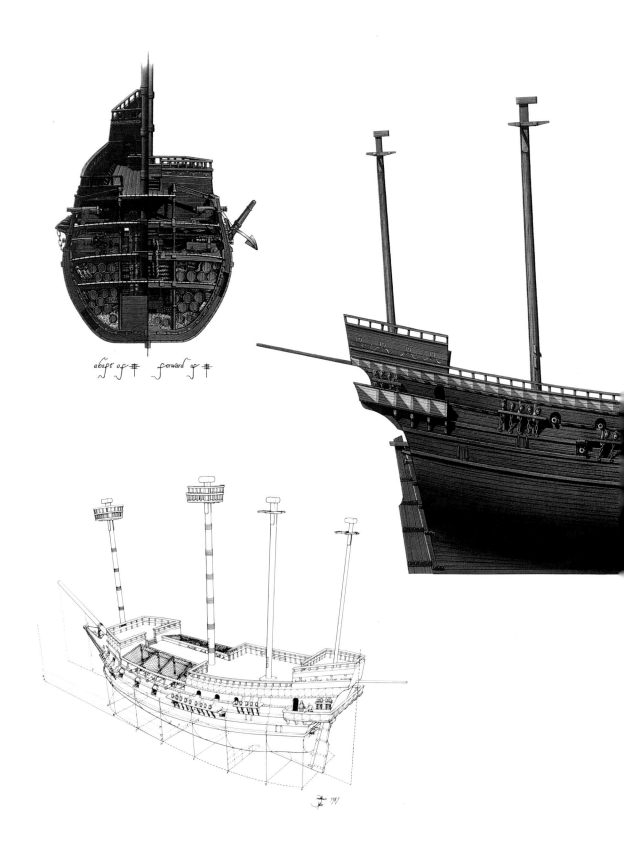

abaft of ⊞   forward of ⊞

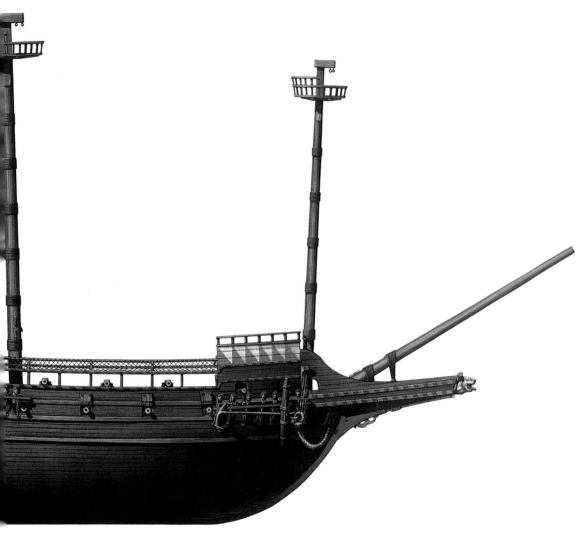

9. Artist's reconstruction of the hull of an English race-built galleon, circa 1588. Compared with the earlier great ship, or with the Spanish galleons, the new vessels were low and sleek, and consequently able to sail closer to the wind. Their cladding was of oak or elm planks about three inches thick, and the green-and-white decoration was a favourite Tudor motif.

In the cross-section (*top left*), wooden casks of food and water can be seen stored on their sides, bung-upwards, on top of the ballast in the hold and on the orlop deck. Above that is the gun-deck, carrying the ship's heavy ordnance, and above that again the upper deck, with the secondary armament.

The drawing (*left*) shows prominently the nets slung above the ship's waist to protect members of the crew stationed there from enemy trying to board.

8. *Previous page:* Artist's reconstruction of a race-built English galleon of 1588 running before the wind. Her mainsail is furled, but the crew have set their spritsail, foresail, foretopsail and main topsail, as well as the mizen and bonaventure mizen. The main armament on the gun-deck is visible through the open ports, whose lids have been fastened in the raised position.

10. Queen Elizabeth in triumph: the Armada protrait by Gheeraerts.

Chapter Six

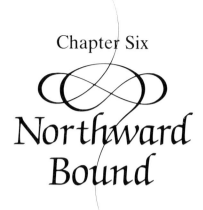

Northward Bound

Whatever his own doubts, Medina Sidonia made steady progress; by 9 May he was able to send the King a complete statement of the fleet and all who were to sail in her. This showed a grand total of 130 ships and 30,693 men. To the War Council in Madrid it seemed sensible – though it would strike us as very odd now – to publish every detail of the fleet and its armament. Clearly the aim was to create intimidating propaganda, and this may well have been achieved; but the practical result was that a copy of the list was in the hands of Burghley, in London, before the Armada even reached Land's End.

With departure at last in prospect, the Duke issued his orders for the voyage. Having reiterated that the 'principal reason' for the campaign was the King's desire to serve God, he gave his own rules for securing the goodwill of the Almighty. All ranks were to be confessed and absolved before they sailed, 'with due contrition for their sins'. Blasphemy was forbidden, on pain of 'very severe punishment to be inflicted at our discretion'. A fresh prohibition was placed upon the embarkation of women, 'public or other', since their presence constituted another 'offence to God'. Every morning the ships' boys were to say their '*Buenos Dios*' at the foot of the mainmast, and at sunset the '*Ave Maria*'.

To reduce the number of feuds and fights, the Duke proclaimed a truce and 'took into his own hands' all 'quarrels, disputes, insults and challenges' for the duration of the voyage and a month afterwards, expressly commanding that the truce was not to be violated, directly or indirectly, 'under pain of death for treason'. Four hundred years after the event, the naivety of some of his recommendations is still painful: 'It is of the greatest importance . . . that there should exist perfect good feeling and friendship between soldiers and sailors, and that there should be no possibility of quarrels amongst them,' he wrote. 'I therefore order that no man shall carry a dagger, and that on no account shall offence be given on either side.'

He went on to lay down procedure for keeping the Armada together once it was at sea – no easy business, with so many vessels and no means of communication except guns, bugles and flags. Every evening one representative from each squadron was to close the flagship to receive orders and the watchword – and on every such approach due protocol was to be observed:

> The flagship must be saluted by bugles if there are any on board, or by fifes, and two cheers from the crews. When the response has been given, the salute must be repeated.

Should the weather be too wild for new watchwords to be exchanged, the following would be employed:

Sunday	*Jesus*	Thursday	*The Angels*
Monday	*Holy Ghost*	Friday	*All Saints*
Tuesday	*Most Holy Trinity*	Saturday	*Our Lady*
Wednesday	*Santiago*		

The Armada was to head first for Cape Finisterre, and then for the Scilly Isles. No ship might break formation without permission, on 'pain of death and forfeiture'. The same penalty awaited any captain who, having become separated from the Armada, returned to Spain. If anyone did lose the rest of the formation, he was to make for the Scillys and cruise to windward off the islands until the rest of the fleet came up with him. Numerous signals – of sails dipped, flags hoisted, guns fired or lanterns posted – were designated to communicate the sighting of other ships or land, a captain's intention of changing course at night, one vessel's disablement, and so on.

The Duke's secretaries must have been busy, for a copy of his orders – which covered many pages – was sent to every ship in the fleet, and read out aloud on board so that 'sailors and soldiers alike may be informed of them, and not plead ignorance'. At many points in the discourse the Captain General's own lack of experience in command was made embarrassingly clear. To proclaim that 'men of quick sight will always be stationed at the mast-head on the look-out' cannot have impressed the seasoned captains whose first preoccupation this had been all their lives at sea; and in his renewal of the prohibition of truckle beds, the Duke was extraordinarily tactless. If any such beds still existed, he wrote,

> they are to be demolished immediately, and I order the sailors not to allow them. If the infantry possesses them, let the sailors inform me thereof, and I will have them removed.

A few paragraphs earlier he had been ordering army and navy to keep on good terms. Now he was openly inciting one to sneak on the other – a particularly foolish and unfortunate move, liable to exacerbate the antagonism which anyway existed between the two arms of the service, the soldiers regarding themselves as superior, even at sea, and looking down on the sailors as drudges whose job was not to fight but merely to run the ship.

At about the time as Medina Sidonia's orders were read out, there was produced an inflammatory pamphlet designed to stir up hatred of England and enthusiasm for the Enterprise. It is no longer clear whether this was an official or private publication; but it is hard to believe that its exaggerated language and overblown appeals to religious fervour had much effect on the 30,000 already committed, by choice or compulsion, to the Enterprise.

Its message was that their mission would be easy, because it would enjoy divine support: 'God, in whose sacred cause we go, will lead us. With such a Captain, we need not fear.' Also in their company would go the saints of Heaven, 'and particularly the holy patrons of Spain'. Awaiting them in England would be 'the aid' of numerous Catholic martyrs, not least 'the blessed and innocent Mary, Queen of Scotland', to say nothing of 'myriads of workers, citizens, knights, nobles and clergymen . . . who are anxiously looking to us for their liberation'.

> God is stronger than the devil [said the peroration], truth stronger than error, the Catholic faith stronger than heresy, the saints and angels stronger than all the power of hell, the indomitable spirit and sturdy arm of the Spaniard stronger than the drooping hearts and lax and frozen bodies of the English. . . . Courage! Steadfastness! And Spanish bravery! For with these the victory is ours, and we have nought to fear.

In spite of this rousing paean, Heaven did not immediately oblige the Spaniards with what they needed most – an easterly wind to take them down the Tagus and out into the Atlantic. The weather remained as bad and boisterous as if it had been in December. Medina Sidonia, however, was not down-hearted. 'God ordains all things,' he wrote to the King on 14 May. 'He knows best.' The Duke had been fortified by his conversations with Antonio de la Concepcion, a holy friar in the monastery of San Benito at Loyos, who felt so certain that the Lord would vouchsafe them a great victory that he asked Medina Sidonia to tell the King as much – which he did.

As the Armada waited and prayed for a wind, the Spanish spies in

Engraving after Breughel, about 1560, of a Spanish *nao* or merchantman, built in the Mediterranean. Many ships of this kind, though not designed for war, were pressed into service for the Armada campaign, but their high bow- and sterncastles made them poor sailers, and put them at a severe disadvantage against the nimbler English galleons.

England were smuggling out daily reports, many of them highly misleading. The English were in such a state (said one) 'as neither they nor their forefathers had ever been in before'. Because their fleet was so weak, they had decided to let the Spaniards land, burn their ships, and attack them on shore. . . . The City of London had offered the Queen £20,000 in cash to increase the fleet by twenty ships . . . Drake was to sail for the coast of Spain on 4 May . . . 'All idle and vagabond persons are compelled to go on board the ships' . . . Drake and the Lord Admiral, with eighty sail, were coming out 'to seek Your Majesty's Armada'. Because messages took at least ten days to reach Madrid, and several more to filter on to Lisbon, none of this last-minute intelligence was of any practical use; but the picture it gave of disarray in England no doubt added fuel to the flames of the Spaniards' expectations.

On 28 May, the eve of departure, Medina Sidonia wrote yet again to the King, rehearsing at length (and in a great muddle) what his tactics would be in the event of various possible moves by the enemy. One was that Drake might fortify himself in Plymouth, wait there until the Armada had sailed past, and then sally out to attack the Spaniards from the rear. As a precaution, the Duke had invented a novel formation – a crescent, with the heavily-armed horns facing backwards, each stiffened by one of the galleasses, and the vulnerable hulks in the centre, where they could be well protected. He himself would lead the centre, supported by the other two galleasses, and thus, 'with the help of God', should be able to deal with any enemy fleet that appeared ahead of him.

At last, late on the evening of 29 May, the fleet weighed anchor. Trumpets sounded across the water as, beneath a canopy of streamers and pennants, the ships began to drift down the Tagus towards the sea. The might of Spain – known officially as *La Felicíssima Armada*, or the Most Favoured Armada, but never as the Invincible Armada – was on its way. Yet still the weather gave no help. Even when the fleet had reached the ocean, which took some time, the south or south-west wind that it needed did not blow, and for day after day it drifted helplessly, not only failing to make progress, but falling away to the south and having to claw its way back. Harassed by his problems, and no doubt feeling lonely in his command, the Duke wrote repeatedly to the King – on 30 May, again on 1 June, and then on the 10th, 13th, 14th and 18th. He complained of the slowness of the hulks, the contrariness of the winds. Before the fleet had been at sea two weeks, many of its provisions had become so rotten and stinking that they had had to be thrown overboard, and water was running short. Soon Medina Sidonia was calling for fresh supplies to be sent after him.

Every day that the weather allowed it, he summoned a council of his senior officers, and by 18 June the pilots were advising him to put into Corunna or Ferrol to replenish supplies. This he was reluctant to do, for fear that soldiers and sailors would desert 'as usual'. Hoping to carry straight on, he sent ahead to Corunna for new provisions, but on the next day, 19 June, he and part of the fleet were forced into the harbour there anyway by a combination of bad weather, bad food and bad water. That night turned really foul, with a gale, fog and high seas; the storm damaged many of the ships caught outside the port, dismasting several, and scattered them to other harbours up and down the coast. Altogether thirty-five vessels, with nearly 8,500 men aboard, went missing. Thus, three weeks after setting out, the Armada came to an inglorious halt.

Medina Sidonia's dismay was almost comical. 'I am looking to everything myself as carefully as I can, with sorrow, as Your Majesty may imagine, at the misfortune that has befallen the Armada,' he told the King:

Notwithstanding my efforts not to enter port, I find myself here, with the best of the Armada out at sea. God be praised for all He may ordain.

Now, once again, he sought to escape the responsibility thrust upon him – not (this time) by asking to resign, but by suggesting that the whole expedition be called off. He had done his best to carry out his orders in Lisbon, he wrote on 24 June, but now that the Armada had been so weakened, he considered it extremely inadvisable to carry on. He was also worried by the fact that his men were so patently inexperienced:

I am bound to confess that I see very few, or hardly any, of those on the Armada with any knowledge of or ability to perform the duties entrusted to them. I have tested and watched this point very carefully, and Your Majesty may believe me when I assure you we are very weak. . . .

I recall the great force Your Majesty collected for the conquest of Portugal, although that country was within our own boundaries and many of the people were in your favour. Well, Sire, how do you think we can attack so great a country as England with such a force as ours is now? I have earnestly commended this matter to God, and feel bound to lay it before Your Majesty, in order that you may choose the best course whilst the Armada is refitting here. The opportunity might be taken, and the difficulties avoided, by making some honourable terms with the enemy.

Coming from the commander-in-chief, it was a monstrous suggestion – almost treason. Yet the King's answer contained no hint of censure. 'My intention is not to desist from the Enterprise in consequence of what has happened,' he wrote from the Escorial on 5 July, 'but, in any case, to carry forward the task already commenced.' The Duke was not to go looking for the lost ships, but to wait in Corunna until they joined him there. Then he was to repair, re-victual and re-water the fleet, and set out again.

This – in due course – he achieved. One party of hulks, wallowing on ahead of the rest, sailed the whole way to the Scillys and cruised up and down there for two days before being fetched back 'smelling of England'

View of Lisbon in 1580. It was here, in the natural inland harbour of the Tagus river, that the Spanish Armada assembled and made ready during the final months of 1587 and the first months of 1588. From here the great fleet of 130 ships, with almost 30,000 men on board, sailed for England on 29 May.

by a pinnace sent to recover them. Other ships trickled in from the places in which they had taken refuge. Men who had fallen ill from eating bad provisions were restored by a diet of fresh food. Repair work went ahead – and along came another peremptory royal order for the removal of all 'partitions, planks, bunks and other erections between decks that may hamper the working of the guns'.

Relations among the high command seem to have been harmonious; but the King took the unusual step of writing direct to Don Pedro de Valdes and other squadron commanders, urging them to help the Duke in every possible way. When Recalde wrote back, he used the occasion to tell the King what his own understanding of their mission was – namely, 'to meet and vanquish the enemy [fleet] by main force', then to cover the crossing of Parma's invasion force, and then to seize a port which the Armada could use as a base. He suggested that Falmouth, Plymouth or Dartmouth would be best, as these lay nearest to Spain, and were well placed to receive the 'highly necessary reinforcements of men and stores' which would have to be sent up from the south. Once the main army was safely established, the Armada might return towards Ushant, meet the incoming reinforcements, take one of the south-western English ports, and 'either push a force inland towards the Bristol Channel or form a junction with the other army'.

These ideas, aiming for a full-scale military conquest, were light-years ahead of any plans entertained by Medina Sidonia, whose sole aim (as expressed to the King) was to sail through the Channel to the Downs and there wait for Parma to make contact with him. This one letter shows how different things might have been if Recalde had managed to win the supreme command.

As it was, Medina Sidonia busied himself with what he was good at – onshore organization. Even in Corunna he was shackled by the King's inability to delegate, by his mania for trying to settle every detail himself. Not content with having appointed his secretary Andres de Alva as a

special *provedor*, or purser, for re-provisioning the fleet, Philip burdened him with a sheaf of thirty-two numbered instructions on how he was to proceed. All purchases – of wheat, flour, fish, meat, oil, salads, vegetables and so on – were to be made where the goods were most plentiful and cheapest. Biscuit for the galleys (which had no ovens of their own) was to be baked as far as possible in ovens belonging to the fleet. 'If necessary, ovens may be hired or loans made for the construction of new ovens, but a calculation of the cost and probable benefit to the Treasury must be made first, and permission obtained for the expenditure.' Biscuit was to be made well in advance of requirements, so that it did not have to be eaten too fresh, 'which is both wasteful and injurious to health'. The money provided – 20,000 ducats – was to be kept in two chests, one at Cartagena and one at Malaga, each with two different locks, 'the key of one lock being kept by the *provedor* and of the other by the storekeeper of the galleys at the port in question'.

Had the King been able to rid his mind of such minutiae, and concentrate instead on a clear exposition of how his forces were supposed to proceed when they reached 'the root of the trouble', the Armada might have been a much more formidable proposition. As it was, the Captain General of the Ocean Sea, far from improving his strategic plans in Corunna, was again bogged down in administrative detail.

His senior captains, not least Recalde, were warm in their praise of his industry; and as he made progress, his spirits lifted, and he was sustained throughout all difficulties by his own religious faith. On 15 July he described to the King, on an unusually enthusiastic note, the special arrangements he had made for all his men to be confessed and absolved, since he did not want them to be deprived 'of this great benefit, both to their souls and bodies'. To forestall wholesale desertions, he had had the crafty idea of ordering the fleet's 180 friars to land on an island in the harbour, where they set up tents and altars for their ministrations. Then, with 'a good watch kept on the island', he had the men landed in companies. 'The soldiers and sailors have done so well that the friars tell me they have already confessed and absolved 8,000 of them,' he reported:

> This is such an inestimable treasure that I esteem it more highly than the most precious jewel I carry on the fleet. On this account, and because the Armada is much improved since we left Lisbon, the men are, as I say, contented and in high spirits.

By 20 July the fleet was once again ready to sail. All except two of the missing ships had rejoined, but sickness, death and desertion had reduced the total number of men by more than 4,000. Adjustments had also been made in the balance of the crews; on the *San Martin*, for instance,

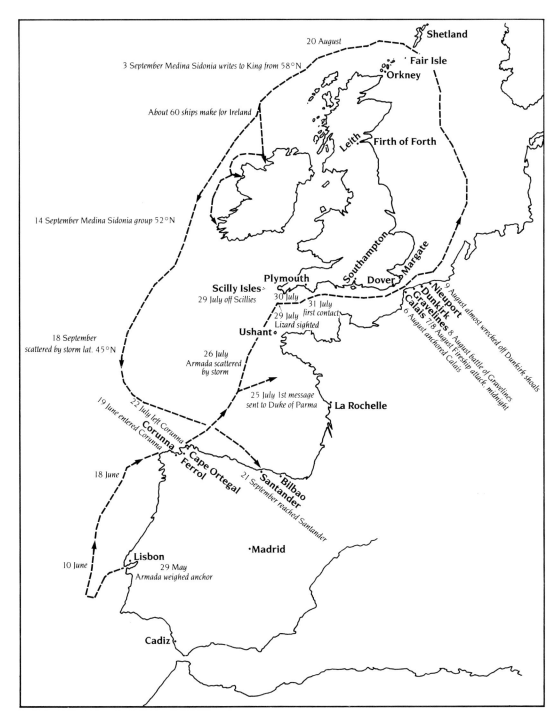

The course of the Armada

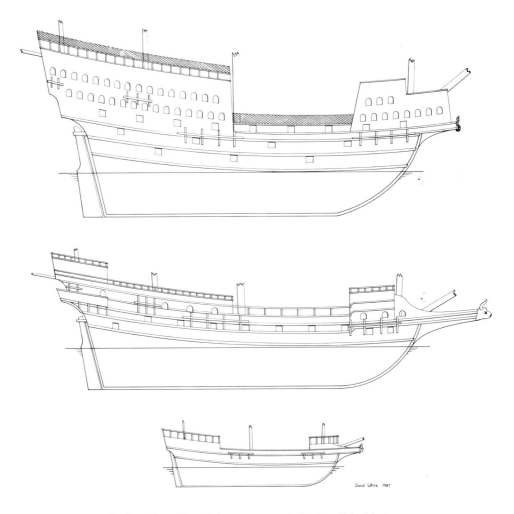

Outboard profiles of three representative English ship types.

Upper   The Great Ship. The floating fortress. The aim of the commanders of these unwieldy vessels was to grapple alongside their opponents and capture them by boarding.

Middle   The Race-Built Galleon. A purely English concept, long, low and highly manoeuvrable, intended to stand off and batter the enemy into submission with gunfire, it literally ran rings around the Spaniards.

Lower   The Pinnace. Fast and handy maid-of-all-work. Used for carrying stores, troops and despatches.

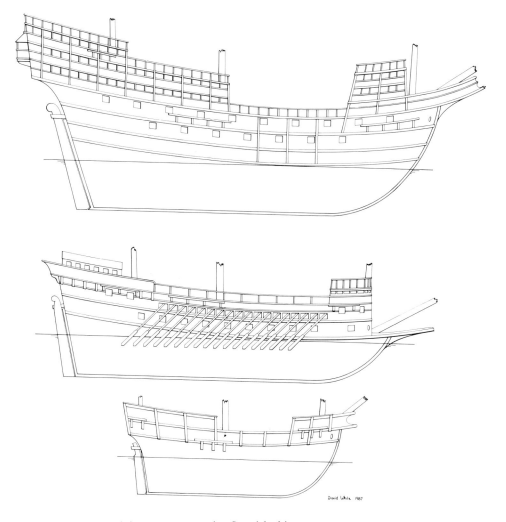

Outboard profiles of three representative Spanish ship types.

Upper   The Galleon. The Spanish version of the Great Ship.

Middle   The Galleass. A hybrid, powered by sails and oars.
It should have been able to outmanoeuvre the race-built Galleons, but in practice failed to do so.

Lower   The Nao. Basically a merchant ship carrying stores
and troops.

the number of soldiers had been increased from 300 to 308, but the total of sailors reduced from 177 to 161 – a change reflected in several vessels. Others had already lost a substantial proportion of their fighting force, among them the galleon *San Felipe*, whose complement of soldiers had fallen from 415 to 331.

Among the high command there existed a dangerous variety of opinion on technical possibilities. All the admirals had been unnerved by the extreme sluggishness of the hulks, which could hardly make headway into the wind, and by now Pedro de Valdes, who had some experience of English waters, must have realized that once such a lumbering convoy had committed itself to a passage of the Channel, it would have the greatest difficulty in beating back against the prevailing westerlies, and that if it ever went past the Straits of Dover, return would be impossible unless the English fleet had already been soundly defeated.

The extent of the Spanish admirals' differences, and their need for an experienced and forceful commander, stand vividly revealed in the minutes of a consultation held aboard the flagship on 20 July to decide whether or not it was safe for the Armada to sail. Having summoned his senior commanders, the Duke 'begged every officer present to give his opinion of the weather for the purpose'.

Don Alonso de Leyva, leading off, suggested that they should consult the sailors, as they were likely to know best. Diego Flores de Valdes did not like the 'evil appearances' of the weather, and said they ought not to sail until it had become really fine: he forecast that a clear period might come in on the 23rd, when there would be 'a conjunction', and he expected the wind to settle in the north-west 'as the new moon came in with it'. Pedro de Valdes agreed that they should wait for the conjunction. Martin de Bertendona said the weather was perfectly all right for sailing as it was: he 'would not wish for better'. Oquendo agreed with the Valdes assessment and said they had better wait. Recalde, who had been studying the elements with the closest attention, said that if the wind remained as it was, they should sail tomorrow, without waiting for the moon. Admiral Gregorio de las Alas said the same. The pilots, summoned later, agreed that if the weather did not deteriorate they should sail next day. In the end Medina Sidonia decided that they should leave at daybreak next morning.

Once more it proved impossible to stick to the plan. Another storm blew up on the night of the 20th, and it was not until the morning of the 22nd that they were able to clear the harbour. Scarcely ten miles out – and before they had started to double Cape Priorio, the headland north of Corunna – a dead calm brought them to a halt. Medina Sidonia feared they would have to put back into harbour; but then at 3 a.m. a breeze sprang up off the land, as though God-given. Growing to a south-east wind, it lifted the Armada not only round Cape Priorio but also past Cape Ortegal, the north-westerly point of Spain. At last the fleet was truly on its way.

Once safely at sea, Medina Sidonia hastened to let Parma know that he was coming. On 25 June he sent Captain Don Rodrigo Tello de Guzman off in an armed pinnace, giving his own projected course and asking Parma to send back a message to say how he should proceed 'for the purpose of effecting a juncture'. For three days the weather remained perfect for a voyage to England. Had three or four of the ships cared to clap on sail (he later told the King), they might have reached the mouth of the Channel by the 25th; but since they could proceed only as fast 'as the scurviest ship in the fleet . . . verily some of them are dreadfully slow', they made less progress.

On the morning of 26 July they found themselves becalmed in dense fog; and this proved to be the lull before a dangerous storm. Heavy squalls from the north-west built up during the afternoon, and the next day brought in a full gale, with driving rain. 'Not only did the waves mount to the skies,' wrote the Duke, 'but some seas broke clean over the ships, and the whole of the stern gallery of Diego Flores's flagship [the *San Cristobal*] was carried away. We were on watch all night, full of anxiety . . . It was the most cruel night ever seen.' For all the *aventureros* and their servants, most of whom had never before been to sea, it must have been a terrifying ordeal. With no practical function to perform, they were nothing but useless passengers.

Thursday, 27 July, broke clear and bright, but with the sea still very rough. A count of the ships showed forty missing, including all four galleys, whose leader the *Diana* had been in difficulties before the storm began. Shepherding over the next three days rounded up all the other types of ship, but Medina Sidonia never saw his galleys again, and it was weeks before he found out what had happened to them.

As many experienced observers had predicted, they were simply not strong enough for the violent northern ocean. Under the stress of high winds and seas the seams of their planking opened and they started to take in water at a disastrous rate. Exactly what happened when they reached the coast will never be known; but it can be said with confidence that their end was *not* as described by David Gwynne, a mendacious Welsh slave who survived. According to him, the *Diana* went down with all hands, and he and his companions, by a great feat of derring-do, killed the Spaniards on board the *Bazana*, in which he escaped to safety. But in fact Gwynne was on the *Diana*, rather than the *Bazana*; his ship did not go down with all hands, but limped towards Bayonne, where she ran aground and was wrecked. In the confusion he and some fellow-slaves escaped to Rochelle, where he fell in with an Englishman called Eustace

Hart before making his way to England. As Gwynne spoke Spanish, he was sent to Ireland to help with the interrogation of survivors from the Armada who were wrecked there, but he soon proved himself a liar and a thief. Hart described him as 'a lewd and prating fellow', who carried in his pocket verses about England, 'naming the Queen as Bess', and in Ireland, after he had been detected stealing from prisoners, he was sent ignominiously away.

From the tone of Medina Sidonia's despatch to the King, it is clear that he was relieved to have lost no more than the galleys. Even the stronger galleasses, he reported, were 'really very fragile for such heavy seas as these'. When, at 4 p.m. on Friday, 29 July, his lookouts sighted the Lizard, he was so thrilled that he had hoisted to the maintop a standard showing a crucifix, with the Virgin and Mary Magdalen on either side of it. He also ordered three guns to be fired, so that the whole fleet would offer up a prayer of thanks for God's mercy in bringing them so far.

After an infinity of setbacks, he was at long last within sight of his target. Yet by now he had grown exceedingly nervous. Suddenly it came home to him that, once the Armada entered the Channel, it would be highly vulnerable if further westerly gales blew up (as they were almost certain to) and would risk being driven onto the shoals of Flanders. Rather than take that chance – he told the King in a despatch written on the morning of 30 July – he proposed to go no further than the Isle of Wight until he had definite news of how Parma was placed.

His anxiety came through clearly in that message, his last before battle broke out. 'The plan is that at the moment of my arrival he should sally with his fleet, without causing me to wait a minute,' he told the King:

> The whole success of the undertaking depends upon this, and in order that the Duke will be acquainted with it, I will send another pinnace to him as soon as I get into the Channel; and still another when I arrive off the Wight. I am astonished to have received no news of him for so long. During the whole course of our voyage we have not fallen in with a single vessel, or man, from whom we could obtain any information; and we are consequently groping in the dark.

That phrase – a favourite of the Duke's – summed up his position all too well. He assumed quite rightly that Parma's preparations were well advanced; but he could not possibly know that, for reasons which will now never be clear, the Duke would never make any serious effort to come out and meet him.

Chapter Seven

Hearts of Oak

On paper the naval forces which the Queen could deploy looked perilously small. Vacillating as usual, and inhibited by a chronic shortage of money, she had spent as little as possible on the fleet, and had stood down its crews whenever the threat of war seemed to recede. Worst of all, she and the Council had failed to build up the stocks of powder and ammunition needed to fight a prolonged action at sea. In the end it was not intelligent preparation on the part of the Government, so much as the courage and realism of her admirals, that saved the country.

In 1588 England's naval tradition was still in its infancy, for scarcely two generations had passed since the foundation of the Royal Navy by Henry VIII. It was he who for the first time saw a standing navy as the kingdom's main weapon of defence, rather than simply as a transport service; it was he who created the basis of an administration by founding the Navy Board at Deptford in 1546, developed royal dockyards at Deptford, Woolwich and Portsmouth, and forced the Lord High Admiral to go to sea instead of merely enjoying a titular position.

No less important, by installing heavy guns on board his largest ships, Henry brought in a new concept of warfare at sea. Until then battles had been dominated by the idea of charging the enemy in line-abreast, as though the ships were infantry or cavalry on land, with the main strength concentrated in the centre. In such contests the principal weapon was the galley, powered by oars and armed with a metal beak on the prow; the aim was to ram an enemy ship, grapple with it, and carry the fight to close quarters – as had been done with such success at Lepanto. Under Henry VIII this medieval tactic gave way to the notion of heavy guns firing broadsides from a distance, and with the new idea came another radical innovation – the development of the great ship, which had the bulk to carry not only a large crew and complement of armed soldiers, who could board enemy vessels and fight at close quarters if necessary, but also the heavy ordnance to deliver a destructive punch from long range.

These half sections show the structure of
the framing and planking of the hull and
the positions of the decks. They are of the
same ship as in Fig. 3 but at twice the scale.

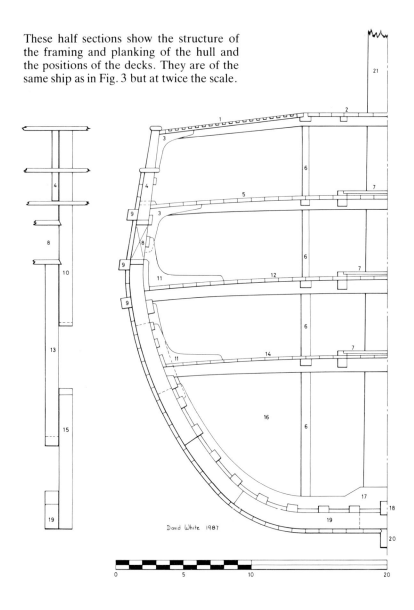

David White 1987

1 Grating
2 Gangway
3 Knee
4 Top timber
5 Upper deck
6 Pillar
7 Hatchway
8 Gun port

9 Wale
10 Third futtock
11 Standard
12 Second orlop (gun deck)
13 Second futtock
14 Orlop
15 First futtock
16 Hold

Fig. 1   Half section through the rider ahead
of the mainmast, looking aft.

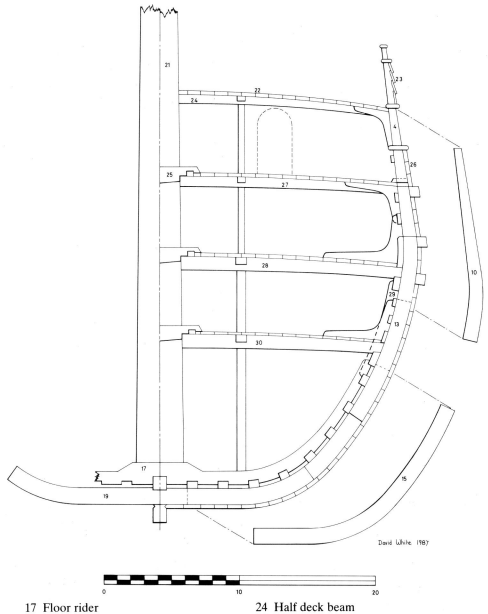

David White 1987

17 Floor rider
18 Keelson
19 Ground timber (floor)
20 Keel
21 Main mast
22 Half deck
23 Half deck bulwarks

24 Half deck beam
25 Mast partner
26 Upper deck bulwarks
27 Upper deck beam
28 Second orlop (gun deck) beam
29 Breast rider
30 Orlop beam

Fig. 2   Half section through the rider abaft
the mainmast, looking aft.
Scale: 1/4″ to 1′ (1/48).

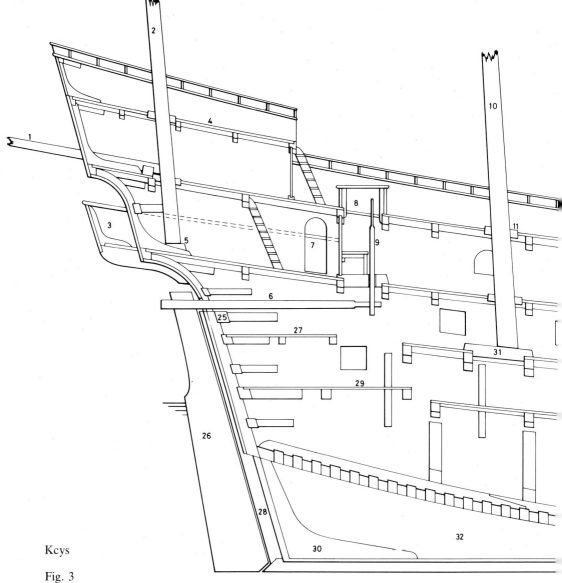

Keys

Fig. 3

1 Outlicker (boomkin)
2 Bonaventure mizen mast
3 Gallery
4 Poop
5 Bonaventure mizen mast step
6 Tiller
7 Gallery doorway
8 Helmsman's shelter
9 Whipstaff
10 Mizen mast
11 Mast partners
12 Half deck

13 Main mast
14 Main hatchway
15 Middle line gangway
16 Grating
17 Upper deck
18 Gun port
19 Fore castle
20 Fore mast
21 Stem
22 Bowsprit
23 Beakhead
24 Grating

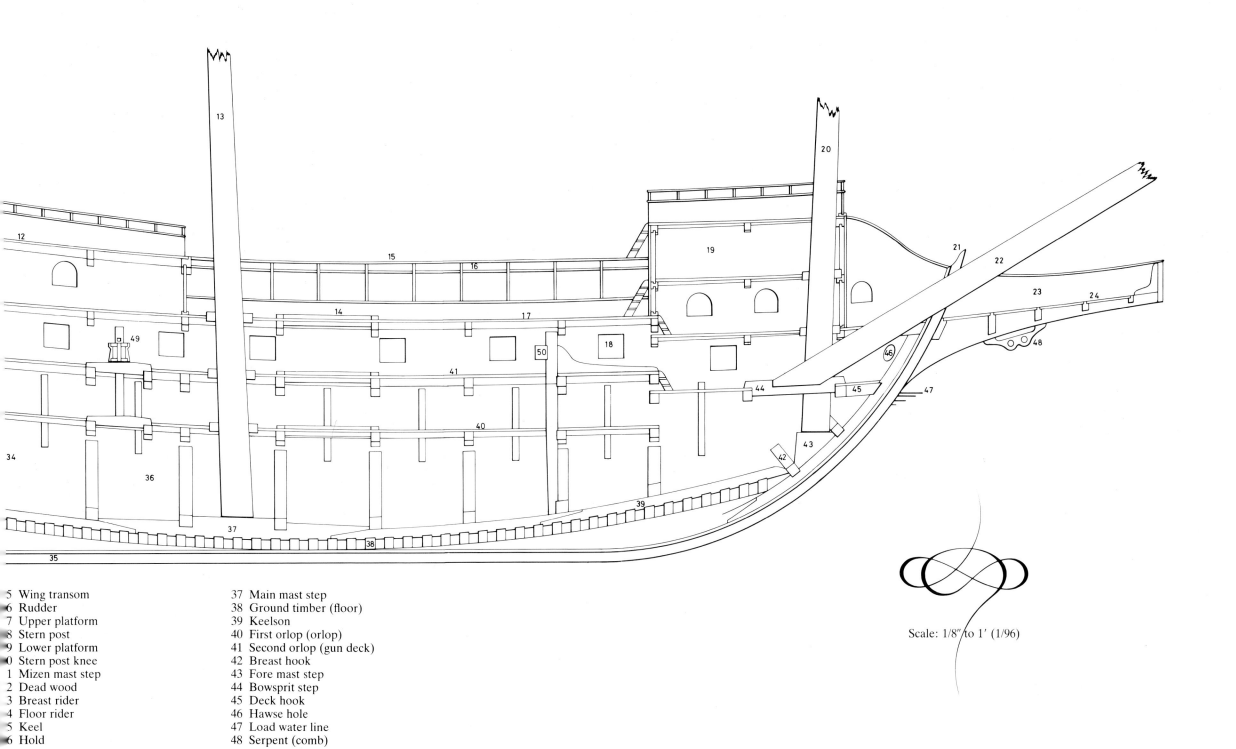

5 Wing transom	37 Main mast step
6 Rudder	38 Ground timber (floor)
7 Upper platform	39 Keelson
8 Stern post	40 First orlop (orlop)
9 Lower platform	41 Second orlop (gun deck)
0 Stern post knee	42 Breast hook
1 Mizen mast step	43 Fore mast step
2 Dead wood	44 Bowsprit step
3 Breast rider	45 Deck hook
4 Floor rider	46 Hawse hole
5 Keel	47 Load water line
6 Hold	48 Serpent (comb)

Scale: 1/8″ to 1′ (1/96)

Longitudinal section (inboard profile) of a
typical English Race-Built Galleon c1588.

There is insufficient evidence available to be able accurately to reconstruct a *specific* ship; so that this section, along the middle line, is only a reconstruction of the layout and structure of a *typical* English race-built Galleon.

It cannot be said to show exactly how these ships were built, as once again there are not enough data available, and although all the known facts have been incorporated into the design, gaps have remained.

By producing a design from scratch it has been possible to fill these gaps in a logical and practical manner and in the style of the time. The result is a ship that not only agrees visually with known criteria but is technically sound, unlike many other so-called reconstructions. In other words,

it is basically stable and possesses sufficient strength.

By comparison with its contemporaries, it has a greater length-to-breadth ratio and finer lines, making it faster. Its fine-run aft would create a better flow of water past the rudder, giving it a quicker response to the helm and increasing its manoeuvrability.

A well-balanced sail plan, with comparatively greater lateral resistance, would enable it to sail closer to the wind, and make less leeway.

The high superstructures of the English Great Ships and the Spanish Galleons resulted in them making considerable leeway. The Armada campaign demonstrated the outstanding ability of the race-built Galleons to sail – and remain – to windward of the Spanish ships.

Confrontation between the English and French fleets in Portsmouth harbour, 1545. It was on this occasion, witnessed from the shore by Henry VIII, that his 700-ton flagship *Mary Rose* suddenly rolled over and sank. Nearly half her hull and many of her contents – preserved in astonishing condition by immersion in mud – were recovered in an eleven-year excavation, culminating in 1982, and are now on show in Portsmouth. They form a unique time-capsule of Tudor life at sea.

Martin Frobisher (left), a tough Yorkshireman, was bitterly jealous of Drake, probably because his own voyages of exploration in search of a North West Passage had not brought him the wealth and fame that Drake enjoyed. It was to John Hawkins (right), who became Treasurer and Comptroller of the Navy in 1573, that Elizabeth principally owed the strength of her warships. An expert in design, he was a leading advocate of the race-built galleon, and thus one of the principal architects of victory over the Armada. Both men were knighted by Howard on board the *Ark Royal* during a lull in the battle.

FORBISHERVS ouans NEPTVNIA regna frequentat
Pre patria at tandem glande peremptus obit

Qui vicit totiens in fructis classibus hostes
Ille magis HAVKINS vitam reliquit in Indis

99

For all the ideas and enthusiasm of Henry himself, under his successors the navy declined. Unlike King Philip, who encouraged the construction of large ships in Spain by giving grants of six ducats a ton for every ton over 300, Elizabeth left things to private enterprise, with the result that in 1588 her navy contained only thirteen ships over 400 tons, and only thirty-eight vessels in all.

The fact that most of these ships were in excellent condition was due largely to the diligence and foresight of one man – John Hawkins of Plymouth, who, after spectacular slaving and trading voyages to the West Indies, had settled down in England and had been appointed Treasurer and Comptroller of the Navy in 1573. Under his guidance the fleet had been imaginatively modernized and strengthened.

Hawkins was a deceptive character: on the surface he was all charm and courtesy, and something of a dandy, but behind this polished facade his mind worked away on many levels simultaneously. Thus, as an ostensible friend of Spain, he had been deeply involved in the Ridolfi plot of 1570, in which he pretended to the Spaniards that he was going to provide ships to cover the invasion of England by Alva; yet he managed to keep Cecil and the Queen informed of what he was doing with such skill that he never aroused the suspicion of the plotters.

His own experience at sea gave him an exceptional insight into ship design, and it was due mainly to his advocacy that the English moved away from the concept of the high, top-heavy great ship which had dominated the past fifty years to the novel idea of a lower, slimmer 'race-built' galleon, which, although it did not present so threatening an appearance, had the inestimable advantage of being more weatherly, or able to sail closer to the wind. This one quality – the superior nimbleness of the new ships – was one of the most important factors in deciding the fate of the Armada.

The rival advantages of bulk and speed fuelled one of the longest-burning controversies of Elizabethan naval architecture. John Hawkins's son Richard, who himself became a leading authority, retained a nostalgic admiration for ships of the old type, 'for majesty and terror of the enemy', and for their ability to carry heavy ordnance, as well as large crews. On the other hand Sir Walter Raleigh (who fought in the Armada campaign as a young man) was strongly against them, arguing that their high stern and bow castles gave them 'all ill qualities', making them 'extreme leeward' [prone to slide downwind] and liable to 'labour and overset'.

The point was that the new ships were designed for a new purpose. Whereas the great ship – especially to the Spaniards – was in effect a floating garrison, whose object was to grapple with and board an enemy so that a land battle could be fought at sea, the race-built galleons were mobile gun-platforms intended to be able to *keep away* from opponents for as long as they wanted, so that they could choose their range and bombard them from whatever distance best suited their ordnance.

Major improvements to the Navy as a whole had been brought in since 1583, when a commission had reviewed ships and stores, reorganized the yards at Rochester and Chatham, set the charges for routine maintenance at £4,000 annually (which the Queen thought monstrous) and decreed that at least one new front-line vessel should be built every year. As a result, the fleet had been strengthened by the addition of five new galleons.

In 1588 the newest of all – appropriately enough – was the flagship, which had been built for Sir Walter Raleigh in 1587 and sold by him to the Queen, before her launch, for £5,000. Originally the *Ark Raleigh*, she became the *Ark Royal*, or *Ark* for short. She was a race-built galleon of the most modern type; her keel was probably 100 feet long, wth a $33\frac{1}{2}$-foot rake forward and a 6-foot rake aft, giving her a total length of $139\frac{1}{2}$ feet, a breadth of 36 feet, and a rating of 800 tons. Her frame was entirely of oak, the beams jointed and held together by trennails, or wooden pegs; she was planked with oak inside and out, each skin being three or four inches thick, and the seams of the outer skin caulked with pitch. Almost certainly she was designed not from any plan, but by eye and rule-of-thumb.* The outside of the hull was probably natural oak colour, and the only decoration the coat of arms she carried on the taffrail, high on the stern. The gun-deck, which ran the whole length of the ship, carried her main armament, which amounted to forty-four guns in all. In the Armada campaign she was manned by a crew of 270 mariners, 34 gunners and 126 soldiers – a total of 430.

The next newest ship was the *Rainbow*, built in 1586, on lines much like those of the *Ark Royal*: the naval historian William Monson, who himself served in the fleet against the Armada as a volunteer, described her as 'low and snug in the water' and 'like a galleass'. The 500-ton *Revenge* dated from 1577 and was designed on the same principles. Several of the older vessels had been reconstructed to bring them into line with modern ideas, among them John Hawkins's own command, the *Victory*, which had been launched in 1561 and, twenty-five years later, had been 'altered into the form of a galleon' at a cost of £500.

It would have been dangerous for an enemy to take the relatively small numbers of the Queen's ships as an accurate indication of the nation's sea power, for the State fleet could be reinforced in times of crisis by considerable numbers of merchant vessels, privately owned and by no means badly armed. Not only had the country's fishermen built up a huge fund of sea-going experience during their regular voyages to Iceland, and more recently to the Newfoundland banks; the privateers

*The earliest known plans of an English warship were drawn by Matthew Baker in 1586, but these are thought to be theoretical, rather than sketches of an existing vessel.

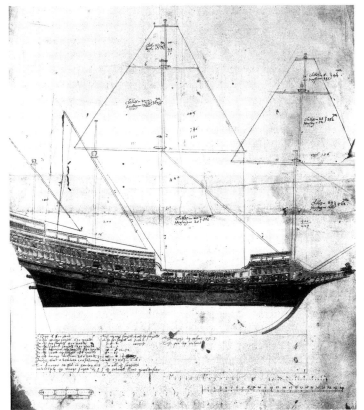

Drawing of a sixteenth-century English galleon, and her sail plan, probably by the master shipwright Matthew Baker. This is one of the earliest plans known; but analysis of the dimensions shows that it was a theoretical sketch, rather than a portrait of any working ship, and it is probable that most of the vessels that fought against the Armada were designed not on the drawing-board but by rule of thumb.

Elizabethan shipwrights at work, from *Fragments of Ancient Shipwriting* by Matthew Baker, published in 1587.

had sailed and fought in distant waters, and amounted to a formidable navy on their own. Thus for the final battle with the Armada, when ships of all provenances had been gathered together, the English fleet amounted to 160 sail, and altogether nearly 200 ships took some part in the campaign.

The officer in supreme command of it, the Lord High Admiral, was Charles, Lord Howard of Effingham, a tall, lean man of 52, with a long, bony face that accurately hinted at his aristocratic lineage. Not only was he a cousin of the Queen – as had been his first wife, Catherine, the daughter of Lord Hunsdon; he was also connected by birth or marriage with many leading figures in government and society. His sister was married to Sir Edward Stafford, the English ambassador in Paris, and several members of his family held lesser posts in the fleet.

Just as Medina Sidonia had been chosen for his social eminence, so Howard owed his position partly to the excellence of his background; but, unlike the Spanish duke, he was no last-minute substitute, brought in to fill a gap. Far from it: his father, Lord William Howard, and two of his uncles had all been Lord High Admirals before him, and he himself, after useful experience at sea, had been appointed to the command in 1585. To many people it seemed that the office had become almost hereditary in the family.

The Howards had already had some dealings with the Spaniards. One of Lord William's tasks had been to meet Prince Philip and escort him into Southampton when he came to marry Mary in 1554. Another had been to command a squadron which escorted the Emperor Maximilian's daughter Anne of Austria when she sailed from Zeeland in August 1570 to become Philip's fourth wife. Nominally, the English force had been a guard of honour, but its real purpose had been to make sure that Anne's powerful Spanish flotilla did not attempt anything while they were close to the English coast; and the Lord High Admiral is said on that occasion to have forced the Spaniards to 'stoop gallant, and to veil their bonnets to the Queen of England'.

Charles Howard was trained on land and at sea by his father, and from an early age he enjoyed the confidence of the Queen. According to the historian William Camden, Elizabeth 'had a great persuasion of his fortunate conduct', and 'knew him to be of a moderate and noble courage, skilful in sea matters, wary and provident . . . industrious and active, and of great authority and esteem among the sailors'. Another excellent trait was that he never held rigid views, but had the common sense to take advice from seamen more experienced than himself. In the felicitous phrase of the historian Thomas Fuller, the Queen had a navy of oak 'and an admiral of osier'. Blessed with a good sense of humour, and aggressively patriotic, Howard faced the threat of the Armada with far greater confidence than Medina Sidonia could ever summon to the task of attacking England.

He was also a lively natural writer, who often coined stirring phrases in his letters and battle reports – as when he described how his ships, tossed by a three-day, 'extreme, continual storm' in Plymouth Sound, had 'danced as lustily as the gallantest dancers in the Court'. Another of his interests was the theatre, and he was patron of the company to which the violent young poet and playwright Christopher Marlowe attached himself.

One of his most engaging features was the robust confidence which he placed in the sturdiness of the English ships. He swore he would be happy to sail to Rio de Janeiro in the little *Swallow*, built in Henry VIII's time, 'in the wildest storm that could blow', and when the galleon *Elizabeth Bonaventure* went aground at Flushing in 1587, he was perfectly delighted at the way she survived the accident.

Launched in 1561, rebuilt in 1581, the *Elizabeth Bonaventure* had seen more than twenty-five years' hard service, not least as Sir Francis Drake's flagship on his voyage to the West Indies in 1585 and 1586, and in his raid on Cadiz a year later. By the beginning of 1588 she had been condemned, because of her age, but with the threat of an attack by Spain looming she was reprieved, and confounded the pessimists by proving uncommonly robust. There was a note of relief, almost of surprise, in the report which Howard sent to Burghley in March, describing how she had run aground on a sandbank, 'by the fault of the pilot', as his squadron put into Flushing to ride out a gale:

> The next tide, by the goodness of God and great labour, we brought her off, and in all this time there came never a spoonful of water into her well. My Lord, except a ship had been made of iron, it were to be thought impossible to do as she hath done; and it may be truly said that there never was nor is a stronger ship in the world than she is. . . . She is twenty-seven years old; she was with Sir Francis Drake two voyages . . . and this is one of the ships which they would have come into a dry dock, now before she came out. My Lord, I have no doubt but some ships which have been ill reported of will deceive them as this ship doth.

Howard's commission, drawn up in Latin in December 1587, invested him with the widest possible powers for the defence of the realm, appointing him,

> Our lieutenant-general, commander-in-chief and governor of our whole fleet and army at sea, now fitted forth against

Like his opponent Medina Sidonia, Lord Howard of Effingham, Lord High Admiral of England (here portrayed in Garter robes), was of most distinguished lineage, being a cousin of the Queen, and connected by birth or marriage with many leading figures at the Court. Yet he was also a professional seaman, and was appointed to supreme command of the English fleet in 1585. In the year of the Armada he was 52.

the Spaniards, their allies, adherents or abettors, attempting or encompassing any design against our kingdoms, dominions and subjects.

Yet although he was Lord High Admiral in name and deed, he was not the man whom the Spaniards saw as their supreme enemy. The principal object of their respect, fear and hatred was his Vice-Admiral, Sir Francis Drake.

Astrolabe made for Sir Francis Drake by Humphrey Cole.

Sir Francis Drake – an unusually animated portrait. When the threat of invasion was imminent he was all for carrying the fight to the enemy and attacking the Armada before it could leave the Spanish coast. His plan almost succeeded, being thwarted only by a last minute change of wind.

Howard was an able and admirable commander, but Drake was a genius. In 1588, aged about 43, he was at the height of his ability and renown. The seventeenth-century historian John Stow left a vivid glimpse of his stature:

> He was more skilful in all points of navigation than any that ever was before his time, in his time or since his death. He was also of perfect memory, great observation, eloquent by nature, skilful in artillery . . . His name was a terror to the French, Spaniard, Portugal and Indian. Many princes of Italy and Germany desired his picture. . . . In brief he was as famous in Europe and America as Tamberlane in Asia and Africa.

This magnetic explorer, warrior and commander of men had been born about 1545 on a farm at Crowndale, near Tavistock, in Devon, the eldest child of a well-to-do yeoman family who had been established in the area for generations. In speech and outlook he was brought up, and always remained, a West Country man; but when he was still a child his family found themselves caught up in the violent Catholic backlash which greeted the enforced introduction of the New Prayer Book on Whitsunday 1549. Driven from home by riots, they fled first to Plymouth and then to Kent, where they went to live in a hulk on the Thames, perhaps on Gillingham Reach, below Chatham.

Three fundamental influences were paramount in forming Drake's character. One was the fact that from as early as he could remember he lived on or near the water: ships and sailing became his whole life. The second was that his father, a lay preacher, gave the boy most of his education at home, from the Bible, with the result that he became imbued with the principles of the Protestant faith. The third was that he grew up in the middle of the violent religious struggle that disfigured Queen Mary's reign. With a campaign of terror raging, and Protestants being burnt at the stake in Smithfield, children could not remain immune from the political and religious tensions of the day: they snowballed the suite of the Spanish ambassador and fought mock combats between the Prince of Spain and Sir Thomas Wyatt, who had led a brief rebellion in the hope of preventing Mary's marriage to Philip, and had been executed in April 1554. So highly-charged were these exchanges that in one of them the boy playing the role of Philip was nearly hanged.

The lasting effect of such boyhood experiences was well summed up by Drake's magisterial biographer Sir Julian Corbett:

> We can see the making of the man in whose hatred of Spaniard and Papist there was always a sweetening of the

love of God, in whose most high-handed and least defensible exploits there sounds a note of piety that rings sincere, and with whose moods of most reckless daring was always mixed some sober calculation and something of a child-like faith that Heaven was listening to his prayers.

Because Edmund Drake was poor, and had eleven children, he sent Francis to sea early on a coaster plying in the Channel. If the experience was tough, it brought handsome rewards – first in the form of the coaster itself, which the owner bequeathed to his young apprentice on his death as a reward for diligence, and more generally in a taste for the sea that launched Francis on a glorious career as privateer, semi-licensed pirate, admiral of the Queen's navy, and national hero.

Of all his early adventures, the one that most fired him with an implacable loathing of the Spaniards was their treacherous attack on himself and his cousin John Hawkins in the harbour of San Juan d'Ulua, on the coast of Mexico. This happened in 1568, when he was 22 or 23. The expedition, whose main purpose was to collect slaves from Africa and sell them in the West Indies, had sailed from Plymouth in October 1567, and until that point had been successful. Then, however, it was caught in a deceitfully-planned ambush from which Drake was lucky to escape. Having been separated from the other ships of the little convoy, he sailed back into Plymouth alone at the end of January 1569, vowing a lifetime's revenge upon the dogs of Spain.

In the next twenty years he made or took advantage of countless chances to exact reprisals; yet in enemy eyes two of his exploits stood out above the rest in terms of their audacity and the offence that they gave. The first was his voyage round the world – the earliest English circumnavigation, second only to that of Magellan – which he made between 1577 and 1580, and the second his raid on Cadiz in 1587.

In purely commercial terms, the circumnavigation was an unprecedented success: the haul of gold, silver and jewels that Drake brought home in the *Golden Hind* repaid his backers (of whom the Queen was one) forty-seven times their original stake. Yet its moral effect was even greater. In the eyes of Philip's subjects the most damaging feature of the voyage was that Drake had sailed not merely into, but right through, that sector of the globe which the Pope in his Bull of 1570 had assigned to Spain. That he should have violated the Spanish Main was bad enough; but that he should have penetrated that holy of holies the Pacific, captured his treasure off the coast of Peru and come home unscathed, was an inconceivable insult. In so doing he was seen to have struck a most damaging blow against the Counter-Reformation, which in Europe had been threatening to sweep all opposition before it: from the moment of his return he was recognized as one of the most vigorous and dangerous champions of the Protestant cause.

His homecoming was fraught with difficulties, for his depredations had strained relations between England and Spain almost to breaking point; single-handed, he had brought about a national crisis. So when, after he had sailed into Plymouth on 26 September 1580, the Queen immediately summoned him to Court, spent six hours closeted with him, and later knighted him on board the *Golden Hind* at Deptford, she gave open and final defiance to the King of Spain.

Suddenly Drake was *the* royal favourite, and a national hero. 'His name and fame became admirable in all places,' wrote Stow, 'the people swarming daily in the streets to behold him.' Books, portraits and ballads were published in his praise, and his 'opinion and judgement concerning maritime affairs stood paramount'. One incident, from April 1588, gives a good idea of how his renown had penetrated Europe. From Venice a contact of Walsingham's wrote to say that he had fallen in with a young gentleman of Naples who was going to Flanders 'to have a share in the spoils of England'. This casual acquaintance told him that a portrait of Drake had just been brought out of France,

> which, being given to a painter to refresh, because the colours thereof were faded in the carriage, was so earnestly sought after to be seen that in one day's keeping the same, the picturer made more profit by the great resort from all places to behold it than if he had made it anew. About it were written these words: *Il Drago, gran corsaro Inglese.*

In England, the Spanish ambassador reported bitterly that the Queen 'shows extraordinary favour to Drake and never fails to speak to him when she goes out in public, conversing with him for a long time . . . she often had him in her cabinet; often, indeed, walking with him in the garden'. According to Francis' brother John, he was sometimes seen talking to her nine times in a single day. In the words of Sir Julian Corbett: 'The arch-pirate had become the popular hero, the centre of growing confidence in the national strength and contempt for the power of Spain.'

His great voyage made him rich, and with part of the proceeds he bought Buckland Abbey, a former monastery some twelve miles north of Plymouth, which had recently been converted into a grand private house by Sir Richard Grenville.* The price – £3,400 – was astronomical for the time. No doubt his sudden wealth increased his arrogance and ostentation; his enemies complained of his 'high, haughty and insolent carriage'. Yet it is clear that, for most people, there was something immensely appealing in his personality. He was stocky and broad, with a

---

*The house, now owned by the National Trust, is maintained as a memorial to Drake, and contains many of his possessions.

round head and reddish-brown beard. Stow describes him as being 'of a cheerful countenance, well favoured, fair', with eyes 'round, large and clear'. He gave an immediate impression of energy, and also of straight-forwardness, and for all his success he never lost the vital ability to talk naturally to people of every rank. Having walked with the Queen in her garden one day, and argued on equal terms with Howard about how to tackle the Armada the next, he could gossip with mariners in Plymouth on the third as if he were still one of them. Don Francisco de Zarate, a Spanish officer whom he captured, remarked on the 'skill and power of his command', and reported that 'he treats them [his men] with affection, and they him with respect'.

Just as the motto which he chose for his coat of arms – *Sic Parvis Magna* – reflected his own career ('Great things from small beginnings'), so on shipboard he insisted that social rank meant nothing. In a speech made at a critical point during his circumnavigation, he laid down a fundamental precept to his crews: 'But, my masters . . . I must have the gentlemen to haul and draw with the mariners, and the mariners with the gentlemen.' His insistence on this principle, and his own ability to prac-tise it daily, were of incalculable benefit in the Elizabethan navy.

Bolstered by his new status, Drake pressed ever more strongly for permission to launch a really damaging attack on Spain – either by intercepting the treasure fleets as they came in from the West Indies, or by putting in direct assaults on the harbours of the mainland. 'Not a day passes that he does not say a thousand shameless things,' reported Mendoza to the King on 1 March 1582, 'amongst others that he will give the Queen 80,000 ducats if she will grant him leave to arm ships to attack Your Majesty's convoys.'

He finally got his chance in April 1587, when, with typical but still astonishing audacity, he led a specially-formed raiding party into the harbour of Cadiz and created havoc among the mass of ships assembled there. Escaping unscathed, he captured Sagres Castle, near St Vincent, and destroyed more than 100 fishing boats, together with the entire stock of barrel-staves. As a pre-emptive strike, his attack could scarcely have been more successful, since it set back Philip's preparations for the Armada for months. Yet again, as after the circumnavigation, the moral effect was even more damaging than the physical. The attack gave the defenders a terrible shock. Now to the Spaniards Drake seemed more than ever an agent of the devil – not metaphorically, as the term would be understood today, but in the most literal, physical sense. Because he was a heretic, it was more than likely that he was working with Satan, and furthering his designs upon the earth. Protected by magic powers, he was the most formidable enemy that could be imagined.

It was only natural, after such exploits, that he felt he should have been given supreme command of England's navy against the Armada; yet so strong were his patriotic instincts that he fought down disappointment and rendered Howard the most loyal service imaginable.

Not that everyone in England appreciated his abilities: perhaps his bitterest critic was that other outstanding sea-captain Martin Frobisher, who in the Armada campaign commanded the galleon *Triumph*. A tough Yorkshireman, whose hard, dark eyes glare out uncompromisingly from his portraits, Frobisher came from a good family, and was a man of many interests, but because his father died when he was only 10, he missed formal education and grew up barely literate, only just able to sign his name. Trading in the Mediterranean as a young man, he became a skilful seaman and an outstanding navigator. For years he dreamed of finding a North West Passage to Cathay and of peopling its shores with English colonists; he made three distinguished voyages to the Arctic in search of it, in 1576, 1577 and 1578, giving the name Frobisher's Strait to what is now known to be only a deep bay in the coast of Baffin Island. In 1585–86 he sailed with Drake to the West Indies, but he never enjoyed commercial or piratical success on anything like the scale that Drake himself achieved, and was always short of money – so that the mainspring of his dislike was almost certainly jealousy.

Nothing alarmed and exasperated the admirals more than the Queen's habit of laying up ships, and disbanding their crews, whenever international tension eased. After Cadiz the *Elizabeth Bonaventure*, *Golden Lion*, *Rainbow* and *Dreadnought* were all paid off and emptied of stores and ammunition. By the end of 1587, however, alarm had mounted again to such a level that on 31 December Howard was ordered to sea to defend the realm. After further stops and starts, a new disposition was made on 15 January 1588 which decreed that the main fleet of sixteen ships was to remain at Queenborough (at the mouth of the Thames) in the charge of the Lord High Admiral. Nine, under Sir Henry Palmer, were to cruise the Narrow Seas – that is, the Straits of Dover – and three were to be based at Portsmouth under Sir Francis Drake to guard the western approaches.

In those days a ship was taken into dry dock only if she was to be completely rebuilt. All other maintenance and repairs had to be done on station, and that February, in the teeth of freezing winds, Drake's vessels were overhauled without ever going out of service. Work went ahead at Plymouth day and night, as one after another they were hauled ashore so that the crews could labour on them during each low tide, burning off the accumulated weed in a process known as 'breaming', and re-caulking with pitch and tallow. At seven o'clock on the evening of 27 February William Hawkins, Mayor of Plymouth, reported to his brother John that the *Hope* and *Nonpareil* were both 'graved, tallowed and this night into the road again; and the *Revenge*, now aground, I hope she shall likewise go into the road also tomorrow'. The operation was proving very expensive, Hawkins warned, for they were having to work 'by torchlight and cressets [basket-lights], and in an extreme gale of wind, which consumes pitch, tallow and firs abundantly':

> We have and do trim one side of every ship by night and the other side by day, so that we end the three great ships in three days this spring. The ships sit aground so strongly and are so staunch as if they were made of a whole tree.

As if to bear out the prophecies of an exceptional year, the weather continued phenomenally wild. From aboard the *Vanguard* in The Downs (the anchorage between North and South Foreland, protected by the Goodwin Sands, off the east coast of Kent) William Winter wrote to tell the principal officers of the Navy that although he had only been at sea a short time, the wind had 'so stretched our sails and tackle, torn many of our blocks, pulleys and sheevers [pulley-wheels] . . . as a man would never believe it unless he doth see it; these be the fruits the sea brings forth, especially in this time of year'.

Gales or not, Winter was full of aggression:

> Our ships doth show themselves like gallants here. I assure you it will do a man's heart good to behold them; and would to God the Prince of Parma were upon the seas with all his forces, and we in the view of them; then I doubt not but that you should hear that we would make his enterprise very unpleasant for him.

Howard was in equally buoyant mood. Returning from Calais, where the captains of two French ships just in from Spain had reported 'wonders of the Spanish army', he told Burghley:

> I protest to God, and as my own soul shall answer for it, that I think there were never in any place in the world worthier ships than these are, for so many. And as few as we are, if the King of Spain's forces be not hundreds, we will make good sport with them.

More important than bravado was the fact that the new *Ark* was handling well: 'We can see no sail, great or small, but how far soever they be off, we fetch them and speak with them.' A few days later he reported the immense loyalty and enthusiasm which had greeted him on his quick visit to Flushing. When, in an impromptu public-relations exercise, he had opened the English galleons to the public, the response had been overwhelming. 'My Lord,' he told Burghley, 'I think we have had aboard our ships, to view and look on them, 5,000 people in a day.'

For the crews at sea that bitter spring, life was exceedingly uncomfortable. As Howard himself wrote, many of the men were 'but ill-apparrelled', having only the single set of working clothes which they had been forced to buy from the purser when they came on board with an advance from their pay of 10s. a month. Their garb consisted of baggy breeches made from linen or canvas, woollen or worsted stockings, shirts, doublets and leather jerkins, and Monmouth caps, which looked like Tam O'Shanters. Once the men had joined their ship they were not allowed to undress, let alone to wash. The result was that those not already verminous became infested with lice, and therefore prone to outbreaks of louse-borne diseases such as typhus.

Because the threat to national security was manifest, many of the mariners in 1588 were volunteers, and therefore of better calibre than the scrofulous rogues and vagabonds normally pressed into service by the Navy's recruiting agents. Even so, the men were a rough lot, ninety-nine per cent illiterate, and most of them unskilled.

The discipline to which they became subject was no gentler, and punishments barbaric. By the first official orders for use in ships at war, which had appeared in 1568, the penalty for absence from daily prayer was twenty-four hours in irons, that for blasphemy a marlin spike – 'viz. an iron pin, clapt close into their mouth and tied behind their heads, and there to stand a whole hour, till their mouths are very bloody; an excellent cure for swearing'. A proven thief was to be dipped into the sea from the bowsprit three times, 'and let down two fathoms within the water and kept alive'. Anyone who drew a weapon against another man on board was liable to lose his right hand, and a murderer would be thrown overboard bound hand and foot to the body of his victim.

Life on board, besides being tough, was unhealthy in the extreme. The shortage of good, fresh food was one prime cause – and on long voyages crews inevitably fell victim to scurvy or beri-beri from lack of vitamins. Equally disastrous, however, was the utter disregard of hygiene and the failure of most commanders to see the need for it.

On a galleon the captain and his senior officers enjoyed the luxury of cabins high in the stern, and one or two of the ship's most important specialists – the carpenter and the surgeon – had little cubbyholes of their own in which they slept and stored their equipment.* But the majority of the crew lived, slept, worked and ate on the main gun-deck, where headroom was limited to six feet at the most, and ventilation poor. Sometimes they had canvas screens which could be rolled up to clear the

*Many details of ship construction and life on board in the Tudor navy have come to light with the recovery of Henry VIII's flagship the *Mary Rose*, which sank off Portsmouth in 1545 and was brought back to the surface in 1982, her hull and contents miraculously preserved by burial in the mud of the Solent.

deck or let down to form temporary cubicles. By the time of the Armada some slept in hammocks, which were not officially issued until 1597, but which were already creeping in, their excellent potential having been spotted by John Hawkins in the West Indies, where they were known as 'hammacoes'. Those not fortunate enough to own 'netting' had to sleep on the bare deck: in the past they had sought to soften the oak planking with bundles of grass and hay, but these had recently been banned because they formed such a fire hazard. They kept their few possessions in wooden chests.

For the relief of nature, the men resorted to the 'necessary seat', which was no more than a wooden plank, with holes cut in it, built out over the water from the beakhead. At sea, when the ship was heeling over or sailing into the wind, the sides of the bow must have become plastered with excrement – and as members of the crew were all too often stricken with diarrhoea, the effect can be imagined. Inboard, at the sides of the gun-decks, were the urine-tubs, permanently kept full – by order – for use in case of fire (not because anybody considered urine a better extinguisher than water, but simply to save the labour of constantly emptying the tubs and refilling them from the sea). 'Chain two hogsheads to the sides of the ship', said the regulations, 'for the mariners to piss into, that they may always be full of urine to quench fire with, and two or three pieces of old sail ready to wet in the piss.' In rough weather the contents inevitably slopped over, trickled down through the lower decks and seeped into the ballast, there joining all the other filth which had worked its way down from above.

It is not clear how much cooking was possible on board. Certainly every large ship had a kitchen – not yet known as a galley – and this was sited (to minimize the danger of fire) in the least salubrious part of the vessel, on top of the ballast in the hold. A wood fire, burning on a hearth of bricks and blown by bellows, fuelled by brushwood or the staves of emptied casks, heated large cauldrons, in which soups and stews were no doubt brewed up; but in rough weather, or in battle, the crews presumably had to eat what they could raw.

Even when victuals could be got on shipboard in good condition, meals must have been deadly monotonous, for rations were minutely prescribed, month in, month out, by memoranda from the Council. On flesh days – Sundays, Tuesdays and Thursdays – each man got 2 lbs of fresh beef, salt beef, mutton or pork, 1 lb of biscuit or $1\frac{1}{2}$ lbs of bread, and a gallon of beer. On fish days – Wednesdays, Fridays and Saturdays – he got the same biscuit and beer, but in place of the meat a quarter of a stockfish or one eighth of a ling, a quarter of a pound of cheese and an eighth of a pound of butter. On the remaining day of the week – Monday – he was reduced to 1 lb of bacon and 'one pint of pease' for each meal.

Obviously the provisions were best when they were fresh, and became steadily less palatable towards the end of each victualling period. From the few comments that survive, it is clear that much of the food was disgusting, even before it had been invaded by weevils or started to go bad. Unscrupulous contractors naturally tended to bulk up their meat-casks with parts of animals which they did not dare palm off on more fastidious customers, and it was common to find cheeks, ears, feet 'and other offal of the hog' among more familiar cuts of pork. The cheese was often said to be of such rock-like durability that buttons carved from it served every bit as well as ones made of metal. Small wonder that in June 1588 William Winter wrote to Walsingham from aboard the *Vanguard* asking if he could get one of his 'good friends hereabouts near the seaside to bestow a buck upon me and Sir Henry Palmer'. Somehow, in spite of his myriad preoccupations, Walsingham managed to arrange the favour – and in the middle of the Armada battle Winter slipped into one of his despatches:

> The best store of victuals that I and Sir Henry Palmer have at this time is your Honour's venison, for the which we humbly thank you.*

The smell in and around the ship must have been overpowering, particularly in sheltered harbours, whenever there was no wind to blow it away. It was here, in port, that the threat to health was most acute, for the crew's eating-bowls, spoons and drinking-mugs were all made of wood, often cracked, and the men washed their utensils with water drawn up from the harbour – in which all the ship's waste products, as well as the corpses of anyone recently expired, were already decomposing.

No one was more keenly aware than Howard of the risks posed by keeping men on shipboard for long periods. He knew only too well that the mass French invasion of 1545 – when over 200 ships had threatened the Isle of Wight – had been shattered not by any counter-offensive on the part of Henry VIII's navy, but simply by a disastrous outbreak of food-poisoning among the French crews, which had sent them scuttling for home; and now, early in 1588, he must have seen that the Queen's passion for economy did have at least one beneficial effect, in that whenever she ordered the ships to be taken out of commission, it meant that the crews got a break and could recover their health on shore.

Even so, his worst fears began to be realized at the end of March, when disease again broke out in the fleet, the *Elizabeth Bonaventure* being one of the worst hit ships. On 7 April the Privy Council wrote to the President of the College of Doctors of Physick, asking for the names of physicians who could be sent to deal with the new epidemic, but no

---

*The fact that two haunch-bones of a fallow-buck, right and left, were found among the debris in the wreck of the *Mary Rose*, which sank in 1545, shows that Winter was by no means the first officer to think of supplementing his rations in this way.

record survives of what, if anything, they achieved. Their chances of doing any good were minimal, for medical knowledge and practice were pitifully inadequate. Again and again the practical experience won by sea captains on long voyages had been squandered and forgotten. Thus although Drake understood the body's need for fresh fish, vegetables, fruit and clean water, and landed his crew to get such things whenever possible during his circumnavigation, his practical knowledge was not translated into regulations for the Queen's ships. Similarly, Richard Hawkins spotted the vital fact that orange and lemon juice cured scurvy, but his discovery was not followed up scientifically for 150 years.

Chapter Eight

Heave and Ho

From the start Howard had been extremely sceptical about the chances of the peace commission which had gone to Flanders. 'There was never since England was England such a stratagem and mask made to deceive England withal,' he had written to Walsingham at the end of January. 'For my own part, I have made of the French King, the Scottish King and the King of Spain a Trinity I mean never to trust or be saved by.'

Now, with the threat of an epidemic nagging at him, he became further agitated as rumour began to pile on rumour. By the middle of March conflicting reports were reaching Plymouth every day. Some were obviously gross exaggerations: the Armada consisted of 450 ships, said one. On board it were 85,000 men and a fantastic quantity of stores, including 26,000 butts of wine and more than four million pounds of cheese. Other intelligence seemed more reliable. Two ship-captains from Lisbon told Frobisher that the King of Spain's fleet would certainly leave Lisbon for the Groyne (Corunna) on 25 March. On 20 March a messenger travelled specially from Dunkirk to warn Howard that 'a Scottish gentleman out of Spain' had just delivered to Parma a packet from the King, bringing the news that the Armada would sail on the 30th of the month, 'with the light moon'. According to this latest message the fleet numbered 210 vessels and carried 36,000 soldiers. In April a message arrived from Rouen reporting that all shipping in Spain had been halted until the Armada had sailed, so that news of its departure should not leak out.

Even if details varied, every rumour pointed to the fact that an immense invasion fleet was on the point of sailing. Urging the Queen to make her own ships ready, Howard produced one of his most memorable phrases. 'All that cometh out of Spain must concur in one to lie,' he remarked, 'or else we shall be stirred very shortly with heave and ho.'

Drake, by then, was clamouring to be gone on another pre-emptive strike. Writing to the Council from Plymouth on 9 April, he apologized for bothering them again, but insisted that it was his conscience which had made him put pen to paper:

> As God in his goodness hath put my hand to the plough, so in his mercy it will never suffer me to turn back from the truth.

With fifty sail, he said, he would do more damage on the Spanish coast than a far larger fleet could achieve in home waters, and the sooner he was gone, the better. Howard supported him, and, when no decision came from Greenwich, told Walsingham how sorry he was that 'Her Majesty is so careless of this most dangerous time':

> I fear me much, and with grief I think it, that Her Majesty relieth upon a hope that will deceive her and greatly endanger her; and then it will not be her money nor her jewels that will help.

When the Queen sent down a list of questions, through Walsingham, asking Drake how the enemy forces assembling in Lisbon 'might best be distressed', he replied to her directly, addressing her as 'Most Gracious Sovereign'. He did not produce any specific plan, but recommended that she should 'command him away' at once.

> For I assure Your Majesty I have not in my lifetime known better men, and possessed with gallanter minds, than Your Majesty's people are, for the most part, which are gathered here together, voluntarily to put their hands and hearts to the finishing of this great piece of work; wherein we are all persuaded that God, the giver of all victories, will in mercy look upon your most excellent Majesty and us your poor subjects.

Drake then coined an aphorism which many later commanders have borrowed or embellished: 'The advantage of time and place in all martial actions is half the victory; which being lost is irrecoverable.' But at once he went on to lay down an indispensable precondition of departure – that his ships must be adequately stocked with food. 'An Englishman, being far from his country and seeing a present want of victuals to ensue,' he warned, 'will hardly be brought to stay.'

In the weeks that followed, the slow supply of victuals almost proved disastrous to the English fleet. Some historians pin the blame on the Queen, believing that it was she who deliberately stopped food getting through, either out of parsimony or as a deliberate measure to keep her ships in home waters and so preserve the slender chance of a peace agreement being reached. Other writers claim with equal conviction that the Queen was not concerned with victualling, but that the shortages were caused by administrative incompetence and the sheer physical difficulty of transporting large quantities of food to the places where they were needed.

It is true that Elizabeth hated spending money, and that inflation had driven prices sharply upwards, putting an extra strain on the Exchequer. In the past twenty years the price of wheat had risen from 12s. to 33s. 4d. the quarter, and that of beef from 1d. to $2\frac{1}{2}$d. a pound. In May 1586 Edward Baeshe, General Surveyor of the Queen's Victuals for the Sea Causes, reported that the cost of victualling four ships for three months' service would be £2,623, instead of the £2,100 estimated and contracted for.

Yet a greater blow to the fleet than inflation was the untimely demise of Baeshe, who had managed the Navy's victualling skilfully for forty years, but in 1586 felt unable to continue any longer. He asked to retire, and died so soon afterwards that there was no time for him to pass on his lifetime's knowledge. His successor, James Quarles, had been clerk of the Royal Kitchen, but was scarcely experienced enough to manage the infinitely more complex task now facing him. The result was that from the beginning of 1587 most of the work of victualling the fleet fell on his deputy, Marmaduke Darell.

The job – difficult anyway – became a nightmare as the crisis developed; for in response to the threat of the Armada the numbers of English seamen built up rapidly, and by the beginning of August Darell – who had no commissariat to help him – was required to produce sustenance for more than 16,000 men in 200 ships scattered along the south coast the whole way from Plymouth to Dover, at a cost of not more than 7d. per man per day. Not only had the food to be collected from far afield and brought to each depot by means of the most primitive transport, over execrable roads; it had also to be stored (in oak-staved casks, without any form of refrigeration) at the height of the summer. No doubt Darell's task was to some extent eased by an order which went out from the Council to Deputy Lieutenants and others charging them to give 'Marmaduke Darell, gentleman, a servant of Her Majesty in household', their 'uttermost aid and assistance' in collecting provisions and transporting them to Plymouth 'or other place upon the sea coast, where he shall appoint'. But even with such backing, he faced appalling difficulties.

Another problem was the Navy's habit of victualling ships for a month at a time. The job of carrying stores aboard was a slow one, taking four or five days in good weather, up to ten in bad; and Howard now pointed out that the traditional pattern could be dangerous, for if the Armada happened to arrive at a point when the ships had only two or three days' food left, the defenders would be caught in a severe predicament. It was even possible that the Spaniards, alerted by agents as to which the most damaging day would be, might deliberately time their arrival to maximum advantage. Howard therefore pressed Walsingham and Burghley to have the ships victualled for six weeks rather than a month. 'For the love of God let the Narrow Seas be well strengthened, and the ships victualled for some good time,' he wrote to Walsingham on 2 July:

> This one month's victual is very ill, and may breed danger and no saving to Her Majesty; for they [the ships] spend lightly seven or eight days in coming to meet their victual and in taking of it in; and if the enemy do know of that time, judge you what they may attempt.

The enemy knew a good deal, and were straining to find out more. 'In accordance with Your Majesty's orders . . . I am using every effort to penetrate the designs of the English armaments,' wrote Mendoza to the King from Paris on 15 March; and it must have struck him as a miracle when, at the end of month, the entire English order of battle – ships, crews, armaments – landed in his hands. The document emanated from Howard, who sent it to his brother-in-law Stafford, the ambassador in Paris, probably with instructions to pass it on, in the hope that the exaggerated size of the fleet outlined in it would give the Spaniards pause. On 28 March an anonymous agent in London reported that the 'ministers of the false religion' were swearing that if the King of Spain entered England by force of arms, he would 'leave no English person alive between the ages of seven and seventy'. A week later there was better news to relate: a cannon had exploded on Drake's flagship, killing thirty-five men and wounding seven, and the English looked upon the accident as an evil omen.

In the Low Countries, on the other hand, Parma was having a bad time. On 20 March he wrote to tell the King of the 'lamentable and astonishing mortality' among his troops:

> This is the greatest pity in the world; so many have died, and so many more are still sick. Out of the 28,000 or 30,000 men I hoped to ship, in truth I cannot find now more than 17,000. I am endeavouring to raise fresh men in Germany.

By then, he said, the 'matter of the Enterprise' had become so public that there was no point in trying to conceal Spanish intentions by pretending that his army was designed for some purpose other than invading England. The only thing that *might* confuse people, he thought, would be to prolong the peace talks. On a cynical note he added: 'Many persons think that, since the English commissioners have crossed the sea for the purpose of entering into communication with us, something must come of it.'

It is clear that by then he saw the talks as a useful charade, and was expecting war. Yet still he was less than whole-hearted in his enthusiasm for the invasion, frequently hinting that he had premonitions of disaster. Elizabeth and her Council would certainly have been encouraged if they had known how he was vacillating. Equally, they would have been glad to know that he had run dangerously short of cash. 'Unless I have money to meet requirements here, we shall be face-to-face with a mutiny of the men and irreparable disorders,' he told the King – and he leant on what he knew would be the weakest spot in his royal master's armament by adding: 'It may be that God desires to punish us for our sins by some heavy disaster.'

Unlike many of the young bloods who had clamoured to take ship in Lisbon, Parma had thought realistically about what would happen when (or if) he landed in England. Far from expecting the conquest to be easy, he predicted that he would have to fight 'battle after battle'; that he would inevitably lose men to wounds and disease; that he would have to leave port and garrison towns strongly defended, and keep open his lines of communication – with the result (he warned the King) that in a very short time his force would be so much reduced 'as to be inadequate to cope with the great multitude of enemies, and unable to push forward. This would give time to the heretics and other rivals of Your Majesty to impede the enterprise and event to bring about some great disaster without my being able to remedy it.'

None of these warnings had the slightest effect on the King's plans. In his mind at least, his colossal Enterprise was already on the slipway; and as Parma's force dwindled daily, he calmly continued his long-range intrigues, despatching Colonel Semple and the Earl of Morton via Paris to Scotland, whence (he hoped) they would advance into England as soon as the Armada hit the country from the south. They were going on an 'excellent mission', he told Mendoza on 24 April:

> You will continue to encourage them, more especially in the intention of crossing the English border when they see the country attacked in another quarter.

The King's instructions were executed with perfect efficiency. Sent on their way by help from Mendoza and Parma, the Scottish traitors sailed from Dunkirk in a fishing boat and found winds so favourable that they reached their homeland only four days later. A small vessel took them ashore, and their transport turned round and went back without ever being seen from the coast.

Chapter Nine

False Starts

By early summer it was clear to the Privy Council that the Spanish attack would not be long delayed, and on 17 May they passed a resolution which handed effective, immediate control of the Navy to the Lord High Admiral, who was to deploy his ships as he 'thought meet, upon such intelligence as he shall receive from time to time'. His task was to impeach (that is, frustrate) any attempt at a landing in Ireland, Scotland or England – and yet although the resolution appeared to give him full, independent authority to act as he saw fit, he was still hampered by criticism and restraint from London.

His first move was to take his own squadron westwards, to put himself closer to the Armada's most likely line of approach. On 31 May he told Burghley, with the wind 'serving exceedingly well', he cut sail at the Downs – that is, cut the yarn that bound the sails when they were furled – having assigned to Lord Henry Seymour the ships appointed to guard the Narrow Seas:

> And so parting companies the same morning athwart of Dover, and with a very pleasant gale all the way long, came and arrived this day [June 2], about eight of the clock in the morning, at this port of Plymouth, whence Sir Francis Drake came forth with sixty sail very well appointed to meet me.

Howard's aim was to stay for two days, watering the fleet, and then 'God willing, to take the opportunity of the first wind serving for the coast of Spain', to 'watch the coming of the Spanish forces'. But for day after day, week after week, he found himself pinned in Plymouth by lack of victuals and adverse weather.

His vexation mounted steadily. So short was he of food that when the *Mary of Hamburg* put in on her way to London with a cargo of rice, almonds and other goods, he 'caused the said rice to be stayed and taken for H.M.'s use'. Word had just come from fishermen of Cape St Vincent that the Spanish fleet was likely to sally forth with the first south or south-west wind – and now that the wind *was* in the south-west, Howard felt certain that they must be on their way.* His intention was still, if he could, to catch them on their own coast,

> And therefore, God willing, the first wind that will serve to put us out, we will be gone towards them . . . God send us a wind to put us out; for go we will, though we starve.

In spite of his calls on the Almighty, the right wind did not blow. The English fleet set out once, but hardly were they well into the chops of the Channel before they ran into south-westerly gales. For seven days they battled with the storm, but then the wind went fully into the west, and they were forced to run for home. Thereafter the weather continued unbelievably wild for the time of year. As Howard explained in another letter, he simply could not afford to put out in a westerly gale, for fear that he be 'driven to the leewards' and forced to take shelter in the Isle of Wight or one of the harbours further east. As the days went by he began to be alarmed that the Armada might be heading for Ireland or Scotland, and indeed might have already landed. The best news he could send Walsingham was that his Vice-Admiral had been giving him loyal support:

> I must not omit to let you know how lovingly and kindly Sir Francis Drake beareth himself; and how dutifully to Her Majesty's service and to me . . . which I pray you he may receive thanks for, by some private letter from you.

Howard's temper, already strained, was in no way eased by a message that Walsingham forwarded from the Queen on 19 June. Her Majesty was afraid that if the Lord High Admiral ventured far south the Spanish fleet might slip past him unseen and 'shoot over to this realm'. It would therefore be safer for him to 'ply up and down in some indifferent place between the coast of Spain and this realm'.

This futile suggestion – as vague as it was useless – drew a stinging riposte. Howard hoped (he told Walsingham) that Her Majesty did not imagine that their decision to go to the coast of Spain had been taken lightly. Had his fleet reached Lisbon, he said, the Spaniards would never have dared to sail for England at all, leaving him 'on their backs'. Pointing out that the Queen's proposal was utterly impractical, he added sarcastically:

> But I must and will obey; and am glad there be such there [at Court] as are able to judge what is fitter for us to do than we here.

*His intuition was correct. The Armada had left Lisbon on 29 May.

The medallion seal of the town of Southampton, one of the many ports that contributed to the defence of the realm in 1588.

Meanwhile, in the Straits of Dover Lord Henry Seymour was no less harassed by the unbelievable weather. 'Such summer season saw I never the like,' he wrote to Walsingham. 'I find no manner of difference between winter and summer, save that the days be now longer' – and he presciently remarked that, if the Spaniards did come, they would be 'as greatly endangered by the raging seas as by their enemies'. In such conditions his task of keeping an eye on ship-movements in the Channel was almost impossible. 'I do what I can to lay in wait for the vessel that should go out of Dunkirk to Spain,' he wrote, 'but it is a hundred to one she may escape me.'

As the Queen dithered, and Drake strained at his leash, the coastal towns had begun to answer as best they could the Council's demand for small ships. One of the most vigorous responses came from William Courteney, master mariner of Dover, who wrote to Walsingham early in April asking him to 'take into Her Majesty's service' between fifteen and twenty hoys, or coasters, of 120 tons and upward. Each was furnished with between twenty and twenty-five mariners, as well as fifty or sixty soldiers, and armed with four or six guns.

In strong contrast was the reply from the Isle of Wight. 'The island is utterly unprovided of any warlike ships or vessels fit for employment in such services,' wrote the Governor, Sir George Carey, from Carisbrooke Castle. Hull was equally unhelpful: the best ships of the town were already abroad, and the local mariners, 'to the number of ninety and four', had already been pressed to serve in Her Majesty's navy. As a result, the town could not meet the Council's demand 'until God send the ships and mariners (now being abroad) to be comen home'.

It is impossible, now, to know how genuine these protestations of difficulty may have been, but some people, it is clear, positively refused to contribute to the defence of the realm. Thus although the town of Lyme furnished a pinnace, and agreed that the 'charge should only rise upon those persons that are set in subsidy to Her Majesty', the people of Axminster refused to put in any money at all. Similarly in Norfolk, although King's Lynn contributed two vessels, the 'chiefest' people of Blakeney, Cley and Wiveton were 'unwilling to be at any charge near the furnishing of a ship'.

From London a Spanish informer reported that 'they are drawing fifty men from each parish, at the cost of the city, to send on board the ships; 4,000, they say, being obtained this way. They give to each man of these a blue coat, whilst those who remain here [probably he meant the soldiers] receive red ones.' Thus, day by day, the English fleet was growing.

With intelligence reaching Plymouth erratically, Howard took some time to learn that the Armada had finally sailed from Lisbon on 29 May. Nor did he hear, until many days after the event, that the Spanish fleet had put back into port at Corunna to reorganize. The first positive evidence of an enemy approach came on 27 June, when one of the pinnaces which he had put out to lie in a screen sighted some twenty Spanish ships, with red crosses on their sails, off Scilly. These were the leading hulks of the Armada, which had wallowed on ahead of the main formation to their original rendezvous, without knowing that the main body of the fleet had been forced into harbour. The English suspected this, but could not be certain that the rest of the Armada was not close behind them.

The news finally shocked the Council out of its paralytic indecision. A despatch restored to Howard his full liberty of action. The victualling ships for which he had so long been waiting at last reached Plymouth. The wind went into the north-west. On 3 July he wrote to tell the Queen that they had been furiously loading stores:

We all went to work to get them in, which I hope shall be

done in twenty-four hours, for no man shall sleep nor eat till it be despatched; so that, God willing, we shall be under sail tomorrow morning . . .

For the love of Jesus Christ, Madam, awake thoroughly, and see the villainous treasons round about you, against Your Majesty and your realm, and draw your forces round about you, like a mighty prince, to defend you.

That same evening, from 'aboard the *Ark*, this Sunday, at twelve of the clock at night', he told Walsingham that, God willing, he would cut sail within three hours. 'Good Mr Secretary,' he wrote, 'let the Narrow Seas be well strengthened. What charge is ill spent now for security?'

In the early hours of 4 July the fleet at last was able to sail. Yet again the wind let them down, swinging to the south-west and turning them back. All they could do was to spread out across the Channel, with Drake on the left, closest to France, and wait for the Armada to appear. In the words of Sir Julian Corbett, 'the position was radically wrong, and based on the old fallacy that a fleet of ships could defend a pass, like an army or fleet of galleys'. If the Spanish ships did come over the horizon, they would inevitably bear down on the English with the wind behind them and hold every advantage.

Nobody saw the dangers of the position more clearly than Drake. His instinct was still to go for the kill on the Spanish coast, and when definite news came in that the Armada was storm-bound in Corunna, he became so desperate to sail down and smash it that he took the unusual step of delivering Howard a written protest.

On 17 July the wind went into the north, fair for Spain. A long council-of-war was held on board the *Ark*. In the end the vote was for Drake. At 3 p.m. the fleet headed south. All that night, all the next day and night, the wind held, winging them straight down the Bay of Biscay for their target. The English admirals – Drake above all – were fired with the headiest expectations. In Corunna the massed Armada lay making its final preparations. Had the English caught it there, a most fearful massacre must have ensued. But on the 19th, when Howard almost had the Spanish coast in sight, the north wind died on him, and a gale sprang up out of the south-west. Short as he was of food, he could not loiter indefinitely in such hostile weather – and once more he was compelled to turn for home.

That dash to the south had been fraught with risks. The ships had been seriously under-victualled, and, if their attack had been pressed home, would have had to rely on replenishing themselves from captured enemy stores. In their absence, England had been left with defences dangerously weak. Yet to Sir Julian Corbett the attempt was one of the

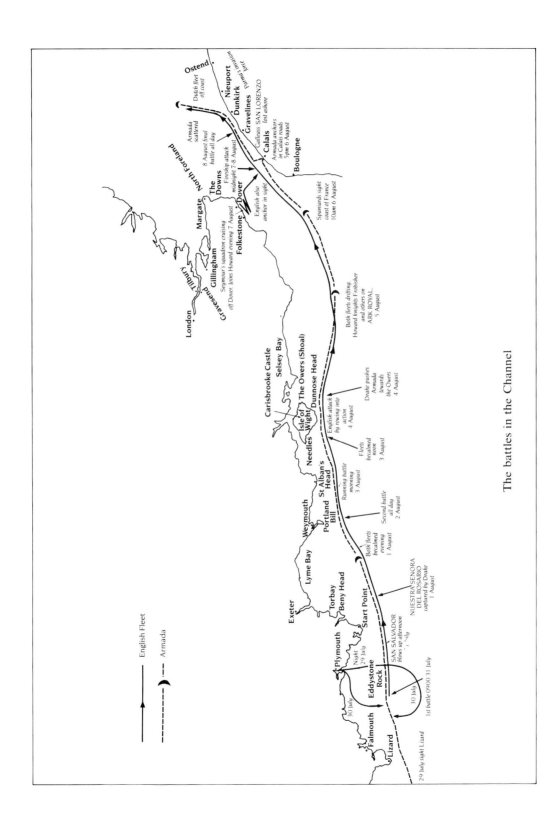

The battles in the Channel

great epics of sea warfare:

> Than that final swoop for Spain at the eleventh hour, no
> more brilliant or daring movement was ever executed by
> naval commander.

That it failed was no fault of Drake or Howard. Like everyone else at
sea in ships powered only by sails, they were at the mercy of the wind.
Yet once they had run north again, they had no alternative but to go back
into Plymouth and await the Armada there.

11. Sir Francis Drake: detail from a painting by an unknown artist. 'He was of low stature, but well set; his chest broad, his hair a fine brown, his beard full and comely, his head remarkably round, his eyes large and clear, his complexion fair, and the expression of his fresh and cheerful countenance open and engaging.'

12. Contemporary map of the Atlantic, showing the track of Drake's voyage to the Spanish Main in 1585-86. Among his many daring raids were the firing of Santiago, the plundering of Vigo, and the capture of San Domingo and Cartagena. His success had a profound psychological effect on Catholic Europe. On his return voyage he brought home the first colonists, whose attempt to settle in Virginia had failed.

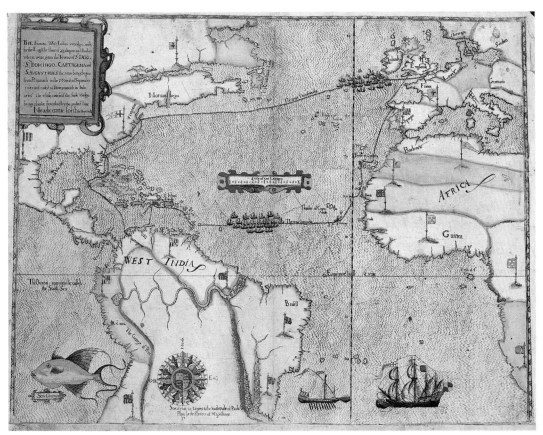

13. Drake at the age of 42: a miniature by Nicholas Hilliard. By the time of the Armada Drake's fame was such that his likeness was in keen demand throughout Europe.

14. Buckland Abbey, Drake's home north of Plymouth, which he bought from Sir Richard Grenville in 1581. The house, now owned by the National Trust, is open to the public as a memorial to Drake.

Chapter Ten

Raising the Bulwarks

On land, the defences were not as weak as some historians have made out. It has been fashionable to contrast the professional skill and organization of the seamen with the shambles that prevailed ashore, and to portray the efforts at home defence as though they were mounted by characters from a Shakespeare comedy. In fact during the past five years, as tension with Spain mounted, the Government had made serious efforts to render the country less vulnerable to invasion.

Most inland towns, it is true, still had no defences, but since 1583 the system of coastal forts had been overhauled and greatly strengthened. Dover, for instance, had been heavily fortified in 1586 and 1587. In 1585 a detailed survey had been made of landing-places along the south coast; as many as possible had been obstructed with bulwarks and lines of stakes, and trenches had been dug to give cover to musketeers. Besides the ordnance already installed in forts, extra guns had been positioned to cover likely beaches, and stocks of gunpowder had been distributed, not merely to coastal towns but to inland centres as well. Some ports had made arrangements to close their harbour entrances with booms or chains.

There was no standing army, but only the trained bands of volunteers, which the Government had instituted in 1573. These were organized by counties, and consisted mainly of well-to-do young farmers, tradesmen and so on – for even in less volatile times it was considered a risk to arm the lower orders of society. Whenever the bands mustered for a few days' training – generally at Easter or Whitsun – their instruction included a strong religious element, the officers in charge being chosen for their Protestant leanings, and being required to make their men attend church. Competitions were held, and prizes given, for marksmanship, and mock battles were fought, mainly for training purposes, but also for entertainment.

When it became clear that invasion was a real possibility, supreme command of the land forces was vested in the Earl of Leicester. According to the distinguished nineteenth-century historian J. A. Froude – one of his most vigorous denigrators – 'a worse appointment could not possibly have been made'. Yet even Froude had to concede that Leicester 'was lifted into a kind of hero by the excitement of the moment'.

All over the country, through their local marshals and constables, the Lords Lieutenant of each county stepped up musters and training. In Huntingdonshire, for instance, 'the ablest men, in property and physique' were required to present themselves to their constables, and those selected for training had no choice but to enrol. On 9 May, the Lord Lieutenant, Lord St John, held a muster at the village of Sapley Leys; all constables were ordered to be present by 8 a.m. bringing along all their trained soldiers, together with their munitions and equipment.

Meanwhile noblemen were contributing forces of their own, among them Sir Edward Wingfield of Kimbolton Castle, who, besides horsemen, had furnished 'a band of 150 footmen well appointed and trained at his own charge to be employed in Her Majesty's service'.

The system of warning beacons, centuries old, was brought to a peak of readiness. The beacons, designed to pass messages swiftly from one summit to the next, consisted mostly of iron braziers set up on long poles, described by William Lambarde, a contemporary, as 'high standards with their pitch-pots', with a sloping ladder to give human access. Some were much bigger than others, requiring several trees for their construction, and some, in flat areas, were merely iron baskets set up in church steeples; the system covered not only the coasts, but all inland areas as well, so that in the event of an enemy landing, news of it would pass to every part of the realm within a few hours. During the summer the beacons were usually manned for twenty-four hours a day in the maritime counties – and certainly now, with a crisis approaching, they were watched day and night.

Watchers on the coast were on the lookout for suspicious sails, those inland for smoke by day, fire by night. The chore of maintaining vigilance day after day, night after night, week after week, when nothing happened, was carried out by rotas of local people; most watchers were furnished with some kind of shelter, but they were forbidden the company of a dog, in case it should reduce their alertness. In an attempt to avoid unnecessary scares, an elaborate system of checks and counter-checks had been devised – only if fifty or more sail were sighted approaching the coast, for instance, was the full alarm to be raised – but in spite of the carefully-graded scale of correct responses, false alarms were by no means uncommon.

In the summer of 1588 the call to arms was reinforced by energetic promotion of rumours. Among the Armada troops were ninety hangmen, said one: the Spaniards' declared aim was to murder every English male and brand in the face every child under 7 years of age. Emotive official proclamations reminded the people of what was at stake. 'Every man will stand in fear of the firing of his own house and the destruction of his family,' said one Council minute. What had to be defended were 'lives, liberties, wives, wealth, children and country, and especially the true gospel of Christ'. Quoting this in a speech to local gentry, Sir Henry Cromwell of Ramsey exhorted his listeners to 'lay aside all malice and privy grudges' and 'join hands and hearts together in the united bands of amity and unity, thereby the better to defy those enemies of ours that have sworn our destruction'. Later, as the likelihood of attack increased, he reminded all the copyholders in his manor of the old feudal law whereby, at times of invasion or rebellion, they were bound to serve him, on pain of forfeiting their land, 'as the lord must serve the king'.

The Government was greatly handicapped by not knowing where the Spaniards intended to land, and the counties along the south coast, each claiming that it was the most likely target, began to clamour for extra support to be drafted in from outside. The natural reaction, when the alarm went up, would be for everyone to rush to the shore and defend it as best they could; but in 1587 the Government issued new orders designed to ensure a more disciplined deployment: only the trained bands were to oppose the initial landings, and everyone else was to wait for particular orders. If the defenders were driven off the coast, they were to fall back in orderly fashion, laying the country waste as they went, burning crops, destroying bridges, herding farm animals before them, and generally 'hold the enemy busied night and day with continual alarms, in such sort as they should give them no rest'.

On 17 May Antonio de Vega, the Spanish agent in London, reported that the 6,000 men raised in the capital were meeting for drill twice a week. 'They are certainly very good troops, considering they are recruits,' he wrote, 'and they are well armed.' Probably these were the cream of the makeshift army; and the fact that in country districts musters were conducted on the picturesque, amateurish lines of some medieval pageant is suggested by a note from Lord St John. Calling for fifty pioneers and thirty carts – 'all horse-and-carts to be ready to serve Her Highness at an hour's warning' – he went on to recommend colours for the soldiers' uniforms:

> Myself would have the footmen's coats to a light popinjay green colour garded with the colours of their captains, and the horsemen's to be of a straw colour, garded with white and red.

In the event, the county of Huntingdonshire mobilized 914 men, besides the 150 furnished by Sir Edward Wingfield. Other counties, however, were far less well endowed: the Deputy Lieutenants of Carmarthen reported to the Council that 'on account of the poverty of the county' it was only with the greatest difficulty that they could persuade their people to provide arms and ammunition. Weapons everywhere were primitive (they included some firearms, but many more pikes, bills – a form of battle-axe – swords, daggers and bows and arrows); training was sketchy, and the authorities were no doubt right in their expectation that the amateur force would prove a poor match for the veteran professionals under the command of Parma.

Apart from the trained bands, nobles rallied to the call with units of their own and hastened to show off their horsemen before the Queen, 'in the fields afore her own gate, to the great marvel of men'. The first to present himself was the aged Catholic peer Viscount Montague, who, 'though he was very sickly, and in age', professed his resolution 'to live and die in defence of the Queen against all invaders, whether it were Pope, king or potentate whatsoever; and in that quarrel to hazard his life, his children, his land and goods'.

To show his dedication, Montague paraded before the Monarch with his band of nearly 200 horsemen,

> the same being led by his sons, and with them a young child, very comely, seated on horseback, being the heir of his house – that is, the eldest son to his son and heir: a matter much noted of many, to see a grandfather, father and son at one time on horseback, afore a Queen, for her service.

In the end the militia was deployed in four separate armies. One, in the north, was detailed to guard the Scottish border and the east coast north of Harwich. On paper this consisted of 12,000 men. A second, consisting theoretically of 30,000 men, was raised from the maritime counties in the south, to shadow the Armada as it moved along the coast. The third was formed to protect the Queen; consisting (again in theory) of 12,000 men under the command of Lord Hunsdon, it began to assemble outside London in July. The fourth – and main – army was that commanded by Leicester and based at Tilbury, on the north bank of the Thames twenty miles east of London. As with the others, its strength on paper – 17,000 foot and horse – was greater than its strength on the ground; but it was reinforced at the last minute by 1,000 veterans from the Low Countries, and it was certainly the best armed and trained of all the defence forces, for its specific role was to engage Parma's army, which was expected to make the capital its first main target. Morale was evidently high, for Stow reported:

It was a pleasant sight to behold the soldiers as they marched towards Tilbury, their cheerful countenance, courageous words and gestures, dancing and leaping, wheresoever they came, and in the camp their most felicity was hope of fight with the enemy.

At Tilbury – chosen because it was the lowest point at which the Thames could easily be crossed – the bank of the river was fortified with a blockhouse under the direction of Federico Giambelli, an Italian deserter from the Spanish service, who had invented the explosive fireships known as 'hellburners' which had been used with such devastating effect during the siege of Antwerp. Gravesend, opposite Tilbury on the south bank, was also fortified, and the river was blocked by a bridge made of wooden barges, reinforced by ship-masts and chains, which horsemen as well as infantry could cross. This at least gave the defenders some flexibility, for they could not tell on which side of the river Parma intended to advance towards London.

As a further precaution a galley under the command of William Borough was anchored in the mouth of the Thames between Little Sheppey and Little Wakering. His plan if he saw Parma's forces advancing – he told the Council – was to go up-river ahead of him, 'shooting off great ordnance to give warning to the country and army at Tilbury of the coming of the enemy'. When he reached Gravesend, he proposed to anchor between the blockhouses, with his prow to the enemy, and try to stop a landing or any further advance towards London:

> Where, if I be not spoiled and overthrown by the enemy, and that they pass by that place up the river towards London, I will follow after them, by permission of the Almighty, and will do them what spoil I can, so long as life shall last.

Anger was roused, and determination strengthened, by the arrival of smuggled copies of Cardinal Allen's *Admonition to the Nobility and People of England and Ireland*, a pamphlet signed in Rome and printed in Flanders, to be taken across by Parma's troops and distributed after they had landed. This 'vile book', as Burghley called it, exhorted the faithful Catholics of England to rise in arms and welcome their deliverers, blackguarding the Queen as an incestuous bastard born in adultery, the foulest of prostitutes, ruler of a court that was nothing but a brothel, 'infamous, depraved, accursed, excommunicate heretic, the very shame of her sex and princely name, the chief spectacle of sin and abomination in this our age, and the only poison, calamity and destruction of our noble church and country'.

Allen had recently been nominated Archbishop-elect of Canterbury, but his ravings were so exaggerated that many people suspected he had written them under duress. In any case, their effect was entirely counter-productive. Burghley called Allen's effusion 'a roaring, hellish Bull', as if it had emanated directly from the Pope, and Elizabeth's response was characteristically forthright: she issued a declaration condemning the book as 'but the blast or puff of a beggarly scholar and traitor . . . intended as a traitorous trumpet to wake up all robbers and Catholics in England against their sovereign', and exhorted her subjects to pray to God 'for his protection to defeat the malice of her enemies'.

Meanwhile the real Archbishop of Canterbury, John Whitgift, had sent out instructions through his bishops for the clergy to arm themselves with 'lances, light horses, petronels on horseback, muskets, calivers, pikes, halberds, bills or bows and arrows, as in regard of their several abilities might be thought most convenient'. He also issued a special prayer, to be used in all parish churches on Wednesdays and Saturdays:

> Especially, O Lord, let thine enemies know, and make them confess, that thou hast received England . . . into thine own protection. Set, we pray thee O Lord, a wall about it, and ever more mightily defend it . . . We beseech thee to direct and go before our armies, both by sea and land. Bless them and prosper them, and grant unto them, O Lord, thy good and honourable success and victory, as thou didst to Abraham and his company against the four mighty kings . . . and to David, against the strong and mighty-armed Goliath.

As a further precaution, arrangements were made to neutralize known Catholic sympathizers, on whose help the Spaniards were setting such store. The most dangerous were already in custody – the Earl of Arundel, for instance, was safely in the Tower – but there were still at large a great many 'Romanists' who could not be trusted in an emergency. Some of these were now confined in Wisbech Castle and the bishops' palaces at Ely, Downham and Somersam, some in more modest private houses, among them Mrs Mordaunt of Tetworth, who 'was entrusted to the care of her brother, Lord Mordaunt'. Godfrey Foljambe, having arrested his own grandmother, Lady Constance, reported that he had her in safe custody, where her would keep her 'by God's help' until such time as 'she shall be called for'. Others, less fortunate, were dumped in local gaols. The ostensible reason for their internment was the fear that in a crisis Protestants would invoke lynch law against them; but of course the real purpose was to forestall treasonable acts in the event of a Spanish landing.

Not all the preparations went smoothly. At Winchester a row broke out between Bishop Cowper and the cantankerous Marquis of Winchester over the muster of the clergy (which was separate from that of the ordinary militia). The Bishop insisted that he had paraded the armed divines 'under the very nose' of the Marquis; to which the nobleman replied that he knew he was 'well-nosed, yet not so long [as] to reach or smell from Tidworth to Winchester, being sixteen miles distant'. At the height of the crisis the Commissioners of Sewers in Lincolnshire, apparently unmoved by the fact that the Spaniards might descend on them at any moment, complained petulantly to Burghley that their plans for improving land drainage were constantly 'overruled by strangers and foreigners'.

On 28 June the Queen issued a proclamation from Greenwich to all her Lords Lieutenant warning that 'an attempt on the realm' was imminent and calling on them to make still stronger efforts to resist 'these great preparations and threatenings now burst out in action upon the seas'. By then the national spirit was thoroughly roused; people everywhere were hastily buying up pikes, swords and body-armour, and speaking openly of 'the proposed conquest'. Even to those deep in the hinterland, buried away in farms and cottages, busy trying to salvage the hay-harvest between squalls of rain, their peril was clear.

In spite of many nervous predictions about what might happen if Catholic invaders arrived, a great wave of patriotism swept through the land when the moment came. Lord Morley spoke for the nation when he told the Council how ready he was to defend his 'natural and sweet country'.

Chapter Eleven

Contact

The English were taken by surprise. They had expected the Armada for weeks; by means of secret agents and their own scouts they had tried endlessly to anticipate the Spaniards' movements; but they were utterly caught out when at last the enemy came. Howard and Drake were both trapped where they would have least wanted to be, in harbour at Plymouth, still struggling to victual their ships and replace men lost to disease.

The first contact was made by the English pinnace *Golden Hind*, whose captain, Thomas Fleming, had been sent to cruise in the protective screen. At 3 p. m. on Friday, 29 July, he came flying into Plymouth to say that he had sighted a mass of ships off the Lizard, scarcely fifty miles to the south-west. What he had seen, in fact, was the squadron under Don Pedro de Valdes which had outstripped the rest of the Spanish fleet; but there could be no doubt that the main Armada was just beneath the horizon.

Indestructible legend has it that, when the news arrived, Drake and the Lord High Admiral were at bowls upon the Hoe, and it was there, on the flat-topped plateau commanding the Sound, that Drake made his immortal remark: there was time to finish the game, he said, 'and to beat the Spaniards after'.

It would take an author of reckless self-importance to deny that the story has truth in it. Since the tale was first told in a pamphlet published in 1624, it must have been current during the lives of men who fought in the Armada campaign, and would surely not have survived if it had been entirely unfounded. It is, at any rate, more plausible than the myth that has Drake, when the bowls were finished, calling for an axe and a block of wood, baring his arms, chopping the wood into pieces and throwing the bits into the sea, whereupon every one became a fine ship as it hit the water.

The point was that, no matter where the Spaniards might be, the

English fleet could not go out immediately, for the wind was south-west, blowing straight up the Sound, and the tide was flooding in. Until it began to ebb, the ships were prisoners. Even so, it is hard to believe that the officers continued their game for long: Howard, normally the most prompt and reliable of informants, sent no word that day to Walsingham or the Queen of the momentous news that had arrived – which suggests that he was in a great hurry.

It was no easy matter to get all the men to sea. Sir Richard Hawkins (son of John, who captained the *Victory* against the Armada) gave a graphic account of the difficulty he had in routing out his crew when he wanted to leave Plymouth in the *Dainty* in 1593:

> And so I began to gather my company aboard, which occupied my good friends and the justices of the town two days, and forced us to search all lodgings, taverns and ale-houses. For some would ever be taking of their leave and

Drake and Howard playing bowls on Plymouth Hoe – a reconstruction by Frank Moss Bennett, 1944.

never depart; some drink themselves so drunk that except they were carried aboard, they of themselves were not able to go one step; others, knowing the necessity of the time, feigned themselves sick; others to be indebted to their hosts, and forced me to ransom them; one his chest, another his sword, another his shirts, another his card and instruments for sea; and others, to benefit themselves of the imprest [money] given them, absented themselves . . .

No doubt in 1588 the men moved more sharply, galvanized by the threat of invasion. Yet it must still have been a scramble to get everyone embarked. If Mary Drake was staying in Plymouth, she would have had time to wish her husband God-speed; but if (as seems more likely) she was at home in Buckland Abbey, twelve miles to the north, farewells would have been impossible.

The English officers had no knowledge of Medina Sidonia's orders, or of the Armada's plan of campaign. But now they assumed that they were in imminent danger of being attacked in Plymouth: with the wind as it was, an assault on the harbour, led by the forward-firing galleasses, and probably rammed home by fireships, was potentially the most effective tactic for the Spaniards to adopt. The urgent necessity was therefore to get the ships out to sea as fast as was humanly possible.

As soon as Captain Fleming came ashore, a signal beacon was lit to send the news leap-frogging through the kingdom. First in the daylight by plumes of smoke, then in the dark by fires shining, the message was sent winging from headland to headland, from one hill-top to the next. In his all-too-brief lay 'The Armada' Macaulay vividly evoked its passage not merely along the coasts, but through the heart of England:

> *From Eddystone to Berwick bounds, from Lynn to Milford Bay,*
> *That time of slumber was as bright and busy as the day.*
> *For swift to east and swift to west the ghastly war-flame spread.*
> *High on St Michael's Mount it shone, it shone on Beachy Head.*
> *Far on the deep the Spaniard saw, along each southern shire,*
> *Cape beyond cape, in endless range, those twinkling points of fire.*

The poet imagined 'the bright couriers' leaping over Stonehenge, Longleat, Cranborne, Beaulieu, to the capital itself, and on towards the north:

138

*All night from tower to tower they sprang, they sprang
    from hill to hill,
Till the proud peak unfurled the flag o'er Darwin's rocky
    dales,
Till like volcanoes flared to heaven the stormy hills of
    Wales . . .
Till Skiddaw saw the fire that burnt on Gaunt's embattled
    pile,**
And the red glare on Skiddaw roused the burghers of
    Carlisle.*

As the fire ran on, all over England men turned sleepily out of bed, ran to wake their neighbours, assembled their arms and equipment, and began heading through the night for their pre-arranged muster points. But none worked harder than the seamen in Plymouth, who during the night, by herculean efforts, managed to warp no fewer than fifty-four ships out to sea, fighting the wind all the way; the fact the Lord High Admiral himself heaved at the ropes with the best of them gave an enormous boost to morale. 'I dare boldly say', wrote Fuller, 'that he drew more, though not by his person, by his presence and example, than any ten in the place.' By dawn on Saturday, with the wind still south-west, the bulk of the fleet was beating out of the Sound.

Howard's aim – as in every phase of the nine-day battle that ensued – was to work round to windward of the Spaniards and stay there, so that the English ships would be able to make maximum use of their mobility and call the tune in manoeuvring for a fight. Once the Armada was downwind, none of its ships, with the possible exceptions of the four galleasses, would be able to claw back towards the English fast enough to constitute a real threat. For ships powered only by their sails, to occupy the upwind station – or, in technical terms, to hold the weather-gauge – was of paramount importance.†

Luckily for the English, the morning of 30 July was wet and misty. If the visibility had been better, they would have been in some danger; but in the thick drizzle the enemy did not spot them, and by early afternoon Howard was near the Eddystone rocks, some nine miles from the coast and fourteen miles south-south-west of Plymouth. There the fleet hove-to and waited under minimum sail, knowing that the Armada was still somewhere

---

*Lancaster Castle.

†The account of the battles which follows is a synthesis of earlier descriptions and interpretations, not least those by Sir Julian Corbett, whose championship of Drake as England's master-strategist sometimes reached ludicrous proportions. It should be emphasized that no one can now be sure precisely what moves each ship made, and that an element of conjecture is necessarily involved. Even at the time there was by no means general agreement about what had happened. The striking disparity shown by the accounts of Spanish survivors shows how different the same events appeared from different viewpoints within the fleet.

to the west, but not certain how far it would have advanced. Then, at three in the afternoon, scanning through the murk, they got their first sight of the enemy, and again, as Howard put it, did what they could to 'work for the wind'.

The Spaniards, for the moment, had not seen them (probably because the English sails had been mostly furled when visibility was clearest). On board the *San Martin* a council-of-war was arguing about what to do next. At dawn that morning the Spaniards had found themselves so close to the English coast that they had seen people reacting to their presence and lighting signal fires. Because they had not spotted any sign of the English fleet at sea, they assumed that it – or at least Drake's squadron – must be in Plymouth, and were debating whether or not they should attack the port. Already Medina Sidonia had sent Ensign Juan Gil off in a rowing boat to gather more precise intelligence; and now, as they drifted on eastwards, Don Alonso de Leyva strongly urged that they should try to surprise *El Draque* in his lair. Most of the admirals seem to have supported him, not least Recalde, who from the first had advocated that the Armada should seize one of the western ports, and Don Pedro de Valdes. The one man resolutely opposed to the idea was Medina Sidonia, who invoked the express orders of the King that he was to proceed straight to his rendezvous with Parma off Margate, if possible without fighting, and not to be deflected from his course even if he found that Drake had got behind him.

By one account, all the senior officers in the end agreed with the Duke; by another, they decided to attack Plymouth in spite of his reservations, thinking that they would have little trouble capturing the port. Either way, the Armada continued on its course until in the evening its lookouts at last spotted a number of ships to leeward. By then the day was dying and the light so poor that the vessels could not be counted, but so large a formation could only be the English fleet, or part of it. They were out, after all. They had escaped from the trap.

At once the Spanish admirals realized that their position was radically different from the one on which they had built their plan. Their safest ploy now was to furl their sails and stay where they were until daybreak, hoping that they would thus remain upwind of the English; but when they sent messages to Medina Sidonia suggesting this, he simply kept going. As Don Pedro later put it in a letter to the King, 'he neither took resolution nor made me answer', but hoisted a small amount of sail and carried on.

Still worse, he conceived the idea that the only way to make sure of the weather-gauge was for the whole fleet to go about and head back towards the Atlantic. With difficulty his admirals persuaded him that to do this in the dark would cause chaos. His anxieties were increased by the return of Ensign Gil, who came back in the early hours of the morning with four captured English fishermen and the news that the bulk of the English fleet had indeed got clear of Plymouth the previous night. Knowing, now, that he had already lost the initiative, Medina Sidonia cast anchor for the night.

This suited Howard admirably. Unlike the Spanish commander-in-chief, the Lord High Admiral was not burdened by orders pages long. On the contrary, he had no explicit orders at all, and was free to use his initiative as events dictated. Thus, when the weather cleared and the moon rose, he saw exactly where the Armada was lying, and did what he could 'to work for the wind', making sail and beating away to the south-south-west, down the Channel. Later in the night the wind shifted more into the west, and this enabled him to complete his encircling movement so effectively that before dawn he had gained the weather-gauge.

While he was on the move, the English ships which had not been able to clear Plymouth harbour the previous night were also under weigh. It is no longer clear which officer was in charge of this party; whoever he was, he assessed the position perfectly, and instead of following Howard's track to seaward of the Spanish fleet, turned hard to starboard round Rame Head and kept close inshore, beating directly into the wind between the Armada and the land.

The Spaniards, though they had failed to see Howard moving, did spot the leading light of the inshore squadron, and watched it throughout the night, supposing it to be the vanguard of the main English fleet – a belief reinforced, when dawn broke, by the fact that several of the largest English galleons were of the company. Afterwards, the Spaniards were convinced that these ships which passed to the north of them had been sent as decoys, to distract their attention.

As the light came up, Howard got his first clear sight of the Armada, and he correctly assessed its strength at about 120 vessels, 'whereof there are four galleasses and many ships of great burden'. Yet his own laconic report gives no hint of the excitement and dread that he and his men must have felt at that tremendous sight. It was by far the largest fleet that any of them had ever set eyes on; and even if they did not see it in terms as poetic as Camden, who described it as 'sailing with the labour of the winds and groaning of the ocean', they must still have been astounded by what looked like a line of fortifications stretched across the sea, topped with battlements and towers flying coloured flags innumerable.

Yet their amazement was nothing to that of the Spaniards. Having spent the night gazing towards the land, they suddenly found that a far larger body of ships was directly behind them, to windward. Such was their surprise that at first they thought this was another fleet altogether, which had come out of Dartmouth; but whatever it might be, it was already coming in to the attack. There was no chance of making evasive manoeuvres. The Armada had to fight, and when Medina Sidonia fired a gun to signal battle formation, his ships drew together to form a huge crescent, with the two horns pointing backwards and inwards like the pincers of a scorpion.*

Thus it was that at 9 a.m. on Sunday 31 July 1588 the two nations at last came to grips, some five miles west of the Eddystone Rocks, in the first round of the battle that decided the fate of Europe. None of those taking part could know that a new era in sea warfare was about to begin. No one alive had ever been in a fight between two such heavily-armed forces. It must therefore have been reassuring to see proceedings open with an archaic ritual, in which, as though at some medieval tournament, the Captain General of the Ocean Sea hoisted his sacred banner to the masthead, and the Lord High Admiral of England sent his pinnace, the *Disdain*, to bear his personal defiance to the Spaniard, which it delivered with a single shot from one of its puny guns.

Thereafter, old tactics sharply gave way to new. There was no general charge in line-abreast such as had smashed the Turks at Lepanto. Led by the *Ark Royal*, advancing downwind in line-ahead formation, the English galleons put in a pin-point attack on a single target, the *Rata Encoronada*, flagship of Don Alonso de Leyva, which was guarding the southern horn of the Armada's crescent. As each ship came within range, she turned across the wind, fired a broadside, sheered off and got out of the way, to be followed in quick succession by the second, third, fourth and so on. As they were firing, the leading ship went about and came back on the opposite reach to deliver her second broadside.

Just as the English had at first been alarmed by the Spanish formation, and by the speed with which it had been adopted, so now the Spaniards were disconcerted by the ease and nimbleness with which the enemy galleons manoeuvred, closing the range, turning, firing, and bearing off without ever risking themselves at close quarters: a sinister foretaste of what was to come. The Spaniards fired back, of course, but they got not the slightest chance of doing what they wanted, which was to close and grapple. Some of the reasons for the English ships' superiority were visible to the naked eye: they were obviously slimmer and lower in the water than their opponents. But the Spaniards could not see one feature that contributed greatly to their performance – the shape of their hulls on either side of the keel towards the stern. There, where other vessels bulged, the race-built galleons were fine-lined, with the result that a much better flow of water passed by the rudder and made the ship answer more readily to her helm.

Another immediate cause of concern, to both sides, was the ineffectiveness of the big guns. Until that moment relatively few of the men in either navy had been in a full-scale gun battle at sea. Now the crews saw for

*There has been much debate about the precise nature of this formation. Some historians have argued that it was not a crescent, but something more angular; but a crescent was what it looked like both to the sailors who opposed it and to spectators on land, and there are numerous references to it in contemporary literature.

the first time how exceedingly difficult it was to direct a bombardment accurately.

The main armament, ranged in batteries along the gun-deck, fired through square ports fitted with thick, hinged port-lids. Even before smoke began to billow, the view from within the deck was severely restricted by the narrowness of each port, half of which was filled by the barrel of the gun. At any one moment only a tiny square patch of sea or sky was visible.

The guns were mounted on heavy wooden carriages, each with four wheels of solid ash or elm, and they were aimed by means of the most primitive adjustments. For ranging right or left, the whole carriage had to be slewed, and for changing the elevation, wooden wedges called quoins were inserted or removed. Even with a crew of eight or ten to a gun, loading was a slow and laborious business. With each shot fired, a violent recoil thrust the carriage sharply inboard, its movement damped by ropes running from ring-bolts in the deck to shackles on its sides. After each discharge the gun had to be run fully inboard and sponged out. Next the crew poured powder down the barrel, followed by a wad of oakum or ropeyarn, then by the shot, then by another wad, before they ran the gun out again. The gunner then primed his piece by filling the touch-hole with fine powder which he carried in a horn on his belt; and to fire it he took his linstock – a forked wooden stick often carved to resemble a snake or

Bronze demi-cannon recovered from the wreck of the *Mary Rose*, which sank in 1545. The wooden carriage and wheels are modern reconstructions, but the gun itself is in excellent condition. Although this weapon was cast nearly half a century before 1588, it is probably not much different from those which defeated the Armada, for little progress in gun-founding was made during that time. On the Spanish side, some at least of the big guns were as old, if not older (see page 75).

143

crocodile – with the burning match fixed in the end, and applied it at arm's length to the touch-hole.

No matter how well-trained the crew, the process took time. Even the actual detonation was slow, and if in the split second that the powder took to explode the ship hit a big wave or started rolling into a trough, the most careful aim would inevitably be spoilt. Much depended on the direction of the wind. A ship firing from downwind – as the Spaniards were in this first encounter, and most of those that followed – was at a double disadvantage. First, the smoke from its own broadsides blew back in the gunners' faces, obscuring their vision; and second, because the vessel was leaning over away from the wind, the elevation of the guns was automatically increased, so that it was hard for them to fire low enough.

Yet another problem was the sheer inaccuracy of the weapons themselves. Even among the skilled English makers, gun-founding was still an imprecise art, for the barrel of a large piece was cast round a central core, which was then withdrawn, and there was no method of polishing the bore. The lack of precision meant that the cannon-ball had to be a good deal smaller than the diameter of the barrel, and under the stress of powder exploding it tended to bounce from one side of the barrel to the other (especially if hardened deposits of burnt powder had accumulated), so that it might easily fly out at a slightly different angle from that in which the gun was pointing. Internal irregularities might also impart to it a high-speed spin, so that it would curve in flight. (One compensation for these deficiencies was that gunners could – and did – make use of captured enemy ammunition, secure in the knowledge that it would be more or less the right size.)

For all these reasons, the first engagement between the *Ark* and the *Rata* inflicted little damage on either side. Soon the battle spread, as Drake in the *Revenge*, Hawkins in the *Victory* and Frobisher in the *Triumph* attacked Recalde's *San Juan de Portugal*. The rapidity of the English fire threw several of the Spanish captains into a panic. As Pedro Coco Calderon, the fleet purser, reported, 'certain ships basely took to flight, until they were peremptorily ordered by the flagship to luff and face the enemy'. Recalde, in contrast, had no intention whatever of running away. Having skilfully marshalled his escorts to protect the Armada's rear, he ordered his own ship about, in defiance of the general order to continue, and in a deliberate attempt to lure the English to close-quarters. A few minutes later he was cut off. One after another English ships came past, bombarding him from close range, concentrating their fire on him, while the rest of the Armada sailed on.

Seeing his Vice-Admiral in trouble, Medina Sidonia turned back into the wind to help him. So too did the *San Mateo*. By then, however, the inshore squadron of English ships had united with the main fleet, and it, too, came into action, bearing down on the *San Mateo*. So brisk was the manoeuvring of the English, so intense their bombardment, that two hours passed before Medina Sidonia could rally enough reinforcements to bring Recalde relief. By then the *San Juan* had taken a good deal of punishment: her hull had been holed, her foremast twice hit by cannon-balls, the mainstay severed and other parts of her rigging crippled. A number of men had been killed or wounded by shot and flying splinters. The 360-odd soldiers massed on board her got an unpleasant first taste of their own helplessness: eager though they were for action, there was nothing whatever they could do except keep out of the way of the sailors and gunners, and pray that the hurtling metal and wood would not hit them.

At 1 p.m. Howard flew the signal to break off the engagement. He must have been satisfied by the way things had gone so far, but judged it better not to risk a full-scale engagement. Already one major threat had been eliminated: by hustling the Armada on its way, the English had made sure that it could not attack Plymouth, for the Spanish ships were already too far downwind. Yet Howard was very much aware of the power at Medina Sidonia's command. 'We made some of them to bear room to stop their leaks,' he told Walsingham in a letter sent off that evening, 'Notwith-standing, we durst not venture to put in among them, their fleet being so strong.'

Nobody needed to tell the people of Plymouth what was happening, for they could see with their own eyes. The town had spent the past twenty-four hours in a state of high excitement, for the Armada had come into view the evening before, and when, as William Hawkins reported to the Council, the Lord High Admiral and his squadron 'passed to the sea', the English fleet had gone out of sight for the time being. During the night pinnaces had come in from Howard to bring word of what he was doing, and in the morning he had reappeared, 'to the windwards of the enemy', and giving them fight. Assuming – from the violence of the bombardment – that Howard would need reinforcements, Hawkins had been assembling all he could lay hands on. 'We have thought most meet to send forth such as the town and country will yield,' he told the Council, 'and in that behalf we have provided divers ships and bottoms to carry them so fast as they come.'

Yet it was not men that Howard wanted. His most pressing worry – already – was that ammunition would run out. 'Sir,' he added at the foot of his letter to Walsingham, 'for the love of God and our country, let us have with some speed some great shot sent us, of all bigness; for this service will continue long; and some powder with it.'

All through the early afternoon of 31 July Medina Sidonia manoeuvred in fruitless attempts to recover the wind. As his hulks drifted steadily on, he beat and tacked with his fighting ships, but the English fleet held off without difficulty, content to make sure that the Spaniards went well past Plymouth. In his own report to the King on the events of that first day the Duke remarked uneasily that the enemy ships were 'very swift and well handled, so that they could do as they liked with them'.

Later in the afternoon his problems were suddenly compounded by two serious accidents. First Don Pedro de Valdes's flagship the *Nuestra Señora del Rosario* fouled another of the squadron, the hulk the *Santa Catalina*, breaking her own bowsprit and bringing down the foresail. When Don Pedro fired a gun to summon help the Duke himself went about to his assistance. Then at 4 p.m., while the crippled vessel was withdrawing into the centre of the Armada to carry out repairs, a huge detonation went booming out over the water as the *San Salvador*, vice-flagship of Oquendo's squadron, exploded. So violent was the blast that it shattered the whole of her stern and blew off the two upper decks of the stern castle, killing 200 men, hurling guns overboard and setting the ship on fire. Many of the men were killed outright; others jumped into the sea in terror and were drowned.

The cause of the explosion has never been properly established. According to Calderon, Captain Pedro Priego, one of the military commanders on board, had beaten a German gunner, who in a rage went below, saying that one of the guns had got wet and would have to be fired – whereupon 'he discharged the piece and threw the port-fire into a barrel of gunpowder'. A similar but more picturesque version of the disaster was given by the contemporary Italian historian Petruccio Ubaldini: according to him, the ship was sabotaged by a Flemish master-gunner, who had been insulted by the captain of the ship's military contingent, perhaps about his wife:

> Whereupon the perplexed man, seeing himself among such a kind of people as not only made him serve their turns at their own pleasure, but disgraced him in as vile a manner as if he was a slave, despairing both of life, wife and young daughter . . . set himself on fire in a barrel of gunpowder, procuring thereby . . . a cruel revenge of his injuries received by one man.

The result was cruel indeed. Apart from the men who had been killed, a great many were hideously burnt. Again Medina Sidonia had to come about to succour a stricken vessel. The *San Salvador* was of special importance, for she carried not only the Armada's Paymaster General, Juan de Huerta, but also chests of money. Rowing boats now got lines on her and towed her round so that her blazing stern was downwind and the fire could be prevented from spreading further. Others ferried the 'principal persons' on board to other ships. They also took off some of the wounded, including Captain Priego, who had been badly burnt. Both Huerta and his money were saved.

The English, scenting blood, moved up as if to attack again, but the Spanish ships took up covering positions so quickly that once more Howard flew the signal to retire. Soon the fires on the *San Salvador* were under control, and two galleasses towed the smoking wreck to temporary safety in the heart of the fleet.

By then – perhaps five o'clock – the breeze from the north-west had freshened. The Armada made sail again and began to move on faster. But then the increasing stress of wind and sea brought down the *Rosario*'s damaged foremast, which broke off at deck level, fouling the mainmast as it fell and rendering the ship unmanageable. Don Pedro de Valdes flew a distress signal – and he never forgave his commander-in-chief for what happened afterwards. Medina Sidonia claimed that he went about once more and tried to pass Don Pedro a hawser, but that as the sea was too rough and the wind too high for him to manage it, he was forced to sail on. Don Pedro, however, in a bitter letter to the King, claimed that although he had fired off three or four guns to signal his distress, the Duke had abandoned him completely:

> Although he was near enough to me, and saw in what case I was, and might easily have relieved me, yet would he not do it; but even as if we had not been Your Majesty's subjects, nor in your service, discharged a piece to call the fleet together and followed his course, leaving me comfortless in the sight of the whole fleet, the enemy being but a quarter of a league from me; who arrived upon the closing of the day; and although some ships set upon me, I resisted them and defended myself all that night till the next day, hoping that the Duke would send me some relief, and not use so great inhumanity and unthankfulness towards me; for greater I think was never heard of among men.

Other evidence shows that this outburst was exaggerated. What Don Pedro did not know was that the architect of his abandonment was not Medina Sidonia but his own cousin Don Diego de Valdes. Medina Sidonia wanted to reduce sail and remain in company with the *Rosario*, but Don Diego persuaded him that to do so would be madness, as, if he did, the *San Martin* would become separated from the rest of the fleet during the night, and the Duke 'would find himself in the morning with less than half the Armada'. After a protracted argument, Medina Sidonia gave in and ordered a small detachment, including one galleass, to fall back and guard the cripple, while he himself sailed on.

The capture of the *San Salvador*, which blew up on the afternoon of 31 July, and was taken by the English next morning. This engraving by John Pine, after one of the tapestries commissioned by Howard, shows the Armada in its crescent formation, with a galleass on its seaward horn in the foreground, closely pursued by the English. In fact, by the time the Spanish ship was captured, she had become unmanageable and had been left behind.

The decision was clearly a difficult one, and Don Diego was later severely censured for it; but the outcome might have been different had the captains of the guard-ships shown more fight. As it was, they turned and ran when threatened by the little *Margaret and John* of London, whose captain, John Fisher, recorded simply, 'They all fled at our approach.' Deserted by his escorts, Don Pedro drifted on. Later that evening men in

the main fleet heard three or four shots from the direction of his ship, but they had no means of telling what they signified, and it was not until survivors from the Armada struggled home to Spain at the end of September, more than six weeks later, that any of his friends or colleagues found out what had happened to him.

At 9 p.m., as the slow summer darkness came in, the *Margaret and*

John moved alongside the towering, dark hull of the *Rosario*, but 'by reason of her greatness, and the sea being very much grown,' the crew could not board her without the risk of damaging their own ship. Their captain reported:

> And therefore, seeing not one man shew himself, nor any light appearing in her, we imagined that most of her people had been taken out; and to try whether there were any aboard or not, we discharged twenty-five or thirty muskets into her cagework at one volley, with arrows and bullet. And presently they gave us two great shot, whereupon we let fly our broadside through her, doing them some hurt.

After this brisk exchange – the shots heard from the main body of the Armada – the *Margaret and John* cast about and hung in the wind close by. The crew heard a voice calling in Spanish, apparently from a man in the water, but when they launched an eight-oared boat to search, they found nothing. Then, at about midnight, they saw the Lord Admiral make sail, and 'fearing his lordship's displeasure if we should stay behind the fleet', they too made sail and left the *Rosario* to drift.

So ended the first day's exchanges. If these were inconclusive, there could be no doubt the English had scored most points. One of the officers, Henry White of the barque *Talbot*, felt that the first attack had been 'more coldly done than became the valour of our nation and the credit of the English navy', but none could deny that the superior sailing ability of the English ships had been convincingly demonstrated. Two important enemy vessels had been disabled, and another badly damaged, and the rest of the Armada had been hustled past Plymouth. This fact alone had done something to clarify the Spaniards' objectives. They could not now be heading for Ireland: their target must be somewhere on the south coast of England – perhaps the Isle of Wight, if nowhere closer. No doubt, as he himself came abeam of Start Point that evening, Drake's mind was casting on along the coast whose every headland and bay and beach he knew, calculating where the enemy fleet was most likely to put in. Ahead of them lay the grand sweep of Lyme Bay, and just into it, beyond Berry Head, were first-class landing-places in Tor Bay. Were these what the Spanish commanders had in mind?

That night, on Howard's instructions, Drake wrote to Seymour (whose squadron was guarding the Straits of Dover) telling him to put his ships into 'the best and strongest manner', and scribbled under the address, 'Haste, Post Haste.'

The battle tactics tried by the English that day must have been planned and perfected over the past few months by Drake and Howard, principally Drake, whose experience of sea-fights was second to none. But his ideas were so novel that they surprised and disappointed many people in high places, not least the Queen, who a few days later got her Council to send the Lord Admiral a querulous 'memorial . . . of such things as Her Majesty doth desire to be informed of'. Among many other questions was this:

> What causes are there why the Spanish navy hath not been boarded by the Queen's ships? And though some of the ships of Spain be thought too huge to be boarded by the English, yet some of the Queen's ships are thought very able to have boarded divers of the meaner ships of the Spanish navy.

The cause was simply that Howard and Drake had decided that boarding was too dangerous, and would play into the enemy's hands. Monarch and Council, safe in their comfortable, dry, stable accommodation in London, entirely failed to grasp the magnitude of the task which their admirals were facing out at sea. They did not realize that any attempt to fight an old-fashioned battle would almost certainly have been disastrous. It says much for the vision of the English admirals that they saw this clearly, and stuck to their plan. Years later, in his *History of the World*, Sir Walter Raleigh (who had taken part in the Armada battle) endorsed their wisdom resoundingly. If Howard had not been better advised 'than a great many malignant fools . . . that found fault with his demeanour', he wrote, 'had he entangled himself with those great and powerful vessels, he had greatly endangered this kingdom of England'.

For Medina Sidonia, the day had been extremely harassing. It is true that, apart from his two casualties, the Armada was intact and proceeding towards its rendezvous, as planned; but he had been given an unpleasant taste of the enemy's sailing skill, and he was clearly in a nervous state when he wrote a letter to Parma from on board the *San Martin* 'two leagues off Plymouth'.

If the object of the English had been to fight, he said, 'they had a good opportunity of doing so today'. But it seemed, instead, that they were bent on 'delaying and impeding' the Armada. The Duke's intention was therefore, 'with God's help', to continue the voyage and not let anything divert him, 'until I receive from Your Excellency instructions as to what I am to do and where I am to wait for you to join me'. He continued:

> I beseech Your Excellency to send with the utmost speed some person with a reply to the points about which I have written to you, and supply me with pilots from the coast of Flanders; as without them I am ignorant of the places where I can find shelter for ships so large as these, in case I should be overtaken by the slightest storm.

This plea the Duke intended to send at once by the hand of his Ensign Juan Gil; but for some reason the *patache* could not leave that night, and the cry for help went off next day.

Chapter Twelve

Hide and Seek

Elizabethan naval operations normally shut down at night, for the lack of visibility and difficulties of communication usually rendered effective action impossible. For a fleet even to change course in the dark was regarded as very dangerous, as compasses were none too accurate, and the risk of collision was high. Yet the night of 31 July was anything but normal. For one thing, immense issues were at stake; and for another, visibility remained exceptionally good right through the few hours of darkness between about ten and three.

The fact that Captain Fisher of the *Margaret and John* was able to see Howard make sail at midnight shows how bright the moonlight must have been. The Lord High Admiral's concern was at all costs to keep in close touch with the Armada, and to be in position for an immediate attack should the Spaniards start to deploy for an attempt on the Isle of Wight. Having briefed his captains at a council-of-war, he awarded the honour of leading the pursuit to Drake; and when the fleet made sail at midnight, it was the *Revenge* which went ahead, showing a lantern on her poop for the rest to follow.

To this day no one has established exactly how the plan – apparently so simple – went dangerously wrong. After a while the leading light vanished. Some of the English captains hove-to; others slowed down by shortening sail; but Howard kept on, in company with the *Bear* and the *Mary Rose* – either because his lookout had unwittingly started to follow a different light, or because he could see the Spanish ships anyway. The result was that when dawn broke, soon after 3 a.m., he found himself almost within shot of the Armada, off Berry Head, with the rest of his own fleet left far behind. Not until the middle of the day did he discover how he had been misled; then other ships closing up to him explained what had happened – but no record survives of how he reacted to the news.

It was Drake who had brought the Lord High Admiral so close to disaster. His action immediately gave rise to acrimonious dispute, and it is clear that many people never believed the story he told.

He claimed that, as he followed the Armada, he had suddenly spotted sails out to sea on his starboard quarter, heading down the Channel in the opposite direction. Suspecting that they might be some of the Spanish ships which had gone about and were trying to win back the weathergauge, he had felt compelled to challenge them; but before he had swung away off course, he had extinguished his poop lantern so as not to throw the rest of the English fleet into confusion. With him went the *Roebuck* and a couple of pinnaces.

Drake's enemies doubted the reality of those evanescent sails in the moonlight, believing that he had invented them as an excuse to turn back and claim the crippled *Rosario* as a prize. But they did exist, and belonged to some German merchantmen from Hamburg, one of whose captains, Hans Buttber, later confirmed that his ship had been boarded by the English during the night, and that he was still in company with Drake when the English admiral came upon the *Rosario* early in the morning.

This Drake did as he sailed eastwards again to catch up with the rest of the English fleet. Closing on the helpless galleon, he sent a pinnace to demand her surrender. At first Don Pedro refused, but when he dis-

Don Pedro de Valdes surrenders to Drake: a Victorian impression.

154

covered who his opponent was, he yielded, considering it an honour rather than a disgrace to give himself up to the most famous mariner of the day. In his own words, from his letter to the King,

> I went aboard him, upon his word. . . . He gave us his hand and the word of a gentleman, and promised he would use us better than any others that were come into his hands, and would be a mean that the Queen should also do the like; whereupon, finding that this was our last and best remedy, I thought good to accept of his offer.

After elaborate exchanges of courtesies, Drake did his captive proud, keeping him on board the *Revenge*, allowing him the use of his own cabin, and introducing him (next day) to Howard. He also brought on board the 52,000 gold ducats that the *Rosario* had been carrying, and her silver plate. As usual, his luck had been prodigious, for, although he could not possibly have known it in advance, the *Rosario* was one of the richest ships in the Armada, and by far the greatest prize that fell into English hands. The ship herself, with 400 prisoners on board, was taken into Torbay in the charge of Captain Whiddon of the *Roebuck*.

The incident drew fierce criticism on both protagonists. Don Pedro was attacked for giving up his ship and treasure so tamely. There was nothing wrong with his guns, and had he decided to sell himself dearly, he could at worst have delayed Drake and kept him out of the main battle area for several hours. At best, he might have inflicted serious damage on the *Revenge* or the *Roebuck*, or both. It was said that he had reacted partly out of pique, goaded by his contempt for Medina Sidonia, who had ignored his advice at Corunna and then, when his ship was disabled, callously abandoned him. (His anger would have been better directed against his cousin Diego de Valdes, for, as we have seen, it was he who persuaded the Duke to sail on.)

Drake's enemies, among whom none was more vociferous and hostile than Martin Frobisher, accused him of gross irresponsibility. To turn back in search of a prize (they said) was the act of an incorrigible pirate. It was indefensible for England's Vice-Admiral to flout his orders and put the entire fleet at risk purely for private gain. Frobisher was so angry and jealous that he swore he would make 'the coward spend the best blood in his belly'. Another special grudge was borne by Captain Fisher of the *Margaret and John*, who was actually in conversation with the Lord Admiral, seeking permission to go back and claim the *Rosario*, which he had found and engaged during the night, when up came a pinnace with the news that Drake had already taken the prize.

In Drake's defence, it was claimed that on the previous afternoon neither he nor his crew had even seen that Don Pedro's ship was in difficulties, so that their falling-in with her was entirely fortuitous. Even if it was, Drake should certainly have sent word to Howard before abandoning his station during night. He could easily have despatched a pinnace with a message explaining that he had seen sails to seaward and was going to investigate. Why he did not, it is impossible to say; but it is very hard to believe that in this moment of national crisis he simply forsook the strict discipline which he had maintained until then and suddenly reverted to the reckless opportunism of his youth.

The one certain fact is that Howard never publicly censured him for his conduct; whatever the Lord Admiral may have said in private, there is no trace of any displeasure in the official despatches. On the contrary, there was a feeling that Drake, with his habitual good fortune, had brought off a typical master-stroke, capturing not only a Spanish admiral and one of the Armada's most important ships, but a badly-needed extra supply of powder and shot along with it. Some people – among them the historian Ubaldini – even felt that Drake had been guided to his prize by the hand of God, and in general the capture of the *Rosario* so early in the campaign sent English morale soaring.

The ship's stores were extremely valuable. In due course eighty-five pipes of Jerez, Candia and Ribadavia wine were taken from her, some of it 'eager' (sour), but some good. There were also fifty pieces of brass ordnance, the heaviest a demi-cannon weighing 5,230 lbs, and a chest of jewel-hilted swords which the King had sent as gifts for the English Catholic peers. Of more immediate use were her eighty-eight barrels of powder and 1,600 shot, which were sent straight out to the English fleet.

The *Rosario*'s 400 seamen and soldiers were far less welcome. For the time being they were kept on board, but their mere presence in the harbour at Torbay caused anxiety to Sir John Gilbert and Sir George Carey, who had to take charge of them. Writing to the Council to ask 'what shall become of these people, our vowed enemies', they pointed out that:

> The charge of keeping them is great, the peril greater, and the discontentment of our country greatest of all, that a nation so much disliking unto them should remain amongst them.

Later, having had no instructions, Carey wrote again to say that he would have been very glad if the Spaniards 'had been made water spaniels when they were first taken'. By then their provisions were running out; their fish was stinking so foully that it could hardly be eaten, their bread was full of worms, and nobody could be prevailed upon to give them anything: 'The people's charity unto them (coming with so wicked an intent) is very cold.'

Interrogation of them all, from Don Pedro down, produced little precise information about the Armada's plans. There were said to have been eight renegade Englishmen in the ship, but three of these, including the pilot, had slipped away in a boat just before she was captured, saying that they were going to fetch help.

Even the Admiral knew nothing about the place where the invading army was to land, except that it 'would be ordered by Parma'. Vicente Alvarez, the ship's captain, said he thought that Parma himself was the man 'that should take upon himself the conquest of England'. But he could give no answer to questions like, 'Whether their meaning [intention] were to take the City of London; and what they meant to have done if they had taken it.' Nor could he say 'Whether the King of Spain would have retained this realm for himself, or given it to some other; and who that is?'

Soon after 11 a.m., before Drake had even caught up with the fleet, another prize fell into English hands. When the *San Salvador* began to fly distress signals to show that she had become unmanageable and was sinking, Medina Sidonia decided to empty her and send her to the bottom. Everything salvageable was brought off, but the *pataches* ordered to scuttle her were driven back by English ships, and Lord Thomas Howard, nephew of the Lord High Admiral, was detailed to take possession of her. Such was the devastation, with burnt, mangled limbs and bodies everywhere, and the air unbreathable from the stink of roasted flesh, that he spent only a short time aboard her before Captain Fleming towed her off to Weymouth. In Stow's graphic phrases, 'pitying their extreme misery, but not being able to stay aboard through extremity of stench,' Howard 'caused the remainder of those scorched men to be set ashore'.

In Weymouth the *San Salvador* gave the local authorities almost as much trouble as the *Rosario*. She was so badly 'splitted and torn' that ten men had to work her pumps continually to keep her afloat, and she drew so much water that she could not enter the harbour. The crew, which included four Germans and one German woman, were described as diseased and naked, and more died every day from a combination of wounds and sickness. Nevertheless, the ship yielded 141 barrels of gunpowder, each of 120 lbs, which were sent off to the Lord Admiral, and 2,246 great shot for cannon, demi-cannon and culverin. The one major disappointment was that there was no sign of the 'chest of great weight' which was rumoured to be in the forepeak. The English got what they called 'some inkling' of its presence, but even though they went to the trouble of removing part of the ballast, they could not find any treasure.

While the English fleet reassembled, Medina Sidonia was re-grouping the Armada into a new formation. Knowing by now that both Howard and Drake were behind him, and the squadron under Seymour somewhere ahead, he decided to increase the strength of his rearguard as much as possible, in an effort to ensure that the enemy should not prevent his union with Parma. As Recalde's ship was still out of action and under repair, he combined the two backward-pointing horns of the fleet into a single division containing forty-three of the Armada's best ships, including three of the galleasses, and ordered Don Alonso de Leyva to take charge of it, while he himself continued to lead the vanguard.

He must, by then, have been in a highly neurotic state, for he summoned all the sergeant-majors of the fleet to the *San Martin* and ordered them to take to every ship in the Armada his instructions specifying the exact position which that vessel was to occupy. The sergeant-majors were also given orders, in writing, that they were immediately to hang any captain whose ship left its place, and they took with them the Provost Marshals and hangmen necessary for carrying out the order.

Considering that the Armada had so far maintained formation well, and that no losses had been incurred by lack of discipline on the captains' part, the Duke's order seems excessively severe. It looks very much like the over-reaction of a weak character unable to think of any more constructive way of tackling the immense problems which confronted him. In any case, the Armada continued on its way, in perfect order, until in the evening the wind died away and left both fleets becalmed, not much more than a long cannon-shot apart.

When the moon rose, the Spaniards saw that one group of English ships had become separated from the rest; in the dead calm, they were powerless either to rejoin the main fleet or to receive any help from it – at last, a sitting target for the galleasses. Leyva, Oquendo and Recalde all urged Medina Sidonia to launch an attack without waiting for daylight. The Duke agreed, and despatched Oquendo to bear his order to Don Hugo de Moncada, commander of the galleass squadron, taking with him a promise that Moncada would have an estate of 3,000 ducats a year if the attack succeeded.

Why was it necessary for the Captain General of the Ocean Sea to offer a subordinate such a lavish bribe in an attempt to make him carry out an order? Simply because Moncada was in a sulk. That morning, when dawn had revealed Howard alone among the Spanish fleet, he had sought leave to attack the English flagship; but Medina Sidonia had refused him permission, on the grounds that the privilege of attacking the enemy's supreme commander was his alone – or, as the seventeenth-century naval historian Richard Hakluyt put it, 'because he was loth to exceed the limits of his commission and charge'. It was precisely this kind of squabbling over archaic, aristocratic privileges that King Philip had hoped he would eliminate by appointing Medina Sidonia to his command; but now, when realistic, altruistic decisions were needed, neither the Duke nor Moncada proved capable of making them. In petulant retaliation Moncada refused to do anything at all, and the opportunity of a galleass attack was missed.

So the second day and night of the conflict came to an end without any clash between the fleets. Howard's main concern was still to keep the Spaniards on the move, and that evening he sent the Earl of Sussex, who was in command of the castle and town of Portsmouth, an urgent request for reinforcements:

> I pray you send out unto me all such ships as you have ready for sea at Portsmouth. . . . They shall find us bearing east-north-east after the fleet. We mean so to course the enemy as they shall have no leisure to land.

Later he added a paragraph which contained an uncharacteristic mistake. He wrote:

> Since the making up of my letter there is a galleass of the enemy's taken with 450 men in her; and yesterday I spoiled one of their greatest ships, that they were fain to forsake it. I pray your Lordship send Her Majesty word hereof with speed, as from me. . . . The messenger saith there is an hundred gentlemen in the galleass which was taken, who for the most part were noblemen's sons.

No galleass had been captured. It seems certain that Howard was referring to the carrack *Rosario*, which he had heard about but not seen, and in the stress of battle did not notice that his secretary had described the ship as a galleass. But, once ashore, the rumour immediately gained strength, as rumours do: within three days Leicester was writing to Walsingham from Tilbury and praising God that the Lord Admiral had 'taken either the Admiral or Vice-Admiral and the great galleass, besides one great ship sunk'.

Chapter Thirteen

Portland

The English officers all knew that in the Channel at that time of the year the wind was liable to follow the sun – to start up in the east at dawn, work round to the south, and finish in the west; but probably even they were surprised by the speed with which a brisk north-east breeze blew up at 5 a.m. on Tuesday, 2 August. This was by no means what Medina Sidonia wanted for continuing his advance-to-contact with Parma; indeed, from his position south-west of Portland Bill, he could not make progress at all with such a wind. On the other hand, it was ideal for an attack on the English fleet. For the first time – by a fluke – the Armada held the weather-gauge; as Hakluyt put it, 'the Spaniards had a fortunate and fit gale to invade the English', and the fact forced Howard to make a rapid move soon after five. Battle broke out almost at once, and a series of running engagements lasted until the evening.

The English led off northwards or north-westwards, towards the land, in an attempt to outflank the Spaniards and regain the weather-gauge; but Medina Sidonia and the four galleasses stood away on the same bearing so quickly that they forced Howard to go about and head back out to sea. Further manoeuvring developed into a controlled English attack. Howard led a dozen of his ships, including the *Victory*, the *Elizabeth Jonas* and the *Nonpareil*, in line-ahead across the bows of Leyva's division as the Spaniards came downwind at him, strung out in line-abreast. As the range closed to little more than musket-shot – perhaps only 100 yards – each English ship opened up with her broadside, and their fire was so hot that the Spaniards were happy to fall away astern of the rear-most vessel, the *Nonpareil*. It is clear that, as on Sunday, the English came within range, fired, and sheered off, determined to keep their distance; but the Spaniards interpreted their movements in an entirely different way, claiming that Martin de Bertendona's flagship the *Regazona* (the biggest vessel on either side) had come so close to grappling with the *Ark Royal* that Howard and all

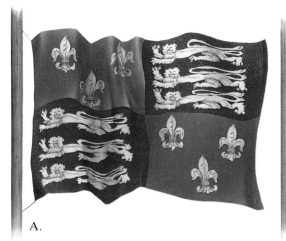

A.

D.

B.

E.

C.

15. Flags: A. Queen Elizabeth I's Royal Standard.
B. Personal standard of Lord Howard of Effingham, Lord High Admiral.
C. Personal standard of Sir Francis Drake.
D. The flag created for the Spanish Armada.
E. Personal standard of the Duke of Medina Sidonia.

16. Death and destruction on the gun-deck: artist's reconstruction. The gunners' view through the ports was severely limited.

his followers had been forced to abandon their assault and flee downwind.

In the account which he wrote for the King, Medina Sidonia commended no fewer than eleven ships which tried to close with the *Ark*; but, as he added bitterly, 'it was all useless, for when the enemy saw that our intention was to come to close quarters with him, he sheered off to seaward, his great advantage being in the swiftness of his ships'. It was a shock for the Spaniards to find that even with the wind behind them they still could not catch their nimble opponents. Like overweight bulls, they charged again and again, only to find that the matadors had feinted out of reach.

Gradually a general mêlée developed, with heavy, continuous firing from both sides. Through their repeated efforts to regain the weather-gauge, the English ships became split up. Confusion was increased by the fact that, as the sun rose and the air grew warmer, the wind kept shifting round; for a while it blew from the south-east, so that the whole, sprawling battle drifted north-westwards into Lyme Bay, where the clouds of smoke and thunder of artillery gave thrilling entertainment to hundreds of spectators along the shore.

The English commander closest to land, and also the one in greatest potential danger, was Martin Frobisher, who had anchored the *Triumph* in the lee of Portland Bill along with five of the London merchantmen. Either he hoped that the battle would drift past him, so that he would be left upwind, or he was lurking there as a ruse to lure Spanish ships on to the shoal of rocks known as the Shambles. These lie two miles east off the Bill, and at some stages of the tide a deadly race of almost four knots sets in towards them: any ship trying to attack the *Triumph* would have to cross it. Whether or not Medina Sidonia was aware of the risks, he came up alongside Hugo de Moncada's galleass, and as he was running beside her yelled something which 'was understood to be the reverse of complimentary', ordering him to press home an attack on Frobisher and make every effort to close, 'using both sail and oar'.

Moncada went, with all four galleasses, and a fierce engagement developed, the *Triumph* manoeuvring skilfully and holding her attackers off with her long-range culverins. Presently Howard, seeing (or at any rate thinking) that Frobisher was in difficulties, set out with a line of ships to his relief. Before he could reach him, however, his rescue plan was divined by Medina Sidonia, who led sixteen ships of his own to cut the Lord Admiral off. Then, looking back, the Duke saw that Recalde's *San Juan*, repaired but still under-strength, had been surrounded by a dozen English attackers, so he passed back word to his followers to go about and help him, while he sailed on alone to reinforce the galleasses.

Now came the clash between flagships for which Medina Sidonia had been waiting – the single combat with the enemy commander-in-chief which his antiquated notions of chivalry told him was his right alone. Two different explanations are given of how it came about. In one, the Duke abandoned his plan for attacking Frobisher and deliberately headed for the *Ark Royal*; in the other, Howard abandoned his plan for rescuing Frobisher and deliberately made for the *San Martin*. Either way, as the flagships came past each other, Medina Sidonia struck his topsails, challenging the *Ark* to stand and fight. But instead of grappling and boarding, Howard simply gave him a broadside from close range and sailed past. The next ship in the English line did the same, and the next, and the next. When all had passed and bombarded, they came about and gave the *San Martin* a salvo from their other sides.

So scattered was the Spanish fleet by then, and so heavily committed in various skirmishes, that for more than an hour the flagship was left to battle on her own. Her gunners worked valiantly to keep their attackers at a distance, and from one side of the ship alone they fired off more than 100 shots, which seemed to them an immense number; but by the time more Spanish ships struggled to the rescue, the *San Martin* was in a bad way, with the holy standard shot in half, much of her rigging cut to pieces, and her hull punched full of holes. Frobisher, meanwhile, had extricated himself from his tight corner; the galleasses, which may have been in trouble with the current, withdrew, leaving the *Triumph* almost undamaged.

As Howard put it, 'after wonderful sharp conflict the Spaniards were forced to give way and to flock together like sheep'. By then the wind had predictably gone round to the west, and the re-formed Armada was able to resume its slow cruise eastwards. Howard was so short of powder and shot that he could not launch another attack, but simply had to let them go.

From the confusion of that day's fighting there emerges one vivid little anecdote which has the ring of truth. Just as Medina Sidonia gingered up Moncada with a few well-chosen words as he sailed past him, so Howard goaded a subordinate into action with a verbal tirade. According to Hakluyt, during 'the most furious and bloody skirmish of all', when the Lord Admiral was surrounded by enemy ships, he spied one of his captains, George Fenner of the *Leicester*, and shouted across the water to him, '"Oh George, what doest thou? Wilt thou now frustrate my hope and opinion conceived of thee? Wilt thou forsake me now?" With which words he being inflamed, approached forthwith, encountered the enemy, and did the part of a most valiant captain.'

Both sides counted the day a victory of sorts. The Spaniards felt they had acquitted themselves well in the first major action, giving as good as they got; and the English had shown that even when caught downwind they could still outsail the invaders. Yet on both sides, equally, the day had exposed serious inadequacies, the most serious of which were in the gunnery.

After twelve hours of intermittent action, and the expenditure of what Howard described as 'a terrible value of great shot', much of it at close range, neither fleet had managed to put a single one of the enemy out of action. For the Spanish, who hoped all along to capture ships by boarding, the failure was perhaps not so surprising; but for the English it was a severe disillusionment, as their faith was pinned on the destructive power of their great ordnance. Even if they had not thought they would be able to sink the great Spanish galleons and carracks immediately, during a battle, they had certainly hoped that they would disable individual ships, so that one after another they would have to drop out of formation, and the Armada would be progressively weakened by its losses.

Many attempts have been made to explain the ineffectiveness of the gunnery. Some authors claim that it was because, until the battle of Gravelines, the English never really came to close quarters; but this theory is plainly contradicted by accounts of the attack on the *San Martin* off Portland, which show that on his first pass Howard at least was extremely close. Another theory is that the main armament of the English – the long-range culverins – lacked penetration, and that the hulls of the Spanish ships were so massively thick – up to four feet of solid oak – that the 17-lb cannon-balls could not break through them. This sounds unlikely.

For one thing, the skins of oak planks with which ships were clad, inside and outside the frames, were normally from four to six *inches* thick – a total of twelve inches at most; and it is hard to conceive of a ship with sides four times as heavily-armoured. Any vessel so built would have consumed a phenomenal amount of timber and been of a phenomenal weight. Supposing the ships had more reasonable cladding – only if an incoming culverin-shot struck the side immediately outside one of the frames would the woodwork be robust enough to stop it.

It is true that some Spanish accounts speak of shots having lodged in the hulls without penetrating; but it is probable that these were rounds from small-bore weapons. The fact that well-aimed culverin shots *must* have been able to penetrate is confirmed by the results of trials carried out at Woolwich Arsenal in 1651. (Although this was sixty years after the Armada battles, neither guns nor powder had been improved, and the loads used in the tests were smaller than those fired in 1588.) At Woolwich iron shots from demi-cannon, culverin and demi-culverin were fired at butts of oak and elm nineteen inches thick ranged in three banks, the second forty-two feet behind the first, and the third twenty-four feet

Manoeuvres off Portland Bill and the Isle of Wight. After what Howard called 'a wonderful sharp conflict' and the expenditure of 'a terrible value of great shot' off Portland on 2 August, the two fleets drifted on before a gentle west wind. On the morning of 3 August another brisk battle developed when Drake, in the *Revenge*, attacked the flagship of the Spanish hulks, the *Gran Grifon*, on the seaward horn of the Armada. Four centuries later, the recovery of flattened bullets from the wreck of the *Gran Grifon* on the coast of Fair Isle proved that the English had come close enough for their musket-balls to embed themselves in the hulk's woodwork.

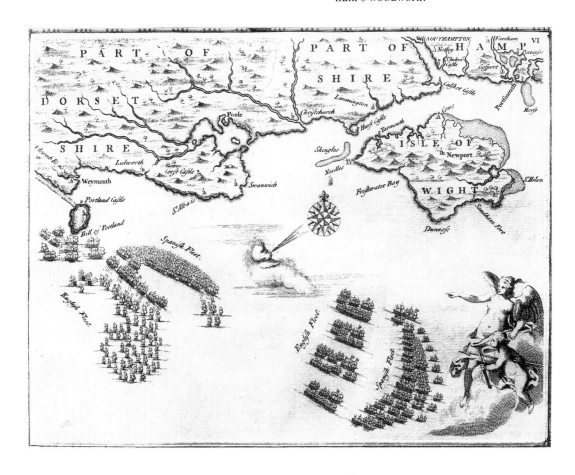

behind the second. Almost all the shots burst clean through butts one and two and lodged in butt three – a striking demonstration of their power at point-blank range.

In any event, Spanish accounts show that in 1588 many shots did penetrate. The fact that the ships receiving them did not sink was due largely to the divers, with whom every large vessel was equipped. These intrepid men went down over the side to plug leaks with lead plates or lumps of oakum, and their efforts were obviously effective enough to keep the amount of water the ship took in to manageable quantities.

A graphic description of the impact made by various types of shot was given by Richard Hawkins, who reported (from his own experience) that 'smaller shot' like that of culverin, demi-culverin and saker 'passeth through and maketh but his hole and harmeth what lyeth in his way'. Shot from cannon or demi-cannon, by contrast, 'shaketh and shivereth all it meeteth, and with the splinters, or that which it encountereth, many times doth more hurt than with his proper circumference'.

It was thus fortunate indeed for the English that the Spaniards managed to hit them so rarely – and it is clear that the Armada's gunners, most of whom were Italian and German, were severely handicapped by their lack of experience at sea. There is no doubt that the English were far better trained, and could re-load and fire at least three times as quickly, perhaps as fast as every six minutes. But one suspects that, with the built-in inaccuracy of the guns compounded by other factors such as sea and ship movement, smoke, changes of course and wind, and stress of being under fire, even they sent a high proportion of shots far wide of their intended mark. (For instance the ball that split the Armada's holy standard, though good for English morale, must have flown about seventy feet above the *San Martin*'s waterline, where it presumably had been meant to strike.)

That said, no small number of shots did find their target. In the battle off Portland Bill the Spanish put their casualties at fifty dead and sixty injured. Not all these were caused by the enemy: two gunners were killed by a premature explosion after they had failed to sponge the hot cinders out of their barrel before re-loading, and two more badly burned in another identical accident. But just as the *San Juan* had been riddled on the first day, so now the *San Martin* was full of leaks. It is said that she had received fifty shots in her hull; how many went through, it is not known, but her divers had to work through the night repairing the holes made by those that did.

On the Spanish side another factor, unsuspected at the time, may have contributed to the débâcle. Although most of the Armada's heavy guns were made of bronze, and well enough founded, chemical analysis has now revealed that the cast-iron balls which they fired were of markedly inferior quality. Perhaps because of the last-minute rush to increase stocks of ammunition, perhaps because of idleness or dishonesty or just plain ignorance on the part of the makers, the shot had been 'quenched', or cooled down quickly in water, after it had been cast – a process which would render the iron brittle. This in turn would be liable to make the ball distort under the high pressure generated by the powder charge exploding behind it; the flight of the missile would then be even more erratic than if it had been perfectly spherical, and on impact against anything solid it would be liable to shatter. No contemporary witness speaks of shot breaking up in this way – but for anybody on board a ship under fire it would be very hard to see what was happening; and if many of the Spanish cannon-balls did disintegrate, it would explain why damage to English ships was so light.

The Spanish admirals certainly did not know why their guns were so ineffective; but the day's experience convinced Medina Sidonia that he must fight no more, if he could possibly avoid it, before joining forces with Parma. In a testy note written that evening to Moncada, he first berated him for incompetence (or wilful disobedience?) and then announced a new plan:

> A fine day this has been! If the galleasses had come up as I expected, the enemy would have had [his fill]. The important thing is for us to proceed on our voyage, for these people [the enemy] do not mean to fight, but only to delay our progress. In order to prevent this, and enable the Armada to keep on its way with safety, it is advisable that it should sail in two squadrons, vanguard and rearguard.

In view of the enemy strength behind him, the Duke decreed that the rearguard was to be reinforced by 'the best ships in the fleet', half under the command of Recalde and half under Leyva. As a further insurance, they were to be strengthened by Moncada and three of the galleasses, while he himself led the vanguard supported by the fourth galleass. In this new deployment the Armada sailed on towards St Alban's Head and the Isle of Wight.

By then, on land, a huge wave of patriotism had sent volunteers pouring into the ports along the south coast, many of them physically alerted by the thunder of the day's engagement, which had been audible for miles inland. Just as the Spanish noblemen now drifting helplessly up the Channel had been drawn to join the Armada by dreams of loot and glory, so now young English bloods came flocking (in Hakluyt's description) 'as unto a set field, where immortal fame and glory was to be attained, and faithful service to be performed unto their prince and country'.

Chief among them were the Earls of Oxford, Northumberland and Cumberland, Sir Thomas and Sir Robert Cecil, Sir Walter Raleigh and Sir William Hatton, besides many other knights and gentlemen. With Lord Cumberland came young Robert Carey, later the first Earl of Monmouth, who described in his memoirs how, when 'the King of Spain's great Armado came upon our coast, thinking to devour us all', he and Cumberland took post horse and rode straight to Portsmouth, where they found a frigate which carried them to sea. For a whole day they sailed in search of the fleets, and, when they eventually sighted some ships, discovered they were in the middle of the enemy. 'Finding ourselves in the wrong, we tacked about, and in some short time got to our own fleet, which was not far from the other.' At first they went on board the *Ark*, but 'finding the ship much pestered [with people] and scant of cabins', they transferred to Captain Reyman's ship, where they were 'very welcome, and made much of'.

Nor were the volunteers all English. Among the distinguished foreigners was Sir Horatio Palavicini, the Genoese banker who had made his fortune in England, largely through handling government business, and had been knighted the year before. That night, from the Court, he wrote to tell Walsingham that his 'zeal constrained him' to depart immediately for Portsmouth,

> there to embark and join the Lord Admiral, where I hope to be present in the battle, and thereby a partaker in the victory or to win an honourable death, thus to testify to the whole world my fidelity to Her Majesty.

Admirable though it was in theory, Palavicini's enthusiasm shows that he, like the Queen, had no conception of the kind of warfare that Howard was trying to wage. Like all the other volunteers, he saw himself somehow bolstering the ranks of the defenders, fighting gloriously in hand-to-hand combat. In fact the last thing that the Lord Admiral needed was a rush of enthusiastic amateurs, who could only get in the way, whether they came aboard the ships already with the fleet or put out to join it in small vessels of their own. What he did need, desperately, was powder and shot; the battle off Portland had run his reserves perilously low, and demonstrated the utter inadequacy of the stocks with which the Navy had started the campaign. After that, his next most pressing need was of fresh food, to replenish the stores which had never been properly topped-up; for the moment his crews were making do by 'scantying', or sharing the normal rations for a mess of four people among six.

Some 150 miles to the east, off Dover, Lord Henry Seymour was also being besieged by what he described as 'worthy gentlemen' who had come 'to serve Her Majesty with the venture of their lives'. Easily the most notable – not least on account of his height and good looks – was Sir Charles Blount, the 25-year-old son of Lord Mountjoy, who had instantly attracted the Queen's notice when he came to Court in 1583, and had been knighted by Leicester for his service in the Low Countries in 1587.

Word had already reached Seymour of the early English successes – the capture of the two ships – and he was itching to join the fray. 'I am most glad of this most happy beginning of victory, but most sorry I am so tied I cannot be an actor in the play,' he wrote to Walsingham from aboard the *Rainbow*, 'a pretty way in the sea in Dover Road, but shifting further north':

> But if the Duke [of Parma] be as good as his threats, he will now show his courage. . . . I pray God it may be my fortune to light upon himself . . . but I fear me this manner will daunt him.

None of the admirals at sea – neither Spanish nor English – knew where Parma was at that moment. Medina Sidonia hoped he was already on the coast, about to sally forth; but in fact he was inland at Bruges, where Don Rodrigo Tello reached him that day. Afterwards Parma told the King that when Tello arrived 'the troops and munitions were waiting . . . and everything was made ready'; but, as will soon be apparent, the statement was highly misleading.

In England, where it was assumed that Parma must be on the point of coming out to cross the Channel, preparations for defence had been rushed ahead. It is not known how many of the hoped-for forces actually mustered; but all over the country the militia had assembled, and the trained bands assigned to the defence of the south coast had been shadowing the Armada as it moved up the Channel, aiming to cover each possible landing-place in turn. In Kent the force was split into two parts, one going to defend the coast and the other to guard Canterbury. At Tilbury, Leicester had already assembled 4,000 footmen, 'as gallant and as willing men as ever was seen', and himself was working among them to strengthen the river forts and lay out their camp. His one cause of irritation was the behaviour of Sir John Norris, who had gone to Dover to organize the defences there and had failed to return. 'If you saw how weakly I am assisted,' Leicester complained to Walsingham, 'you would be sorry to think that we here should be the front against the enemy, that is so mighty, if he should land here.'

He went on to console himself with thoughts which, ironically enough, were shared to the letter by the commanders of the invading forces, and might just as well have been uttered by them:

> But I see the mighty God doth behold his little flock, and will do all things to His glory, not regarding our sins.

Chapter Fourteen

A
Strolling Fight

Through the early hours of Wednesday, 3 August, the wind kept on gently from the west, pushing the Armada steadily forward. The English, following close behind, were now more certain than ever that the enemy must be planning an attack on the Isle of Wight, which they intended to take and occupy as a base. With every hour and mile that passed, it therefore became more important to make a decisive strike that would throw the Armada off course.

Howard's main problem was his shortage of powder and shot: he had sent ashore urgently for more, but until fresh supplies arrived, he could scarcely commit the fleet to a full-scale engagement. Nevertheless, when dawn came up to reveal the Armada's rearguard, under the command of Recalde, not far ahead of him, Drake did not hesitate to close up and attack. The escorting galleasses tried to drive him off by firing their stern-guns, and the Spanish ships in general, under orders to keep going forward, were reluctant to break formation.

Then the *Gran Grifon*, flagship of the hulks, began to straggle in the wake of the crescent's seaward horn. Although a large ship of 650 tons, and well armed with thirty-eight guns, she was a poor sailer. In the light following breeze the *Revenge* had no difficulty in overtaking her, coming up abreast, giving her a broadside, going about, giving her another salvo, and then, as she crossed behind the hulk, raking her from stern to stem. As Recalde led a small flotilla to the rescue, battle spread to the whole of the Spaniards' right rear formation. By the end of it the *Gran Grifon* had been so badly knocked about – with her rigging shot up, and forty holes through her hull – that one of the galleasses had to haul her to safety in the middle of the Armada.

In this short action, lasting not much more than an hour, the Spanish lost sixty dead and seventy wounded, most of them on the *Gran Grifon*. The fact that casualties were more numerous than in the multiple, twelve-hour engagement of the day before suggests that the English had taken a decision to make every shot count by coming in to as close a range as possible. (The recovery from the wreck of the *Gran Grifon*, four centuries later, of flattened musket-bullets which had embedded themselves in her woodwork, confirms that the action really was a close-quarter affair.) The Spaniards claimed that the *capitana* attacking them – by which they probably meant the *Revenge* – had her main yard cut in two by a cannon-ball. Whether or not this was wishful thinking, English accounts did not even mention the engagement, let alone any damage to Drake's ship.

At noon the wind died away to nothing. The fleets drifted in full view of each other, no more than a mile apart. As the Needles came into sight on the Spaniards' port bow, Medina Sidonia must have been in a torment of indecision. It was now nine days since he had despatched Don Rodrigo Tello to the Duke of Parma with the news that the Armada was on its way. No answer had come back, no word about the invasion army's preparations or plans. Yet now – if the wind got up – the fleet was within a couple of days' sail of Dunkirk, where Medina Sidonia expected, and greatly hoped, that he would find Parma waiting.

How many times, as he approached the Isle of Wight, did the Duke re-read the supplementary, secret orders which the King had sent him in Lisbon on 1 April? The more he studied them, the more unsatisfactory they must have seemed; for, having pointed out what a good base the island would make for the Armada, the King had forbidden him to land there unless something went seriously wrong. 'If . . . the Duke should be unable to cross to England, or you unable to form a junction with him', Philip had written,

> You will, after communication with him, consider whether you cannot seize the Isle of Wight, which is apparently not so strong as to be able to resist, and may be defended if we gain it. This will provide for you a safe port for shelter. . . .
> It will therefore be advisable for you to fortify yourself strongly there.

Medina Sidonia's experience on the voyage up from Spain had shown him how vulnerable the Armada was to storms; now he was in enemy waters, and his pilots knew all too well that there was no harbour on the Flemish coast that could accommodate ships which drew as much water as the Spanish galleons. If, at any time henceforth, a westerly gale blew up, the fleet would risk being driven helplessly through the Straits of Dover, clean past its target, and up into the North Sea, from which it would be very difficult, if not impossible, to return.

With the haven of the Isle of Wight in view, the Duke must have felt a powerful temptation to land and wait until liaison with Parma had been established, especially as his council-of-war held off the Lizard had decided to proceed no further than this unless good contact had been made. Yet there in his orders, immediately after the King's eulogy of the island's usefulness, was a specific prohibition on doing what now seemed so obvious: 'On no account will you enter the Wight on your way up, nor before you have made every possible effort to carry out the main idea.'

A man of greater authority might at this critical point have defied his monarch, invoking factors which had not been foreseen before the fleet sailed; one feels that Recalde would have, and Leyva, and certainly Drake, had any of them been in Medina Sidonia's position. But the Duke lacked the force of character to do any such thing. Before he left Lisbon he had promised the strictest possible compliance with his orders, and now, propelled by the dead hand of the royal bureaucracy, even at a distance of nearly a thousand miles, he carried on and led the Armada to its doom.

During the afternoon, as the fleets drifted in the calm, the English high command made a revolutionary innovation. The fight of the day before had thrown them into chaos; in marked contrast with the Spaniards, who had contrived to maintain their basic squadron formation and to protect the slow-moving hulks even in the heat of battle, Howard's fleet had lost its co-ordination. Some tighter and more positive organization was needed, especially as volunteers had increased the English numbers to about 100 ships, and the newcomers, though eager to be of service, were unfamiliar with naval procedure.

The English admirals had been impressed by the Armada's efficiency, and after a council-of-war on board the *Ark* they divided their ships into four squadrons, under Howard, Drake, Hawkins and Frobisher. The first two were obvious choices, and Hawkins a natural third; the promotion of Frobisher to squadron commander seems to have been a tribute to the skill and courage he had shown the day before – and it is possible that the fourth echelon was brought into being partly to provide another top-level position for him to occupy. To make this major change not merely in mid-campaign, but with the enemy in sight and almost in gun-shot, says much for the flexibility of the English. Far from being suffocated by a blanket of orders from Queen or Government, they were free to act as they thought best.

With the new organization came a new idea: to attack the Spaniards simultaneously at four different places, and try by this means to disrupt any plans they might have for landing, or at least to break up their steady advance. It was agreed that six merchantmen from each of the new formations should attack, at different points and all at once, during the night – itself a concept of daring and originality.

As it turned out, this scheme was frustrated by lack of wind, for the breeze died into another calm which persisted throughout the night. Dawn on Thursday, 4 August, found both fleets still drifting on; but by now the Armada was so close to the Isle of Wight that the English felt it necessary to launch an attack on the stragglers by the desperate expedient of lowering row-boats and hauling one or two galleons into range.

The rearmost Spanish ships were the galleon *San Luis* and the carrack *Santa Ana*. The closest pursuers were ships of Hawkins's squadron, which had themselves towed forward into such close range that the rowers were 'beaten off with musket-shot'. The manoeuvre carried a high risk, not merely for the unprotected oarsmen, but for the big ships as well, since this was perfect galleass weather: the calm might have been designed for the powerful marauders, as at last it gave them a chance to do what they had been vainly trying to achieve for the past four days – grapple and board one of the enemy.

Sure enough, back came three of the galleasses to the rescue, accompanied by Leyva in the *Rata Encoronada* and some other vessels. The Lord Admiral in the *Ark* and Lord Thomas Howard in the *Golden Lion* had themselves towed forward by their long-boats to the fray, and there set in a dogged engagement, during which the big guns seem to have been rather more effective than usual – no doubt because the decks from which they fired were relatively stable and the targets all-but immobilized.

There is something medieval about the stately tempo of this encounter. For several hours the combatants pounded away at each other, surrounded by other ships in full view but unable to move or intervene. Howard thought he had the better of the exchanges, and his account of them was tinged with unusual self-satisfaction. 'There were many good shots made by the *Ark* and the *Lion* at the galleasses in the sight of both armies, which looked on and could not approach, it being calm,' he recorded. The English ships fought the galleasses for 'a long time and much damaged them, so that one of them was fain to be carried away upon the careen [that is, listing], and another, by a shot of the *Ark*, lost her lantern, which came swimming by, and the third his nose'. Howard claimed that it was only when the wind got up, and the rest of the Armada came back to the rescue, that the galleasses escaped.

The Spanish saw things differently. To them Howard's battle was a mere skirmish, from which the galleasses extricated the other ships. Of greater consequence in their eyes was another action which developed as the first was ending. In this second engagement a vessel which they described as 'the enemy's flagship' attacked the *San Martin*, 'firing off its heaviest guns from the lowest deck, cutting the trice of our mainmast and killing some of our soldiers'.* The English assailant, it seems certain, must have been Frobisher in the *Triumph*, who had been closest to Dunnose Head, apparently trying to cut between the Armada and the eastern approaches to the Solent, and now had been carried ahead of the rest of both fleets by the strong inshore current.

He was very nearly caught, for when a breeze at last began to stir, it came not from the east or south-east, as he might have expected, but from the south-west, putting him directly downwind of the main body of the Armada. Threatened by several of the biggest Spanish ships, including the *San Martin*, the *San Juan* and the *Gran Grin*, Frobisher lowered his standard and fired his guns for assistance.

Other English ships sent long-boats to his aid, and soon eleven of them were frantically striving to haul him out of trouble. The Spaniards thought they had a kill. 'We made sure that at last we should be able to close with them, which was our only way of gaining the victory,' wrote Medina Sidonia in his official report. But Frobisher's luck held. At the last possible moment the wind freshened. The *San Martin* and others were closing in when suddenly the *Triumph*'s sails filled and (in the words of another Spanish account) 'she got out so swiftly that the galleon *San Juan* and another quick-sailing ship – the speediest vessels in the Armada – although they gave chase, seemed in comparison with her to be standing still'. Quickly the wind became strong enough for Frobisher to run back inshore of the enemy and rejoin the rest of the British fleet. To the Spaniards his escape was a severe disappointment.

Meanwhile yet another separate engagement was in progress on the Armada's seaward wing, where Drake and Hawkins were harassing the right-hand horn of the crescent. First the little Portuguese galleon *San Mateo*, then the much larger *Florencia*, bore the brunt of their attacks; but almost certainly neither captain realized that, besides bombarding individual ships, Drake and Hawkins were deliberately manoeuvring the whole Spanish fleet into an area of extreme danger.

No one knew better than they the perils of the Owers, a wide shoal, with a few rocks breaking the surface, some ten miles east of the Isle of Wight. If the Spanish ships, with their deep draught, could be driven on to it, they would meet a gigantic disaster. So Drake and Hawkins kept on, chivvying and hustling the enemy left-handed towards the land.

But now it was Medina Sidonia's turn for a stroke of luck. Suddenly his pilot, or one of his top-men, spotted discoloured water to port and became aware that they were in acute danger. Firing a signal gun, the

*The significance of 'firing off its heaviest guns from the lowest deck' is hard to determine. The phrase suggests that the English had not used their main guns until then; but this seems most unlikely. It is more probable that the remark applies only to the *Triumph*, which was one of the more old-fashioned English ships, and may have had its main gun ports so close to the water that they could be opened only in calm weather. It was injudicious opening of the port-lids which sank Henry VIII's ship the *Mary Rose* in 1545.

Duke stood away to the south-east and led the Armada clear, heading out into the Channel for the coast of France. By the time the English had reformed, they were far behind, but probably content to let the enemy go, for now it was clear that the Spaniards were not aiming to enter the Solent, and the defenders were again perilously short of powder and shot.

Still there was no comprehension on land of what the Navy was doing – no grasp of the tactics with which Howard and Drake had so successfully exasperated the Armada high command. 'The Queen's Majesty is informed that the enemy is very well provided of shot [musketeers],' wrote the Council to Howard that day. She had 'given order that a good number of the best and choicest shot' of the trained bands in Kent 'should be forthwith sent to the seaside' so that if necessary they could 'double man the ships' both in the main fleet and in Seymour's squadron.

This was the last thing that Howard wanted. He had absolutely no need of more musketeers. In fact, with food already so short, they would be worse than useless to him in the kind of war he was waging. Already, the day before, he had turned away a hundred new men sent out in a pinnace from the Isle of Wight. What he wanted was not extra small-arms fire-power, but more ammunition for his great guns.

Yet somehow the rumour spread on land that he was hampered by lack of men. 'Good Lord, how is this come to pass, that both he [Seymour] and my Lord Admiral is so weakened of their men?' wrote Leicester that same day in a querulous note to Walsingham:

> I hear their men be run away, which must be severely punished, or else all soldiers will be bold . . . I beseech you assemble your forces, and play not away this kingdom by delays.

Leicester might be edgy; but nobody can have had a more nerve-racking day than Sir George Carey, Governor of the Isle of Wight, who, along with many lesser mortals, had watched the battle throughout. At eight o'clock that evening – when, to his profound relief, the Armada had sailed out of sight – he wrote to Lord Sussex from his headquarters in Carisbrooke Castle, saying that the cannonade had been so fierce 'that it might rather have been judged a skirmish with small shot on land than a fight with great shot on sea'.

In the Spaniards' view, the day's action was at least as severe as Tuesday's, and they put their casualties at fifty dead and seventy wounded. According to Carey, 'there hath not been two of our men hurt'; but how he knew that already is not clear – and in any case it can scarcely have been true after such violent exchanges. Even so, the damage-estimates made by both sides seem to have been exaggerated:

175

certainly the galleasses which Howard fancied he had almost put out of action resumed their stations, and there is no mention in English reports of the *Triumph*'s rudder having been wrecked, as the Spaniards claimed (although, with skilled carpenters on board, and almost the entire ship made of wood, it was possible to carry out all but the most drastic repairs).

That evening Medina Sidonia sent off another despatch to Parma, this time by hand of Captain Pedro de Leon, in which his appeals for powder, shot and above all an early rendezvous took on an urgent note. He explained that the Armada had been delayed by constant skirmishing, and that the enemy had 'resolutely avoided coming to close quarters . . . although I have tried my hardest to make him do so'. As a result of the constant bombardments he was running short of ammunition:

> If the weather does not improve, and the enemy continues his tactics, as he certainly will, it will be advisable for Your Excellency to load speedily a couple of ships with powder and balls of the sizes noted in the enclosed memorandum, and to despatch them to me without the least delay. It will also be advisable for Your Excellency to make ready to put out at once to meet me, because, by God's grace, if the wind serves, I expect to be on the Flemish coast very soon. In any case, whether I be further detained or not, I shall require powder and ball, and I beg Your Excellency to send them to me at once, in as large a quantity as possible.

By the morning of Friday, 5 August, the wind had again fallen to nothing. During the night the English fleet had caught up, but now, as the two fleets drifted in sight of each other, Howard did not bother to press home an attack by means of rowing boats, as he had the previous morning, for today the Armada was well out to sea, and there was no immediate danger of the Spaniards making an attempt to land.

Instead, he took advantage of the lull to stage a ceremony on board the *Ark*, where he knighted Frobisher, Hawkins, Lord Thomas Howard, Lord Sheffield, and Captain George Beeston of the *Dreadnought*, all of whom had distinguished themselves in the battles. Clearly the awards were made as a celebration of victory, and it hardly matters whether Howard meant to salute the events of the day before, or the fleet's general success in denying the Armada any chance of landing. Either way, English morale was high – and it was pushed still higher by the advent of golden news from France. During the day a message came by pinnace to say that no invasion was being planned by the Duke of Guise and his faction. Until then the English had feared that Guise might take advantage of the Armada's arrival to launch a diversionary raid on the south coast; and to know that this possibility could be discounted removed a substantial worry.

The same ship brought other news, harder to evaluate. At the mere appearance of the Armada in the Channel, rumour had gone blazing down through France to the effect that England was conquered. In Paris the egregious Mendoza fell victim to an over-optimistic report from agents in Havre de Grace and Dieppe, routed through Rouen, which said that the Armada had scored a great victory over Drake on 2 August. Passing it on to the King, he hoped unctuously that 'God will allow it to be followed by many other victories, making use of Your Majesty's arms to save our holy Catholic faith, as He has hitherto done'. In England, where his name lent itself to many punning accusations of 'mendacity', he was bitterly reviled; and in Paris, according to Stow, he excelled himself when he

> entered into Our Lady Church, advancing his rapier in his right hand, and with a loud voice cried 'Victory, victory,' and it was forthwith bruited that England was vanquished. . . . [Soon] the Spanish faction in many nations had divulged that England was subdued, the Queen taken and sent prisoner over the Alps to Rome, where barefoot she should make her humble reconciliation.

Alas for the Captain General of the Ocean Sea! Not only had word run far ahead of deed: he still had heard nothing from Flanders, and by now he was deeply alarmed. Yet again he sent word to Parma, this time despatching the pilot Domingo Ochoa with a verbal message, asking for cannon-balls of 4, 6 and 10 lbs, and requesting that the Duke should immediately send out forty flyboats to join the Armada, 'and so by their aid to enable us to come to close quarters with the enemy'. Ochoa was also told to impress upon the Duke 'the necessity of his being ready to come out and join the Armada *the very day it appeared in sight of Dunkirk*', [author's italics].

Away went Ochoa with this pressing appeal. But still, as the fine summer day wound down, no answer came. What Medina Sidonia could not know was that his second messenger, Ensign Gil, had that day reached Parma in Bruges. The Duke promptly sent orders for his flotilla of boats to be brought inshore, and the embarkation of his troops to begin; but, as his letters to the King make clear, his behaviour during these critical days was strangely ambivalent. In retrospect it looks very much as if he never meant to sail, and made no serious attempt to do so. Whether the embarkation was carried out as a drill, or to impress Ensign Gil, it led to nothing. Parma himself did not move up to the coast until two days later.

A key element in the containment of Parma's invasion force was the deployment of the Dutch navy under the command of Justinus of Nassau. With their thirty-five shallow-draught vessels designed specifically for these waters, able to sail in and out of the sandbanks that were death to ships which drew more water, the Dutch were lying ready in the hope that Parma *would* come out, and that they would have an easy target in his mass of overloaded, flat-bottomed barges. So eager were they for a fight that in recent months they had come positively to resent the presence of Lord Henry Seymour and his squadron based in the Narrow Seas. Seymour had been altogether too active for their liking; they imagined that by his energetic patrolling he had been keeping Parma in, and denying them their chance of a famous massacre.

Exactly where the Dutch ships were on 6, 7 and 8 August is no longer clear. Certainly Parma did not know; but his letters to the King harped on the fact that 'constant advices' were informing him that 'the enemy has a large force of armed vessels on this coast to oppose our coming out'. The existence of this deterrent was, and remained, his main reason for not emerging. Unluckily for Medina Sidonia, he did not know the state of affairs on land. Had he done so, he would surely have called a council-of-war and tried to work out some fresh plan. But as it was, when the wind got up from the south-west on the evening of Friday 5th, he merely sailed on towards Calais.

Next morning, after a stormy night, the day dawned grey and blustery, and heavy showers blew up from the south-west. With the wind astern, the Armada had closed up in good order; but at first light the Spaniards found the enemy, as ever, hard on their tail. No shots were exchanged, however, and the English seemed content to drive their quarry on. At 10 a.m. the Spaniards sighted the coast of France, somewhere near Boulogne.

On board the Armada there were sharp differences of opinion about what they should do when they reached Calais, only twenty miles short of Dunkirk. The majority of the admirals were for sailing on – presumably in the hope of meeting Parma that much sooner. Medina Sidonia, on the other hand, was told by his pilots that if he went any farther the currents 'would force him to run out of the Channel into Norwegian waters'. Once that happened, his chance of making the vital rendezvous would be gone. So he decided to anchor off Calais – and this he proceeded to do at five in the afternoon. Seeing the Armada unexpectedly come to a halt, Howard also anchored, immediately upwind, within culverin-shot of the nearest ships.

For the citizens of the town, it was.the most amazing sight ever seen. They came out to stare by the hundred, among them the Mayor, M. de Gourdan, and his wife, who drove out in a carriage to the shore in the

The harbour, fort and town of Calais, off
which the Armada anchored on 6 August,
and from which the people came 'thick and
threefold' to observe the fleet. After the
fireship attack on the night of 7–8 August,
the disabled galleass *San Lorenzo* ran
aground on the harbour bar, right in front
of the town's walls, and was captured by
the English, her captain, Don Hugo de
Moncada, being killed by a bullet between
the eyes.

expectation of watching a good battle. Medina Sidonia was uncertain
how the French would respond to the close proximity of so huge a force
from Spain; but when he sent Don Pedro de Heredia to bear his respects
to the Governor and offer him friendship, he was rewarded by a return
visit from Gourdan's nephew, and the presentation of a handsome basket
of fresh provisions.

Such civilities may have brought some small immediate comfort, but they could do nothing to lessen the very great anxiety by which Medina Sidonia was gripped. Now, if ever, the inadequacy of the plans came home to him. Here in the open roads of Calais his huge fleet was no safer than if it had been on the edge of a precipice; if Parma did not come to his aid immediately, either the English fleet or merely a storm from the west could push it over the edge. It was an indication of how morale was faltering that during the evening Simon Henriquez and Juan Isla, master and pilot of the hulk *San Pedro Menor*, deserted to the enemy.

Realizing by now that it was too dangerous to remain in the open sea indefinitely, Medina Sidonia had developed the clear idea that he and Parma should 'go together and take some port where this Armada may enter in safety'. In yet another missive, sent by hand of his secretary Geronimo d'Arceo, he besought the Duke to move quickly:

> I have constantly written to Your Excellency, giving you information as to my whereabouts with the Armada, and not only have I received no reply to my letters, but no acknowledgement of their receipt has reached me. I am extremely anxious at this, as Your Excellency may imagine. I feel obliged to beseech you, if you cannot at once bring out all your fleet, to send me the forty or fifty flyboats I asked for yesterday, as, with this aid, I shall be able to resist the enemy's fleet until Your Excellency can come out with the rest. . . .
>
> As I am uncertain whether this messenger will arrive in time, I only again supplicate Your Excellency to accede to my request, as it is of the utmost importance for carrying out the desired object in the interest of God and His Majesty.

Medina Sidonia's worries were increased still further by the arrival on Saturday evening of thirty-six more English ships, including five big galleons, which came down from the north-east and anchored alongside Howard at about 6 p.m., making the English fleet in all 120 strong. The Spanish imagined that the newcomers were under the command of John Hawkins, but in fact they were the ships led by Lord Henry Seymour in the *Rainbow*, defying his latest order from the Council, which had been to lie in wait for Parma off Dunkirk.* As when it sent down the royal command to double-man the ships, the Government had again demonstrated its failure to grasp the most obvious naval principle. To have lain off Dunkirk would have been both futile and dangerous, for the first gale would either have wrecked Seymour on the Flemish coast or forced him

---

*The Spanish belief that this was Hawkins, with whom they had been fighting for days, shows how vague they were about the enemy's ships and flags. Although they could identify an *almirante*, or flagship, they evidently could not tell whose command it was. The English were better informed, for Howard had the loquacious Don Pedro de Valdes on board, to help with identification.

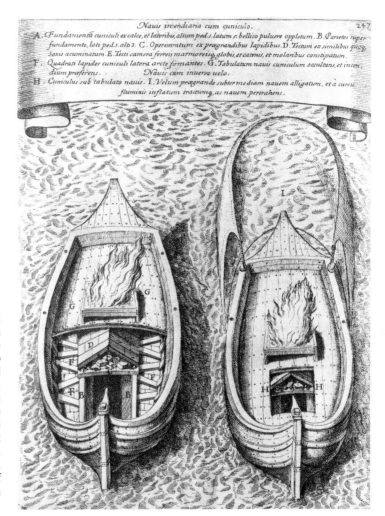

Sixteenth-century illustration to show the principles on which fireboats could be loaded and rigged. These two were floating mines, armed with gunpowder and rocks, which would fly out when the ship exploded. In contrast, the fireships which flushed the Armada from its anchorage at Calais were ordinary vessels, sacrificed for the occasion, smeared with pitch and full of spare timber, and sent off with their guns fully loaded.

to flee northwards off his station. The place from which to blockade Parma was Dover, for from there the English ships could swoop down and have the slow-moving invasion flotilla at their mercy. So angry had Seymour been that he had gone back to the Downs to protest and to stock up with food – but before he had even had time to start loading, a pinnace came flying in with urgent orders from Howard to join him. As Seymour's veteran colleague William Winter of the *Vanguard* described it, 'forthwith we made sail and gat out, not having time to relieve ourselves with victual, and bare over with the French coast.'

It was his squadron's first sight of the Armada – and deeply impressive they found it. Old Winter later described to Walsingham how they had seen the 'Spanish army anchored to the eastward of Scales Cliffs, very round and near together', and it was this density of their grouping that gave him (as he claimed) the idea of attacking the huge fleet with fireships. At 9 p.m. that evening he went on board the *Ark* and proposed the plan. 'His Lordship did like very well of it,' he reported; but while the two men 'were reasoning of this matter in his Lordship's cabin, there did drive with the tide aboard my Lord's ship the *Bear* and three others, who were all tangled together, so as there was some hurt done by the breaking of yards and spoil of tackle'.

The damage, however, was slight, and the confusion was soon sorted out. But the idea of fireships had been set in motion. It may have been Winter's alone; more likely others thought of it too, particularly Drake, for this very device had been used against him by the Spaniards at Cadiz the year before, and a few days earlier Walsingham had sent down an order to Dover, for fishing boats to be assembled against this very task. Here, off Calais the position was ideal for a fireship attack, the English lying upwind and upcurrent of a mass of unwieldy ships packed close together. Whatever its origin, it was the master stroke which finally broke the Armada's long-held discipline and sent it wallowing on the road to destruction.

Chapter Fifteen

The Fireships

Sunday, 7 August was the day that snuffed out the Armada's chances of success. Nobody on the Spanish fleet knew it, but it was then that the commander-in-chief of the land forces, on whose co-operation they depended so heavily, finally admitted in a letter to the King that he had no hope or intention of playing his part in the invasion.

For Medina Sidonia the day began badly. At 5 a.m. the wind started to rise, bringing in showers from the south-west – a sinister portent which suggested that the Armada might be forced to move on, whether its leaders wanted to or not. Then at dawn Captain Rodrigo Tello came back from Dunkirk, bringing the first news of Parma. This was by no means reassuring. Although he had expressed great joy at the arrival of the Armada, he had not come to Dunkirk by the previous night (when Tello had left there), and the embarkation of men and stores had not begun. Nor was the letter he sent to Medina Sidonia in the least helpful. Twice during the day the Duke wrote back to him in terms of increasingly naked desperation.

In the first letter he begged Parma to hasten his coming-out 'before the spring tides end', and added: 'The general opinion is that it will be very inadvisable for the Armada to go beyond this place.' The second letter went by hand of Don Jorge Manrique, the Armada's Inspector General, whose task was to represent to Parma the urgent need for providing the fleet with a port, 'without which it will doubtless be lost, as the ships are so large'. The message betrayed its author's fears all too clearly. 'It is impossible to continue cruising with this Armada,' the Duke wrote, 'as its great weight causes it to be always to leeward of the enemy, and it is impossible to do any damage to him, hard as we may try.'

Yet before this appeal was even on its way, Parma had in effect declared that he did not intend to help. In an extraordinarily dis-ingenuous letter to the King he frequently repeated how eager he was to help, but in the next breath explained why it was impossible to do so.

When Ensign Gil had arrived, he wrote, he had given orders 'that the boats should be brought in-shore and the embarkation commenced. This was done with all speed, and will shortly be completed.' (This was a very great exaggeration, if not an outright lie.) Meanwhile, Parma continued, he himself had remained in Bruges 'to close up affairs and write despatches' (a most unconvincing reason). He then had the nerve to add:

> If the Duke succeeds in getting to a place where I can assist him, Your Majesty may be sure that I shall do so, and, as soon as the passage across is free, no opportunity shall be missed.

The Duke was already at Calais, as Parma knew. A few hours' sailing would have brought him to Dunkirk. It was outrageous of Parma to write 'if the Duke succeeds in getting to a place where I can help him'. He was already in easy reach.

> Nevertheless [Parma went on], the constant advices I am receiving inform me that the enemy has a large force of armed vessels on this coast to oppose our coming out, but doubtless they will depart before the Armada arrives.

Here he contradicted himself in the course of a single sentence. First, he cannot come out because the coast is blockaded by enemy vessels. Second, these will doubtless go away when the Armada arrives . . . but still he cannot come out. Yet this inconsistency was nothing compared with the admission that followed:

> To judge from what the Duke says, it would appear that he still expects me to come out and join him with our boats, but it must be perfectly clear that this is not feasible. Most of our boats are only built for the rivers, and they are unable to weather the least sea. It is quite as much as they can do to carry over the men in perfectly fair weather, but as for fighting as well, it is evident they cannot do it, however good the troops in them may be. This was the principal reason why Your Majesty decided to risk sending the Armada, as in your great prudence you saw that the undertaking could not be carried through in any other way . . .

Sycophantic, evasive, misleading, Parma was now saying in effect that the whole plan on which the King had based his invasion had been impossible from the start. Next day, still in Bruges, goaded by his conscience and seeking to justify his lack of co-operation, he wrote to the King again, in still more unsatisfactory terms.

'I have news that the Duke, with the Armada, has arrived in Calais roads,' he began. 'God be praised for this!' Here, straight away, was a subterfuge. He had known that the Armada was at Calais when he wrote the day before, for he mentioned inadvertently that he had already had the Duke's letter of the 6th, telling him this. In any case, he went on, protesting far too much:

> I, for my part, will exert every possible effort to fulfil my obligation, and will duly co-operate with the Duke and assist him to the full extent of my power. But it appears that he still wishes me to go out and join him with these boats of ours, and for us, together, to attack the enemy's fleet. But it is obviously impossible to hope to put to sea in our boats without incurring great danger of losing our army.
>
> If the Duke were fully informed on the matter, he would be of the same opinion, and would busy himself in carrying out Your Majesty's orders at once, without allowing himself to be diverted into another course. Suffice it to say that I will, in all things possible, endeavour to please him . . .

This last suggestion – that the Duke had not been carrying out his orders – was monstrous. If anything, he had erred in sticking to them too slavishly. But then, in seeking to justify himself, Parma perhaps showed more of his hand than he meant to:

> The men who have recently come hither from the Duke, not seeing the boats armed or with any artillery on board, and the men not shipped, have been trying to make out we are not ready. They are in error. The boats are, and have been for months, in a proper condition for the task they have to effect, namely, to take the men across. . . . The boats are so small that it is impossible to keep the troops on board of them for long. There is no room to turn round, and they would certainly rot and die. The putting of the men on board these low, small boats is done in a very short time, and I am confident in this respect there will be no shortcoming in Your Majesty's service . . .

Even if these remarks were not downright lies, they certainly stretched the truth. Three days later, Juan Manrique – a member of Parma's army – at last gave a glimpse of the real state of affairs at Dunkirk, when in a letter to Juan Idiaquez, the King's secretary, he wrote:

> The day on which we came to embark, we found the vessels still unfinished, not a pound of cannon on board, and

nothing to eat. This was not because the Duke of Parma failed to use every possible effort – for it would be difficult to find another person in the world who works half as hard – but because both the seamen and those who had to carry out the details openly and undisguisedly directed their energies not to serve His Majesty (for that is not their aim), but to waste his substance and lengthen the duration of the war.

Was Parma, then, sabotaged and let down? If he was, why did this forceful and able commander allow so vital an operation to drift along without proper supervision? That it was not under proper control is confirmed by an anonymous report from Rouen, written on the same day as Juan Manrique's letter above. 'There has been very bad management with the Flemish ships, which cannot be ready for another fortnight,' this said. The chaos resulted

> from the neglect of the commissaries, whose one care has been to steal all they could . . . The Dunkirk ships are short of sailors, in consequence of the neglect they have shown towards them. They [the sailors] have even been dreadfully ill-treated. The whole of the fame gained by the Duke of Parma in the past is forfeited by this great neglect, and this will cause the Spanish fleet to be lost, if God does not come to its aid.

Mercifully, Medina Sidonia did not know how bad the position was at Dunkirk. He had quite enough worries anyway. Some time in the morning the Mayor of Calais sent out his nephew to the *San Martin* with the present of fresh provisions; but he also brought warning that the Armada was anchored in a dangerous position, because the cross currents there were very strong. Encouraged by the friendly attitude of the French, the Duke sent his *provedor*, Bernabé de Pedroso, ashore with the paymaster and 6,000 ducats in gold to buy food and medicines for the fleet. According to Stow, on land 'the Flemings, Walloons and the French came thick and threefold to behold the fleet', and soon a lively trade was in progress between the officers and the shore:

> Fresh victuals straight were brought aboard. Captains and cavaliers for their money might have what they would, who gave the French so liberally as within twelve hours an egg was worth five pence, besides thanks.

During this comfortable lull the English were hatching their plan. Howard put out his flag to summon a council-of-war early, and it was decided to make an attempt with fireships that night. At once Sir Henry

Palmer was despatched to Dover, where he was to appropriate suitable vessels. He lost no time. During the day he recruited nineteen boats – some of which may already have been prepared, after Walsingham's order – and at midnight he himself embarked in one of them and set off 'laden with bavens [faggots], and every boat one barrel of pitch of their own'. Yet these, as it turned out, were not needed, for Howard and Drake decided that they could not wait for Palmer to return, but must strike sooner.

The sight of boats plying between the Armada and the shore made them nervous. What was this traffic between French and Spanish? Were messages being sent on post-haste, overland, to Parma? Fearing that Palmer would not be back that night, the English high command decided to make up fireships of their own. Drake led the way, sacrificing his own 200-ton *Thomas* (for the destruction of which he later claimed £1,000 compensation). Hawkins offered another. A third was the barque *Talbot*, belonging to Henry White, who afterwards mourned the little ship's loss to Walsingham: 'Now I rest like one that had his house burnt, and one of these days I must come to your Honour for a commission to go a-begging.'

Altogether eight ships were made ready, five of them from Drake's western squadron. There was so little time that stores and guns were left on board – but at least the guns served some purpose, as they were left loaded, so that they would go off when the conflagration on board became hot enough, and thereby increase the enemy's confusion.

On board the Armada ships morale fluctuated sharply. The occasional movements which the Spaniards could see in the English fleet made them suspect that something sinister was afoot, and there was a general presentiment of danger. At about 4 p.m., to their astonishment, they saw an English pinnace making straight for them, and in particular for the royal flagship. Once in range, it fired four rounds into the *San Martin*, went about, and made off with no damage other than a hole in its topsail, punched by a culverin-shot from Hugo de Moncada's galleass *San Lorenzo*. The watching Spaniards were shaken by its impertinence and audacity, and by the speed with which it manoeuvred. Later they saw a new flotilla of nine vessels joining the enemy, and towards sunset a group of twenty-six ships moved close inshore, putting themselves directly upwind of the Armada.

For the senior Spanish officers the sense of impending disaster was increased, some time in the evening, by the arrival of a message from Medina Sidonia's secretary Geronimo d'Arceo, in Dunkirk, who sent word that he did not see how Parma's force could be ready in less than a fortnight. To prevent morale collapsing altogether, this dire news was converted into a rumour that Parma would arrive the next day. When darkness fell Medina Sidonia suspected a fireship attack so strongly that he put Captain Serrano on special guard-duty in a pinnace, with an extra anchor and cable, and orders to divert any fireship that he might see approaching.

The English waited till midnight. Then, when the tide had turned and the current was running with the wind, they set their deadly convoy in motion. One man remained on board each ship as long as he dared, and the fires were not lit until the last possible moment. Then, as the flames ran rapidly along the smeared trails of pitch and into the bundles of faggots until the ships were blazing, the eight brave men jumped into rowing boats and skimmed away into the dark.

At first the Spaniards saw only two points of light coming at them; but, almost before the alarm had been raised, there were suddenly eight, closing rapidly on them down the wind and tide, sails ruddy in the glow of the flames, fire climbing the tarred rigging. As the fires increased, cannon began to explode in huge bursts of flame and sparks. In the dark the sight and the noise were terrifying. One Spaniard vividly described how dreadful the ships looked, 'spurting fire and their ordnance shooting, which was a horror to see in the night'.

Panic set in, fuelled by memories of the fireships known as 'hellburners' which at the siege of Antwerp, only three years before, had detonated with such cataclysmic explosions that they had blown more than a thousand Spanish soldiers to pieces. Now Medina Sidonia rapidly sent out an order for ships to cut anchor cables and disperse, but 'with an intimation that when the fires had passed they were to return to the same positions again'.

The instruction was hopelessly optimistic. It is clear that Medina Sidonia did not lose his head, for, although at first confronted by a knot of ships which had become entangled, he himself got clear, sailed a few miles to the north, anchored again and rode out the night. Many of his captains, however, simply fled. As the fireships bore down on them, Hugo de Moncada's galleass fired a shot to raise the alarm – as if it were needed – and ships which had been riding head-to-wind, suddenly freed from their moorings, turned sluggishly across the wind and current. In the mêlée the *San Lorenzo* caught the cable of the *San Juan de Sicilia* in her rudder and wrenched it clean off, so that she became unmanageable. The rest of the Armada struggled towards open water, leaving more than 300 anchors on the sea-bed. In spite of the chaos, the fireships passed harmlessly between the Spanish ships and drifted on to the shore, where they continued to burn throughout the rest of the night and the following day. But if they did no direct damage to the Armada, the long-term harm they wrought upon it was incalculable, for in the words of one Spanish officer,

> Fortune so favoured them [the English] that there grew from this one piece of industry just what they counted on, for they dislodged us with eight vessels – an exploit which, with 130, they had not been able to do nor dared to attempt.

It is impossible not to speculate on what might have happened if Parma had been standing by in Dunkirk, fully prepared and eager to go. Had he been in a constructive frame of mind, he would surely have got word to Medina Sidonia more quickly, to tell him he was ready.

As he rode at anchor off Calais, Medina Sidonia knew that he had the entire English fleet to the west of him, so that the Armada lay between them and Dunkirk. Had he been more strategically alert, he would surely have realized that this was the moment for the invasion army to sail, for the English were more than twenty miles from Parma's crossing line, and even if they had found out that the Spanish invasion army was on the move, the Armada could surely have obstructed them for long enough to give Parma a clear passage. Had Medina Sidonia sent ahead – privily, at night – a small force consisting perhaps of one galleass and two or three galleons, powerful enough to keep the Dutch off, with orders for Parma to embark and sail at first light, the first phase of the Enterprise might after all have succeeded.

In reality it was fatally crippled by the combination of Medina Sidonia's lack of initiative and Parma's lack of enthusiasm. Within his limits, the Captain General of the Ocean Sea had done the best he could; he had brought the Armada to within a short distance of its agreed rendezvous, without serious losses, and there is not the slightest doubt that he was comprehensively let down.

Chapter Sixteen

Gravelines

Until dawn broke, the English could not tell how effective their night attack had been; but at first light they saw to their delight that it had driven the enemy clean out of his lair. The anchorage ahead of them was empty, and only a scattering of Spanish ships was visible in the distance. With the wind freshening from the west behind him, veering to the north and backing to the south, Howard made sail at once and set out after the enemy. For the first time the full strength of the home fleet was gathered together, and now, with the Spanish ranks thoroughly broken, they could at last go for the kill. Already their plan had been made – to follow up whatever disruption they had managed to achieve with an all-out assault, Howard giving the first charge, Drake the second and Seymour the third.

Medina Sidonia, meanwhile, had found with the coming of daylight that he was almost alone. Having managed to anchor again and ride out the few remaining hours of darkness, he intended that the whole fleet should return to their former station and recover their anchors and cables. But dawn showed that this was out of the question, for most of his ships had been swept far to the east, and, with wind and current both from the west, it was physically impossible for them to come back. He therefore weighed anchor and went after them, with the English gaining on him every minute.

It was obvious that battle would break out the moment the English closed the range. Yet now, for the first time in nine days, Howard made a serious mistake. Until that moment his judgement seems to have been admirable; all the surviving accounts suggest that he had remained cool and calculating through the earlier phases of the campaign. With the enemy fleeing in disorder, however, his normal discretion deserted him, and instead of pushing through the agreed plan of action, he allowed himself to be diverted by a subsidiary target, much as Drake had done during the night when he had abandoned his brief to lead the English fleet and gone off after the shadowy German vessels out to sea. In extenuation, it is only fair to point out that Howard, like all his colleagues, had been in action on and off for more than a week, and had probably had very little good sleep in the time, so that by then his judgement may well have been impaired by exhaustion.

As he forged after the main body of the Armada in the grey early light, he sighted the galleass *San Lorenzo* over to starboard, close inshore, struggling to pull herself clear of the bar of Calais Harbour. Undoubtedly she was a target of the first importance: already during the campaign she had demonstrated her power and versatility in a dozen actions, and now it must have seemed highly desirable to put her out of commission once and for all. 'There was no better ship in the Armada for fighting in these parts,' said a contemporary Spanish report. 'She is alone enough to face twenty of the best English ships, and draws so little water that she could easily enter Dunkirk.'

Even so, it must have been clear to Howard that the monster was already *in extremis*. From a distance he probably could not see that she had lost her rudder, but she was obviously out of action and therefore tactically irrelevant. She could safely have been left to struggle while he led the attack on the ships that were still mobile. The temptation, however, was too great, and the *Ark Royal* peeled off to starboard, out of the pursuit, followed by the rest of her squadron.

As the sun rose, a vicious little battle broke out, right under the castle of Calais. Don Hugo de Moncada had deliberately made for the port, sending ahead a messenger to the Governor to ask for asylum under the town's shore battery while he carried out repairs. But the ebbing tide had dumped him on the harbour bar, and the *San Lorenzo* had heeled over on one flank, deck towards the land, so that her big guns on the seaward side were pointing to the sky and could not be brought to bear. She could thus be defended only with hand-weapons. As fifteen or twenty English ships bore down on her, bombarding her first from a distance, members of her crew began leaping overboard and swimming or scrambling for the shore. The Italian sailors and artillerymen went first, and then some of the slaves, who 'made a terrible outcry'. But Don Hugo – some of whose earlier actions had not been entirely creditable – showed great courage and defended her to the last.

Having given her a pounding with his ordnance, Howard sent in a boat with 100 men under the command of Lieutenant Amyas Preston to board her (the big ships could go no closer because of the shallow water). For a while the boat held off, the crew daunted by the high, steep bulge of the canted-over hull. Then, as musket-shots began to pick them off, they went in. First aboard the galleass was William Coxe, master of the barque *Delight*. In the hand-to-hand combat Don Hugo fought valiantly until killed outright by a musket-ball between the eyes. Many men on both sides were slain, and Preston himself severely wounded, before the ship was captured and the remaining members of the crew abandoned her.

Eagerly the boarders stripped her of everything they could shift. According to one account her cargo included 50,000 gold crowns, but according to another only 22,000 were swagged away. By prize-law her contents were now English, but her hull belonged to the country on whose shore she had been wrecked, and when Gourdan saw the victors hanging about on board, with the evident aim of floating the wreck off when the tide came back in, he sent out officers to order them to abandon it. But 'our rude men' – reported Richard Tomlinson – 'knowing no difference between friend and foe', began to abuse them and throw them into the sea, whereupon Gourdan ordered his shore battery to open up on the ship. Three times the English tried to set fire to the stricken hull, but in the end they were driven off, having lost about fifty men, and taking with them three captured Spanish officers for ransom. Only then, after perhaps a couple of hours, was Howard free to sail on and join in the main engagement, which he should have been conducting all along. (The galleass never got free, and in the end was broken up by the French for her timber.)

The battle that raged all day off Gravelines, half way between Calais and Dunkirk, was by far the most intense that any of the combatants had ever seen. It began at 7 a.m., and when it ended at 4 p.m. the Armada was in ruins. The fleet that Hawkins considered 'the greatest and strongest combination that ever was gathered in Christendom' had been shot to pieces, and several thousand of its men were dead.

No coherent overall account of the action exists, although several vivid individual narratives have survived, mainly from the Spanish side. Yet the main features of this momentous day, on which the English navy won its first major victory at sea, are clear enough. The wind blew steadily from the west, fresh but not of gale force, perhaps veering occasionally to the north or backing to the south, and pushed both fleets on through the Straits of Dover. The English always held the weather-gauge, and from an early hour the Spaniards were threatened from both sides simultaneously – from the west by the enemy attacking, and from the east by the proximity of the shoals off the Flanders coast, on to which they were in constant danger of being driven.

The main action began when Medina Sidonia, having tried but failed to rally the Armada round him, and being told by his Flemish pilots that all would be lost if he went much closer to the shoals, brought the *San Martin* up into the wind and offered action. His aim was to steady the fleet's headlong flight, his long-term hope being that if he could somehow

17. The Armada in action against the English, as imagined by a contemporary artist. On the right is Howard's *Ark Royal*, in the centre (with the red-and-yellow striped flag) Seymour's *Rainbow*. The ship with the broken mast between them is the *Nuestra Señora del Rosario*, the first to be captured by the English. From the shore on the left, the Queen watches the battle.

18. Off Calais, midnight on 7-8 August. The fireships secretly prepared by the English bear down on the Armada moored in serried ranks. Such was the Spaniards' panic that they cut their cables and abandoned 300 anchors in their haste to escape.

19. The treacherous reefs and headlands of the Blasket Islands, off the Dingle peninsula in Co. Kerry, where Martinez de Recalde brought his galleon *San Juan de Oporto* for respite, and where the *Nuestra Señora de la Rosa* was wrecked, disembowelled by a submarine pinnacle of rock.

Drake's chest, preserved in Berkeley Castle, Gloucestershire. On the inside of the lid is a representation of the *Golden Hind*, in which he made the first English circumnavigation of the world between 1577 and 1580. After his return the Queen knighted him in a ceremony on board at Deptford; the ship was put on show there in a specially built shed, and scholars of Winchester College incised laudatory Latin verses on her mainmast.

hold the English off, he would still be upwind of Dunkirk, and might yet manage to make his rendezvous with Parma. As before, he was behaving with courage and good sense.

As he luffed, his ship became perilously exposed, being accompanied only by the galleon *San Marcos*, and at once Drake came straight in to the attack, as one Spanish source described it 'with great fury . . . approaching within musket-shot, and some time within harquebus-shot'.

There is no doubt that Drake led the opening attack, closely followed by Hawkins and Frobisher, each admiral at the head of his squadron. But it seems that, having given the *San Martin* his bow guns and a broadside, Drake pressed on to break up a threat which he could see developing

Drake's Drum, preserved at his former home Buckland Abbey, north of Plymouth. The drum, said to sound supernaturally in times of national peril, inspired Henry Newbolt to the celebrated poem in which he imagined Drake keeping an eye on England from the other side:

Drake he's in his hammock an' a
    thousand mile away,
  (Capten, art tha sleepin' there below?)
Slung atween the round shot in Nombre
    Dios Bay,
  An' dreamin' arl the time o' Plymouth Hoe . .

Take my drum to England, hang et by the
    shore,
  Strike et when your powder's runnin' low;
If the Dons sight Devon, I'll quit the port
    o' Heaven,
  An' drum them up the Channel as we
    drummed them long ago.

Drake he's in his hammock till the great
    Armadas come
  (Capten, art tha sleepin' there below?)
Slung atween the round shot, listnin' for
    the drum,
  An dreamin' arl the time o' Plymouth Hoe . .

ahead. His immediate purpose was to stop the scattered Armada from re-forming, and in this he was only partially successful, for some fifty of the best Spanish fighting ships did manage to beat out into deeper water and take up their familiar crescent formation. As the battle progressed, their flagship drifted on and rejoined them. (It may have been this action of Drake's which provoked the bitter outburst from Frobisher, who after-wards accused his colleague of having come 'bragging up at the first, indeed, and gave them his prow and his broadside; and then kept his luff and was glad he was gone again like a cowardly knave or traitor – I rest doubtful which – but the one I will swear'. It seems that Frobisher, either out of jealousy or from tactical ignorance, failed to realize what his colleague was trying to achieve.)

As the running fight developed, the Armada struggled to preserve its defensive formation and at the same time to work northwards, into the open sea. The English sought to cut out and surround individual ships nearest to them, but also to chivvy the whole fleet forward on to the coastal banks.

In the strong breeze the disadvantages of fighting from a downwind position were severe; for one thing, because the Spanish ships spent much of the time heeling over, away from the wind, the guns on the side facing the enemy were pointing skywards, and therefore difficult to bring to bear. This alone must have contributed to the fact that English casualties were so light – although a more decisive factor was the Spaniards' shortage of ammunition. They began the battle with little and ended it with almost none. Yet perhaps their most serious handicap of all was one of which they were not aware: the defective nature of their ammunition. Here, fighting at really close quarters at last, their heavy, ship-smashing cannons should surely have been able to do substantial damage – yet they did not. Was it because the brittle cast-iron balls simply broke up on contact?

Medina Sidonia's critics later claimed that he spent the whole day cowering in his cabin, surrounded by sacks of wool for protection; but this is manifestly unjust, and there is no evidence to suggest that he did anything but direct operations with guts and tenacity. For part of the time, at least, he was in that most exposed position of all, the main-top – the circular platform built round the mainmast – and one Spanish account described how, in attempts to slow down the dangerous rush to the east, 'he kept luffing up continually upon the enemy's fleet, transfigured and shrouded in the smoke of his guns, which he ordered to be fired with the greatest rapidity and diligence'.

Nor did any of his compatriots let him down. To a man they fought magnificently, and many individual deeds of heroism were recorded; but the English had the better of almost every exchange – partly because their ships were so much more manoeuvrable, mainly because they held the weather-gauge throughout, and so were able to initiate attacks as they chose.

According to Pedro Coco Calderon, the Armada's purser (and a staunch supporter of Medina Sidonia), the *San Martin* was under continuous artillery fire for nine hours, from 7 a.m. to 4 p.m., and during that time more than 200 cannon-balls struck her hull, masts, sails and rigging, killing or wounding twenty sailors and forty soldiers, and disabling three of her guns. One 50-lb ball went clean through her, and so many holes were punched in her planking between wind and water that two divers, working all day with tow and lead plates, could hardly control the inflow of water. To the crew, it sometimes seemed that the entire English fleet was attacking them alone.

The Portuguese galleon *San Felipe*, commanded by the veteran soldier Don Francisco de Toledo, was smashed up still more severely. Surrounded at one time by seventeen English vessels, and bombarded from all sides simultaneously, she had her rudder disabled, her foremast broken, and more than 200 men killed. When Don Diego de Pimentel bravely brought his galleon the *San Mateo* to her rescue, she too was raked by a hail of shot. Her upper works were shot away, the spars and rigging a tangle of wreckage; yet her crew remained full of fight, and when an enemy ship came so close alongside that an Englishman leaped aboard, the Spaniards instantly cut him to bits.

The air was evidently alive with lead, for the rigging of many ships was sliced to shreds, and several men were killed or dismembered by cannon-balls. Among the distinguished individuals so struck down were Don Pedro de Mendoza, who was killed outright by a great-shot; Felipe de Cordoba had his head shot off, and Don Pedro Henriquez had a hand carried away.

For every member of the Armada, the day turned into a nightmare. It does not take much imagination to feel the desperation of the gun-crews as, deafened and exhausted, they finally found themselves defenceless for lack of ammunition; or of the surgeons, working down in the dim, stinking bowels of the hold – the safest place on board – overwhelmed by the flood of hideously wounded men for whom they could do little or nothing. There seems no reason to doubt the report which described the decks of one Italian ship as awash with blood, which was running out of the scuppers. A great many men were drowned, some flung overboard by the violence of collisions, some jumping in attempts to save themselves. The English fished out a few, in the hope that they might prove worth ransoming, but most were never seen again.

For the 180 friars on board, it can only have been an appalling ordeal: besides having to master their own fears, they had also somehow to allay the terrors of the dying. 'Yea, in the end,' wrote Padre Geronimo de la Torre,

> I saw myself in such sore straits that day that it was a miracle of God we escaped; for since the ships were so scattered and could not help one another, the enemy's galleons came together and charged us in such numbers that they gave us no time to draw breath.

But for nobody on board can the experience have been more shattering than for the noble young volunteers, especially the group on Don Alonso de Leyva's carrack. Seasick, terrified, helpless, and (worst of all) frustrated by the fact that they could not take part in the fight or do anything to discomfort the enemy, they could only watch death and destruction strike all round them, as their dreams of wealth and glory were finally blown away. And what of Don Pedro de Valdes, still a prisoner on board the *Revenge*? He too must have endured agonies, seeing his ships and countrymen so brutally savaged. Curiously enough, one man who seems to have been very little affected was the young poet Lope de Vega, whose biographers describe him sitting serenely among the hail of bullets, impervious to the danger and continuing to write his poems in the most hellish circumstances. No matter that the blast of the big guns several times carried his papers away: compelled (as he himself recorded) 'to exercise his pen', he wrote in the Prologue to 'Angelica's Beauty', 'There, on the waters, between the rigging of the galleon *San Juan* and the flags of the Catholic King, I wrote and translated these little verses from Turpino.'

By afternoon the *San Mateo* was crippled and unserviceable, with a high proportion of her crew dead or wounded, and Medina Sidonia sent *pataches* to take off the remaining men. This they did, but Don Diego de Pimentel refused to abandon his ship, and when night came she was last seen falling away towards the Dutch coast. A similar fate befell Don Francisco de Toledo and the *San Felipe*, which had five of her starboard guns dismounted, and another spiked by an Italian gunner, who was afterwards killed. Calderon left a graphic account of the ship's distress:

> In view of this, and that his upper deck was destroyed, both his pumps broken, his rigging in shreds and his ship almost a wreck, Don Francisco ordered the grappling hooks to be got out, and shouted to the enemy to come to close quarters. They replied, summoning him to surrender in fair fight; and one Englishman, standing in the main-top in sword and buckler, called out, 'Good soldiers that ye are, surrender to the fair terms we offer thee.' But the only answer he got was a gunshot, which brought him down in sight of everyone, and the Maestre de Campo then ordered the muskets and harquebuses to be brought into action. The enemy thereupon retired, whilst our men shouted out to them that they were cowards, and with opprobrious words reproached them for their want of spirit, calling them Lutheran hens, and daring them to return to the fight.

The English were by no means short of spirit; nor, as Calderon thought, were they under 'orders from the Queen that, on pain of death, no ship of theirs was to come to close quarters with any of ours'. The Queen was eager that grappling *should* take place, and that prizes should be won. The orders to stand off had been issued by Howard and his admirals – and they were executed with admirable discipline, to deadly effect.

By late afternoon many Spanish ships had been reduced to floating wrecks, their rigging destroyed and their ammunition gone. Besides, about fifteen of them had been cut off from the rest of the Armada, and these now looked certain to fall victim to the enemy, who were closing in for the kill. Finally, it seemed, the English restraint was about to be rewarded with some glittering prizes.

Yet it was not to be. At the last moment the Spaniards were saved by the arrival of a violent squall, which at 4 p.m. suddenly buffeted both fleets with a blast of wind and torrential rain. The English saw the storm coming and turned away to meet it. For quarter of an hour further action was impossible, as visibility was blotted out; and in that lull, which must to the Spanish have seemed heaven-sent, they fell so far away downwind as to put themselves out of the enemy's reach, at least for the time being.

Yet still they were in dire trouble. Even when the fiercest of the storm had passed, wind and sea remained high, and it became impossible to carry out any more repairs, so that the *San Martin* herself was in danger of going down. At least one ship had been so badly damaged by gunfire that she sank there and then. This was the *Maria Juan* of Recalde's squadron. She signalled for assistance, but when rescuers reached her they found that, with the hull already settling in the water, the crew had taken to the spars and rigging, and only one boatload of eighty men could be saved. Down she went, with the rest of her ninety seamen and 180 soldiers.

For all her defiance, the *San Felipe* was also doomed. Of her 360 soldiers sixty had been killed and 200 wounded, and her hull was riddled. At 7 p.m. she fired shots to summon help, and the hulk *Doncella* came alongside to take off survivors. Captain Juan Posa, who was with them, then said that the hulk herself was going down, whereupon Don Francisco jumped back on to his own ship, shouting out that if he was going to be drowned, he would rather it happened on the galleon than on a hulk. He too was borne away into the murky twilight towards the shore, and Medina Sidonia gave him up for dead.

In fact he survived, for the ship managed to limp into harbour at Nieuport, where he and the remains of his crew disembarked. The galleon was then captured by the Dutch, who took it to Flessingen; but there a great press of people swarmed on board, drawn by reports that the ship was carrying excellent Ribadavian wine. This the raiders tackled with such relish that they quite forgot that the ship had been shot full of holes; and when she suddenly rolled on her side and sank, 300 of the revellers were drowned.

Don Diego Pimentel also survived. After drifting helplessly all night, he ran on to a shoal near Flushing, and at dawn was attacked by more than twenty Dutch boats; and although the ship was already disabled, with many of its crew dead and most of the rest injured, he held out gallantly for six hours. Eventually, in the words of the Spanish historian C. Fernandez Duro, 'he gave himself up to the force and persistence of his enemies, the Spaniards selling their lives and their liberty so dearly that it will remain eternally an example of courage and valiant resistance'. Don Diego himself was held in prison until a heavy ransom was paid. The English captain William Borlas, who took part in the action, boasted to Walsingham: 'I was the means that the best sort [of Spaniards] were saved', and he had no qualms about adding: 'The rest were cast overboard and slain at the entry.'

The English emerged from the battle of Gravelines by no means unscathed. The *Revenge* was said by Hakluyt to have been 'pierced with shot above forty times'. Drake's

> very cabin was twice shot through, and about the conclusion of the fight, the bed of a certain gentleman, lying weary thereon, was taken quite from under him by the force of a bullet. Likewise, as the Earl of Northumberland and Sir Charles Blount were at dinner . . . the bullet of a demi-culverin brake through the midst of their cabin, touched their feet and struck down two of the standers-by.

Every ship sustained damage of some kind. The number of casualties is hard to ascertain, since it was deliberately played down so that the crews could go on drawing rations for some of the men who were dead. Yet most estimates put it at only about 100, of which perhaps half were killed in the storming of the galleass; and the fact that the Government grant for distribution among the wounded amounted to no more than £80 shows that their number also was very small. Among those killed was Captain Coxe of the *Delight*, who had shown such valour in the attack on the *San Lorenzo* a few hours before, but whose luck now ran out. As Ubaldini put it, 'Within a little while after, he lost his life by a great piece of ordnance, fortune not being correspondingly favourable unto his courage.'

It was by far the most furious fight in which any of the English had ever been. 'Out of my ship there was 500 shot of demi-cannon, culverin and demi-culverin,' Winter reported to Walsingham, 'and when I was farthest off in discharging any of the pieces, I was not out of shot of their harquebus, and most times within speech one of another. . . . When every man was weary with labour, and our cartridges spent and munitions wasted – I think in some altogether – we ceased and followed the enemy.' Winter himself was hurt when one of his demi-cannons recoiled so violently that it hit him on the hip, and injured him badly enough to prevent him attending Howard's council-of-war next day.

Howard himself, who was not given to exaggeration, confirmed Winter's assessment:

> Some made little account of the Spanish force by sea [he told

Walsingham], but I do warrant you, all the world never saw such a force as theirs was; and some Spaniards that we have taken, that were in the fight at Lepanto, do say that the worst of our four fights did far exceed the fight they had there.

Harassed as he was by acute shortage of food and countless other problems, the Lord Admiral found time to send out a derisive message for the Spanish ambassador in Paris:

Sir, in your next letters to my brother [-in-law] Stafford, I pray write to him that he will let Mendoza know that Her Majesty's rotten ships dare meet with his master's sound ships; and in buffeting with them, though they were three great ships to one of us, yet we have shortened them sixteen or seventeen, whereof there is three of them a-fishing in the bottom of the seas.

On the evening of the 8th, with the Armada already in ruins, the Duke of Parma at last rode into Nieuport. There (he reported to the King) 16,000 men had been shipped on to the assault boats during the day, and when he arrived 'the embarkation of the men was so forward as to be practically completed'. Without waiting, he pushed on to Dunkirk, where he found 'the men on the quay and everything ready, so that by evening matters would be completed there also'. He claimed, in other words, that his force had been ready to sail.

Yet clearly this was not true. Don Jorge Manrique, who had come with urgent appeals for help from Medina Sidonia, was so far from satisfied with what he saw that he became incensed at the lack of preparation. After a sharp argument with the *provedor* of the Flanders fleet, he met the Duke, who received him with a very bad grace; and when Don Jorge told him that the troops should embark, Parma replied that it was no business of his. Their exchanges became so heated that the Duke had to be restrained by his retainers from laying hands on the messenger. When ordered to return to the Armada, Don Jorge said he would go – and tell Medina Sidonia the lamentable state of affairs on land. Already, however, it was too late, for by the time this argument broke out, the fleet was flying in tatters towards the North Sea, and Don Jorge was stranded in Dunkirk.

The embarkation that took place was no more than a charade. Whether it was supposed to be a rehearsal, or a demonstration to bluff Medina Sidonia's messengers, is not clear; but it was certainly not a serious attempt to send the invasion force on its way. According to Duro, it was so farcical that it caused great mirth among the soldiers, because they were going on board boats which the caulker had not set a hand on, and which were without munitions, provisions or sails. At once some 40,000 men [sic] went on board, packed as it was the custom to pile up and squeeze in sacks of grain.

Even if the boats had been ready, and able to put out (which the wind made impossible), they would merely have sailed into the path of the rampant English fleet, to their certain destruction. But they were not within days or even weeks of being sea-worthy.

The reasons remain infinitely puzzling. Some people thought that Parma had been against the King's plan from the start, because he believed that Spain could not safely launch an invasion of England until the subjugation of the Netherlands was complete. When Parma heard that the Armada had been blown into Corunna (this school of thought held), he convinced himself that the whole plan had collapsed and the campaign been put off; he therefore sent the invasion army inland, where he could maintain it more easily, and at the same time stopped all work on the boats. So stubbornly did he cling to his wishful belief – in spite of repeated messages to say that Medina Sidonia was on his way – that when the Armada reached Plymouth, he was taken by surprise, and had no time to remedy his neglect.

This explanation seems only moderately convincing. Parma was a decisive man of action, not a dreamer, and it is hard to believe that he did not realize that the Armada was coming. His failure to have things ready seems more deliberate than negligent, and certainly when he wrote to the King two days later, on 10 August, his letter contained elements of deception, as well as strenuous attempts at self-justification. Thus although he already knew that the Armada had been defeated off Gravelines, he did not begin with news of the disaster, or even mention it until he had spent several pages reiterating the reasons why he had been unable to send out flyboats to reinforce the fleet, as Medina Sidonia had requested. Then, having at last admitted that the fireship attack had succeeded, that the *San Lorenzo* had been lost at Calais, and that the rest of the Armada had fled in disorder, he descended into unctuous waffle:

> God knows how grieved I am at this news, at a time when I hoped to send Your Majesty my congratulations at having successfully carried through your intentions. But I am sure that Your Majesty knows me to be one of your humblest and most devoted servants, who has laboured hard in this business. . . .
>
> I will only say, therefore, that this must come from the hand of the Lord, who knows well what He does, and can

redress it all, rewarding Your Majesty with many victories and the full fruition of your desires in His good time. We should therefore give him thanks for all things. Above all it is of the utmost importance that Your Majesty should be careful of your health . . .

Evidently Parma's conscience was still troubling him, for yet again he returned to the subject of the men and the boats:

With regard to the embarkation of our troops, some of the officers who have come from the Duke wished to make out that we were not ready, but they were mistaken in this, as it was not possible to ship the men sooner. . . . It was not advisable to keep the men a long time beforehand in these boats, where they could not be controlled as if they were on land, and yet could go ashore when they liked, besides which they would have rotted and died . . .

Rambling, inconclusive and repetitious, the letter all too clearly betrays its author's lack of conviction. There is no doubt that it was Parma's failure to fulfil his role which broke the back of the Enterprise, and equally little doubt that he knew it.

Chapter Seventeen

Chase to the North

The most fortunate members of the Armada were those who had been sent ashore, on various errands, before the action off Gravelines began. One was Juan de Marolin, the pilot, left behind by mistake. Another, Don Jorge Manrique, was left stranded in Dunkirk after he had run his errand. A third was the Prince of Ascoli, allegedly a bastard son of the King. He had been aboard the *San Martin*, and when the fireships bore down on the Armada at midnight Medina Sidonia had despatched him in a *zabra* to carry instructions to other ships. Off he went into the dark in search of the rear squadron, but while he was trying to carry out his orders the flagship sailed away. At daybreak on the 8th he found himself in the middle of the English fleet, with the Armada far downwind.

Sighting a Spanish pinnace, he went aboard and got the crew to clap on all possible sail in an attempt to overtake the *San Martin*, but he was so hotly pressed by English boats coming fresh from the kill of the *San Lorenzo* that he never managed to rejoin his own fleet. At two next morning, when a gale got up, he was forced to run before it, 'he knew not whither', for the rest of the night, without a pilot. At dawn he sighted Calais, but too far to leeward to make the port, and he was blown willy-nilly into Dunkirk. There he found the Duke of Parma, of whom he begged, but was refused, permission to return to the fleet. 'I am very unhappy to be out of whatever events may happen to the Armada,' he wrote to the King. 'But as God has ordained it otherwise, it cannot be helped, and my only wish is to be in some place where I may serve Your Majesty and do my duty in a manner worthy of my birth.'

Having reformed themselves into a crescent in the evening, the Armada's surviving ships ran on north-eastwards through the stormy night under all the canvas that their splintered masts and spars would carry, their crews haunted by the menace of the Zeeland banks ahead. At 2 a.m., when the wind increased to gale-force, Medina Sidonia had the flagship brought up into the blast as close as possible, but still she kept

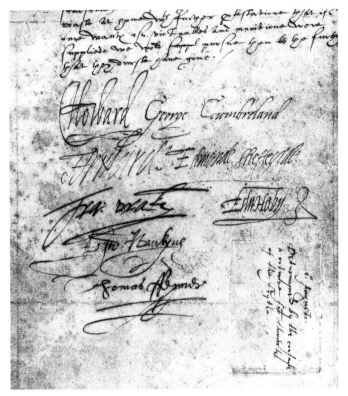

The end of the resolution passed by the English commanders 'to follow and pursue the Spanish fleet until we have cleared our own coast', made on 11 August after the Armada had been scattered at the Battle of Gravelines two days earlier. The signatures of Howard, Drake, Cumberland, Sheffield and Hawkins can all be deciphered

falling to leeward, unable to hold a safe course. For perhaps three hours the ferocious storm kept up, not moderating until after dawn.

Daylight showed that the *San Martin* was accompanied by only a handful of ships, among them the three remaining galleasses and three or four galleons. The rest had been driven far to leeward. Astern, as ever, lay the enemy, following inexorably. To Medina Sidonia it seemed that the end had come. His pilots assured him that it was death to continue as they were going. To go about would be to invite another artillery assault, which he had no means of countering. Some people, it is said, urged him to surrender, or at least to save his own life by escaping in a pinnace.

To his credit, he would do neither, but came round into the wind and hove-to with the galleasses ranged ahead of him, awaiting the apparently inevitable attack. Yet to his amazement, it never came. The English held off, waiting – and suddenly the Spaniards realized why. When they took a sounding, they found they had only six and a half fathoms of water, scarcely ten feet more than the draft of the *San Martin*. There was no need for the English to waste any more powder and shot. The Armada was on the point of being destroyed by natural forces, without another battle.

In desperation Medina Sidonia fired two guns to bring the rest of his ships onto the wind, and sent a *patache* with an order that they should keep close-hauled. This was entirely futile, as they simply were not able to obey the command. The drift to destruction continued. Far gone with frustration and despair, Oquendo and Leyva came alongside the *San Martin* and yelled out at Medina Sidonia that he was a coward. By goading him with insults, they tried to make him fight. They shouted to the soldiers to throw the hated Don Diego Flores overboard.

But their verbal bombardment was in vain. As if in a trance, hypnotized by his impending doom, the Duke sailed on, gripped once again by the fatal passivity which had led him to accept his commission in the first place. Sounding once more, the leading galleass called out a mere five fathoms. The pilots were astonished that they had not already grounded, that such large ships could still be clearing the ocean floor. Everyone on board resigned themselves to their fate. 'It was the most terrible day in the world,' wrote Don Luis de Miranda. 'All the people stood in despair of salvation and expecting to die.'

As the Duke himself wrote, 'God alone could rescue them', and, to their inexpressible relief, it seemed that He did. At the last possible moment the wind suddenly went round – if not, as one overjoyed witness claimed, as far as the south-east, at least to the south – and even the most battered vessels of the Armada were able to make headway towards the open sea. To the English it was an unbelievable and undeserved stroke of luck; but to the Spaniards it really did seem a divine intervention.

Again the chase was on. As the fleets laboured up into the North Sea, at least one more of the Armada went down. Captain Robert Crosse saw a Spanish great ship in distress, and approached it to parley with its master, 'who, being in speech of yielding unto the said captain, before they could agree on certain conditions sank presently before their eyes'.

During the middle of the day there was time for both sides to assess their position. Neither knew the full extent of the other's damage or deprivation. The Spanish did not know that the English were all-but out of ammunition and desperately short of food. Equally, although the English knew they had inflicted many casualties, and sunk three ships and sent others wallowing towards the shore, they could not be sure that the enemy, too, had exhausted his stocks of gunpowder and shot. They fully expected that they would have to fight again. Still less could they tell what the Duke of Parma was planning: for all they knew, his invasion force might at that very moment be poised to come out of the Flanders ports, waiting only for the wind to drop, and the departure of the Armada northwards might be a pre-planned decoy movement, designed to lure the English fleet away from the Channel and leave the south coast unprotected.

As Howard himself reported, 'after the fight, notwithstanding that our powder and shot was near all spent, we set on a brag countenance and gave them chase, as though we wanted nothing'. Yet when he fired off a warning gun and put out his flag to summon a council-of-war, between 3 p.m. and 4 p.m., he was by no means celebrating a victory. Instead, he was cautiously planning the next phase of the campaign. It was decided that most of the fleet should continue the pursuit, but that Seymour and Winter should return to their station in the Straits of Dover, in case Parma were to attempt a crossing. As Winter described it in a letter to Walsingham, they were ordered 'to bear away in the twilight, as the enemy might not see our departing'. Thus at 8 p.m., when the wind had died and veered to the north-east, their squadron ran back through the fleet, 'and truly we had much ado with the staying of many ships that would have returned with us, besides our own company'.

If other captains wanted to turn back, Seymour most certainly did not. Having risked his life in battle with the Spaniards, he told Walsingham,

> I find my Lord [Admiral] jealous and loth to have me take part of the honour of the rest that is to win, using his authority to command me to look to our English coasts . . . I pray God that my Lord Admiral do not find the lack of the *Rainbow* and that company, for I protest before God and have witness for the same, I vowed I would be as near or nearer with my little ship to encounter our enemies as any of the greatest in both armies.

Writing to the Queen the same day, he told her also how he had been 'commanded by my Lord Admiral to return back for the defence of Your Majesty's coasts, if anything be attempted by the Duke of Parma; and therein have obeyed his Lordship much against my will, expecting Your Majesty's further pleasure'. With an ironic flourish – and a curious pre-echo of the English National Anthem – he finished his letter:

> Hoping God will confound all your enemies,
> Your Majesty's most bounden
> and faithful fisherman,
> H. Seymour.

Among the admirals there was a feeling that nobody on shore yet understood the scale of the threat which the Armada posed. Asking urgently for money, ground tackle, cordage, canvas and victuals to be sent to Dover 'in good plenty', Hawkins warned Walsingham,

Your wisdom and experience is great; but this is a matter far
passing all that hath been seen in our time or long before.

Drake, now appointed to lead the pursuit, was in ebullient form,
already looking forward to another fight. 'We have the army of Spain
before us,' he told Walsingham,

and mind with the grace of God to wrestle a pull with him.
There was never anything pleased me better than the seeing
the enemy flying with a southerly wind to the northward . . .
With the grace of God, if we live, I doubt not but ere it be
long so to handle the matter with the Duke of Sidonia as he
should wish himself at St Mary Port among his orange trees.

No doubt the Duke was already fervently wishing himself at home,
for now he was not only in dire physical straits, but faced with a strong
possibility that the Enterprise had failed, and that he might have to make
an ignominious return to Spain. That same afternoon he summoned his
commanders, including Leyva, to decide what should be done, and himself 'submitted the state of the Armada' to them. The question was,
Would it be best to return to the Channel and see if they could after all
join up with Parma? Or should they 'sail home to Spain by the North
Sea', making an anti-clockwise circumnavigation of the British Isles?
Purser Calderon warned his fellow officers that the voyage 'would be a
tremendously laborious one, for we should have to sail round England,
Scotland and Ireland, 750 leagues [2,250 miles] through stormy seas
almost unknown to us, before we could reach Corunna'.

The council voted unanimously in favour of returning to the Channel
'if the weather would allow of it'. The decision was a courageous one, but
the men who took it had no chance of carrying it out, for the south-south-
west wind kept increasing in violence, and the Spanish ships, in their
weakened state, could do nothing but run before it, all that day and
through the night.

Wednesday, 10 August should have been auspicious for them, since it
was the day of San Lorenzo, patron saint of the King. Yet during the
morning the high wind and sea drove the Armada on, and when, in the
afternoon, the gale at last abated, the English made a menacing advance
under full sail towards the Spanish rear. Seeing the threat, Medina
Sidonia struck his topsails to allow his weakened rearguard, under
Recalde, to close up, and fired three guns at intervals – the signal for the
whole Armada to shorten sail and stand by the flagship.

The English feint came to nothing. It is fairly certain that they never
intended to attack (for they had so little powder) and meant only to prey
on the Spaniards' nerves. But this they managed with even greater suc-

cess than they could have hoped. So overwrought was Medina Sidonia by then that he sent out an immediate order for the execution of two captains who had not conformed closely enough to the prescribed formation.

One was Captain Francisco de Cuellar, who had sailed from Lisbon as an *entretenido*, or aspirant captain, and had been given command of the galleon *San Pedro* after the reorganization at Corunna. On the morning of 10 August he had fallen asleep in his cabin, exhausted after more than a week without proper rest. While he was thus unconscious his second-in-command had piled on full sail and deliberately drawn some two miles ahead of the *San Martin* (as other ships had been doing), so that he could then hove-to for a while to inspect for damage and carry out repairs.

The wretched Cuellar suddenly found himself summoned to the flagship, along with Don Cristobal de Avila, captain of the hulk *Santa Barbara*, and immediately condemned to death for disobedience, nominally by Francisco de Bobadilla, the general in charge of the military forces, but ultimately by Medina Sidonia himself. Being a man of some influence, with many friends, Cuellar managed to argue his way out; he was saved by the intervention of Martin de Aranda, who had been deputed to carry out the execution. But Avila had no such luck, and after much insult and cruelty was hanged at the yard-arm, his body then being paraded round the fleet.

The order for the execution was surely that of a badly rattled man. Medina Sidonia also condemned some ships' captains to the galleys, and reduced some military officers to the ranks – because (it was said) they had allowed themselves to drift out of the battle the day before. Yet even if the punishments eased the Captain General of the Ocean's nerves, they did nothing to lessen his predicament.

As they sailed north, Purser Calderon went from ship to ship taking stock of food, wine and water. Apart from the few luxuries imported at Calais, there was very little left to eat but bread, and many of the water-casks had been shattered by gunfire. Presented with his calculations, the Duke put out an order reducing each man's daily ration to half a pound of bread, half a pint of wine and one pint of water. So ignorant were he and his admirals of the northern seas ahead that he offered a French pilot 2,000 ducats if he could bring them safe to any port in Spain.

The English, never sure of their intentions, had thought that their plan might be to land in the Firth of Forth (then known as the Frith) and consummate King Philip's long-drawn-out intrigues with the Catholic faction in Scotland. But by the morning of Friday, 12 August, it was clear that the Frith could not be their target; although the Armada had reached a latitude of 55 degrees, level with Newcastle, the fleet was so far out in the North Sea, towards the Dogger Bank, that it was obviously not aiming for the south of Scotland.

'Considering the wind and the great draught of their ships,' wrote Thomas Fenner of the *Nonpareil*,

> they have no place to go withal, but for the Scaw in Denmark, which were an hard adventure, as the [bad] season of the year approacheth. If the wind by change suffer them, I very believe they will pass about Scotland and Ireland to draw themselves home.

The Knave of Hearts and the Knave of Clubs from a set of playing cards brought out to commemorate the Armada's defeat. Pope Sixtus V is here seen sending off bags of gold, but in fact his offer of a million ducats was conditonal on Spanish troops setting foot in England, and he managed to avoid contributing anything at all.

Soon after dawn on the 12th, Drake called a council on the *Revenge*. Until then Howard had nursed an ambition to put in one final attack on the fleeing enemy – perhaps because his own squadron, which had missed half the battle of Gravelines, had more ammunition left than the other ships. At the council, however, it was agreed that no action could be fought with the exiguous stocks of powder and shot that they held, and the decision was taken to go into the Firth themselves, both to collect fresh water, and to make a show of force that would help keep the King of Scotland's loyalties focussed in the right direction.

A pinnace and a caravel were detailed to continue tailing the Armada until it had cleared Orkney and Shetland – or, if it changed course, to report the alteration at once and come south in search of the English fleet. Then at midday, with a joyous, derisive, valedictory discharge of ordnance, the rest of the English ships swung away to the west and let the enemy go.

Seeing them turn, the Spaniards supposed they were heading back for the south coast – and this in the end was what they did, for next morning the wind went round to the north-west and again changed the whole prospect. With such a wind blowing, it would be impossible for the Spaniards to approach any part of the English coast north of Hull; but they might, if they still had any fight in them, make a dash straight back to the Channel. The English therefore decided to do the same, setting course for North Foreland, where they hoped to pick up sorely-needed supplies.

As they ran south, the wind steadily increased, and when they were off Norfolk went round to the south-west in such a violent gale that the fleet was blown apart. But, forced though they were to run before the storm, the English admirals rejoiced at the wildness of the elements, for they knew that this blast would finally put paid to any chance the Armada had had of landing in Scotland.

When Howard eventually reached the shelter of Margate Road on the 18th, he wrote to Walsingham:

> Where the rest [of the ships] be gone I do not know, for we had a most violent storm as ever was seen at this time of year, that put us asunder thwart of Norfolk, amongst many ill-favoured sands; but I trust they all do well, and I hope I shall hear of them this night or tomorrow.

The ships all came in, battered but safe, to various ports on the east coast; yet still no victory was celebrated, for no one could be sure that the Armada would not return, and Howard's immediate preoccupation was to prevent Queen and Council disbanding his force before the threat had finally gone. The Government's parsimony, he knew all too well, would lead to the quickest possible scale-down of the Navy, and in an attempt to delay the inevitable he wrote to Walsingham:

> I know not what you think of it at Court, but I do think, and so doth all here, that there cannot be too great forces maintained yet for five or six weeks, on the seas; for although we have put the Spanish fleet past the Frith, and I think past the Isles, yet God knoweth whether they go either to the Nase of Norway or into Denmark or to the Isles of Orkney to refresh themselves, and so return; for I think they dare not return [to Spain] with this dishonour and shame to their King, and overthrow of their Pope's credit.
> Sir, sure bind, sure find. A kingdom is a great wager.

That very morning, as her ships were coming home, the Queen left her capital on a royal Progress. She had wanted to visit the coast, to witness at least part of the battle, but Leicester had forbidden it; so now, with her unfaltering touch for making a public appearance at the moment that would do most for national morale, she went to accept Leicester's invitation and inspect the army camp at Tilbury.

Embarking on the royal barge at St James's to the blare of trumpets, she swept down-river, beneath the houses on London Bridge, at the head of a flotilla bearing the gentlemen of her household and the yeomen of the guard. At Tilbury, outside the fort, Leicester had drawn up the capital's main defence force on parade ready for her inspection. Like everyone else, he expected her to move through their ranks in the centre of a large, protective bodyguard; but she astonished them all by insisting that her entourage should consist of four men and two boys only.

First went the Earl of Ormonde, on foot, bearing the Sword of State. Then came two pages, also walking, one leading the Queen's horse, the other carrying her ceremonial silver helmet on a cushion. The Queen herself rode between two mounted retainers – on her one hand old Leicester, her Captain General, and on the other the dazzlingly handsome young Earl of Essex, her Master of the Horse. White was the colour that stamped the spectacle indelibly on the minds of all who saw it: the Queen's horse was white; the two pages were dressed in white velvet. Of white velvet, too, were the Queen's own clothes, and the cushion on which her ceremonial casque was borne. Over her white dress she wore a silver cuirass, and in her right hand she carried a silver truncheon. She rode bare-headed so that the men could see her better; and some kind of jewels – diamonds, perhaps – glittered in her fiery hair.

'Perhaps an objective observer would have seen no more than a battered, rather scraggy spinster in her middle fifties perched on a fat white horse, her teeth black, her red wig slightly askew,' wrote the

Robert Devereux, second Earl of Essex, the Queen's latest favourite in the year of the Armada, and Master of the Horse, who rode beside her when she went to inspect the troops at Tilbury.

American historian Garrett Mattingly:

> But that was not what her subjects saw, dazzled as they were by more than the sun on the silver breast-plate or the moisture in their eyes. They saw Judith and Esther, Gloriana and Belphoebe, Diana the virgin huntress, and Minerva the wise protrectress, and best of all their own beloved Queen and Mistress, come in this hour of danger in all simplicity to trust herself among them.

When the soldiers saw how Elizabeth presented herself to them, they roared approval; and it was either that day or the next – for she stayed the night nearby and insisted on returning – that she made one of the most moving and heroic speeches of her life,

> My Loving People,
> We have been persuaded by some that are careless of our safety to take heed how we commit ourselves to armed multitudes, for fear of treachery; but I assure you, I do not desire to live in distrust of my faithful and loving people.
>
> Let tyrants fear. I have always so behaved myself that, under God, I have placed my chiefest strength and safeguard in the loyal hearts and goodwill of my subjects; and therefore I am come amongst you, as you see, at this time not for my recreation and disport, but being resolved, in the midst and heat of battle to live or die amongst you all; to lay down for my God and for my kingdom and for my people my honour and my blood, even in the dust.
>
> I know I have but the body of a weak and feeble woman; but I have the heart and stomach of a King, and a King of England, too; and I think it foul scorn that Parma or Spain or any Prince of Europe should dare to invade the borders of my realm; to which, rather than any dishonour should grow by me, I myself will take up arms, I myself will be general, judge and rewarder of every one of your virtues in the field
> . . .

According to Leicester, this *tour de force* 'so inflamed the hearts of her poor subjects as I think the weakest person among them is able to match the proudest Spaniard that dares now land in England'. Evidently the surge of patriotic fervour went to her head too, for when, as she sat at dinner among her captains, word suddenly came that Parma was on the point of sailing to the attack, she proposed to remain at Tilbury and await his coming. Only with great difficulty did Leicester and the rest persuade her to return to St James's.

For the moment, the admirals who had scudded home knew nothing of this. They did not even know where the Armada had gone. Drake felt sure that it must have made for Norway or Denmark, and suggested that a responsible person should be sent to the King of Denmark to find out what was happening there. 'What the King of Spain's hot crowns will do in cold countries for mariners and men,' he wrote to Walsingham, 'I leave to your good Lordship, which can best judge thereof.' As for the Prince of Parma – Drake took him 'to be as a bear robbed of his whelps', and reported that the Spaniards had begun to hate him, 'their honour being touched so near'. No doubt Drake got this information from his conversations with Don Pedro de Valdez, and he told Walsingham that the Spaniards had 'nothing to say for themselves in excuse, but that they came to the place appointed, which was at Calais, and there stayed the Prince of Parma's coming above twenty-four hours, yea and until they were fired thence'.

By then gratifying news of Parma's discomfiture had begun to cross the Channel. Lord Willoughby, in command of the Queen's forces in the Low Countries, sent word that the mariners got together by the Duke for his invasion fleet 'refuse the service and are grown into a mutiny'. Parma had had ten or twelve of them executed as an example, but the rest were 'retired and dispersed, and refuse to serve in that sort'. Those who were recaptured cried out that the Duke had betrayed them.

This intelligence was confirmed, a few days later, by the arrival of a man from a village near Dunkirk, who reported that Parma had retired in haste from Bruges 'up into Brabant, as high as Brussels, fearing, as it was thought, some sudden revolt'. Sailors were deserting daily, the messenger said, and 'great dissension' had sprung up between the Spaniards and the Walloons, the Spaniards 'bitterly railing' against Parma in public, and the Walloons vainly demanding their pay, which they were told had been on board the Armada, now 'fearfully fled'.

All this encouraged Drake to feel that the danger had passed, and on 20 August he wrote to the Council:

> I protest to Your Lordships that my belief is that our most gracious Sovereign, her poor subjects and the Church of God hath opened the heavens in divers places and pierced the ears of our most merciful father, unto whom, in Christ Jesu, be all honour and glory. So be it; Amen, Amen.

By then the Armada was far beyond any hope of returning. On the day that Drake wrote his little paean, Medina Sidonia recorded that the fleet 'had doubled the last of the Scottish islands to the north', and with a north-east wind had set its course for Spain. Already the defeated force was in deep trouble. The gale that scattered the English fleet had dispersed them, too: for six days between the 13th and the 18th they sailed through squalls, rain, icy fog and such heavy seas that the crew of one ship could not see the next, and the Armada split up into separate groups. These came together again on the 19th, but that night the weather was so bad that the main body once more lost sight of Recalde and his squadron. By then, to save water, the surviving mules and horses had all been thrown overboard – and a few days later a German captain had the surreal experience of finding his ship surrounded by their floating bodies.

Whenever the state of the sea allowed it, Purser Calderon had been

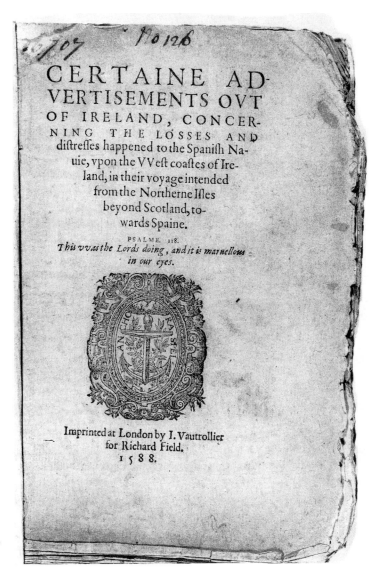

CERTAINE AD-
VERTISEMENTS OVT
OF IRELAND, CONCER-
NING THE LOSSES AND
diftreffes happened to the Spanifh Na-
uie, vpon the VVeft coaftes of Ireland, in their voyage intended
from the Northerne Ifles
beyond Scotland, to-
wards Spaine.

PSALME. 118.
*This vvas the Lords doing, and it is maruellous
in our eyes.*

Imprinted at London by I. Vautrollier
for Richard Field.
1588.

Broadsheet spreading news of
the destruction of the Armada.

distributing what he called 'the hospital delicacies and medicines which he had so carefully preserved in his artillery-pharmacy'. The first request for some came from the flagship, on which many men had fallen ill (almost certainly with food-poisoning). Calderon sent them some rice, 'which present was greatly esteemed', and the Duke begged him to do the same for all the ships that had been in the battle. Calderon was also able to supply Recalde with 'a quantity of delicacies'.

As the Armada headed north, Medina Sidonia had been compiling a diary of the campaign, for later presentation to the King. The document was very much in character – generous in its praise of those who had fought valiantly, sparing in criticism, and never seeking to blame others for the misfortunes that had befallen the fleet. It did not even censure Parma for his failure to appear. Only when the Duke recorded that he had sought advice from Don Francisco de Bobadilla on how to fight the flagship and take up position, and from Diego Flores de Valdes on the general management of the Armada, did he suggest that he had not made all the important decisions himself. Otherwise, he tacitly accepted responsibility for everything that had happened.

When he had brought the diary up to date, on 20 August, he wrote the King a letter which went off by hand of Don Baltazar de Zuniga in a fast despatch boat. The Duke gave his present position, calling urgently for supplies to be made ready at Corunna, and letting fall hints of how bad conditions on board had become. After an outline of the system of rationing, he added:

> Your Majesty may imagine what suffering this entails, in the midst of the discomfort of so long a voyage. We have consequently over 3,000 sick, without counting the wounded, who are numerous, on the fleet. God send us fair weather so that we may soon reach port, for upon that depends the salvation of this army and navy.

The Duke could have made more of the hardships the fleet was enduring. One of the worst was the cold, to which the crews – especially the Andalusians and men from Africa – were quite unaccustomed, and for which they had nothing like enough clothes. In rough weather, with the wind constantly driving spray into the ships, they were wet through and half-frozen all the time. On the pitiable amount of food to which they were reduced, it was inevitable that more of them died every day.

When the Duke wrote his letter, he was clearly still in control, both of himself and (more or less) of the Armada. But as the desperate voyage dragged on, he gradually succumbed to exhaustion and sickness, withdrawing into himself and, for most of the time, into his cabin, so that he made no attempt to hold the fleet together or to exert himself for the common safety. It sounds as if his behaviour was already becoming erratic by 24 August, when he summoned Calderon on board the *San Martin* and asked him what latitude they were in. When the Purser told him $58\frac{1}{2}$ degrees north (some 150 miles north-west of Cape Wrath), he did not believe it, but summoned both the pilot to whom he had offered the 2,000 ducats and Diego Flores – only to find that they confirmed Calderon's estimate.

Already the fleet was breaking up. The Duke asked Calderon if he had heard anything of Don Alonzo de Luzon, but no one had seen his ship for thirteen days. Nor could anyone say where the fourteen ships under the command of Recalde might be. Calderon could only suppose they had drifted further toward Iceland or the Faroes.

The Purser, supported by the pilot, urged that the Armada should give the west coast of Ireland a wide berth. Diego Flores opposed them, saying that they must go in to land and get fresh water; but for once the Duke over-ruled him and took the other two men's advice. The tragedy was that the Spanish ships were in too bad a state, their ability to hold a chosen course too shaky, and their Captain General too enfeebled, for the plan to be followed through.

In the south, meanwhile, rumours were running riot. Two cutters sent by Parma to chase the Armada could not find it, but when they returned to Dunkirk they reported that the fleets had fought a tremendous battle near Newcastle, in which the English had lost many ships. From Rouen – that rumour-factory – a spy wrote to Mendoza clothing this invention with seductive detail: the Spaniards had sunk twenty ships and captured twenty-six 'in perfectly good condition'. The rest of the English fleet had fled 'all in bits and without crews'. Other reports claimed that the Armada was at 'a very fertile Norwegian island', that Drake had been captured when he went alongside the galleass *San Lorenzo*, the same when he went alongside the *San Martin*, that he had had a leg shot off, that he had been wounded in the cheek, that the *Revenge* had been sunk and he had been forced to flee in a small boat, that 'the great sailor John Hawkins has also gone to the bottom, not a soul having been saved from his ship . . . The Queen has entered the field with 30,000 men in great alarm.'

The reality was very different, but not, for the English, much more comforting. Although Drake himself was sound in wind and limb, the optimism which he had voiced proved premature; for although the Armada had gone, the struggle against it left a terrible legacy in the form of an epidemic that inflicted on the English crews far more cruel ravages than anything the Spanish guns had managed to achieve. Howard had come into Margate Road on 18 August, but it seems that he did not land there until two days later – and then he wrote immediately to Burghley, appalled by what he had found:

> My Good Lord,
> Sickness and mortality begins wonderfully to grow amongst us; and it is a most pitiful sight to see, here at Margate, how the men, having no place to receive them into here, die in the streets.

Howard himself had been 'driven . . . of force' to come ashore and see them bestowed in lodgings. The best he could find were barns and outhouses, and, as he wrote, 'it would grieve a man's heart to see them that have served so valiantly to die so miserably'. One of the most wretched ships – once again – was the *Elizabeth Jonas*. In spite of thorough purgings, the infection had now broken out afresh 'in greater extremity than it ever did before', and men were dying 'faster than ever they did'. Howard realized that poor hygiene contributed to the risk of illness. Many of his men had been at sea for eight months on end, with almost no change of clothes in that time, and now he sent urgently for new hose, doublets, shirts and shoes, 'for else, in a very short time, I look to see most of the mariners go naked'. Yet he also believed that the infection on *Elizabeth Jonas* was lodged in the pitch used to caulk her seams; and neither he nor any of his fellow-officers – not even Drake, who had something of a reputation for his medical knowledge – realized that the cause of their distress was simply bad food. They did to some extent blame the beer, which had gone prematurely sour from being brewed with too few hops, but that was the only scapegoat they could think of.

Modern medical authorities agree that the epidemic which struck the English fleet was food-poisoning in its most virulent form, followed in most cases by rapid death from toxaemia. So powerless were the crews to resist it, so useless their surgeon-doctors, that by the end of the month Howard was writing to the Queen from Dover:

> My Most Gracious Lady,
> With great grief I must write unto you in what state I find your fleet in here. The infection is grown very great and in many ships, and now very dangerous; and those that come in fresh are soonest infected; they sicken the one day and die the next.

To the Council he reported that the ships had 'hardly men enough to weigh anchors', and that he had therefore decided to split the fleet in two, one half to ride in the Downs and the other at Gore End, so that he could bring as many sick men ashore as possible. By this means, he said, he could be ready for service within a day, if news should arrive that the Armada was on its way back. But he also had to report the 'great discontentments' of his crews, who had been expecting to receive their full pay, and were disgusted at being given only part of it.

In the middle of this crisis news came from Sir Edward Norris, who had been pursuing the Armada, that the Spaniards were definitely returning. How the rumour gained credence, it is no longer possible to say; but it could not have arrived at a worse moment. 'God knoweth what we shall do if we have no men', wrote Howard to Walsingham. Relief came at the beginning of September with the arrival of another message to say that on 18 August a fishing bark had seen a fleet of nearly 100 'monstrous ships' heading westwards between Orkney and Fair Isle, and that because the wind had remained in the south-east for seven days after that, there was no longer any chance of the Spaniards landing on the mainland of Scotland.

It was indeed a miracle that, in the felicitous phrase of Francis Bacon, the Armada, 'this great preparation', had 'passed away like a dream'; for by mid-September, when Hawkins sent Burghley a statement of losses, the *Triumph* had only 325 men out of her complement of 500, and the *Bear* 260 out of 500 – and this after both ships had been repeatedly re-manned. For the *Elizabeth Jonas*, whose complement should also have been 500, Hawkins was able to make no return at all, since every attempt to keep men alive in her had failed. Small wonder that he considered the fleet 'utterly unfitted and unmeet to follow any enterprise from hence' until it had been comprehensively re-fitted and renovated. The total number of deaths is not known, but it is certain that disease killed at least ten times as many men as had fallen victim to the guns of Spain.

Every ship in the fleet needed repairs of some sort; most were leaking through damaged or decayed timbers, and many had lost their boats. Yet the amount of serious damage inflicted by gunfire was extraordinarily small. The *Revenge*, belying her reputation as an unlucky ship, had come through the campaign without serious misfortune, but she had to have a new mainmast, the old one having been damaged by shot. The *White Bear* needed new mainmast, foremast, bowsprit, main yard, fore yard, spritsail yard and bonaventure mast, besides a new boat and a new pinnace. The *Triumph* had lost her long-boat at sea, and one of her silk ensigns had been carried off by Frobisher as a souvenir.

The strain of fighting, and then of countering disease and discontent, began to show among the officers. The fact that Howard had given Drake such a large share of responsibility – in the view of some historians he had almost surrendered command of the fleet to him – provoked Frobisher and Seymour to paroxysms of jealousy. Matthew Starke, one of the *Revenge*'s crew, swore he had heard Frobisher abusing Drake in Lord Sheffield's bedroom at Harwich, accusing him of cowardice and threatening that he would 'make him spend the best blood in his belly' if he did not hand over a fair share of the treasure which he had captured from the *Rosario*. Seymour wrote irritable, ironic letters to Walsingham and Burghley. Drake himself felt obliged to tell Walsingham, in his tortured, barely comprehensible style, that he and Howard had got on famously during the Armada campaign. It was perhaps an illustration of the difference in temperament between the adversaries that whereas the

Spaniards allowed personal rivalries to influence their actions during the battles, the English did at least manage to master theirs until afterwards, and therefore to fight more coherently.

Many a row broke out about money – either because the naval officers could not wring pay for their men out of the Council, or because of the labyrinthine bureaucracy with which the Government sought to control the disposition of captured assets. Hawkins complained vigorously to Burghley when accused of embezzling seamen's pay – 'I am sorry I do live so long to receive so sharp a letter from your Lordship' – and prayed that he would never have to handle pay again: 'God, I trust, will deliver me of it [the job] before long, for there is no other hell.' Howard, too, was incensed by suggestions that he had appropriated part of the treasure captured in the *Rosario* for himself, when in fact he had been forced to use the money to pay his men.

> I did take now, at my coming down, 3,000 pistolets, as I told you I would [he wrote to Walsingham]; for, by Jesus, I had not £3 besides in the world, and had not anything could get money in London; and I do assure you my plate was gone before.

It is sad to find no record of any kind that either Queen or Council showed gratitude to the men who had saved the nation. No doubt when Howard and Drake first returned to Court, Her Majesty had gracious words for them, and she bestowed fine presents on them at New Year. But no official gesture or message seems to have gone out to lesser mortals; and even the ultra-loyal Burghley could not suppress his irritation at the way in which the monarch blithely credited her infallible Leicester, who had done almost nothing, with repelling the entire attempted invasion.

Such was the State's thirst and need for money that even before anyone in London knew for sure where the Armada had gone, the Queen was demanding that Drake should again try to intercept the Spanish treasure fleets; and the taste of triumph was soured by realization that meanness had bungled the job. The naval officers all felt that if they had gone into the campaign with abundant stocks of powder and shot, instead of with miserable half-rations, they would have sent most of the Armada to the bottom. 'Our parsimony hath bereaved us of the famousest victory that ever our navy might have had at sea,' wrote Henry White to Walsingham; and Walsingham himself endorsed his verdict when he remarked: 'So our half-doing doth breed dishonour and leaves the disease uncured.'

Chapter Eighteen

Ireland

Once the English knew that the Armada has passed between Orkney and Shetland, they could be almost certain that it would come down the coast of Ireland on its way home to Spain; and it seems extraordinary that the Council did nothing to alert its far-flung garrison in the west to this possibility. But no official advice of the battles in the Channel was sent – indeed, not even any word that the Armada had passed up the Channel – and only confused reports filtering across from England or Scotland claimed that a huge Spanish fleet had been sent flying. Early in September the Lord Deputy (or Viceroy) Sir William Fitzwilliam wrote from Dublin Castle to tell Burghley that he had heard of the Spanish fleet's passage 'through the Narrow Seas', but he had no word about it from London, and on the 19th he sent a testy note saying that he had not 'of long time' received any news 'touching the Spanish attempts now on foot against Her Majesty and Her Dominions', and suggested that perhaps he should be kept informed of what was happening.

Thus when the first galleons loomed up out of the misty ocean off Donegal, Clare and Kerry, the defence forces assumed that an invasion was imminent. 'Whether they be of the dispersed fleet which are fled from the supposed overthrow in the Narrow Seas, or new forces come from Spain directly, no man is able to advertise otherwise than by guess,' reported Sir Richard Bingham, the Governor of Connaught, from Athlone on 18 September. But he inclined to think that the lack of specific information, and the fact that the ships had appeared from the west, 'doth rather show their coming from Spain'. A mass-landing by Spaniards in Ireland was what the English had long dreaded; and now that this very event was apparently about to happen, panic set in. When seven ships were sighted in the Shannon Estuary, the Mayor of Limerick instantly passed the figure on as seven score; and even Fitzwilliam, who had recently returned to Ireland for his second tour as Lord Deputy, so far lost his head as to describe twenty-four men who had landed at Tralee

The Gentleman of Ireland

The Gentlewoman of Ireland

The Civill Irish Woman

The Civill Irish man

The Wilde Irish man

The Wilde Irish Woman

Inhabitants of the west coast of Ireland, where many of the Armada ships were wrecked: from Speed's *Empire of Great Britain*. The long-haired 'wild Irish man', pictured bottom left, was a stock figure of fun in sixteenth-century theatrical productions.

222

as twenty-four galleons.

Ireland was then an exceedingly wild place, all bog, lough and mountain, whose people had, among the English, the reputation of being savages (a character 'dressed as an Irishman' was a staple figure of fun in theatrical productions). Although the country had been colonized by the English in the twelfth and thirteenth centuries, the invaders had never taken real control over most of it, their influence being confined to the Pale – the eastern counties round Dublin – and to a few fortified outposts. During Elizabeth's reign vigorous attempts had been made to bring more of the country in hand, and to impose on it an English form of constitution, headed by a Council under the Lord Deputy; yet the grip of the English remained precarious, and their efforts evoked nothing but hostility from most of the Irish chiefs, whose ancient clan structure did not adapt easily to foreign ideas, and who felt no ties of friendship, culture or social tradition with their overlords. A few had thrown in their lot with the English – or said they had; but almost all remained hostile and fiercely independent.

With Spain, on the other hand, Ireland had age-old connections. Trade between the two countries had flourished since mesolithic times, not least because the trade-winds gave ships an easy passage up from the south. The fishing-grounds off the west coast were such a strong attraction to Spanish trawlers that during 1572 no fewer than 600 of them were reported to be in action there. In return, the Spaniards brought thousands of gallons of wine, on the importation of which the prosperity of Galway was founded; and in several of the west coast ports – notably Galway, Limerick and Dingle – the Spaniards built themselves handsome, tall houses of stone, so that they had a permanent presence on the island. A further – and to the English of the Reformation very dangerous – link between the two countries was that the Irish were solidly Catholic, and at times of particular oppression would flee to the safe havens in the south. By the summer of 1588 the Bishops of Kildare, Limerick, Ross and Ossory had been exiled to Spain or Portugal, along with hundreds more of their countrymen, and it is thought that on board the Armada alone there were 200 Irishmen, including the Bishop of Killaloe.

For years the English had feared that King Philip or the Pope would finance or organize an invasion of the island – as had happened on a small scale in the summer of 1579. Then, the exiled Sir James Fitzgerald had landed at Dingle with a force of Spanish and Italian mercenaries backed by the Pope. The Earl of Desmond had rallied to his support, and by the winter the province of Munster was largely in rebel hands. Amphibious operations by the Government's forces led to the death of Fitzgerald and the fragmentation of resistance, but in September 1580 a draft of 800 reinforcements landed in the natural harbour of Smerwick on the Dingle peninsula. The attempt was disastrously bungled: trapped and besieged on the promontory of Dun an Oir, the invaders surrendered, only to be treacherously massacred.

On that occasion, eight years earlier, the English had eliminated the threat without much difficulty; but now, they thought, a far larger one was looming. At first they did not realize that the ships coming in from the west were *in extremis*, riddled with shot, battered by gales, their crews racked by wounds, disease, hunger and thirst. Far from being an organized invasion, their landfalls were entirely haphazard, determined in some cases by a pilot's sketchy knowledge of the coast, but usually by sheer force of weather. Like the summer, the autumn of 1588 was exceptionally wild; one big storm came in on the tail of the last, the worst of all being that which started on 20 September, and which caused most of the wrecks.

Some of the Spanish ships did not even manage to sail as far as the Irish coast. One such was the *El Gran Grifon*, the hulk under the command of Juan Gomez de Medina which had sustained seventy hits to her hull in the action off the Isle of Wight, when she fell behind on the seaward wing of the Armada. In spite of her damage, she managed to stay with the fleet all the way up the North Sea; but on or about 20 August she and three other ships parted company from the rest somewhere north of Shetland. The little group of four battled south-westwards into constant headwinds, their seams opening ever-wider under the stress of the big northern seas. On 1 September the hulk *Barca de Amburg* signalled that she was about to go down, and her company of 250 was taken off just in time. Three nights later the *Castillo Negro* (another hulk) vanished, never to be seen again. The *Grifon*'s last companion, *La Trinidad Valencera*, also disappeared, leaving her to struggle on alone.

Until 7 September she wallowed on to the south-west; but then she was hit by a ferocious storm, which was more than she could face. Weakened and half-waterlogged as she was, she would have gone down if she had crashed on into the waves. The only alternative was to run before the wind. This she did, flying first for three days to the north, then for three days to the south-west (heading, to the crew's great joy, for home), then inexorably back to the north-east, the ship being knocked about so violently that the crew were battered and exhausted, besides being desperately short of water. At last, by what seemed to them divine intervention, they reached Fair Isle, between Orkney and Shetland, on 27 September; and although their ship went down there, all 300 of the survivors managed to escape to Scotland.

Many months went by before they knew it, but they fared much

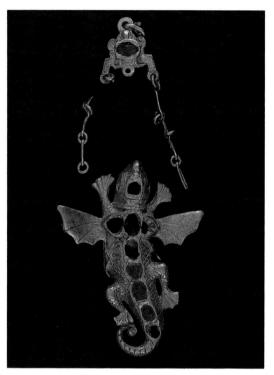

20. Jewellery recovered from the wreck of the galleass *Girona,* which sank with the loss of some 1,300 lives at dawn on 26 October 1588 off Lacada Point, Co. Antrim. *From left:* a gold salamander set with rubies; portrait cameo carved in lapis lazuli and mounted in gold; gold receptacle in the form of a book, which was found to contain *Agnus Dei* – pellets of wax and consecrated oil believed to have miraculous powers of protection.

These and many other finds – heavy guns, roundshot, navigational instruments, tableware – were salvaged from the site by Robert Sténuit and a team of divers in 1968 and 1969, and are now in the Ulster Museum.

21. *Following page:* Design for a tapestry commemorating the defeat of the Armada.

better than many of their compatriots in the main body of the fleet. Soon after he turned south to head for Spain, Medina Sidonia (as we have seen) issued orders that the Armada was to give Ireland a wide berth, and that no one was to go ashore without his express permission. It was a sound enough decision, and those captains who were able to follow it did not get into trouble on the Atlantic coast. The *San Martin*, for instance, never sighted Ireland at all, and Pedro Coco Calderon's hulk the *San Salvador* (which kept company with the flagship) stayed far enough out to avoid the only land the crew saw, which was an island, perhaps Achill or Innisbofin. By 14 September this group had laboured past the Blaskets – the westernmost point of Kerry – and were safely on their way home.

Yet about 60 of the ships – either because they became separated from the rest in one of the storms, or because their captains took a deliberate decision to go in search of water and food – did approach the coast, with terrible results. Even if they had been in good condition, they would still have been at very grave risk from the inaccuracy of their charts. These were probably based on the map of Ireland drawn by Ortelius, the Flemish cartographer and mathematician who had been appointed geographer to King Philip in 1575; and of their many deficiencies by far the most deadly was their misrepresentation of the shape of Sligo and Mayo. They gave the impression that the coast of these two counties ran roughly north and south, and altogether failed to show that it sticks out sixty miles due westward into the Atlantic, with Erris Head at its north-western point. The Spaniards were aware that they would have to round this headland – which was known to them as Cape Clear – but their charts were so misleading that many of them took Rosean Head, in Donegal, for their most westerly point, and thought that once they had doubled this landmark they were safe – whereas in fact they were only heading down into Donegal Bay. By the time they realized their mistake, they were trapped in the bay by the prevailing westerly winds. This one error alone led to the destruction of eight or nine ships.

The physical hazards of cliffs, rocks, tides and on-shore gales in any case made the western coast highly treacherous; what the Spaniards could not know was that, for political reasons, this part of Ireland, known as Connaught, was the most dangerous in which they could have landed, since it was ruled by a man who seemed to derive positive satisfaction from the slaughter of his enemies, whoever they might be at the time. Sir Richard Bingham had been a mercenary warrior all his life. He had fought for the Spaniards at Lepanto, and against them at Terceira. When first appointed Governor of Connaught in 1584 he had let loose such a reign of terror against the Irish that he soon became known as the Flail of Connaught. At a battle on the River Moy he made it his business to supervise the execution of over 1,000 women and children; and so fiendish did his behaviour become that the previous Lord Deputy, Perrott, sent him in disgrace to the Netherlands. Soon, however, he was back, reinstated and if anything more bloodthirsty than before.

To a killer of this stamp, and indeed to his ageing superior Fitzwilliam, the arrival on the Irish coast of thousands of the Queen's enemies seemed literally a God-given occasion for further slaughter, a divine licence to murder. 'Since it hath pleased God by his hand upon these rocks to drown the greater and better sort of them,' wrote the Lord Deputy to the Privy Council in London, 'I will, with His favour, be His soldier for the despatching of those rags which yet remain.' Later he reported with satisfaction to Burghley that 'God hath fought by shipwrecks, savages and famine for Her Majesty against these proud Spaniards.'

Bingham scarcely needed the authority of the Lord Deputy's edict, which appointed him 'to take all hulls of ships, treasures, etc., into your hands, and to apprehend and execute all Spaniards of what quality soever'. One feels that he would have gone ahead anyway. It was entirely in character that, to intimidate the locals, he put out a proclamation announcing that all Spanish prisoners must be handed over to the authorities within four hours of capture, on pain of death.

Thus, though they could not know it, the Spaniards who crawled ashore from wrecks anywhere within reach of Bingham's stronghold in Galway were coming to almost certain extinction, and only those whom providence landed farther afield, in areas beyond the range of his troops, stood much chance of escape. No matter that they might give themselves up, without resistance, and have no aggressive intentions: they were the Queen's enemies, and that was that.

Clearly the English believed that there were compelling practical reasons for killing all their prisoners. There was no space to keep them in gaol, and by their sheer numbers the Spaniards could have constituted a threat, especially if the Irish had had the guts to help them; yet even now, 400 years later, it is impossible to feel anything but guilt and horror over the massacres that ensued. The natives were by no means blameless: having long looked for the coming of the Spaniards as their best chance of escape from English tyranny, the Irish succumbed – when the moment arrived – to their own rapacity, and instead of welcoming the castaways, stripped them of valuables and clothes and left them to their fate. Some even joined in the official slaughter – and none more enthusiastically than the giant Melaghlin McCabbe, who was said to have killed eighty Spaniards with his gallowglass axe. Only a very few of the Irish gave the castaways active help. In their defence it can be argued that they were intimidated by the threats and presence of the English; but even so their behaviour remains such as to make their descendants squirm.

Easily the most vivid account of what it was like to come ashore in that hostile environment was written by Captain Francisco de Cuellar. Having narrowly avoided death by hanging in the North Sea, he now had a second and even more miraculous escape, which he afterwards described in a long narrative.

The *Lavia* (on which he had been since his arraignment) successfully rounded Erris Head, but then, after riding at anchor for five days, was blown ashore by a tremendous storm on to Streedagh Strand, north of Sligo. Two other ships were swept in with her; on the gently-shelving beach, hemmed in on either side by rocks, they grounded some way from the shore, and within the space of an hour all three had been smashed to pieces by the waves. It was, Cuellar reported, 'a most terrible spectacle'. More than 1,000 men were drowned, and fewer than 300 reached the shore. There, hungrily awaiting the survivors, was a crowd of local people who had been gathering for days, drawn by the sight of the ships off the coast:

> The land and beach were full of our enemies, who were going about skipping and dancing for joy at our misfortune. Whenever any of our men reached land, 200 savages and other enemies rushed upon them and stripped them of everything they wore, leaving them stark naked, and without any pity beat and ill-used them.

Clinging to the wreck, unable to swim and wondering how best to save himself, Cuellar saw a great number of his comrades die before he himself reached land. Most of the Spaniards were non-swimmers, and many succumbed to the sheer weight of gold sewn into their clothes, or slung about their necks in chains, which dragged them under water as they floundered towards the shore. Others, in desperation, flung their chains and money into the sea before they set out. None perished more pitiably than Cuellar's companion Don Diego Enriquez, who with several others climbed down into a small tender, taking 16,000 ducats' worth of jewels and gold crowns with him, and had the hatch caulked down over his head in the hope that he would float ashore safely. Immediately, however, seventy other men flung themselves on top of the little craft, making it top heavy, and inevitably it overturned on its way to the beach, where it lay upside-down for a day and a half:

> By this mishap the gentlemen who got in under the little deck perished within . . . [At last] some savages came to it and rolled it over in order to take out some nails and bits of iron, and breaking the deck they took out the dead men. Don Diego Enriquez breathed his last in their hands. They

stripped him and took the jewels and money that were there, letting the bodies lie without burial.

In the end Cuellar climbed on to a wooden hatch-cover the size of a table, accompanied by the Judge Advocate. When a huge wave sent them under, Cuellar clung on, but his companion was so weighed down by gold crowns sewed into his doublet and hose that he sank, crying aloud to God as he drowned. Cuellar was washed ashore, 'praying to our lady of Ontanar' (apparently a shrine near his home in Segovia), bleeding, exhausted and unable to stand because his legs had been crushed against a baulk of timber. He was wearing a gold chain worth more than 1,000 reals, and in his doublet had forty-five gold pieces (two months' pay) which had been given him at Corunna; but, perhaps because he looked so wretched, the natives left him alone, and in the evening someone took pity on him to the extent of covering him with rushes to keep him warm. By then there were more than 600 corpses on the beach, and already crows and wolves had begun to feed on them.

Recovering a little during the night, he set off in search of a monastery which he had somehow heard was nearby; but there he was greeted by a sight no less grotesque than the one he had left on the shore. The buildings were in ruins, and the bodies of twelve Spaniards hung in the church, 'dangling from the iron grates within the church windows'.

Moving on, Cuellar was stripped of his money and clothes, but also given some milk and oatcakes, and went on his way naked except for a bit of mat and some fronds of bracken. For a while he was held captive by a blacksmith, who made him work as a slave, and he was never safe until he reached the territory of the man whom he called 'Manglana' and described as 'a very brave soldier'. This was Dartry MacClancy, whose burning hatred of the English made him one of Bingham's most tiresome enemies, and who sheltered many Spaniards in his castle Rossclogher, at the end of a promontory which stuck out half a mile from the south shore of Lough Melvin, before sending them on along a chain of safe-houses towards the north-east. With this splendid wild chieftain Cuellar spent three months, and the Spaniard left some memorable pictures of him and the other 'savages' among whom he sheltered. They liked the Spaniards well, he reported, because they knew 'we had come to fight the heretics and were their deadly enemies', but their habits tended to be primitive:

The nature of these savages is to live like beasts among the mountains . . . in huts made of straw. The men have big bodies, their features and limbs are well made, and they are agile as deer. . . . They wear their hair down to their eyes. They are good walkers, and have great endurance.

The main pastime of the Irish, Cuellar reported, was robbing one another. He described them as constantly at war with the English garrison, and recorded how, when pressed, they abandoned their homes and took to the hills with their women and cattle. In this he knew what he was talking about, for during his sojourn with MacClancy the chief did that very thing, leaving his Spanish guest in the castle when a contingent of English arrived. From the shore of the lough half a mile away, the Government force did all it could to scare the defenders out – among other things hanging two Spaniards in their view. But in the end the English were forced to retreat by prodigious falls of snow, and Mac-Clancy returned so delighted that he pressed upon Cuellar the offer of his sister in marriage. That was too much. The Spaniard felt it was time to leave, and he escaped first to Antrim, then to Scotland, and finally to Flanders, which he reached in October 1589. There he yet again had extraordinary luck, for the ship that brought him and 270 other Spaniards from the north was ambushed by a Dutch vessel at the bar of Dunkirk harbour. Many of the passengers were killed, and Cuellar reached the shore half-drowned, wearing nothing but a shirt.

Only a small proportion of his countrymen were as fortunate, for the great majority of those who did not drown in Ireland were executed, if not the moment they came ashore, then within a few days of landing. One of the first ships to be wrecked was the 1,100-ton carrack *Trinidad Valencera*, which had accompanied the *Gran Grifon* for as long as she could, but grounded on a reef of the Inishowen Peninsula in Glenagivney Bay, Co. Donegal, on 14 or 15 September. After lying there for a day or two, she broke her back and was smashed to pieces. The military commander Don Alonso de Luzon got ashore safely, and made herculean efforts to ensure the safety of his survivors, buying ponies for them to eat, making contact with a local bishop, and parleying with the Government troops, who here happened to be Irish; but after a skirmish that lasted all night, he was tricked by perfidious guarantees of safe conduct into ordering his men to hand over their arms – whereupon they were stripped naked, compelled to spend a night in the open, and then, the next morning, massacred by lance and bullet in the middle of a field. Some 300 died, and 150 fled across country, many of them wounded. Of the survivors about 100 eventually escaped to Scotland. Don Alonso and a handful of officers – spared because of their potential ransom value – were marched a hundred miles to Drogheda and there interrogated, but several (including Don Alonso's younger brother) died on the way, and only two – Alonso and one other – seem to have survived.

Even this disgraceful episode, ghastly as it was, seems less cold-blooded than the murders which took place in Galway. When the 300-ton hulk *Falcon Blanco* was wrecked on a reef in the entrance to Ballynakill Harbour, there were no English troops in the immediate area, and the survivors – who included Don Luis de Cordoba and his cousin Don Gonzalo de Cordoba – were at first given shelter by local people. But then they were handed over to the English troops in Galway, where the gaol was already packed with other castaways.

Bingham himself came from Athlone with a warrant to put the whole lot to the sword; and after setting aside fifty 'of the better sort' (including the two Cordobas) as ransom subjects, he did just that. At St Augustine's monastery, on the hill outside the town, he supervised the butchery of 300 men. The only two who escaped were smuggled out to the Aran Islands. The people of Galway, appalled by what had happened, waited until the troops had gone, and then came out to make shrouds and help bury the dead. Later the Pope sent them his forgiveness, but, in the words of a modern historian, Niall Fallon, 'even this failed to erase the memory of a terrible day in the city's history. Spanish fishermen still come to kneel in prayer at the mass grave of the Armada men.' Nor did most of the fifty men saved for ransom escape. When Fitzwilliam heard that Bingham had spared them, he furiously denounced him for disobeying orders, and all were put to the sword except the Cordobas, who were eventually ransomed.

Another vessel thought to have been wrecked in the same gale as finished the *Falcon* was the 1,100-ton *El Grangrin*, vice-flagship of the Biscayan squadron, which was swept on to the rocks of Clare Island, south of Achill Island, in the middle of the entrance to Clew Bay. Of her complement of 300, nearly two-thirds were drowned in the wreck, and the 100-odd who struggled on to the island, though first spared by men of the O'Malley clan, were later massacred when they tried to escape to the mainland.

No one fought harder for survival than the flaxen-haired Don Alonso de Leyva, who was to have taken over command of the Armada if Medina Sidonia had been killed, and on whom such high hopes had rested. The *Rata Encoronada* had been severely damaged at Gravelines, and the gales she met during the north-about passage weakened her so much more that on about 18 September her crew decided they must head in to the Irish coast. But she had one major advantage over other ships, in that, besides the young noblemen and their servants, and several Irish clerics including the Bishop of Killaloe, she carried a pilot who knew the coast. She was thus able to keep clear of Erris Head and find her way safely to Blacksod Bay, some twenty miles further south. As she came in, the crew had to bury at sea the body of Maurice Fitzgerald (the exiled son of James Fitzmaurice Fitzgerald) who 'was cast into the sea in a fair cypress chest with great solemnity before Torane'.

A party of fifteen, sent ashore to reconnoitre, did not last long: the men were captured by locals, stripped of their clothes, handed over to the English and executed at Galway. But next day, when the ship was blown ashore on to the shelving beach of Fahy, at Ballicroy, by the great gale of 20 September, the whole of the rest of the crew got ashore and fortified themselves in Doona Castle.

For the first time a sizeable force, consisting of perhaps 700 well-armed men, had gained a foothold in Ireland. News of its presence flew quickly to Bingham, but he, luckily for Leyva, was already so extended by calls for assistance from up and down the coast that he could not take any immediate action. No doubt he feared, or at any rate pretended, that the Spaniards were bent on aggression; but in fact their only motive was to escape, and after they had joined forces with the crew of the *Duquesa Santa Ana*, which had also anchored in the bay, they all piled on to the 900-ton hulk and sailed out again, hoping to reach Scotland.

With 1,000 men on board – nearly three times her normal complement – the ship was grossly overcrowded. At the first attempt to put out, she was driven back by the wind, but then managed to sail clear of the coast of Mayo and ran back to the north-east. She had not gone far, however, before she was caught by another westerly gale, and wrecked in Loughros More Bay, Donegal. Leyva was injured, having his leg crushed against the capstan so badly that he could not walk or ride, and had to be carried ashore.

Now, at least, the refugees were among people inclined to help them, for this time they had landed in Tirconnell, one of the last strongholds of the Gaelic chieftains Hugh Manus O'Donnell and McSweeney ne Doe, who had held out against the English more vigorously than their southern neighbours. It was bad luck for the Spaniards that both chiefs' freedom of action was at that moment severely circumscribed: Perrott, the former Lord Deputy, had managed to kidnap O'Donnell's son and one of the McSweeneys, both of whom were held hostage in Dublin, so that the chiefs were not able to give much overt help. Yet over the next nine days, which the Spaniards spent in and around the ruins of a castle on the island in Kiltoorlish Lake, McSweeney did send them food. Again, rumour inflated their presence into a threat to the whole English presence in Ireland: a huge force of Irish and Spanish was said to be marching south, and Fitzwilliam called urgently for reinforcements to be sent over from the mainland.

Nothing could have been farther from Leyva's thoughts than aggression; and when he heard that there were three Spanish ships in the harbour at Killybegs, twenty miles over the mountains to the south, he at once set out to join them, having himself carried in a litter by four of his men. On the south side of the peninsula a disappointment greeted him,

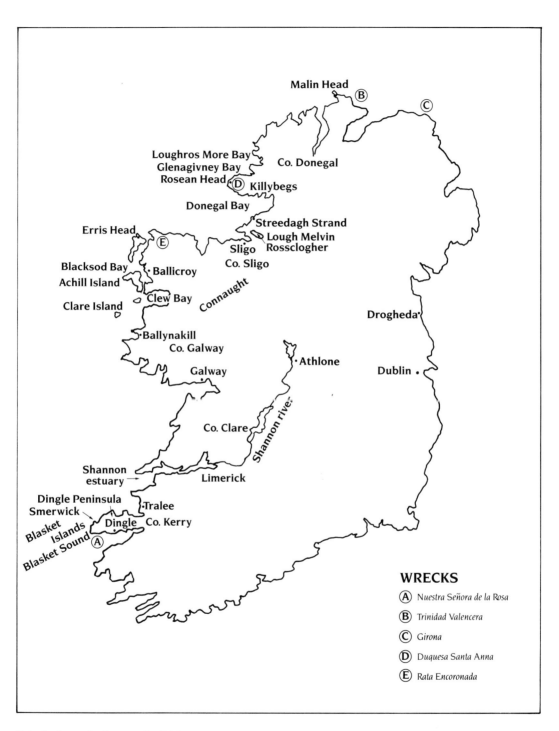

Principal wreck sites on the Irish coast.
(At least fifteen more have been identified)

for he found that only one ship – the galleass *Girona* – had survived; but at least she could be made seaworthy with timbers from one of the vessels that had sunk. While they were patching her up, the crew took out most of her big guns so that she would be able to carry the greatest possible number of men.

By now the combined force of Spaniards was 1,500 strong, and McSweeney ne Doe's neighbour McSweeney Bannagh had trouble feeding so large a number. He was therefore relieved when, on 26 October, they crammed 1,300 of their men on board the *Girona* – leaving behind 200 for whom there was no space – and sailed out on the falling tide, hoping once more to reach Scotland.

Again fate seemed to smile on them, only to turn vicious a few hours later. Having run easily before a west wind past Malin Head (the most northerly point of Ireland), the galleass was caught by a rising gale which went round to the north, blew her inshore, broke her makeshift rudder and smashed her on the coast of Antrim, near the Giant's Causeway. Just after midnight on 26–27 October she struck the rocks off Lacada Point broadside on. She may have turned right over with the impact; in any case she broke up within a few minutes, and all but nine of the 1,300 men aboard were drowned or battered to death in the raging darkness. So, in their third shipwreck, Leyva and his young followers at last were swept to their doom.*

Meanwhile, in the south-west, another of the Spanish leaders, the gallant old Recalde, had come perilously close to extinction in his galleon the *San Juan de Portugal*. Almost alone of his compatriots in the fleet, Recalde had been to Ireland before, for he had escorted the papal reinforcements which had landed at Smerwick in 1580. Now he returned to the area he remembered well, forced in by desperate shortage of water and food.

In company with the galleon *San Juan Bautista*, he anchored in Blasket Sound, some eight miles south of Smerwick, and managed to take on water; but on 21 September a storm came in with such violence that the flagship dragged her anchor and drifted down to collide with her neighbour. As the crews struggled to disentangle their vessels, yet another ship appeared – the *Nuestra Señora de la Rosa*, vice-flagship of Oquendo's squadron, fleeing in dire trouble before the storm, with her sails in tatters. Although she managed to heave-to, her single anchor could not hold her when the tide began to ebb from the sound, and she started to drift dangerously with the race. One of her officers, crazed with fear, drew his sword and ran the Genoese pilot through, 'saying he had done it by treason'. But it was the sea, rather than human failure, which

*The remains of the wreck were discovered in 1967 by the Belgian nautical archaeologist Robert Sténuit, who returned with a diving team in 1968 and 1969, and recovered a great number of items, including gold coins, chains and buttons, jewellery, silver forks, bronze cannons and cannon-balls of stone and iron. The finds are now in the Ulster Museum in Belfast.

finished the vessel. Striking a submarine pinnacle of rock not shown on any map, she effectively disembowelled herself, and sank with terrible speed – a disaster witnessed by Marcos de Aramburu, captain of the *San Juan Bautista*:

> In an instant we saw that she was going to the bottom, trying to hoist the foresail, and immediately she went down with the whole crew, not a soul escaping – a most extraordinary and terrible occurrence.

In fact one man did escape – a young Italian called Giovanni, son of the pilot, who was washed ashore on a board and greatly excited the English by telling them that among the men drowned had been the Prince of Ascoli, whom he described as having worn white doublet and breeches and russet silk stockings. This slender young man, with hair 'of an acorn colour brushed upwards', and very little beard, sounds a striking figure; he had come aboard at Calais, but who he was – or whether he was invented under pressure by Giovanni, who was interrogated three times – will never be clear. The Prince of Ascoli (as already recorded) had been left stranded in Dunkirk; but the English did not know that, and now word went out that the bastard son of the King was drowned.

Of course, the man whom the English most hoped to capture and ransom was the Duke of Medina Sidonia. Rumours spread that he had been lost 'in the great ship off Torane', and then that he had been 'in the great ship which received 600 from land at Ballicroy', which the English thought must certainly have sunk, as the weather had been atrocious and the ship 'marvellously pestered with such numbers of men'. (They were confusing Medina Sidonia with Leyva.) Yet still there was a chance that the Captain General of the Ocean Sea might come ashore, and against that event the Earl of Ormonde sent out instructions that if he did, he was 'to be kept without irons' and to be given his own horse to ride.

Having witnessed the destruction of the *Nuestra Señora de la Rosa*, Recalde managed to put to sea again, and continued his journey south, although he himself was crippled by sciatica, and his company was in a parlous state. According to Emanuel Fremoso, a Portuguese who had landed from the *San Juan* and been captured, at least 100 of the crew were 'very sick, and do lie down and die daily', and the coxswain 'very sad and weak'.

As they sailed away, an appalling number of their countrymen lay dead along the Irish coast. Writing to Burghley at the end of October, Sir Geoffrey Fenton described how during a recent visit to Sligo he had 'numbered in one strand of less than five miles in length above 1,100 dead corpses of men which the sea had driven upon the shore', and how local people told him that other beaches were similarly strewn with bodies, although not in quite such numbers. It will never be known exactly how many Spaniards were drowned off and on the coast, or murdered in Ireland, but at least seventeen ships were wrecked on the coast, and the number of dead certainly exceeded 6,000.

The English, though profoundly relieved, were staggered by the scale of the disaster. When the Lord Deputy went on a tour of the north in December, he was obviously shaken by the sights he saw. The bodies had gone from the beaches by then, but as he rode along the shore he passed a mass of timber from wrecked ships, 'more than would have built five of the greatest ships that ever I saw, besides mighty great boats, cables and other cordage answerable thereunto, and some such masts for bigness and length as, in my own judgement, I never saw any two could make the like'.

To Fitzwilliam, it was a miracle that God had overthrown 'those that fight against His Church and Her Majesty', and Bingham echoed his verdict, giving thanks for 'the wonderful handiwork of Almighty God', who 'hath drowned the remains of that mighty army . . . by great and horrible shipwrecks'. For the English, the chief annoyance was that so many valuable big guns had been lost with the wrecks, and that so much treasure had been carried off by 'unworthy persons', from whom, as experience showed only too clearly, it would never be recovered.

'Pray consider the distress of this Armada after so terrible a voyage, and the urgent need for prompt measures of relief,' wrote Medina Sidonia to the King on 3 September. The *San Martin* was then still in 58 degrees north latitude, west of the Outer Hebrides, north-west of St Kilda. Already the Duke was prostrate in his cabin with fever and dysentery; his men were dying every day. Yet almost three more weeks went by before at last he sighted Spain.

Until the 18th, in latitude 45, he still had sixty ships in company; but then a great storm scattered them, and after it only eleven were left in sight. In this small company they sailed grimly on until at last, on the 21st, they sighted land, which was said to be the island of Cizarga, only twenty miles from Corunna; but at the last moment they realized they were near Santander, more than 250 miles to the east, and they had to enlist the help of some small local craft to pull them clear of the coast before they anchored off Point Enoja. Almost two months to the day since they had left Corunna, the survivors returned to Spain.

The Duke felt so ill that he did not even wait for the ship to come into harbour, but went ashore leaving Diego Flores in charge. 'The troubles and miseries we have suffered cannot be described to Your Majesty,' he wrote in a pathetic letter to the King, begging for fresh supplies and for leave to lay down his command. His ship alone had lost 180 men to disease, and everyone else on board was ill. Three of the four pilots were dead. Of the sixty personal servants with whom he started out, only two were left. He himself was 'in no condition to attend to business of any sort', having come back 'almost at my last gasp'.

Even before he knew about the appalling loss of life in Ireland, he was utterly defeated. The strain of the voyage had turned his hair prematurely grey, and as soon as he had been humanely released by the King from any obligation to present himself at Court, he set off for San Lucar, his home in the south, through a country plunged into mourning. He travelled in a closed litter to avoid recognition, but was plagued nevertheless in the towns through which he passed, such as Medina del Campo and Salamanca, by boys shouting insults and throwing stones. 'Hey, coward – to the tunny fishery!' they cried, and, in one place, 'Look out – Drake's coming!' All over Spain he was execrated as the cause of the disaster, and the historian C. Fernandez Duro recorded how Father Juan de Victoria collected complaints about him from 'generals, field-marshals, captains, ministers, soldiers', all of whom agreed that he had 'lost the honour, reputation and fame of Spain and of his own person and house as well, being cowardly and always dreading dying'. This verdict – as the narrative should have shown – was far from just; but the Spaniards could not know that the two men they ought to have blamed were Parma and the King.

Recalde also reached Spain, sailing into Corunna in his galleon, accompanied by two pinnaces, but he was broken in body and soul, and died within ten days of arriving. Oquendo was the same: although he reached the port of Pasajes, at San Sebastian, he was so overcome with grief and mortification that he refused to see any of his family – even his wife and children – and died six days later, on 2 October. A letter poignantly records the Spaniards' great joy at being back in their own warm sunshine, at the sight of grapes against a white wall, and the taste of fresh bread; but for many of them the relief was too late.

In a quirk of historical repetition – for it was Oquendo's vice-flagship the *San Salvador* which had blown up in the Channel – the ship in which he had come home exploded in harbour at Pasajes. According to Douro, it blew up with such a fantastic report that much of it was hurled into the air – as was half the crew. A negro servant of Oquendo's flew 'the distance of a harquebus-shot' and landed on a scrub-covered mountain, from which he descended two days later, deafened and terrified. It is thought that the accident killed about 130 men.

In all only fifty-four ships returned to Spain, out of 130, and losses were estimated by Duro at between 8,000 and 9,000 men. Much has been made of the superhuman self-control and imperturbability with which

Philip received news of the catastrophe; but the stories that he merely praised God and went on writing are almost certainly apocryphal. It is far more likely that the scale of the disaster was borne in on him only by degrees, and that weeks went by before its impact fully sank in. Moreover, there is evidence that the King did feel the setbacks deeply. 'This war moves him,' reported Hieronimo Lippomano, the Venetian ambassador in Madrid, on 6 September. 'He lives very retired and gives audience to no one.' He certainly did all he could to relieve the suffering of bereaved families, with pensions and grants; and with the one exception of Don Diego Flores de Valdes, who was briefly incarcerated at Burgos, he seems to have blamed no one. On 13 October he wrote to all the bishops and archbishops of his dominions saying that he himself had given thanks to God for His mercy in allowing so many of the Armada to reach home, and that the disaster would have been greater but for the prayers which had been offered up 'so devoutly and continuously' on the Armada's behalf.

For ordinary people the truth was made even harder to swallow by the rumours of Spanish success that had been let loose by Mendoza. These spread right through Europe. On 27 August the Senate of Venice voted to send the Spanish ambassador a minute recording: 'From many quarters we hear of the success of the Armada, and we rejoice. We order you to offer our congratulations to His Majesty.' The message was endorsed by a huge majority: Ayes – 186, Noes – 1, Doubtful – 1. Edmund Palmer, an English merchant, reported to Walsingham how he had happened to be present when letters were read out in San Sebastian announcing that Howard and Drake had been captured, Plymouth, Portsmouth and the Isle of Wight all taken, and the invaders 'thought in a few days to be in London'.

> As they did read, some said of me, 'See how the dog looks at the news' . . . The town made great feasts all that day, running through the streets on horseback, with rich apparel and vizards on their faces, crying with loud voices, 'That great dog Francis Drake is a prisoner, with chains and fetters'; and at night the town was made full of bonfires, with other their dances accustomed, reviling at Her Majesty with villainous words, and when they could not do any more, with stones they brake down all the windows of my house.

Disillusionment, when it came, was shattering – particularly the news that Drake was still at large. Palmer vividly described another incident, a few weeks after the first. 'I would yon man were Francis Drake,' said a Spaniard, snatching up a harquebus which he did not realize was loaded, and pointing it at a passer-by. 'How I would hit him!' he cried –

> and so drew up the snapchance and levelled at the man, and
> down fell the cock and off went the piece and killed the man,
> who spake not one word.

Chapter Nineteen

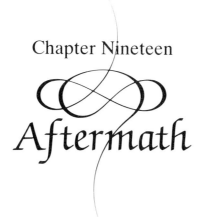

Aftermath

In England the defeat of the Spanish Armada was greeted with immense relief and signalled with prolonged celebrations, among them two services of thanksgiving at St Paul's. For the first, in September, captured Spanish banners were exhibited (as Stow described it) 'on the lower battlements' of the church, and one streamer, 'wherein was an image of our Lady with her son in her arms', was 'held in a man's hand over the pulpit'. The second service was attended by the Queen, who came to St Paul's in a grand procession, riding in 'a chariot-throne made with four pillars, behind to have a canopy, on top whereof was a Crown Imperial, and two pillars before, whereon stood a lion and a dragon, supporters of the arms of England, drawn by two white horses'. In general there was a feeling that God had given His verdict in favour of England and Protestantism. Elizabeth herself composed a song, or hymn of thanks to God, which was sung before her at St Paul's in December ('He made the winds and waters rise/ To scatter all mine enemies'); she also sat for a commemorative portrait, and ordered the minting of a silver medal which bore her profile on one side, a ship at sea on the other, and the legend, *Afflavit Deus et dissipati sunt* (God blew, and they were scattered).

Yet soon it began to seem that the victory, momentous as it was, had changed very little. It did not even end the war with Spain. Far from it: the English, flexing their new-found muscles, threw themselves into the struggle with greater vigour than before. For some months they argued about how best to exploit their supremacy at sea. Hawkins wanted to blockade the coast of Spain and drive the country to bankruptcy by cutting off her silver imports. Drake favoured an attack on Lisbon, designed to spark off rebellion in Portugal. In the end the second course was chosen, and in April 1589 a fleet carrying 20,000 men set out; but, apart from the capture of Vigo, the expedition was a fiasco . . . So the war continued, sputtering on and off inconclusively for another fifteen years.

All the same, when seen in a more distant perspective, the victory of 1588 clearly had positive results. Most obviously, it ensured that England remained Protestant, not merely for the time being, but for centuries to come. The English Catholics, who had waited and watched to see what the outcome of the struggle would be, accepted what seemed a divine verdict and transformed themselves into moderate Anglo-Catholics or High Churchmen. The wavering James VI of Scotland also accepted the verdict, and by remaining Protestant thereafter made sure of his own smooth accession to the throne of England, on Elizabeth's death, as James I. Across the Channel, the defeat of the Armada put new heart into the Protestant cause: it made certain that Philip never recovered his lost provinces in the Netherlands, and in effect broke the back of Spain. In France, it eventually brought Henry of Navarre to the throne.

Had the struggle gone the other way, things would have been profoundly different. If the Armada had defeated the English fleet in the Channel, if Parma had performed as he should have and landed in Kent, if his army had marched to London, if he had captured the capital and the Queen, installed the Infanta in her stead, and forced the country to return to Catholicism . . . the imagination runs riot at the conceivable consequences.

The political and religious history of much of Europe would certainly have taken a different direction, at least for the time being. A wider-reaching possibility is that the whole of North America would now be Spanish- rather than English-speaking; for the English efforts to plant colonies in the New World, which Raleigh had started in 1584 with an expedition to explore the territory that he named Virginia, and continued in the 1590s, would surely have been taken over by the conquerors. At home, the budding genius of William Shakespeare – whose Sonnet 107, 'The Mortal Moon', was almost certainly written in 1589 to commemorate the crescent-Armada's eclipse – might have been suppressed, or at least diverted from the career that brought forth such incomparable literary riches.

Fantasies apart, fate dealt the leaders of 1588 a wide variety of hands. Leicester lasted the shortest time of all, falling ill and dying at Rycote, in Oxfordshire, on his way to take the waters at Buxton, in September 1588, the very hour of victory. The Queen, who had wanted to make him her Viceroy, was distraught, and for years kept his last letter by her bed.

Drake also met an untimely end, dying of dysentery and being buried at sea near Nombre de Dios, in the West Indies, in 1595, when he was barely 50. His name and achievement, however, have survived so triumphantly that he is scarcely less famous in 1988 than he was 400 years earlier.

No premature death claimed Howard, who, after the capture of

Cadiz in 1596 was created Earl of Nottingham in recognition of his outstanding service, and remained Lord High Admiral well into the reign of James I. In 1619 he resigned at the age of 83, but retained, by special patent, the precedence which his post had given him. He died aged 87, in possession of all his faculties, not very wealthy (according to Fuller) but having kept seven houses in full operation.

Immediately after the Armada battles he commissioned the Italian journalist–historian Petruccio Ubaldini to write an account of the campaign. This was published in the winter of 1588–89 as an Official Relation of the proceedings; but Drake evidently objected to it on the grounds that it glorified the Lord Admiral excessively, at his own expense, and a second edition, published in August 1589, presented a more comprehensive and balanced version, including material contributed by Drake himself. Howard also commissioned from Cornelis de Vroom a series of tapestries depicting various stages of the action. These were later sold to King James, who presented them to the House of Lords, where they were destroyed by a fire in 1834 – but not before engravings of them had been made by John Pine.

Like Howard, some of the ships which took part in the campaign enjoyed remarkable longevity. Drake's flagship the *Revenge* was sunk by Spanish guns in the Azores in 1593, though only after she had won undying glory under the command of Sir Richard Grenville in a battle made immortal by Tennyson and others. But the old *Elizabeth Bonaventure* was not broken up until 1610, after more than fifty years' service, and the *Victory* survived until 1608.

The Duke of Medina Sidonia also served on for many years. Whatever feelings of personal humiliation he may have suffered, he was never publicly censured or demoted, and continued to act as Captain General of the Ocean Sea until his death – probably in 1611, after which the post passed to his son. To the end, his association with any major naval or military undertaking remained unfalteringly disastrous. When the English raided Cadiz in 1596, he was again in charge of the defence, and again managed to be absent at the critical moment, as he had in 1587. As Froude cuttingly remarked, 'he ventured back only after the English had gone, and was again thanked by his master for his zeal and courage'.

Philip himself died a terrible death – no less fearful, one feels, than that suffered by St Lawrence on the gridiron, whose upturned legs the corner towers of the Escorial represented. In 1598, at the age of 71, having seen almost all his own grand projects disintegrate, and his country brought to the verge of bankruptcy, the King found his own body beginning to rot. Malignant tumours broke out all over it, and the pain became so excruciating that he could not bear even the touch of cloth. For the last fifty-three days before his death on 12 September he lay without a proper wash or a change of garments; but he died gazing at a crucifix, with his faith unbroken, and was buried in a coffin made of wood from a galleon which appropriately enough had fought against the English.

Elizabeth's end, though more merciful, was also wretched, for she had been grievously hurt by the treachery of her latest favourite, the Earl of Essex, who was executed for treason in 1601, and she died two years later in loneliness and misery. In spite of the triumph over the Armada, and although she outlived her arch-enemy Philip, she never again knew peace with Spain.

She could not see the events of her reign with the detachment that we can now employ; but it is clear to us that 1588 did, as the prophets had expected, turn out to be a climacterial. For the English, however, it did not bring the disasters presaged; rather, it was a year of new hope, of fresh vigour and confidence – and such was the sense of escape that in 1601, when John Chamber published a treatise against astrology, he suggested that all of that trade should have '88' branded on their fore-heads, 'that when they meet they might laugh at one another, as did the Aruspices in old time'. But, he went on,

> Howsoever they might laugh, it was no laughing matter to the Catholic King and his invincible navy, who will be famous for that exploit till '88 come again.

Four centuries later, the exploit still exerts an undying fascination, and legends about it survive with extraordinary strength in all those parts of Britain to which the Armada came close – the south-west (Plymouth particularly) and the south coast of England, the west coast of Ireland, the islands and Highlands of western Scotland. The tale of the Witch of Beinn a' Bhric – a hill in north-west Inverness-shire – is more fanciful than most, but a good indication of the power with which the saga has gripped men's minds.

Ask any local what happened to the Armada, and he will tell you. When invasion threatened, the Witch of Beinn a' Bhric summoned the Witch of Mull from across the sea, and the Witch of Moy from close at hand, and held a meeting on the slopes of her home mountain. By one account the three hags met at the Witch's Seat – a rock like a natural arm-chair on a ridge going up to the summit – and there cast their spell. By another, they stirred the Witch's Well, a spring in the big corrie on the northern side of the peak. Whatever the rendezvous, their incantations proved effective, for they produced a tremendous storm that blew the Spanish fleet to destruction.

Medal struck to commemorate the defeat of the Armada. The inscription reads: FLAVIT ET DISSIPATI SUNT – [GOD] BLEW AND THEY WERE SCATTERED.

243

Sources

Any modern author writing on the Armada is immeasurably indebted to the energy and scholarship of Martin Hume, the soldier-turned-historian who took up writing in middle life, and in 1898, at the age of 55, became Editor of the Spanish State Papers at the Public Record Office in London. Of partly Spanish descent, and known to his friends as 'Don Martin', he translated, collated and published a great mass of manuscript papers preserved in, or originally belonging to, the Spanish national archive at Simancas. Volume IV of the *Calendar of Letters and State Papers relating to English Affairs*, which covers the period of the Armada's preparation and voyage, alone runs to half a million words – six or seven times the length of this book – and constitutes a gold-mine of contemporary reports from diplomats, spies and military commanders. This invaluable source enables those who cannot read medieval Spanish to observe the daily reactions of the Duke of Medina Sidonia as he led the Armada to its doom, and the evasions of the Duke of Parma as he struggled to explain away the fact that his invasion force was not ready.

Another useful Spanish source, although much coloured by the opinions of the author, is *La Armada Invencible* by C. Fernandez Duro, a sea-captain who collated the memoirs of participants and published them in 1884.

On the English side, a particularly valuable service was performed by Professor J.K. Laughton, who trawled through the immense archive of original documents in the Public Record Office and published a rich selection in *State Papers Relating to the Defeat of the Spanish Armada*, which came out in two volumes in 1894.

PRINCIPAL PUBLISHED SOURCES:

Aramburu, Marcos de, 'Account' in *Proceedings of the Royal Irish Academy*, Vol. 27. Dublin, 1908.

Aubrey, John, *Brief Lives*, edited by Oliver Lawson Dick. London, 1949.

Boynton, Lindsay, *The Elizabethan Militia*. London, 1967.

Bradford, Ernle, *Drake*. London, 1965.

Byrne, M. St Clair, *Elizabethan Life in Town and Country*. London, 1934.

Calendar of State Papers (Domestic), Vols 200 (April 1587)–218 (November 1588).

Calendar of State Papers (Foreign Series), Vol. XXII, July–December 1588, edited by R.B. Wernham. London, 1936.

Calendar of State Papers (Ireland): Elizabeth (Vol. 4), August 1588–September 1592, edited by H.C. Hamilton. London, 1885.

Calendar of State Papers (Scotland), Vol. IX, September 1586–March 1589, edited by W.K. Boyd. Glasgow, 1915.

Calendar of State Papers (Spanish) relating to English Affairs, preserved in or originally belonging to the Archives of Simancas, Vol. IV, Elizabeth, 1587–1603, edited by Martin A.S. Hume. London, 1899.

Calendar of State Papers (Venetian), Vol. VIII, 1581–91, edited by H.F. Brown. London, 1894.

Camden, William, *Annales, or the History of Elizabeth*, translated by R. Norton. 1635.

Camden, William, *Britannia*, translated by Philemon Howard. London, 1610.

Campbell, J., *Lives of British Admirals and Eminent Seamen*. London, 1779.

Carey, Robert, First Earl of Monmouth, *Memoirs*. Edinburgh, 1808.

Clarke, Sir George, and Thursfield, J.R., *The Navy and the Nation*. London, 1897.

Corbett, Julian S., *Drake and the Tudor Navy* (2 vols). Longmans, 1898.

Corbett, Julian S., *Fighting Instructions, 1530–1816*. Navy Records Society, 1905.

Cuellar, Captain, *Captain Cuellar's Letter*, translated by Henry Dwight Sedgwick, Jr. New York, 1895.

Duro, Cesareo Fernandez, *La Armada Invencible*. Madrid, 1885.

Fallon, Niall, *The Armada in Ireland*. London, 1978.

Ffoulkes, C., *The Gun-Founders of England*. London, 1969.

Froude, J.A., *The Spanish Story of the Armada*. London, 1891.

Froude, J.A., *English Seamen in the Sixteenth Century*. London, 1895.

Froude, J.A., *History of England*, Vol. 12, Chapter 71. London, 1870.

Fuller, Thomas, *History of the Worthies of England*. London, 1840.

Guilmartin, J.F., *Gunpowder and Galleys*. Cambridge, 1974.

Hakluyt, Richard, *Principal Navigations*, Vol. 2. Glasgow, 1903.

Hardy, Evelyn, *Survivors of the Armada*. London, 1966.

Harrison, William, *Elizabethan England*, edited by L. Withington. London, 1899.

Hotson, Leslie, *Shakespeare's Sonnets Dated*. London, 1949.

Howarth, David, *The Voyage of the Armada: the Spanish Story*. London, 1981.

Hume, Martin A.S., *Philip II of Spain*. London, 1934.

Hume, Martin A.S., *The Year after the Armada* and other historical studies. London, 1896.

Hurault, André, Sieur de Maisse, *Memoirs*, translated by G.B. Harrison and R.A. Jones. London, 1931.

Keevil, J.J., *Medicine and the Navy*. London, 1957.

Lambarde, W., *A Perambulation of Kent*. First published 1570. New edition, London, 1970.

Laughton, J.K., (Editor), *State Papers Relating to the Defeat of the Spanish Armada* (2 vols), Navy Records Society, 1894.

Lewis, Michael, *The Spanish Armada*. Batsford, 1960.

Lewis, Michael, *Armada Guns*. London, 1961.

Lloyd, Christopher, *The British Seaman, 1200–1860*. London, 1968.

Martin, Colin, *Full Fathom Five*. London, 1975.

Monson, Sir William, *The Naval Tracts of Sir William Monson, Vol. 1*, edited by M. Oppenheim. Navy Records Society, 1902.

Nichols, John, *The Progresses and Public Processions of Queen Elizabeth, Vol. 2*. London, 1823.

Noble, W. Mackreth, *Huntingdonshire and the Spanish Armada*. London, 1896.

Platter, Thomas, *Travels in England 1599*, translated by Clare Williams. London, 1937.

Raleigh, Sir Walter, *History of the World*. 1614.

Read, Conyers, *Mr Secretary Walsingham*, Vol. 3. Oxford, 1925.

Rowse, A.L., *The England of Elizabeth*. London, 1951.

Southey, Robert, *Lives of the British Admirals, Vol. 2*. London, 1833.

Stow, John, *Annales, or a Generall Chronicle of England*. 1631.

Ubaldini, Petruccio, 'Discourse' in *Naval Miscellany Vol. 4*. Navy Record Society, 1952.

Williams, Neville, *Elizabeth Queen of England*. London, 1967.

Woodrooffe, Thomas, *The Enterprise of England*. London, 1958.

UNPUBLISHED SOURCES:

National Maritime Museum
Collection of Printed Books and Manuscripts. Files REC/1, REC/40, HSR/HF, WEL/3, PHB/1, ADL/QF/4, LEC/1.
Public Record Office.
State Papers Domestic, Vols 200–218.

Illustration Acknowledgements

Colour plates:

Bord Fáilte (Irish Tourist Board), 19; Bridgman Art Library, London, 5.10; British Museum, London, 6, 12; National Maritime Museum, Greenwich, 3, 7, 11, 13, 18, 21; Prado Museum, Madrid, 4; Ulster Museum, Belfast, 20; Weidenfeld and Nicolson Archive, London, 1, 2, 14; Worshipful Society of Apothecaries of London, 17.

Black and white illustrations:

The illustration on page 28 is reproduced by gracious permission of H.M. the Queen.

Alba Collection, Madrid, page 20; Ashmolean Museum, Oxford, page 13; Bodleian Library, Oxford, page 34; Bridgman Art Library, London, endpapers, page 137; British Museum, London, page 204, 242; The Duke of Bedford, Woburn, page 25; Mansell Collection, London, page 31 above, 33, 52 above, 66, 106 below, 148, 149, 164; The Marquess of Salisbury, page 53 below; Musée Royale des Beaux-Arts, Brussels, paged 50; Museo Navale, Madrid, page 61; National Maritime Museum, Greenwich, page 84, 87, 98, 99 above, 99 below, 105, 106 above, 106 below, 181, 209 left, 209 right, 212; National Portrait Gallery, London, page 31 below; Palazzo Barberini, Rome, page 15; Pepysian Library, Magdalen College, Cambridge, page 102 above, 102 below; Pitti Gallery, Florence, page 22; Plymouth Museums and Art Gallery, page 154, 194, 215; Science Museum, London, page 124; Sudeley Castle Collection, Gloucestershire, page 29; Ulster Museum, Belfast, page 74; Weidenfeld and Nicolson Archive, London, page 17 above, 24, 36, 38 above, 38 below, 40, 41, 42 above, 42 below, 44, 46, 48 above, 48 below, 179, 193, 222.

Endpapers:
Map by John Pine, 1739, showing the route of the Armada, Bridgman Collection, London.

Index

256

A CHART
shewing the several
Places of Action between the
ENGLISH and SPANISH Fleets,
with the Places where several of
the SPANISH Ships were destroyed in their return to SPAIN,
North about the
BRITISH ISLANDS.

SI · CONTRA · STIMVLOS · CALCITRARE · &

NON · LÆDOR · V

FRANCE

FLANDERS

HOLLAND

NORWAY

Jutland